THE SKELETONS IN OUR CLOSET

SINCLAIR A. MACABRE

First paperback edition October 2025

Book design by Warickaart

ISBN 978-0-9756222-4-7 (paperback)

ISBN 978-0-9756222-5-4 (ebook)

Published by Sinclair A. Macabre

sinclairamacabre.carrd.co

For my love, who never stopped believing in me.
And for those who struggle to see the fire in the darkness—I see you, I
know you. You got this.

— • —

Hello dear reader, important warning:

THE SKELETONS IN OUR CLOSET is a Dark Romance/Fantasy story, meaning there will be darker themes and tropes within. Here is a list of what to expect:

Manipulation

Familial Abuse

Explicit Sexual Content

Death by Execution (Hanging)

Murder

Gore/Blood

Needles

Mention of Being Drugged

Mention of Self Harm (scars)

Depression

Madness

Hallucinations (light)

— • —

PEOPLE & RACES:

Daedalus (day-da-liss)

Mikhalis (mik-ah-liss)

Irsa (ear-suh)

Minos (mihn-ohs)

Xekelon (zek-eh-lon)

Luceri (loo-sair-eye)

— —

PLACES

Nemoure (nem-or)

Laia (lay-uh)

Vira (veer-uh)

Lur'ala (lure-ah-la)

Makor (mah-core)

Part

ONE

1

— · —

MAGIC IS a curious, hungry thing.

A single chain of green lightning snakes between my fingertips, arcing back and forth in quick succession as I lean back against my black pillows. The magic is simple—something I learned when I was younger, much younger than now, though I still can't help but find entertainment in making the energy dance over my skin. It crackles with every snap, raises the hair on my arms in a wave as it passes across the pads of my fingers, searching curiously for the next landing point.

My mother would likely disapprove if she saw me using it solely to amuse myself, but it's easy to conjure in boredom, and easy to replicate to create actual damage.

This one would not devour a person, as some of the spells I know could—but it's amusing to note how even with it being so small, it aches to become *more.*

Magic is easy after so many lessons in it, so many different versions of how to conjure it, how to speak in its tongue. It lives and breathes in every part of me, thrumming through my veins in time with my pulse. Sometimes, I count the beats of it in the same way I would the tempo of my songs. It is the heartbeat of my entire world, of all cities I've ever been to and of every person I've ever met.

Most creatures wield a natural magic within them, though each is unique in its own way—all different elements and variations. They call it "soul magic," for the soul itself is what powers such a thing. I have always found it fascinating.

As much as magic is a hungry thing, so too am I. Always searching for more, always stuffing my nose in a book to grab at that little scrap of something new.

A deep sigh leaves me in a rush at the murmuring sound of conversation just outside my door, pulling me from my thoughts and emptying my lungs entirely the second I recognize my mother's voice. Displeased, as usual, though that's never hard to guess.

My eyes walk from the lightning to my furniture, checking each object for any signs of disturbance, grateful to see my intricately-carved black dresser and nightstand still covered with the small items I used last: a mostly empty teacup, a handful of rings, a book of anatomy laid open to whatever page I had left on.

It's a habit at this point, to note and categorize each item around me the moment I hear my mother's voice nearby. To memorize where everything is and compare it to my latest memory.

A strange and annoying habit, for certain, but one I cannot help unconsciously doing. Too often things disappear or are moved or misplaced. Whether it is her or the house that does it, I do not know, but I have long since accepted the compulsion. Now it is a means of settling myself and preparing for whatever the woman might bring in her wake.

As the muffled conversation beyond the door trails off to an end, an uncomfortable silence falling over the room with only the crackle of my magic to fill it, I will the lightning from my hands. It leaves with a trail of static, dissipating into a little flash of light before it disappears entirely.

My mother is alone when she steps into the room, so I've no clue if it was my father or a servant she'd been speaking to in the hall. Though it hardly matters.

Her dark lips are already pressed in a firm line, and the waves of her just-as-dark hair frame her sharp-angled face in cutting shadows. When her mismatched eyes land on me—one a blinding pink and the other so dark it swallows the pupil entirely—they are blank and foreboding.

I'm not surprised by the expression. It's become a guessing game for me to imagine which emotion she'll show up with next—perfectly neutral, angry, or empty of anything at all. At least this one is easy enough to parse.

Morgana folds her arms over her chest, the pale skin of her forearms and shoulders showing in between the pieces of her black, leather armor. It curves around her and juts out in jagged points, almost reminiscent of a carapace, but not quite—a look far more for intimidation than it is anything else, I suspect. Pointed black heels peer out beneath the flare at the bottom of her velvet pants, and the cloak I always expect now sways from her shoulders as she comes to a stop a few feet away from me.

And then there were the markings. Tattoo-like skeletal designs that covered half her body—the same half with her neon eye. They were a unique trait of our family, a trait that started rapidly developing on my own skin over the past few months, swiftly taking over my body as I grew. I tried to ignore them as much as I could, though that was hard to do when they stared back at me each morning in the mirror, and now here with my mother's right in front of me.

"Oh good, Daedalus, you're awake. Get up," she says, reaching back to close the door and leveling me with another look that reeks of disappointment.

I nod hesitantly, pushing myself away from the bed and sitting up before her. Morgana doesn't step closer, simply watching me watch her.

We stare at each other for a long moment, before I finally get the courage to speak. "What is it?"

"We're moving."

My eyebrows raise in surprise as I reach over to the nightstand, picking up a pair of black-framed glasses and sliding them onto my face. *That* was not at all what I expected her to say when she came in here, that's for sure. A bitter taste lays thick in my mouth from her presence, as if I'd sipped poison straight from a bottle—one that she alone created in me, one that will never leave. I hate the uncertainty that swims in my gut, the initial disgust that lays between us, one I've never been sure came from me to her or vice versa.

I should be accustomed to her, but she grates on every nerve as if they'd been exposed for her to pluck at like lute strings.

Morgana gestures for me to stand, and for a moment, I simply watch the motion of her hand before doing so. She eyes me as I pick up my discarded teacup and take a sip, grimacing at the coolness of what was once hot tea. How long has it been since I left it there? I lost track of time. Still, the flood of cool mint wakes me up, washing away the venom resting on my tongue with one swallow.

I set it back down and look over at her, not meeting her eyes. "Why are we moving?"

She makes a noise similar to a scoff and turns on her pointed heels to eye my room in a swift sweep before turning back to face me again, remaining silent. I watch her motions, unsure of what to do next with her simply *staring* at me like this. She doesn't speak for a long while, her expression shifting a time or two—falling somewhere between irritation and complete neutrality before she seems to settle on the right words.

"There is a better school overseas, and they've already accepted your application."

It only feels like half of the truth. There has to be more, but I'm not going to ask. I *can't,* not with her.

My body tenses as her hand extends to me, her long claw-like fingernails pointed toward my chest. "But first," she starts, a tone of disinterest in her voice, "you should train here one last time."

For once, I wish she would sound *happy* to have me trained.

Morgana leaves the room ahead of me, leaving my door open like a spread-wide maw waiting to trap me. Once I step through it, I face magic and weaponry. Once I step through it, I face her ever-present disapproval that I have, for so long, craved to change.

With a nod and a sigh, I follow her, brushing my fingers across the black floral wallpaper on the walls, across thin windowsills attached to tall crystalline windows. Sunlight floods through them in vibrant rays, warming my body as I pass, glancing outside at the city beyond.

The City of Magic, or so it's been called.

Countless smoothly- paved streets wind through buildings ranging between towering skyscrapers, squared-off shops, cathedral-styled buildings that weren't in fact churches—once painted in sharp grays, pale purples, yellows, oranges, and blues, now faded and dull in the dying light. The city was vibrant once, but after quite a few years, I've watched it slowly become colored in melancholy pastels. It's still beautiful, but it feels strange these days.

Like a faded sunset, marked by graying clouds.

I let my eyes drop to the street closest to our home, the Macabre Manor, watching people outside as they duck away from the iron gates and hurry through the gates of their own homes nearby. No one lingers around our home, not that we mind, and I know it's likely because they imagined they'd be cursed. Maybe they thought the world they knew would shatter to a halt if they even looked at the manor, or that if they saw the bright eye belonging to one of their archmages, they might shrivel into nothing.

She has a reputation, my mother, but then again, so does my family as a whole.

Morgana eyes me over her shoulder as she leads me up a flight of stairs and down a similarly colored hallway, the ring of her heels sharp and almost rhythmic to my music-primed ears. My fingertips tap along with them on my thigh, brushing over the velvet of my slacks with each movement, filling the quiet between them.

The room she leads me to—for what will hopefully be the last time—is wide and mostly empty between the gray walls. Six black, marble pillars frame the center of the room, three lined up on either side to create an isle of sorts, separating the training area from the rows of weapons hanging off the back wall. Each detail is intentional, precise. Marbled tile floor, so as not to interrupt the smooth gait of our movements. A singular burnished-gold chandelier dripping with glittering gems that hangs between the pillars, casting vibrant enough light that it keeps the shadows at bay with ease.

I know this room like the back of my hand—each crack or crevice in the floor, the gold streaks in the pillars. I know where my weapon lays still, waiting for me.

And, I know where my trainer will be, standing in the center of it all, directly beneath the chandelier.

Morgana guides me forward, her hands achingly tight on my shoulders as we stop before the man. Silas, the only trainer that we've kept over the years—since he has been the only one who can keep up with how fast I learn—stands slightly shorter than me, with sun-kissed tan skin and a shock of slicked-back white hair on top of his head. No wrinkles other than slight maturity lines around the eyes and mouth, and because of that I've never been able to place how old he truly is, only that he must not be *too* old, judging by the fact that he's elven.

His irises remind me of cool blue rivers, a clear sky around the void of his pupil, swimming with intrigue and something kind. Something *far* kinder than I'm familiar with.

Morgana speaks to him over my head before she releases me from her grasp, moving to stand at the entrance of the room. I watch her through strands of my black hair for a moment before stepping up to Silas, retrieving a longsword for today's training from his hand and lifting it up to my face. It's nothing too fancy—glossy silver steel with a black, simple handle, caging in my hand.

I peer at the blade, eyeing my own reflection in it for a moment too long. It creates a slight waver to my tan skin and the bits of hair falling in my face, making the sharp angles of my cheekbones and jaw appear softer, easing the shadowed bags under my golden eyes that hide beneath my family's skeleton-like bone marks. It doesn't show my forcibly-straight posture, or the too-long and too-skinny form of my body. Just my face. Just my sad, tired face.

I almost appreciate the sword-me more than the one I see in the mirror.

Silas turns his body to point his silver rapier at me, and I could almost smile, if such an expression belonged on my lips.

2

THE MOVE happens fast, too fast, with little explanation for why we are leaving Makor in the first place other than something about a better school for me. Before I know it, we've left the City of Magic and Lur'ala as a whole; crossing the rough seas on a ship bigger than any I've ever seen, and all I can do is watch my life vanish before my eyes, swallowed by the waves carrying me away.

Nemoure, also known as the self-proclaimed, 'City of Glamour', seems enticing, at least. From what little I've studied of it, or its continent of Vira, it is almost as highly magical as Makor, but twice as big. Some rumor it to be nothing but trouble; some rumor it to hold daring promises; some even say it hides dark secrets under the glitter and the gold. It all makes me curious, every single little drip of information.

According to the maps and books, the sprawl of the city supposedly takes up nearly half of Vira on its own and is split into three connected parts—the richer end to the right called the Upper Circle, middle class in the Center, and the shadier end to the left dutifully named the Lower Circle. Though there are some who say

11

the Upper is titled the 'Penumbra' for its gilt-gold brilliance, and the Lower is titled the 'Umbra' for its clinging shadows.

Nicknames I rather like, truthfully.

According to my research, my new college is set in the perfect epicenter of the Upper Circle, and is apparently one of the highest-end magic schools in the entire *world*. That fact alone is hard to believe after my brief attendance at Inkwell—the only school worth the caliber in Makor. Even so, it's hard *not* to be intrigued by it.

Still, despite my reluctant excitement and intrigue about the possibilities Nemoure could offer me, one thing continues to bother me about the move. My mother was an influential mage in Makor—so why the sudden departure? Why did she tell us nothing as we were ushered onto the boat with barely a word and no goodbyes? Why had she not given sooner notice, or even so much as a hint? Why did it feel so much like we were running away from something?

I cannot not help thinking that something must have happened, that my mother had done something wrong, and it eats away at me as I pace the upper decks of the ship at night.

What could she possibly have done that would cause her to leave the city she came to power in?

Roughly two weeks pass before we lay eyes on land again, and I'm more than grateful for the reprieve of being trapped atop the ocean with nothing but my parents, the random crew members, and my racing mind to keep me company.

A golden shoreline of sunlit sands marked by docked ships finally crawls into view, reaching out to us from where it hugs the edge of the massive city. It's nearly impossible to take it all in at once, no matter which way I look—crowds of skyscrapers rising above scores of other towering buildings, all glittering with vast amounts of windows and well-polished walls. Like an ocean of its own, sprawling and deep and full of life.

Nemoure'. I can hardly believe I'm only seeing one section of the Upper Circle, one gate of the many surrounding the area.

"It certainly gives Makor a run for its money," Mikhalis, my father, says, offering me a grim smile that is not at all reassuring.

As the ship docks and we start to walk away from it toward our welcoming guide, Morgana waves a hand and rips open a sickly-green portal in front of us, her power singing to my own. The energy of it hums in my veins, stirring my magic as if reaching right into me—so I keep myself away in case it actually would. My mother's arcana has always felt like drowning, too thick and too persistent. *Too close.*

She takes our luggage and passes it through, and in the brief moment I feel electric with her power, she closes it and it all vanishes from my grasp.

Magic is hungry, but so am I, in some cases. *Even* for hers.

Our guide, a delicate-looking elven women, smiles at us as we approach her. "One moment, please," she states, holding up her hands before our small trio. I shudder as a sudden wave of magic crosses over my body, passing under my skin and meeting my own so swiftly, I could've sworn she was *searching* me. The power is surprisingly intense, and it only rattles me less when I notice my parents' shoulders are also hunched against it.

She glances toward the walls on either side of the docks with a faltering look of concern before smiling again, clasping her hands at her waist. "Ah, you are the new mages arriving here! We look forward to your presence in our city. Welcome to Nemoure."

Mikhalis hums as he starts to walk ahead of me. His tanned skin glows in the warmth of the sun, and because of it, I can't help but look over him, surprised by how healthy he looks under the glow—from his graying black hair swept back over his head, to the 'X' shaped scar at his right temple that cuts around his eye and over his cheekbone, down to his neat salt-and-pepper beard. Often times, he looks somber in his quiet state of being, but not now. Now he looks serious, with his dark eyebrows drawn down over his golden eyes and his mouth in a firm line. Almost angered, in a strange way.

I got most of my looks from him, with my mother's harsh angles and height. To this day, I still do not know how to feel about that.

Luckily for me, I had greater distractions than that of my inherited genetics.

Every building in Nemoure is dark and glossy, I learn quickly, some with multicolored paint around the edges of windows or differently colored doors that I take note of as we walk from the docs to the city proper. It feels wrong, after living in the painted sunset and sunrise of Makor, seeing how dark the buildings are here. They feel far less personal, much more intimidating and oppressive in their glamorous sharp looks. We pass open bakeries and shops for high-end clothing, a café smelling of rich coffee, a wizardry shop I don't catch the name of fast enough. I breathe in old book pages and fresh bread, sage and smoky incense, flowers from a florist across the stone street.

We don't stop for any of them, but they excite me all the same.

A circular fountain rests in the heart of the Penumbra, placed in a rounded courtyard in front of the school I'm to be attending—Whitestone College. The fountain appears made from smooth white marble, cool water pouring from the uppermost platform and spilling over until it fills the base. I drag my fingers through droplets on the outer rim, watching golden coins wink and shiver through the ripples of the constantly-moving waves.

Even this, feels magical. The very air crackles with it faintly, getting thicker the closer we get to the school.

I step forward to walk beside Morgana as we approach Whitestone, casting my gaze up to it. The building itself is shaped much like a cathedral, composed of pure white stone that glitters in the right lighting, almost marble-like in appearance. From what I can glean of the roof, it appears to be covered in dark shingles, even lining the tops of the four spires that mark each corner. Wide arched windows, loosely covered by white cloth curtains, surround both sides of a larger circular window high above the main door.

I squint a little at the glare of the sun shining off it, trying to note the design of the stained glass before giving up and returning my eyes to the heavy wooden doors before us.

Mikhalis pushes through easily, using one arm to hold the door to the side as we quickly follow.

A towering man with stone-gray skin, pure white eyes, and swept-back dark hair offers us a forced smile as we enter—and only once we get close enough, do I notice the charcoal-colored draconic wings sprouting from his back and the pair of horns standing out from his head. "Good afternoon. You must be the Macabres," he says, authoritative and firm.

His voice, deep and gravelly, jolts my attention back to his face and away from his body. My mother takes over talking to him before I can greet him in return, swiftly moving on to enrolling me in classes and what we should know about the place. I know she's only doing it to save face. If there's anything I know well about her, it's that she's already thoroughly researched Whitestone, from classes to classmates to teachers. She probably knows everything to do here, and everyone walking in the corridor with us.

Some might say it's creepy. Morgana would say it's "for our own good."

I did the same thing, so I can't hold it against her.

I turn away from them and my father, taking in the surrounding hall and the people crisscrossing over the marble floor. All across the room, elven students bustle around us—some in robes, some in suits, some in colorful extravagant outfits I could never imagine myself wearing. Jewelry glitters from hands and pointed ears; some have intricate makeup surrounding their eyes and painting their plump lips. Most carry armfuls of books, but quite a few only have cups in one hand while they gesture with their other, laughing and conversing with whoever they're walking with.

Morgana always says "Friends are distractions" or "they'll take away from your studies." Watching all these people now, jealousy blooms in my chest, fierce and painful—I've never had anything like they all have. I've never experienced what it's like to drink tea or coffee from a paper cup while laughing with a group, or dressed in a way that would capture everyone and anyone's attentions. I've never had the experience of leaning against the statue in the center of the room, smiling lazily at a girl or boy like I can see happening just a few feet away.

New anxiety forms underneath the jealousy, making my hands shake as Morgana calls for me to follow them.

The man—now introducing himself as the dean of the school, Xekelon—waves for us to follow him down the hall and towards a room with a heavy oak door. My eyes widen at the sight of an imp working at the desk in front of it, her skin bright red, a thin tail resting in a sort of curly-q behind her as she looks up and smiles at me. She's likely the size of my forearm at most from the tips of her horns to her toes, dressed in a black skirt and white button-up shirt, her golden hair pinned back out of her face.

Xekelon glances back at me as he starts to walk into his office, letting out a low chuckle. "Don't mind Shirley. She's my secretary."

Is that truly her name, or is he lying?

I nod uncertainly, shooting a wary glance between my parents before following them into the room and sitting in one of the black leather chairs waiting by the door. It isn't that Devils are of any distaste to me, only that I've heard how they tend to be. Overly ambitious, sometimes aggressive, willing to take over planets and drive the original inhabitants underground. I can't place if the Dean is one, but the energy surrounding him is heady with a sort of potential I'd imagine is close enough.

Trust your mother, Daedalus.

The dean moves to sit behind a wide mahogany desk, tucking his massive wings back as he gathers a pile of paperwork and places it in front of Morgana. His office is surprisingly neat—painted deep red with a singular standard light on the ceiling, a few stacks of paper lingering on the desk, gray file cabinets hugging the corner to his right, and a wide, square window on his left allowing him a nice view of the courtyard and plenty of sunlight.

It wouldn't be the *worst* place to work, I suppose, but I wouldn't choose it myself. Not even with my slight enjoyment of paperwork.

I watch him as he continues speaking to my parents, studying the deep blue tie against his white button-up for a moment before my mother absently hands me a piece of paper to fill out and draws my attention away.

The form is the usual for schools and easy enough to complete—age, school history, what I already knew, what my grades were at past colleges. My leg shakes restlessly as I slide the clipboard back over to the dean, glancing nervously to my mother as she completes her own, then back to Mikhalis.

My father nods at me, and not much else.

Xekelon passes over my class schedule, as well as a map with the locations of each class already marked, and I look it over curiously before Morgana can take it, grateful to see that the classes are all about the same range as what I'd had in Makor—I don't think I could handle being in anything lower. If I was, I'd probably surpass my classmates far more than I should, and it would be boring. *Very* boring.

And besides, it would mean that all my studying and practice at home would have been for nothing, and I'm not about to have that.

Morgana dismisses me with a wave of her hand, and through my anxiety, a wave of relief crashes over me as I stand up and duck out of the room. I pause in the hall, drinking in the fresh scents of floral perfumes and distant trails of coffee in a swift breath before wondering where to continue on to. A singular desk to my left against the wall holds visitor information I know I won't need, so I don't linger long; instead, I turn back to people-watching, taking the other students in one by one, wondering which ones would eventually be my classmates—

Someone's shoulder connects with my upper arm, bumping me backward into the visitor desk.

My heart stops as I lift my eyes from the floor to the person—or rather, to the ruby-colored irises staring back at me. No words find my lips as I look at him, immediately drowning in the sounds of roaring fire and the glimpse of disgust that flashes across his fine features, a look that quickly disappears in the blink of an eye. He wears a fine white button-up with long sleeves and an impressively tailored crimson vest over it, paired with black slacks that cling to his long legs and knee-high leather boots. A slight bit of eyeliner and shimmery eyeshadow frames those gem-like eyes, his vibrant red hair, falling around his face and down his back in a high pony-tail.

For a moment, I just stare at him, watching his lips move, though hearing only the sound of his fire and my heart, pounding away like the ticking of a clock.

"I said, who are you?" he says, his voice suddenly crisp and clear as all the sound comes rushing back to me. "Did you not hear me?"

"No, I apologize. I'm Daedalus," I reply quickly, swallowing down the urge to continue talking. To ramble, like always. "And you are?"

The man jolts slightly, like I offended him by asking, tilting his upturned nose toward the ceiling and peering at me. Even though I stand taller than him, I still feel like he's looking down at me. "Cain Sidrelle. I'm surprised you don't know that already."

Should I?

I shake my head, letting out an uneasy laugh that's more air than sound. "I'm new to this city. I'm... considerably unaware of the people here."

Cain's eyes narrow at that, but he nods. As he opens his mouth to speak, a masculine voice rings out from the main entrance.

"Oh, good, Cain. You are here."

My eyebrows raise at a shorter elven man who nearly snarls at me for being in Cain's presence as he approaches us. His energy is uncomfortable—squeamish, almost—though he isn't horrible looking, with tousled dark hair and fair skin. Smooth jawline, slight bags under his sharp gold eyes, a cocky tug to his lips that already has me feeling unsettled in his presence.

Before I even have a chance to open my mouth, he's already talking. "Who the hell are you?"

I shift away from him, trying to get away from the radius of the discomfort clinging to him. "Daedalus. Who are you?"

He rolls his eyes, adjusting the bag over his shoulder. "Irsa, are you new?"

I truly want this conversation to be over, so all I do in response is nod.

Irsa smirks and laughs, nodding to himself as he turns to Cain, passing off my existence as though I'm not even here. Just another painting on the wall. "Anyway, Cain, would you join me in the library? Or are you still in a mood?"

Cain's lip curls into a silent snarl, his eyes suddenly flaring to life with a heat that I easily feel through my magic. Sparks dance across my skin, and combined with the sickening feeling from Irsa, I'm almost overstimulated. "No, I have a class. Leave me alone right now."

"Fine, fine. You'll come around eventually," Irsa says, turning away from us. My stomach flips as he disappears up the nearby stairwell, no longer twisting up on itself due to the aura he had—but my anxiety hasn't lessened. I press my hands together, digging my knuckles into my palms back and forth until the piercing sound of Morgana's heels on the stone floor rings out over the hall, pulling me from my nerves.

For someone who rarely ever seems content, the look on her face is nearly pleased for a second, until she notices Cain standing beside me.

"Come along, Daedalus," she directs, moving back toward the two doors and out into the plaza beyond once more. I exhale shakily as I catch up to her and my father, my hands still rubbing over one another as the nerves continue to cling on to me. Unhelped, of course, by the way the students and usual city goers pass by on smooth cobblestone streets, casting curious or confused glances at the three of us. It is only now that I realize how much we stand out against the vibrant colors of this new city, a fact that does not comfort me or my nerves even the least bit.

Our new manor lingers outside the main circle of Nemoure, out of reach of the shops and parties, framed by a vibrant forest and tucked behind a gray stone wall topped with black iron points. The tall matching gate creaks as we push it open, revealing stone walls painted black and a set of dark wooden doors with long vertical handles that swirl into hooks on the top and bottom. The manor itself is surrounded by a vibrant lawn and neatly trimmed hedges. Black shingles and sharp points stand out from the roof, giving an almost church-like appearance that stirs a new discomfort in my stomach.

It almost feels familiar to our former home in Makor, but veers just to the left of being exactly the same—this one being far more outwardly decorated, likely for the perceptions of those in the city, with gardens and gargoyle statues and the neatness of the yard. I don't know if I like it, the stark cleanliness of it all.

One of the doors heaves open before we reach the stone steps leading up to them, behind it standing one of the few servants we brought overseas with us, Shriek—a Luceri, standing shorter than the entire family, with a soft face that always reminds me something of a cherub, her brunette hair tied back in a thick braid falling past her sky-blue shoulder blades. She makes me more curious than any of the others we've kept, due to the fact that she never speaks out loud to any of us. Her messages are always telepathic, and though I haven't had much experience with them, I'm still unsure if it's unusual for Luceri to do so or not.

Luceri are seemingly more common in Makor than here, from what little I've seen of the city so far. They're created from Devils—or devil-touched bloodlines—made by the blood of the fallen angel Lucer, often inheriting horns, tails, and various colored eyes and skin tones from the genes passed down to them. I often found myself relating to them, in a way. To the way they were considered a bit taboo—as if the worst thing they could possibly have done was be born as a devil-blooded creature.

It was sort of sad.

Morgana nods to Shriek as we pass by, turning to face me in front of the stairwell tucked to the left of the fully furnished living room. I force my gaze from her neutral expression to the room; sweeping over two separate velvet couches facing each other, the glass-topped coffee table in between them, and the gray walls only decorated by paintings that blink when I look at them. The legs to the couches and table are all carved intricately, neat faces of humanoid skulls peering back at me from empty eye sockets.

Mikhalis steps past us and into what I assume is the kitchen, letting out a low sigh I'm sure he wanted none of us to hear.

The stairwell is carpeted, black as usual, and I'm more than grateful for it—knowing it will muffle the sound of Morgana's heels as she stalks around, compared to the old manor's pure marble. I trail over the framed pictures along the wall going up to the next floor, not bothering to linger when something—no, *someone*—disappears out of sight at the top of the stairs. Just a quick flicker of dark hair and a cloak, as if I'd seen another version of her, but smaller. Blinking, I stare at the open space, wishing for the shadows to clear for even a second.

My mother clasps her long hands together at her waist, and my eyes follow the motion for a second before darting to the top of the stairs again, searching for the person I know I saw.

As I'm about to conjure a spell to help me see through invisibility, my mother clears her throat. "Daedalus, I have something... *someone*, for you to meet."

A frown finds its way onto my lips without my control as she turns to face the stairs, looking up where I saw the humanoid blur before. One lavender hand curls around the edge of the wall, leading to a pair of irises the color of blood peeking down at us shyly.

My eyes immediately snap to Morgana, waiting for some sort of explanation, but she doesn't look at me. Instead, she beckons the other forward with a motion of her finger and I tense as whoever it is steps out, slowly creeping down the stairs until he's fully revealed from the shadows above.

He looks up at me curiously, past dark, chin-length hair curling in waves around his face and falling over his forehead. His entire body is the same lavender shade as his hand, aside from a twisted crown of obsidian that branches out from the back of his head to his temples, one I swiftly recognize to be the mark of a Witchblood—rare creatures, typically made by deals with hags. Some say they're linked to the Fae, other say it's far more eldritch than anything else.

I've never met one, so I had no idea what to think.

Until now.

I look between them silently, so many questions swimming through my head even as the words that refuse to find their way across my tongue.

Who is this boy? How did a Witchblood come to be in our new manor? In my mother's care? I knew so little about his kind and his abilities. Were they stronger than mine? Would he live longer than me? I'm still unsure of where I stand in the length of my lifespan. If he is Fae in nature or eldritch-magic infused, his could be longer. And depending on our relation, people would know we weren't related by blood, not only by the difference in skin tones.

I shake my head, trying to clear my mind momentarily, before Morgana's gaze finally finds her way to me.

"Bren, say hello to your brother, Daedalus," she states, smiling thinly at us both and sending a shiver down my spine.

Brother.

No friends, no emotions, but no longer an only child.

How? Morgana had shown no sign of being pregnant, and my father had shown no sign of being interested in making her so. Not that it really mattered now, we're in a different city after all—

Instead of saying anything, Bren smiles at me and blinks his bright red eyes, six more forming across the span of his forehead and under the outer corners of his main pair. The whites of his scleras vanish into pure crimson, swallowed by the arachnid he's playing to be. If I didn't know magic the way I did, I would've thought it was real—at least, until he conjures deep red spider-like limbs from his back and beams at us.

Morgana claps her hands in an intrigued way and gestures for more, freezing me in place. I watch in a stunned silence at her approval of the illusory creatures he begins drawing from his sleeves, and at the fact that she gave away that amusement so easily, when she only ever praises me when things are going her way. Even now, I can't tell if she's being true, or if she's trying to make him like her more. I don't know why he's here. I don't know what she's trying to do to me.

A sigh, something far too familiar to me, passes from my lips as I watch Bren, and I regret the sound as soon as it passes my lips. My—*our*— mother looks to me and shakes her head, instantly losing any softness to her face before taking me by the arm and leading me up the stairs. We start to pass Bren, leaving him with the servants and our father, and when he nervously waves at me, I can't bring myself to wave back.

"Where are we going? Why is he here?" I ask Morgana as she walks me down a hallway similar to those I knew in the old manor, feeling strange as my fingertips ghost across the black-painted walls and the frames of shifting paintings.

Her smile is tight when she glances back, her expression once again blank as her grip tightens on my arm. "To train you. Did you think our move would change that?"

I shake my head, unable to pull my arm away from her iron grip. "No, but, why do I have a brother? When did you—where has he come from? Will you answer me?"

Morgana stops in her tracks, spinning to face me so quick her cloak blows out behind her. "Don't question me, Daedalus. Be glad you have anyone at all."

And just as easily, as if she didn't just wield a hot knife against my skin, she continues her stalk down the hall with me in tow behind her.

3

WORD SPREADS fast in Nemoure, or so it seems, after only a few short weeks.

Clutching my books close to my chest, I weave my way through the bodies of my classmates in the hall, heading silently to my next class. Many conversations become whispers, heads turn in the opposite direction or shift to eye me in curiosity—though I know they seem to think we'll curse them with simply a glance. It must be something to do with the dark clothes, the ominous manor, our skeleton tattoos.

I haven't begun to place it yet, though I've been trying to. It's the same as it was back in Makor. People see someone who looks *different*, someone who might fit in a different step of life than them, and they're afraid. They turn to hostility out of fear.

Nemoure is far more intense about the spread of rumors than my former home, however. I've heard every sort of thing whispered behind my back already, from dealings I might have my hands in, or my family's 'deceptions', or the darkness we carry obviously meaning we rose up from the dead and plan to take over.

They really will believe *anything*, sometimes.

I make fully sure to arrive on time to my next science-focused lecture and set my things out exactly as I want, particular and precise. There's a specific rhythm to it— sit down, set my books down on the table, place my notebook to the right of the pile, pen to the left of it, needed textbook in the center. It has been the same for every class, and I don't know why I do it, but it's a compulsion I cannot fight against. If I don't do it this way, my entire desk feels wrong and out of place.

I feel out of place, if I don't do it, and I desperately need to focus being how new I am.

Science has always been intriguing to me, in all its forms and methods. Anatomy, equations, the taking apart to put back together. Making something new from something old, or something dangerous from something simple. It has a certain pace, an excitement that fires in my veins every time I step foot into a classroom—and maybe I have my mother to blame for that, with the lab-like area I discovered accidentally in our former home. The idea of filling vials, needles, playing with chemicals... I love all of it. Every single piece.

That love has helped me in this class so far, as I'm a slight step above the others when it comes to my education in it.

A handful of my classmates pass by without a word, most walking in pairs as they come through the door. I peer slightly over the edge of my glasses to watch them, taking note of their appearances and what little I can grasp of their personalities, either through outfits or makeup or expressions. I've been able to pinpoint who is friends with who, who respects who, who seems to be hated or feared. It's strange, witnessing them all, because *so many* of them seem to just be acting. Part of it is sad, really.

As I look away to start taking down an early set of notes, one specific voice rings through the room with such an authority, it's been catching my attention for days. His magic sparks mine to life, burning holes in the center of my focus with the flames I know he wields. I've met very few people that uses fire as strongly as he does, and gods, does he intrigue me.

Cain Sidrelle.

The most expensive person in every room he walks into, wearing an expression that challenges anyone and everyone to try him. His nose is nearly always pointed slightly upward to the ceiling, and every time I see him, his mouth is set in a firm line that twitches into a cocky smirk or a snarl. It isn't often I witness him smiling, genuinely or otherwise—but even when he doesn't, he still laughs, and his laughter is a song on its own. A wildfire turned into music, if that is even possible.

Cain is ethereal, with a slender body that's closer to my seven feet of height mostly due to his high-heeled boots, his long crimson curls meeting the center of his back familiarly even when it's pulled back into a ponytail.

According to the rumors I've caught wind of, the Sidrelles are the most well-known family in the city—for their riches and for their involvement in the businesses around. Cain, the only son but not the only child, is a top student in the college, and even has a side business of his own already. He seems to be what anyone around would label 'perfect' and seemingly has little problems with anything in his life, but I know that can't be true.

There is something under all of that bravado, and I'm sure of it. *More* than sure of it.

Something in me feels carnally about him, wanting to cut him open and find out what makes him tick, like one of my few experiments. He makes me hungry, pulling the long-forgotten want to bite from deep inside me when I see his pretty pale throat. I don't know what it is, or why he has this effect over me.

He shouldn't, being I hardly know him.

A quiet exhale escapes me at the sight of his vibrancy, watching him trail into the classroom effortlessly with a beautiful blonde elf wearing an emerald green outfit and matching makeup I now know as Marion. Cain's best friend and closest confidante, and probably his fiercest protector. They both glance over at me, quick enough I almost don't even see it, but then Cain pauses. He hesitates at the corner of my desk, his red-nailed fingertips grazing my table—I'm not sure I even dare to inhale again while he stands there, drowning me in him. Drowning me in embers and heat.

"Hi, Daedalus."

His voice draws my gaze up to his face, but I never meet his for more than a second.

"Hello, Cain," I reply quietly, just loud enough for him to hear.

He smiles at me. It's small, no more than a light tug at the corners of his glossy lips, but it's still something. "How are you?" He asks, resting his fingertips on the edge of my desk. "Marion told me you were in today. I wanted to make sure I said something to you."

Why? I want to ask, but the word falls flat on my tongue. "I'm well, I suppose. How are you? You seem... content."

It's true—however true Cain's contentment can be to someone who doesn't really know him, at least. His magic feels calmer today, not so riled the way it was when Irsa made that comment to him on my first day. He shrugs, eyeing me before looking back over at the door. "I am, actually."

"Some might say it's because he got laid," Marion remarks, only to get elbowed by Cain a second later.

I laugh, because I don't know what else to do, then drop my eyes to the jewelry on his fingers. Two intricate gold rings standing out from his middle finger, one carved in the shape of a dragon curling around the upper portion, and the other a simple gold band with a ruby in the center. They stand out against his fair skin and well-manicured red nails, and they certainly make my own black bands feel simple in comparison. "I like your rings, Cain."

Cain's cheeks flush slightly as he looks back down at me with a surprised expression on his face. "Oh, thank you. I picked them out myself."

"You have good taste," I remark, lifting my eyes back to his face, looking at the waves of hair around his eyes rather than directly into them. "That shouldn't be very surprising though, right?"

Cain laughs and opens his mouth to say more, but is quickly interrupted by Irsa hurtling into the classroom with what I assume is a coffee in hand. His odd energy is thankfully muted by the intensity of the Sidrelle inferno I can feel even from where I'm sitting, but the disgusted look he gives me is enough to make me uncomfortable.

"Cain! I brought you a coffee—why are you wasting your time talking to him?" he asks, holding the cup out and turning his bright eyes on Cain instead of me. Thankfully.

I drop my eyes to my book as Cain scoffs, pushing his extended hand away. "I'm not wasting my time, thank you. And keep your coffee. I don't need more."

Behind Irsa, another elven figure appears almost out of his shadow, wearing a black cloak that matches his slightly messy dark hair. A pair of circular sunglasses hides his eyes from my view, but his secretive nature doesn't bother me, not when his lips quirk into a slight smile in my direction. He has darker tanned skin than Irsa, and for a moment, I swear I see stitch-like scars in the planes of his face. His magic brushes against mine, a dark hunger like my own, one I haven't recognized in anyone else. It nearly makes me jolt away, staring up at him through the lenses of my glasses with widened eyes.

"Hello, Daedalus," he whispers in the back of my mind, his gaze never leaving mine. *"I'm Asher, Cain's friend. I'd like to know you more, sometime."*

"Okay," I whisper back to him, because I can't find it in me to say anything else.

A low throb forms in my temple as their mixed energies fade into the space behind me, threatening to become a migraine. It blooms quick, unfolding from my temple to my eye, pounding away like someone with an icepick attempting to chip away at my skull.

Pressing my fingers to it, I excuse myself and start for the hallway. I know what happens when my migraines come on—the pain building and building until I'm sick with it, only to gingerly fade away like it was never there, leaving me feeling emptier than before. It is not something I wish to experience in front of an entire classroom of people.

I pause, leaning into the wall for a moment and exhaling thinly through my nose as another sharp stab cuts through my temple. *Shit.* Quickly, I continue my path down the hall and into the bathroom, tucking myself neatly into one of the stalls. My stomach turns as I sit down on the cool floor, resting my palms against it to try and center myself. Anything to not get sick right now.

The pounding in my head drowns out anything else, but underneath it somewhere, I swear I hear the creak of a door.

"Daedalus? You in here?" The soft, slightly raspy voice breaks clear through the fog, and my stomach turns again at the thought of Cain finding me here like this.

I brush my fingertips under my nose, breathing a sigh of relief when they come away bloodless, before glancing backward at the stall door. "Yes, what is it?"

I can picture him standing out there in his white button-up and red vest, his arms crossed over his chest and his red eyes narrowed and unamused, barely concerned but for some reason *still here.*

Why is he still here? Why did he come at all?

"You ran off all of a sudden. Figured someone should come check on you," he says, and I picture him checking his manicured nails in the bathroom's low lighting. Cain doesn't sound irritated, for once. I could almost trick myself into thinking he sounds caring.

The pounding in my skull eases as I sit up a bit straighter, glancing down at the glimpse of Cain's black leather boots outside my stall. Even though something about him being here makes me want to talk to him—makes me want him to look at me with those intense eyes—I can't let him see me like this, breathless and panicking on the bathroom floor. Not right now.

"Go away, please."

He says nothing at first, and I wonder if he will deny me. If he will stay out there all day, waiting. Then, finally comes his quiet, "Fine."

It takes a moment, but the sound of Cain's boots on the tiled floor echoes through the small room, followed soon by the creak of the door, and then I am left in silence. Pushing upright and away from the toilet, I take another deep breath to put my head back together as the momentary ache settles down, focusing on the sounds around me.

One of the faucets drips a steady metronome into a porcelain sink. Pipes groan quietly inside the walls as someone flushes somewhere above me. Muffled conversation filters through the bathroom door, one of Irsa's cocky laughs reverberating from outside in the hall.

Likely laughing at me, no doubt, if Cain told him why he seemingly followed me.

"Why do you bother with these frivolous emotions, Daedalus?"

The heat that boiled up with my frustration is swiftly swallowed by a cold abyss, curling icy claws around my vertebrae. My gaze darts around the room, searching for where Morgana could possibly be watching from, but I don't feel her anywhere.

"I asked you a question." Her voice is crisp, emotionless.

I close my eyes, biting the inside of my cheek. "I don't know, Mother. I'm sorry."

I swear she scoffs before she speaks again. *"Well, try not to let him get to you further, yes? I—we, don't need you getting distracted, right?"*

My own blood weeps across my tongue as a fang cuts into it, but I barely notice the sting that chases at its heels. "Yes, Mother."

I shake my head, returning to my now empty class to grab my books before moving on to the next, her voice still lingering in the back of my mind.

I hadn't missed the way she'd changed her words. 'We' don't need to get distracted. It's one of her many rules—stay focused, surpass everyone, don't let anyone shake you from your goal. Whatever the goal is, I'm still not sure. Maybe it's to be like her, or just for me to be at the top. All this time, and I still don't know.

My hands rub together slightly, a little wash of nerves running through my veins before I imagine my emotions being tidied up into a glass bottle with a cork, putting them away for now. Maybe for good, if I'm lucky.

The day doesn't pass without seeing Irsa and Cain again, but instead of letting myself slip into watching their actions, I ignore them and everything else around me. I go through classes taking notes, reading passages of books, practicing spells.

I don't feel anything, not even a twinge of interest in Cain when he glances at me in the hall—and before I know it, I'm standing before Silas again.

Our sessions together are practically a dance, spinning around one another, smoothly diving from the swings of our blades. Rhythmically dodging the slim, pointed tips of the rapiers we now both wield when we aim it a little too close, catching each other off guard by nipping the ends against cloth. I know each footstep to take to avoid him, each duck and twist to get into his weakest points—and with my mother watching, I strive for them every time. I *have* to be good. I have to be what she wants.

Silas's blade swings quick, throwing my focus as it cuts into my cheek from the corner of my jaw to the center of my cheekbone. My own rapier drops, and I stagger away from him as the heat of my blood warms my shirt, running in a thin stream down the side of my neck after the initial spray. I open my mouth to speak, to try and say anything at all, but I can't get any words to form fast enough. Before I can manage *anything*, Morgana sweeps over from her spot by the door, anger rolling off of her in sheets as she yanks the rapier from Silas's hand and throws it across the room.

My body flinches as the weapon crashes to the floor with a metallic clang, and again as she glares at him, her mismatched eyes blazing. "Silas, you *know* what we've discussed."

Silas nods, bright eyes closing as he kneels before her, resting a palm over his chest. "I know, Morgana. I apologize, it wasn't my intention—"

"Intention or *not,* he is still spilling blood. I should have you punished." Her voice raises at the start and swiftly lowers, nearly a snarl.

I attempt to sweep the blood from my skin, but it does nothing to make it stop, continuing a hot path down over my turtleneck. "Mother, please, he didn't mean it."

Morgana grabs me by the hand and yanks me from the room, shooting me a look that spells out danger if I continue to speak. A cold warning, wrapped in ice and served directly through her sharp irises. "That doesn't matter, Daedalus. Be quiet."

I glance back to see Silas still kneeling there before she pulls me out of the room and down the hall, leading me to a small chamber consisting of a plush red rug, deep red walls, and a black velvet couch with two bookshelves on either side. One of her relaxing areas, or at least, one of the rooms she decorated herself. She pushes me down onto the couch and shakes her head, her anger threatening to swallow me whole in the energy of her magic—a deep void, reaching for eternity, snapping at my lungs and freezing me in place. The feeling drowns out all thoughts from my head, forcing me to remain as quiet as possible.

One ice-cold hand raises to the wound on my cheek, burning against the heat of my blood, continuing to pool under her palm and drip down onto my thigh. I count each slow drip, remaining unmoving as she heals me, golden eyes tracing the sharp teeth of the half-mask in her skeletal markings. One, two, three, four. One, two, three four. One...

My mind drifts the longer I sit, so still I could nearly be a statue, becoming as blank as the stars in a vacant night sky.

A confused blink as she withdraws her hands and steps back from me, her anger no longer coating my skin.

I raise my fingers to my cheek, brushing the fresh, rough scar carved into my skin.

Morgana smiles at me, but it doesn't reach her eyes. "There, all better dear. Now, go rest."

I can't manage to find the words to answer her, so all I do is nod and hurry down the dark hall, ignoring the eyes of the paintings along the walls as I find my way back to my room.

It's rather large in size, similar to our former home; with a black curtained-off bed covered by velvet blankets and a heap of pillows, dark walls lightly obscured by framed moths and taxidermy bats, a handful of oak bookshelves in one corner with two armchairs by a window layered with rows and stacks of new and old books alike. A long mirror nearly tall enough to reach the edge of the vaulted ceiling faces the wall, standing beside a wardrobe and two wooden trunks, across the room from my doorway.

My eyes finally reach the center of it all, my glossy-black grand piano standing like a homing beacon, drawing me to the velvet bench with familiar ease. The fogginess in my head lingers as I sit down, resting my fingertips over the smooth surface of the keys for a moment before starting to play. The song that flows from me is one I started composing myself, dark and gloomy, swirling from somber to something ethereal as I fly along the keyboard.

It echoes throughout my room, each note pulling me into a deeper focus, the piano aching with me as it always does.

And finally, I am able to breathe.

4

—·—

THE NEXT NIGHT, the college is quiet. So quiet, in fact, it almost sounds as if the bones of the building whisper in the midnight breeze, barely reaching in through the window and to the library's piano I sit by.

I exhale, leaning forward to look out at the city, past the bright wash of moonlight painting over me and the carpeted floor beyond. Nemoure glows beyond the glass pane, gold and multicolored lights shifting and blinking, tempting me to climb out onto the roof just out of sight above me. It calls with gentle hands, waiting for me to witness the scale of it, waiting for me to look out over the horizon and just see.

Maybe if I did, I would allow myself to acknowledge what is bothering me. I know there is something, even if I cannot place what it is. Morgana doesn't allow me to remember.

The thought jolts me to a halt, forcing the slow motions of my hands over the keys to stop entirely. I sigh, withdrawing from the piano and biting the inside of my cheek until it burns, before moving closer to the window instead to watch the city.

I carefully settle on the wide ledge—an uneven balancing act, with one knee up to my chest and the other left to hang over—shifting to rest my head against the cool glass and hating the pain circling my sternum. It clings like a weighted cloak over my shoulders, growling in my gut, waiting. Pacing. Hungering for me to let it know it hurts, it hurts, it hurts.

I likely should have gone home tonight, but having a room here makes it so much easier to avoid the responsibility attached to the word *home*.

I'm more than grateful that the library tends to be more empty at night, allowing me more time to sulk. The scent of old books and paper clings to every breath, touched with a hint of something like lavender as I take another look around, eyeing the shadows just in case someone is hiding there to watch me.

Countless bookshelves line every cream-white wall, stacked with heaps of multicolored books of every size. One half of the library's floor is covered in a solid gray carpet with multiple smaller rugs in shades of blues under the tables, matching the detailed painting of some legendary mage dueling a dragon sprawled across the arched ceiling. The other half of the floor is made up of a light brown oak wood, stretching out to the entry doors and beneath the librarian's desk.

The door leading into the library creaks open, startling me from my study of the room. For a second, nothing moves, and I worry that I've imagined the sound entirely, until Cain steps in from the darkness of the hall, his stride loose and at ease compared to how he usually looks—with the weight of power on his shoulders. My heart pounds uncertainly against my chest as I watch him, and I swallowing down the instant anxiety his presence brings me, before forcing myself to look back through the window in some slim attempt to remain unnoticed.

Something shifts where Cain is behind me, sounding like ruffled clothing. A flinch, maybe, then—"Oh! Ah. Daedalus, I wasn't expecting to see you here," he says, though he doesn't get any closer.

I look back at him, catching him look over his shoulder in the direction of the door, and shift carefully. "Hello, Cain," I reply, a little softer than I mean it to be.

"What are you doing here this late?" Cain asks, stepping into the square of moonlight on the carpeted floor. The pale rays light him up vividly, casting an array of color into my sight against the otherwise dark room—brightening the red of his hair, scattering a glitter in his eyes.

The entire view of him makes my stomach flip with nerves. "I could ask you the same."

"Fair point. I'm getting away from someone." Cain shrugs, looking past me to the city beyond the window.

I know *exactly* who he must be talking about, but I keep my mouth shut. Instead, I sit upright again and readjust my black turtleneck, tugging down the sleeves and moving back onto my feet.

Cain's eyes graze over me, making it impossible to stay still, impossible to *even think.* He always seems to have that effect. "Are you leaving?" he says with a slight frown.

Only now, when I finally *really* look at him, I realize just how casual he appears. His long hair isn't in its usual ponytail, but instead spread out over his shoulders and down his back like a mane, all curls and waves. There is no scarlet vest either, only his loosened white button-up and black slacks—though the ones he's wearing tonight look different than the ones I often see him in. Comfier, maybe. It feels odd to see him this way, undone, almost. Not at his most perfect.

"I was considering it, yes," I admit slowly, before leaning back to rest on the window's ledge again.

As he steps closer, my eyes catch on the glitter of gold and red jewelry across his hands and around his neck, dangling from his long and pointed ears. It adds to the odd allure of him, and it makes me unable to do much more than watch him as he turns to drag a chair over. My body won't allow me to move, freezing to this very spot, unable to decide where to go. Why it had to be Cain, and not someone else—

"Why not stay a moment? We never get the chance to speak." Cain smiles as he sits down in the navy-blue armchair he moved, settling back into it as if it was something more like a throne than a seat in a library.

My hands tighten on the edge of the windowsill as I consider it, and with a soft sigh, I agree, trying my best to relax, despite the nerves skittering under my skin.

I duck my head slightly, so my hair almost curtains me off from him, relieving me from the sight of his beauty for at least a *second*. But something else catches my eye as it falls, and I follow it with a curious frown—a thick gray streak cutting through otherwise black strands.

Since when did I start graying? Was it recent? No, this had to be there for a while with how thick it is. It must be from stress, rather than age, I'm sure, though how I could have missed it—even with my aversion to mirrors—I've no idea.

"What are you still doing awake, Daedalus?" Cain's voice jolts me from my train of thought, and he chuckles low in his throat when I jump and push my hair back over my shoulder.

"I don't sleep well." I swallow as the words leave me, wishing I could've stopped them before they came out. Gods, I can't look at him. He's so Godsdamned intimidating. "Or rest well in any form, I suppose."

Cain nods, eyeing me. "I wish I could say the same, but I need my beauty sleep."

A laugh slips past me, soft and uncertain in the quiet. Some-how, it doesn't surprise me that he considers it beauty sleep, rather than anything else. *How fitting.*

Clearing my throat, I glance at Cain's moonlit eyes and away quickly, studying the patterns of the carpet beneath the piano instead. Finding every ninety-degree angle in them suits me far better than looking at him, but I do wish I at least had a cup of tea or something to keep my hands steady. "Why do you want to speak with me?"

Warmth instantly rushes to my cheeks in mild embarrass-ment at asking, but in all honesty, I know I have little im-portance in the universe that is Cain Sidrelle. At least, I don't gravitate around him or in his circle the way most seem to.

Instead, I came hurtling like an asteroid into his center of gravity, throwing everything off.

"You're new, and too quiet. It makes you different than my friends, I don't know." He shrugs, laughing as one of his ringed hands lifts to twirl a red curl around his finger. "I've wanted to talk to you for a while."

'Would you touch my hair like that?'

The thought blazes through me, creating more heat in my cheeks and the tips of my ears. So much so, that I turn away from Cain so he can't see me, so I don't have to explain why I'm suddenly as red as the shade he wears. Maybe the room itself will swallow me whole for thinking something so inappropriate. Maybe I'll magically disappear below the shadows and run away.

"I see," I say, instead of running off like my body screams to. I glance back at the city before pushing away from the windowsill, shifting my weight from one foot to the other. Restlessly, aimlessly, uncertainly.

Cain's gaze follows the movement, rising from my black leather boots to somewhere at my hip. It shifts in a straight line from one point to the other, connected as if pulled perfectly taut. "Are you bored?"

I shake my head, folding my arms over my chest. "Thinking, mostly."

"What are you thinking about?" He tilts his head to the side, casting a wave of crimson over his shoulder and the arm of the chair. One leg crosses over the other, hitching over the knee, adding a new angle to him. A new degree that my brain calculates quickly, before I register his question.

"Angles, lines." The angles of you, in particular. "Mathematical equations."

Cain laughs, almost sensually. He sounds like he's purring. "You're very strange, Daedalus Macabre."

Something like a smile quirks at my lips, tugging at the corners. I'm blushing again. "So I've been told."

After a brief moment of silence filled by nothing but the shifting of Cain's body in his chair, he eyes me. "So," he says, a light smile on his lips. "What should I know about you?"

Funny, how it feels business-like.

"Well," I start, pausing to hum in thought, a little uncomfortable with the idea of talking about myself.. "I play piano, and I originally came from Makor. I'm the son of a former archmage, so I'm very well-versed in magic. What about you?"

"I don't play any instruments, but I was formerly an athlete in my private school in Midrana. I'm the favorite son of a very rich, draconic father, who is on the council here. So in a sense, we're sort of similar." Cain shrugs a shoulder, the moonlight perfectly catching his eyes as he looks me over. Every second that look is on me, my body *burns*. "I like your tattoos."

I smile, rubbing my hands together. "Oh, thank you. They run in my family."

The smile instantly falters as a sudden wave of something familiar hits me, flooding my entire body.

The feeling of being watched.

Panic twists up in my gut and soars through my veins, causing my legs to move without my command. "I have to go, forgive me."

I nearly trip over myself as I hurry out of the library, hearing Cain mutter to himself in confusion behind me before the door snaps shut between us. Walking briskly down the empty hall, I cast a glare toward the ceiling. "Why can't you leave me alone?"

My heartbeat quickens as whispers of a different kind begin to take form in my head, echoing and reverberating inside my skull. *"Why didn't you come home, Daedalus?"*

I likely made a fool of myself in front of Cain, during what could have possibly been the *one* chance I'd see him alone, and now my mother is making me visibly flinch. What a night. "I was studying late, I apologize."

She doesn't reply right away, leaving me in chilled silence for a moment. *"I saw you with that Sidrelle. You know what I said."*

I close my eyes tight at her statement as I stop at the stairwell, letting out a breath before jogging up them until I reach the floor to the student's rooms. My legs ache by the time I get there, but it's a welcome distraction from my mother's cold voice, so I don't mind it. The hall is painted a cool blue with golden accents lining the edges, and every door is made up of a dark oak wood with a little engraved plaque on them with a number. Navy carpet softens my footsteps as I continue down to my room, glancing at the doors as I pass and studying the little designs some students have carved into theirs.

"I know," I reply quietly. "I didn't plan on speaking with him."

When I reach my room, I fumble with my key for a moment before pushing open the door, leaning my back against it once it's closed behind me.

Another stretch of silence passes, then a slight huff. *"But you did. Regardless, you should come home tomorrow. You missed training tonight."*

"Yes, Mother."

My body trembles from the fade of adrenaline as I push away from the door, feeling a little too small in the expanse of my dorm room. The walls are a pleasant dark gray with a cream ceiling and matching double doors leading to a small balcony across from the entry, a few feet from where my bed sits in the middle of the left wall. On it sits a handful of plush gray and black blankets, some velvet and some not, with multiple matching pillows. I've always had too many pillows. I don't know how I keep acquiring more of them.

A wooden table sits in the corner with a black armchair, greeting me from beside the door, welcoming me over to it like a long-lost friend, waiting for me to go and sit down for hours.

Instead, I ignore it and the black bookshelf next to it, my stomach flipping unsteadily from my mother's words.

Instead, I ignore it, my stomach flipping unsteadily from my mother's words, and make sure the door is locked before ducking into my personal restroom. I brush my fingertips over the dove-gray tiling making up the walls before starting a bath in the white marble bathtub, pausing there for what feels like minutes until I finally make myself move back to the sink.

The bath makes the room bloom with the scent of vanilla—intense at first, but pleasant. My body continues to shake as I stare at myself in the small, triangular mirror above the sink for a long while—studying my scarred skin and the furrow of my eyebrows, following the lines of my face and how they intersect with the black skull markings over it. The darkness of the eye socket markings nearly mask the bags under my eyes, but I know if they weren't there, they'd be the color of bruises.

God's, I hate looking at myself. I don't know why I bothered.

I withdraw for a moment to strip down, folding each garment in a neat pile, one on top of the other. It's become a ritual I have to do every time I undress, regardless of where I am, which some may say could be annoying or frustrating. I don't think it is. Rather, it keeps me somewhat organized if I do.

I glance back at how the markings cover the slender shape of my body, shifting in line with the mirror again and leaning against the sink, finding my gaze locking onto the scars crisscrossing my arms. It drops for only a second to fixate on my knuckles turning pale from how hard I'm gripping the sink's edge, then returns.

My stomach turns worse the longer I look.

Tearing my gaze away before the ache in me deepens, I walk to the tub and turn it off, gingerly stepping into the steaming, clear water. I sink in until my back presses against the bottom of the basin, folding myself under the surface.

It's a strange thing to not need to breathe. I could likely sit here for hours if I chose—there would be no colors or shadows at the edges of my vision, no pressure in my chest telling me to *exhale, sink, sink, sink.* I sigh and breathe slightly out of an early-learned habit from watching my father do it, something I realized when I was younger made people far more comfortable around me. If I didn't breathe, I was given looks and whispers. If I do, people barely notice me.

I consider it, sitting here like this, but eventually decide to sit up and sweep the ropes of wet hair from my face, propping an elbow against the side of the tub to rest my head against instead. Everything in me aches as deeply as the college sounds like it does, but if a hot bath would not help, then I do not know what will.

Somehow, I thought the college might help me feel better when it came to my mother. Somehow, I thought I might hurt less.

Instead, I feel as if I'm the cello that the college is dragging its bow across, making me weep as my mother plucks at my strings.

Will I get any rest tonight?

After a few minutes, I push myself from the tub, grabbing one of the light towels they sent with each room from on top of the toilet and drying myself with it, grimacing at its odd texture. I've never been a fan of how towels feel—somewhat coarse and somewhat soft, almost plush if they're expensive enough, otherwise they're too rough. They're not my favorite thing, by any means, especially being there isn't one consistent texture for them. There are so many towels in the world, why haven't their makers perfected them yet? And some barely absorb anything while others absorb it all—

"Focus, damnit." I thump the heel of my palm against my forehead as I squeeze out my hair, slipping into the main room and up to my wardrobe.

I dress in a pair of black silk pajamas before dragging the small table by my bed to the armchair in the corner, settling down to read instead of going to bed like I maybe should.

Old habits die hard, I suppose.

The next time I look at the window, the sky is turning a mix of vibrant oranges and pinks, indicating that I definitely missed my chance to sleep. Pushing out of my seat—promptly dumping a lap full of crumpled papers onto the floor—I walk over and peer out of it, almost glaring at the city below and all the beauty it holds between its glossy buildings. The multicolored lights and wild parties of the night will end here, becoming whites and yellows as the more formal part of society begins to wake. People will be making coffee or tea to accompany their breakfast. Stores will open, and early-rising customers will excitedly shout 'good morning!' to their cashier or barista or bookseller.

Some will be doing a walk of shame down the street, much to their dismay, clutching their clothes to their chests or adjusting broken straps and clinging to broken zippers . Maybe they're limping from the broken heel on their shoe, or they're simply trying to mask their hangover.

Nemoure may be new to me, but I can guess how it acts all the same. Its bones are no different than anywhere else, after all.

My own exhaustion will likely catch up to me later on, but so long as it doesn't show, I'll be fine.

If it does, if it shows at all, I'll be disappointed—and inevitably, so will my mother.

Gods, I wish I could relax. I wish relaxation would take me now, ease my shoulders, stroke through my hair like it cared. It would let me lay in bed, unbothered by the daylight. Relaxation would hold me until I woke again.

But for now, it leaves me alone.

My gaze sweeps back over the table and the surrounding floor, noting the crumpled balls of paper and books strewn around it like a storm had swept through. Stiff and a bit achy from holding the same position all night—hunched over papers and books, ignoring the pains in my neck and back in favor of continuing my studies—I stretch out toward the ceiling, listening with some amusement to the ripple of cracks down my spine that follows, something messy that makes typical people shudder in its wake. To me, it's just another strange thing my body does. To others, it's horrifying.

Or so I've noticed, by looks shot in my direction.

After changing into a black, long-sleeved shirt and velvet pants, I gather up my books and leave the mess of paper on the floor behind for a later me to deal with. The hall is quiet, still too early for most of my classmates to be awake—many of them will be doing the walk of shame themselves, or they'll be the ones still in bed with a hangover. At this hour, I don't anticipate seeing any of them.

That is, until I turn around after locking my door and nearly bump into someone.

Breathe in, roses. Fresh roses, with still-sharp thorns and un-bruised petals. I need not look up at him to know who it is. The scent is practically seared into my memory by now, its presence leaving me completely unsure of what to do with my hands.

Cain, again. Red, red, red.

"Good morning, Daedalus," he greets. Formal, but not un-friendly.

I lift my gaze from Cain's black, leather boots to his face, eyeing the red lipstick he'd painted on and the way his usu-al ponytail sways behind him. I cannot help thinking that it looked better down. He's much closer than last night—I can almost see every shade of red that make up his crystalline irises now, whereas I could only admire the danger of them from afar before. My heart is pounding so hard, I swear he could probably hear it. "Hello again, Cain."

Cain smiles as he shifts his bag over his shoulder and takes a step back, making me feel oddly self-conscious. Was I too close? I never moved. Oh Gods, I should've moved.

"I wasn't sure if I'd see you after you took off last night," he says, and though it sounds a little brisk, he still seems kind. Strangely, so.

I grimace, visibly, then give him an apologetic look. "I'm sorry for that."

He shakes his head, and his smile changes. Almost warmer, in a strange way. "I wasn't scolding you for it, I was just saying."

I nod, slowly, considering if I could skirt past him and continue on down the hallway or not. I probably could, but his presence is too immense, too heavy, that I find it hard to move. It's almost as if he's cornering me against the wall, and really, it would be better if he pinned me here himself. Not in any intimate way, but to settle my nerves.

"Still. It wasn't very...*right*, of me, we'll say, to leave like that," I offer him.

Cain glances back over his shoulder, seemingly relaxing a little more when the hallway continues to remain empty. "Were you alright?"

A slight clear of my throat, a shift of my weight between my feet. "Yes... something like that."

He frowns slightly, tilting his head at me. "I won't ask more, but... I would like to talk to you again. For longer than last time?"

"I would like that." *I don't know if I can.* "I tend to be awake at most hours, so... it won't be hard to find me."

Cain laughs, and it sends a strange feeling through my chest—a pang, maybe, or a twinge. Something in my heart missing a beat, or my stomach? I can't tell.

"Oh, Cain!"

We both tense at the sudden voice, and Cain rolls his eyes as he turns on his heel to face its owner, my own gaze following quickly behind.

Irsa smiles wide at him, *too* wide. The only color standing out against his otherwise gloomy gray outfit is a deep red rose in his hand—a rose that was probably fresh once, but now looks as if it's going limp simply from his touch alone.

He beams until he spots me in front of him, the expression turning dark and cold for all of a second. "Cain, what are you doing?"

Cain raises an eyebrow at him, his lip curling in unhidden disgust. "Simply saying good morning to Daedalus, not that it's any of *your* business. What do you want?"

Irsa extends the rose to him, and I immediately have to fight off a slight laugh when Cain denies it and pushes his hand away. Every time I see them interact, it usually consists of Irsa trying to impress Cain, or nearly begging him to go somewhere with him. Once or twice, I overheard him mentioning hotel rooms, and something of a slap that followed. It seems to be a continuous ritual between them, one that I'm learning Cain hates.

"Do you have something to say, Daedalus?" Irsa narrows his eyes at me, practically spitting out my name. He must have noticed the twitch of a smile I wore when Cain said no.

Rather than answering him, I force myself to meet Cain's gaze. "I suppose I'll see you in class?"

He nods, smiling pleasantly for a split second. "Of course. See you then."

Not wanting to get trapped in any form of conversation with Irsa, I slip around Cain and hurry down the hall, heading in the direction of the dining area. It's thankfully easy to find once I get down the stairs, simply following the smell of fresh waffles and bacon, and to my relief, there aren't many others at the periwinkle-colored tables this early in the day.

I struggle to focus on anything as I move through the line, hurrying to find my own little space in the hall. A small plate of waffles topped with bright red strawberries and a sprinkle of powdered sugar fills my lungs with sweet vanilla, a welcome change from the dust of the college. A black coffee, and an empty table toward the back corner.

At first, I intend to eat quickly so no one joins me, but a shadow at the corner of the table changes that. I turn to look at the person joining me, pleasantly surprised to see Asher with a similar plate to my own.

"Hello again," he greets, a light curl of a smile forming before he takes a small bite. "I thought you might not mind it if I joined you."

If it was anyone but him, I likely would.

"I don't," I agree, nodding back at him.

Asher nods, continuing to eat in mutual quiet for a moment, then looks back to me. "Why are you in science classes if you're so ahead of everyone, Daedalus?"

The way he asks makes me tense momentarily, narrowing my eyes in his direction. "I experiment more than you might expect. I've recently attempted making a form of adrenaline, but I haven't perfected it yet. *That's* why."

"Shit, really?" Asher replies, sliding down the table until he's directly across from me. His eyes are lit up behind the dark lenses of his sunglasses. "I experiment, too. My last one was trying to blend a humanoid heart with one from the Astral."

"The Astral?" I echo, eyebrows raising. Most things in the Astral are called alien and strange, sometimes monstrous. Eldritch beings live out there, in the cold spaces where no one can find them. It's always intrigued me, that vacuum of darkness, but I haven't yet studied more into it. "Really?"

He nods, smiling a bit wider. "Yes, I'll have to show you sometime."

I nod, exhaling my curiosity. "I'd love to know."

An hour passes before I realize it, and I barely recall walking to my first lecture of the day with the way my mind is so wrapped around the Astral. Even seeing Cain in our shared science class does nothing to pull me from that fuzzy mind space. It's as if my body is moving on its own, ducking in and out of the next few rooms with relative ease, eyes always to the floor.

Once the classes pass by, I make sure to return my books to my room before leaving the college and stepping into the sun-warmed plaza. The sun is setting, casting the cobblestone in oranges and yellows, but the air, now cooling in the shadows of the skyscrapers, still feels content with the summer heat. Casual conversation and bubbling laughter from my classmates spills out around me, telling me they likely feel the same. Instead of lingering in the waning sunlight like I'd like to, I keep my head ducked, and I slip through small groups of people, crossing the stone streets, passing by sweet smelling bakeries and incense-filled shops.

I can't make myself stay still, especially not out here.

A group of elven people in colorful outfits duck away at the sight of me walking toward them, whispering low enough for me not to hear what they must be remarking. To them, I'm a walking premonition of dark times on Nemoure. I still haven't placed why.

One of them, a ginger-haired man with green eyes, catches me looking and laughs. *Harshly.* "What're you looking at, freak? Got something to say?"

I shake my head, steeling my nerves. "No, not at all."

"That's what I thought. Go back to your freaky manor and disappear," he says, and when his friends snicker, he turns to them. "He probably has some kind of fucked-up dungeon in his basement. Fucking creepy."

They sneer at me before moving on, their laughter echoing down the alley they turn into.

With a slight frown, I continue walking, until someone grabs my shoulder from behind and reels me into the brick wall of what looks to be a plant shop. Instinctively, my shadows form in response, and those same people passing us flinch at the sight of them. A familiar, uncomfortable energy flows over my skin like sewer water, and my frustration builds at the feeling of it.

"Hello, Macabre," Irsa sneers, practically spitting out my name in that specific way of his. "I just wanted to have a little chat."

My lips curls in response, and I shove him away from me, desperate for even a breath of relief from how sick his magic makes me feel. "I don't want to speak with you, actually."

He snaps forward, hands grabbing the front of my shirt and forcing me into the wall, hard enough for my back to ache. "I don't care what you want, Daedalus. You're gonna listen to me."

My shadows coil up and around his arms, lingering around his elbows. Like this, I could turn them into barbs, or snap a bone if I needed to. For right now, I make them wait there—a threat without words. "Get off of me."

"No," he growls, gold eyes brilliant with his hatred for me as his magic forms a small knife in one hand, which he holds up against the side of my throat. "Stay the *hell* away from Cain. He isn't yours, he will never like someone like you. Cain is meant for far better things than some foreigner like you."

Foreigner. Is that why Nemoure hates us? I thought it was the type of city to like people like me.

"I can't control what he does," I reply simply, swallowing hard as the edge of his blade touches my skin, making my skin crawl. My stomach turns at the feeling. "And I won't let you control me, either. Leave me alone, Irsa."

My magic surges, just enough to shove him back and clear some space between us. Irsa snarls as he stumbles, nearly tripping over himself before he levels his anger on me again. "I mean it, Macabre."

"I don't care, Irsa." I shake my head, allowing the dark tendrils to circle in front of me, remaining defensive. "You won't do anything about it, anyway."

The clank of armor walking in our direction makes Irsa straighten up, willing his magic away the instant one of the city guards appears around the corner. The pair looks both of us over as they pass, but neither stop to inspect our interaction, or to even listen to Irsa as he greets them.

Irsa levels his eyes on me as he turns on his heel, a bitter smile on his face. "We'll see about that."

And in nothing more than a breath, he's gone.

I let my magic settle again, cursing as I glare at the space he once stood in. Unease shifts under my skin, turning to continue walking in the direction of the manor—and that feeling only grows bigger with every turn and pass down winding alleys and wider streets.

Returning home weighs on me like an anchor in my chest, and each step I take grows slower and slower as I approach, as if someone was continuously wrapping chains around my shoulders and drawing them toward the ground. I pause just outside the property, glancing toward the thick forest that lines the back of the manor's yard in a foolish attempt at ignoring the oppressive iron gate looming before me.

Towering trees shade my eyes from the setting sun, but I still have to squint at the beams of it peeking between the trunks and branches, scattering dappled light over the grass below. My father always murmured about it, reminding him of their shared manor back in Makor, where it was framed by a similar forest, touched by Fae magic.

In the shadows, I swear I catch a glimpse of something flickering before I look away—eyes, or the blinks of fireflies perhaps?

I press my lips into a firm line as I push open the gate, listening to it creak and shudder with the motion. It rattles back into place, officially caging me in, trapping me in my own yard. I swallow as I take a moment to count the gargoyles peering over the roof—a pointless ritual to calm my nerves—before rubbing my palms together and starting slowly up the path to the door.

The vague smell of roses from our small garden rushes to meet me, and the instant thought of Cain it brings makes my hands tremble.

As I open one of the doors to let myself in, Bren darts away from the stairs in a flash of lavender and black as if I were a stranger in his home. I might have called after him if given the chance, curiosity stinging at my fingertips, demanding answers, but the sharp sound of Morgana's heels as she enters the room floods me with a cold dread and washes the thought from my mind before it fully forms.

She eyes me, then strides past me toward the stairwell with a curt jolt of her head. "Oh good. You're home. Upstairs, Daedalus. We need to talk before your training with Silas."

Even through the carpeting on the stairs, the sharp sound of her heels echoes in my ears, consuming my thoughts. *Click click click click.* Stabbing into me, working threads of anxiety into my head with every defined step.

Morgana leads me into the resting chamber she had taken me last time, when Silas had cut my cheek, and gestures for me to sit down before closing the door. "Stay still, yes?"

I don't know why I listen to her. I don't know why I can't bring myself to move away when she cradles my temples, holding me too tight.

He's not what you wanted. He's a pathetic version of what you wanted to make.

Her voice, distinct and angered, rips through me like a blade. I can't move away, staring up at her as her own words echo in my mind. The feeling of her disappointment shatters everything in my chest, not even a hint of false pride to soothe my wound. They sit on repeat, turning again and again, every new utterance creating another injury.

My mind turns foggy, emptied and gutted of thoughts as she works over whatever it is that she wanted. When I realize it, I make a weak attempt to jerk away from her, but her grip remains unyielding. I know what she's after, and I don't understand *why.*

She keeps me there almost gingerly, as if she *wants* me to try escaping, knowing full well I won't be able to. I have to get away. I can't let her take anything, I can't, but nothing is working. My body won't move, not even as I try to shift from her reach again—and before I can make another pass at it, my mind empties. Static roars in my ears, ruffling the overlapping disgust from her own thoughts to the panic in mine.

When she finally lets me go, everything comes back in a rush, my days blurring together between classes, staying up studying, playing my piano. Something in me aches like loss, like grief, causing fresh tears to well in my eyes as I meet her gaze.

"Oh, dear, don't do that. I have a gift for you." Morgana steps away from me after a moment of watching my expression, reaching behind her to take down a medium-sized black jar from one of her bookshelves. Within it appears to be a living shadow, coiling within the glass, twisting and turning as she holds it before the light so I can see. Pride dashes across her face briefly before her neutral and glassy-eyed mask returns, looking back down at me.

She passes the jar into my hands and clasps her hands at her waist, eyeing me. "Drink it."

"What—what do you mean, drink it?" I look between her gaze and the writhing mass of smoky tendrils, swallowing past the sudden dryness in my throat.

Irritation breaks across the emptiness in her eyes, just for a second. "Daedalus. I know best, especially what's best for *you*, don't I? Do as I say."

Feeling almost threatened by her tone, I fight not to show the trembling in my hands as I nod, popping open the lid and tipping the glass against my lips. The shadow instantly shoots into my mouth, rolling over my tongue, tasting of nothing but ashes. It moves like it hasn't been freed in ages, as if she had it trapped there and it was finally tasting freedom in the space of me.

I force my mouth to close, despite the gasp and gag that wants to leave, clenching my jaws so tight it makes my teeth ache, shivering visibly. My stomach twists as I squeeze my eyes shut and swallow, forcing it down my throat—feeling it writhe and dance inside me, flowing swift and quick, expanding the further it drops.

The feeling of it seeping into me is far too strong, filling every space in my body. My left hand opens and closes without my control.

"What was that?" I look up at Morgana again through blurry tears, and she smiles at me.

"Good job. Now, let's get you to your training, yes?" She takes my hands, ignoring my question entirely as she drags me to my feet. The glass jar thumps onto the carpeted floor, and I had half the mind to join it there.

"Mother, what *was* that?" I repeat, nervously, and she stops in the doorway to the training room.

"Trust me, Daedalus." No room for error. Last warning, last chance.

I hesitate, swallowing down another wave of tears. "I do, Mother. I do."

I wish I didn't.

5

—·—

MY OWN reflection stares back at me in the thin slice of blade I've been contemplating for hours, watching, waiting for that old burst of pain to come, but it never does. I never move close enough. My heartbeat pounds in my ears as I sit in this unbearable limbo, feeling my body ache. An age-old urge for a new pain, one I know I can't commit myself to again.

I suppose it should come as no shock that Morgana does not love me. For so long, I have tried to convince myself otherwise, tried to listen to her words and not her actions. I have spent my whole life deluding myself into believing it, believing that the things she did were worth it, that they were best for me.

But there could be no other answer now. No other explanation to her ministrations, to the hurt she's placed on me, to the experiments and the lies. I always thought that maybe, underneath her cold exterior, her heart held something for her oldest son.

That was until she was cupping my face, and I heard her thoughts so clearly, I'd nearly thought them my own.

He's not what you wanted. He's a pathetic version of the thing you wanted to make.

Returning to my dorm room had felt like the only answer to my pain, and so, I've been sitting here since. Sobbing, wishing the world would cave me in, wishing for something better than...*everything.* Wishing someone would maybe care enough to come to my door and walk inside, at least slap some sense into me.

Worst of all, some part of me still wants to pretend that she loves me, that I could be the son she wanted, that I am worth something. I might have even convinced myself of it, if not for the very physical evidence she'd left me as a reminder.

Because ever since that talk with my mother a week ago, the skeletal markings on my skin have become... *living*, in a sense.

Shadows curl around each bone, constantly writhing against the skin it has since been trapped on. They formed after Morgana fed me whatever was in that jar, and with them came a small voice in the back of my mind telling me to do odd things. Try this, try that—things I wouldn't typically do. Violent things.

I haven't acted on them, but whatever the thing is she put inside me wants me to. It wants to feel. It wants to know what it's like to burn, to sit underwater until the lack of breath aches in our lungs, to know what it's like not to be loved by someone we once thought the world of.

That last one is easy enough to provide, apparently. With what she'd fed me, with what she'd *thought* of me, I am practically saturated in heartbreak. Not to mention the memories…

I only realized it this morning, during a small discussion with Cain. It was brief and mostly unimportant, but Cain had offhandedly mentioned a conversation we had a few nights ago, and I couldn't recall anything about it. Not where we were, or who we were around. I didn't even remember talking to *him* as a whole. I could only find Morgana's gentle cradle, palms to my temples, long nails resting in my hair.

The realization was nearly as painful as the heartbreak—the knowledge that she has been messing with my mind, my memories, and I haven't even noticed.

What else has she erased?

Remembering it makes me lose my grip on the dagger, letting it clatter to the floor as another sob lets itself loose from my lungs. A gut-wrenching thing that tears free from my body and shakes the very foundation of me.

Why have I assumed she loved me? She has been doing this the entire time—hurting me, changing me… Even my newest voice I have started calling 'the Rot' is her fault, and she'd called it a gift. I've been rotting forever because of her, and this is just another piece. Another *reason*, to.

I don't want to go back home.

I haven't been back since.

A familiar knock sounds from my door, one I now know means Cain is on the other side—his knock is always rhythmic with the sort of solidity that comes with knowing one's own importance. A knock I'd imagine he practiced on late-night flings or easy boyfriends, rather than a professional kind offered during meetings. A knock I'd imagine him doing against the inside of a doorway, casual and sweet.

I frown at myself in the mirror, struggling to find any way to make myself look better before he lays eyes on me. A strange weight settles on my chest at the sight of the dark bags under my eyes, the vague redness from previous crying, the fragility written all over my frame that I can't seem to shake off.

It's disgusting. All of it.

Somehow, the fragility wants to break out from my skin, turn into something that *isn't* soft. Frighteningly rough.

I will the dagger out of existence and drag my palms over my face before walking to the door. *Who cares if I look like shit?* I know I do, and hopefully Cain won't say anything about it. *Just Gods, let him be alone—*

"Daedalus!" Cain's voice calls clearly from the other side, followed by a sigh. "Open the door, will you?"

I sigh too, pausing with my hand on the doorknob before opening it up to him. "Hello?"

His expression flickers between a smile and a frown for a moment, decidedly stopping on a smile. "I brought your things back for you. You kind of left them in class and never came back, so they suggested someone bring them to you."

"Oh! Ah, thank you... You can come in, if you'd like, though you're probably busy—"

Cain moves past me before I can finish my sentence, setting my books and notebooks on the table by the door. He rests his hands on his hips, ponytail swishing as he looks back and forth at my room, a curious look on his face. "Huh. Not much different than mine."

"What do you mean?" I close the door behind him, eyeing the crisscrossing ribbons keeping his bright red vest tight. I never noticed it was a corset style before. "You mean your room is dark and gloomy as well?"

I still have a sense of humor, I guess.

He pivots easily on his heel, shifting his weight onto one leg and smiling at me. A few loose strands of crimson fall over his forehead, framing his neat eyebrows. "Oh, no, I guess not. I just mean, you know, similar bookshelves and table, the armchair...are you alright, by the way? You look terrible."

I roll my eyes, looking away from him. "Great, thanks."

"No, not like *that*, Daedalus. You really don't look right." Cain frowns, stepping toward me almost a little hesitantly, as if he wanted to reach out but couldn't bring himself to. Like I'm a wild animal he wants to soothe but can't find a way.

I shrug, walking over to the stack of books he returned to me to habitually check each one for any sign of anyone else touching them. "I'm fine."

It's only after assuring the books are untampered with that I glance back at Cain, something squirming in my belly when he purses his lips and furrows his brows. It takes me a moment to recognize the look, and it hits me just how strange it feels to see him with an expression of concern. I should be the last person he should care about like this, or at least, the last person he should be frowning over.

The Rot doesn't care—can't care, I suspect. My mother doesn't care, and she probably never has. The people around me don't because I shut them all out.

But Cain... he does, it seems, in his own quiet ways. And I don't think I'll ever understand why.

I glance at the darkness past my window, eyeing the distant glowing of the city below before folding my arms over my chest. "What time is it?"

Cain sighs softly, taking another hesitant step forward. "It's like seven... what's going on with you, Macabre? And don't lie to me. I know damn well you're not fine."

His voice, tinged with frustration, creates a new simmer in the aching void resting in my gut. My eyes almost threaten to tear up. "I don't know. I don't know what's wrong with me."

He watches my expression, likely noticing the hurried way I blink to keep the possibility of crying away. "Do you want to talk about it?" he asks, quieter than usual.

"I don't know if I can. It's...a lot." I grimace, finally lifting my eyes to his. I don't know why he's still here. "Maybe another time."

Cain doesn't look happy at that, but he nods anyway, crossing his arms. "I'll leave you alone. You're welcome for your stuff."

Please don't go. Don't leave me like this. "I'm sorry, you don't have to. Thank you for bringing it."

He pauses where he's turned toward my door, his eyes darting from my books to me. That strange little hesitation makes me unsure of myself. For a second, he almost seems like he feels bad for how his tone came across. "... Alright."

Relief cracks me open at that. Even if he doesn't stay for long, I'll be glad to have him for a moment longer. "I'll explain more another time, but my relationship with my mother has always been... difficult, we'll say. It was hard today."

Cain nods, looking away again. "I'm not good with the deep shit sometimes," he says, swallowing visibly. "But, mine is hard too. Marrying me off, particularly. She's been trying that for a long time."

"Mine never did that," I say, shaking my head. "Mine keeps me away, in fact."

"I'm not sure if I should say to be glad for that or not." He snorts, tucking his hands in his pockets. "Mothers are tough to break through."

I nod, letting out a thin sigh. "They are."

We fall into an uncomfortable silence, and Cain shifts a little, glancing at the door and to me. Over and over. "I should likely go," he replies, glancing at the expensive-looking watch on his wrist. "I forgot I have an important meeting with my father tonight."

"Right." I smile tightly, looking toward the floor. The topic was obviously too much, too soon. "Good luck with your meeting."

He slips through my doorway and vanishes behind the oak, leaving me to my silence—and I feel myself caving again instantly. My chest feels tight, as if my ribcage is closing in on my heart and lungs, suffocating me slowly.

For the fifth night in a row, I don't get any rest.

The following morning, I go to my classes as I should. I study, write, sigh. Every time I see Cain, I keep my gaze down and try not to catch a glimpse of how he looks at me—like I'm crumbling right there before him.

Maybe I am, and maybe it's hard not to have anyone to turn to. The closest person I really have is Bren, but that would require my returning home, which I do not wish to do. I can't even go *near* him, much less try to express to him how I feel. He's my brother, and I should love him—he's my brother, and I should *try*, but I can't. I can't make myself talk to him, because I don't know what will happen.

I'm angry, hurt, and wearing down so thin all of my threads are worn at the edges.

The classes drag their feet throughout the day, and my focus wanes the longer they go on. I imagine going home, training, hating the look on Morgana's face as I inevitably recall what I finally figured out. In an odd way, I can almost feel her watching over my shoulder—though I know it isn't real. She hasn't watched me in a while.

I'm 110 years old. She shouldn't be watching me anyway, right?

I shake my head as I walk through the streets, crossing over puddles, watching the people scurrying past me through the mist of the rain. I study the variations in their damp hair—some wearing it in curls or straight, some long or cropped close to their head, some slicked back in ocean-like waves. Droplets of water run down cheeks and the backs of their hands, the curl of their lips and long eyelashes. Cheekbones and the cupid's bow curve of mouths glow and glitter with what must be makeup or magic. Even in the gray, rainy day, bright jewels in gold or silver jewelry wink at me from necks and wrists and pointed ears.

My heart winces as I, for a moment, wish I looked half as nice as they do. Jealousy or envy or both sink their teeth into me like wild dogs, tugging back and forth until I feel the cut of them in my skin.

Tension joins them, winding tight until it feels like my spine could easily snap like the hair on a violin's bow.

The closer I get to the manor, the further that tension heightens. I don't know if I'm more tense due to the beauty of the people that surround me, or the fact that I'm finally returning home after so long and don't know what to prepare for. I brush raindrops off the gate before pushing it open, passing them between my fingertips until they inevitably drip onto the ground below, escaping my skin. The manor looms over me, foreboding and far less inviting than something with the word *home* attached to it should be. Shadows stretch further over the yard as if it is leaning toward me, following the light breeze, staring me down. A warning, maybe. A threat, probably. Enter If You Dare.

I study the brick walls and the gargoyles, eyeing their hooked mouths and wings, imagining the leathery way they'd feel if they were alive. Their gaze remains unblinking, staring far off into the distance at other roofs and gates and people. Do they know they're guarding our home, or do they simply sit there because that's where they were placed? I tilt my head, eyeing their clawed hands next.

What would they feel like, if one attacked you?

The Rot rumbles to life in my head, and the scene plays out before my eyes—me, standing here before the manor, watching the gargoyles break free of their crouched positions and shaking crumbled stone to the ground below. Their wide grins only growing wider as they leap from the roof, wings crackling, flying directly to me. One pins me to the ground as the other attacks, raking surprisingly sharp stone claws and teeth over my skin.

I get a glimpse of red blood before one of the doors opens to Shriek waving me in, and my heart plummets into my feet.

My body feels strange as I start walking up the stone stairs, thanking her before continuing inside and up to the next floor. I don't linger in the halls or even my room—making my path like an arrow's point to the training room. The manor is eerily quiet, but I can easily pick up the sounds of distant footsteps and music off in opposite corners of the building. Having grown up so secluded, I quickly learned to figure out whose sounds were whose, between our servants and my parents.

I'm slowly starting to learn the quick tap of Bren's, among the lower steps of my father and the sharpness of my mother.

I focus in on the sharp sting of Morgana's heels somewhere in the lower level, glad to find myself alone with Silas for at least a moment when I enter the room. He watches me walk in, bright eyes lighting up in a way reminiscent of machines when they're turned on again after a long time. The low light glints off the edge of his silver rapier as he drags a rag over the blade, cleaning it, despite not needing to, something habitual and rhythmic to the motion.

"Hello, Daedalus. It's been a little bit, hasn't it?" Silas smiles, his voice echoing in the quiet of the chamber. He always has a warmer tone to his voice that I don't fully understand, but I never try to ask about it. Something about asking makes it feel like it would go away if I did.

"Hello again, Silas. Can we start?" I grab my rapier from the wall as a new wave of impatience settles over me, striding over to the space across from him. Perfectly six feet apart, as always. I know exactly where to set myself by the lines in the tiles.

When I glance back over my shoulder to the door, he follows my gaze and narrows his eyes. "Just us today, it seems," he states.

I nod, swinging my weapon in a distinct arc through the air in front of me. "Thankfully."

Silas nods and tosses the rag he had been cleaning his blade with over his shoulder, sweeping his hand across his slicked-back white hair before pointing it at me. "*Finally,* more like."

There's a moment of hesitation on both sides where we both pause to watch each other, leaned on our heels like predators, but it doesn't last long. In a flash, we dance around one another—silver and white against black, perfect opposites, blades ringing out with a *clang!* each time they meet. I nearly feel like myself for a moment as I sweep across the black marble floor, catching Silas every time he tries to do something sneaky like cut my feet out from under me or knock my blade to the side.

The air grows heavy with our magic, rippling through the room in thick bands of golds and reds and ice blues, warping with every slice of our weapons.

A sudden crash jolts me from my accidental trance, causing the magic to vanish as I step away from Silas to try and find the source of the sound. My eyes land on his rapier, cast onto the floor a small distance from us, alongside a few drops of bright red blood. The scent spirals around my mind, turning my stomach into something ravenous. It unlocks a hunger I haven't felt in years, stirring it from somewhere far down inside me, making my hands clench. My head reels back, jerking sharply in a way that makes fear roll in my gut, something so *familiar* yet foreign.

"It's only my palm. Good swing, Daedalus. You've seriously improved." Silas nods approvingly, holding his right hand over his palm and healing it with ease.

The warmth that floods me is quickly turned cold by my pangs of hunger, and by the Rot asking to be sliced in the same way. "Thank you, Silas."

"You know... you haven't been home in some time, have you?" Silas asks, eyeing me as he picks up his blade, resting it momentarily at his side.

I bite the inside of my cheek, unable to find the perfect words to answer him—so instead, I continue looking at the bit of blood on the end of my rapier. My hunger is never-ending. I haven't felt it in so long, that need to *consume*.

If I wasn't terrified of another person's skin on mine, maybe I would've eaten much, much sooner.

"Daedalus. Are you alright?" My trainer's voice commands me to look at him without saying those exact words, standing close enough that his bright eyes feel as if they might pierce through me.

My body tenses as I step back a little in response, shaking my head to clear my mind. "Yes, I'm fine. Thank you," I say with a sigh, forcing a thin smile. A slight frown tugs on his lips, disappointment passing across his sharp features briefly before I tap my blade against his. "Shall we go again?"

We continue our sporadic training session, ending with Silas's rapier across the room once more. It hits the floor with a bang instead of a crash this time, likely denting the hilt or warping the blade, but he just seems pleased rather than concerned. Breaking the metal in one way or another is easier in rapiers than swords, especially ours. It's thinner. Moldable.

Moldable like me, experimental in how thin the blade and the swirling hand guard is. I can almost picture the way it's most likely bent on the floor, sitting still in the low lighting.

Silas gasps for breath as I back him up against one of the pillars in the room, his hands up in surrender. We stand there for a little too long, the tip of my blade against his chest, just enough pressure to feel the give of his clothing and skin beneath it. The air is charged with something electric and heavy, tingling on my skin as our magic circles us yet again—nearly intimate, nearly too close, too much. I can't think with the rise and fall of his breath, no longer focusing on the numbness in my stomach. My gaze drops to Silas's slightly parted lips and the rabbit of his pulse at his throat, beating quick, quick, *quicker.*

A flicker of red hair, a pale throat instead of Silas's.

"Wow," he breathes, and I yank my sword away from him.

A new shakiness forms in me at his approval and at my own thoughts as I back away from him, moving to the wall to replace my weapon. The echoes of his breathing rattle in my ears, and I dart out of the room before he can say anything further.

My heart pounds, consuming every other sound but my heavy footfalls. I don't stop until I close my door, and I briefly consider pushing the bookshelf in front of the door even after it's definitely locked. I check twice, no, three times to make sure it is, then slump back against it.

Why did Silas's approval feel like that? Why did I think about him like that? It must be the day. No, the week. Many weeks have made me this way. It must be that.

I groan, sweeping my dark hair from my face and pinching the bridge of my nose.

Why did I see Cain, too?

It must be the week.

6

I EXHALE as my father's echoing raven calls reach me and break through the silence of my studying, filtering in slow and steady, like wax dripping from a candle.

"*Daedalus?*" he says, his voice soft, always gentle with me. Maybe he knows how easy I might be to break.

"*Yes?*" I answer, connecting our threads before his can dissipate entirely. His magic shudders against my own, barely strong enough to take note of, but I hold it there with mine. Somehow, I keep us together despite how wispy his has become. "*What is it?*"

"*We have a dinner to attend to, with the Sidrelle family. They formally invited us, if you'd like to meet us there.*"

My heart jolts in my throat at the thought of going to the Sidrelle mansion, standing before Cain and his even more intimidating family, followed by an immediate wave of anxiety. I rub my hands together and sigh, attempting to keep it down as best as I can. "*Now?*"

"*Yes, my son. Your mother is teleporting us and Bren there. She says it's a good idea for us to connect with them... Unfortunately, I agree after our past ties with Minos."* I can nearly picture his sigh, the slight gruff tone to the end of his words. *"Meet us, please?"*

Right. 'Past ties.' My mother spoke of them loosely on the ship to Nemoure, how her and Mikhalis went through college with Minos Sidrelle, the business-formal draconic patriarch of the Sidrelle line, and they were a rather close trio. I was never fully certain if that was the entire truth, but Mikhalis never gave anything away, so I only had my mother's words to go on.

"Alright. I'll head there, then," I reply, then let our magic fall apart, severing the connection.

I don't bother changing my outfit for the dinner—finding my black button-up and matching pants to be fitting enough for something so formal. With one last nervous look at my dorm, I will the portal spell into my hand, carving it open in the center of my living room.

The wavering shapes of my family's dark bodies before on the other side makes my anxiety climb higher, but I force myself to walk through, even when everything in me screams to do otherwise.

The Sidrelle mansion is beautiful, towering above me with cream-white pillars and arched windows, painted a smooth crimson. Every window is framed by white curtains matching the pillars and, glowing from within by the lights of whatever rooms lie beyond them, golden and pale. Rose bushes and neat hedges crowd the edges of the building and disappear down into the yard, filling what I've heard is a massive garden in the back yard.

It smells *incredible*.

Morgana looks over at me with no expression, no kindness, her hands tight on Bren's shoulders. "Glad you arrived, Daedalus," she says, and something about it feels cold and uneasy. "This is too important to miss."

"Yes, I heard," I say, swallowing down my nerves as the brown double-doors slowly swing open.

A pair of elven men in entirely red outfits smile at us on the other side, both holding the doors for us. "Come in, Macabres," the one on the right says, his voice surprisingly melodic. He's brunette where the other is blonde, his sapphire-blue eyes twinkling curiously when I briefly meet his gaze. "We will lead you to the dining room."

Morgana guides us through and passes them, and Mikhalis does the same as I glance in his direction. He, at least, offers me a reassuring pat on the shoulder before we walk in. The doors are closed behind us before the pair stride up in front of our group, leading us down two separate hallways and toward what looks to be a massive dining area.

Just before we enter, a hand catches my arm from the room beside it and I barely manage to stifle a yelp as someone swiftly drags me back, forcing my anxiety into a higher state as I attempt to break from the other's grip.

"Easy, Daedalus, it's me," Cain hisses softly, letting me go the instant he can shut the door. He looks lovely as always in his business-perfect red vest, white button-up, and black slacks. Even his eyeliner is perfect. *Gods.* "I wanted to catch you before we go in there. We're going to need this."

He waves a bottle of amber liquid at me and smiles before popping it open, taking a hearty swig I'm not sure I can match. "Here."

For a moment, I do nothing but stare at him. While I knew I would run into Cain during this visit—it is his house, afterall—I certainly hadn't expected it to be like this. Nor did I expect to be greeted with that rakish smile of his, so friendly and mischievous, accompanied by the heavy bottle dangling between his fingers.

I take the neck of it uncertainly, then knock back a swallow that's not nearly as big as his own, but big enough for me. The alcohol burns on the way down, searing a warm path all the way to my stomach. Drinking it feels perfectly foreign and pleasing, being it's something my mother forbade me from having for my entire life. *It'll dull the senses*, she says. *Don't touch it.* "Gods, what is that?" I ask, wiping a small drip from my lips as it attempts to run down my chin.

"My father's whiskey. We'll have wine with dinner, of course, trust me when I say, you'll be glad for this starter, alright? It's going to be uncomfortable in there." Cain smiles as he drinks down another mouthful, slightly coughing. "I'm glad you came with your family. I couldn't do this shit by myself...speaking of which, watch what you say in front of my father. My family is...well, I'm sure you might know a little. Tough. Judgmental."

Cain's glad I came? Oh. Ohhh.

A slight smile finds my mouth before I can hide it, drinking a hearty swallow when he passes the drink back. This time, it eases my rising anxiety pleasantly, warming my entire body. "I'm glad you're here as well, and I'll keep that in mind."

"Good," he answers, popping the cap back on the bottle and setting it aside. "We should go now. It'll catch up quick, and we'll be drunk if we keep going like this."

I nod, following him from the room and into the dining area, taking my seat across from him. My eyes trail over to where Minos Sidrelle sits at the head of the table, his sharp red eyes peering over at my mother, where she is sitting opposite of him. The most important man in the city certainly makes himself *feel* like it—his posture and energy alone scream how vast his power is, from riches to the draconic burn torching my sinuses. I've heard countless people talking about him, how he's the greatest thing to happen to Nemoure as one of the Counselors, how he's used his riches to invest in the luckiest of businesses. He's cold and calculating, but at the same time, one of the most charming men around.

I force a breath as I go to sit, feeling strange beside my brother. My father and Bren are on either side of her, then myself, while Cain and his mother sit across from us.

The alcohol had been a welcome distraction, brief as it was, but sitting here now, facing down Cain's family and my own? My heart is rattling in my damn chest.

"Glad you two finally turned up," Minos rumbles, eyeing Cain with a look that's something almost curious but stern.

The servants bring out plates of roasted duck, asparagus, baked potatoes, and red wine for our glasses. I swiftly lose track of the growing conversation as I watch them, finding intriguing angles of their elbows and wrists between the plates, finding the curves and arcs as they pour the deep-red drink for us. Every breath smells like basil, garlic, and herbs, and I'm more than okay with that. It's rather pleasant, mingling with the rose scent that always seems to waft from Cain in waves.

Morgana clears her throat sharply, dragging me back out of my sudden focus—but when I look at her, her eyes are on Cain's mother, disdained and almost angered.

"Unfortunately for you, we are not interested in marrying Daedalus to anybody, Celeste," she says, curating the venom in her words. The way she says the woman's name is jarring. I nearly choke on my first sip of wine, and when I look at Cain, his face is slightly reddened. Embarrassed. *This* must have been what he loosely mentioned the other night.

Marrying me? What?

"Oh, really?" Celeste says, swirling her glass with an irritated expression. "Are you sure? That's a considerable loss for your family, if you didn't. You know how Nemoure views you. Taboo. Not exactly trusted, because of how you are."

Morgana's lips twitch as she takes a bite of duck, but beyond that, her face doesn't change. "Yes, I'm positive. Thank you for the offer, but no."

"We don't need to offer that, anyway, Celeste," Minos growls, almost as if we weren't supposed to hear it at all. "We discussed that."

Cain's parents stare each other down for a long moment—so long, I'm sure they're having a silent conversation through magic, so none of us overhear the argument I assume they must be going through.

My wine is gone before I can even process that I drank it all, and one of the servants quickly refills it. Cain looks like he wants to be anywhere but at this table. I glance between our mothers as the tension builds, shifting uncomfortably in my seat, waiting for *anyone* to break the silence. *Anyone.*

"Daedalus," Minos says, low and slow, after too-long of a moment. Testing my name. "What exactly do you do?"

"He's trying to intimidate you. Don't let him. And, quit drinking. You know it will make you slow," my mother says in my head, without me even noticing the magic clicking together.

"Science, primarily," I reply, taking a bite of my food and swallowing before continuing, despite not being hungry in the slightest. "I am a scientist and a mage."

Minos nods, and as he opens his mouth, Cain smirks. "Do you study anatomy?" he interrupts, and though the question seems genuine, his eyes are devious, the smirk on his lips even moreso.

I blush. *Hard.* "I do, yes."

My mother is glaring at me, or him, I can't tell.

"Oh, really?" Cain leans forward, the embers of his eyes trailing from my eyes to my mouth, then farther down to where the table cuts me off. All I can hear is my heartbeat, pounding loudly in my ears. "Interesting."

"Cain." Minos eyes him, and the look obviously means something like *'behave'.* "As I was saying... you take after your mother then, yes? Since she's quite the scientist."

"I suppose I do," I answer with a nod, looking back as the servants return to fill Cain and I's glasses again. *Again. How does this keep happening?* My head feels thick. "I'm well-versed in all areas, but those are my specialties."

Cain snickers, and the sound makes me laugh. *Really* laugh. It's a strange feeling, but I can't stop it, especially not as he starts laughing harder. I try desperately to hide it behind my hand, attempting to seem collected like I should be, but I can't seem to pull myself together again.

Minos groans, shaking his head. "You two can be dismissed. Take your plates, if you'd like. Leave us to our conversation."

I waver slightly when I stand up, both of us polishing our last glass and quickly hurrying out of the room. Cain can't stop giggling as his shoulder bumps into mine, stumbling back down the hall and out of the main doors, where we both nearly fall into sitting on the step.

"Oh, that was terrible," he says, wiping his eyes. "Gods, I'm glad we got out of that."

"Me too," I answer through a breath, shaking my head. "They were going to marry us? I missed that entire topic."

"Ah, my mother was asking about that. Not exactly *going* to marry us, but she wanted to. It's something she does with so many people." He shakes his head, sighing. "Apparently, you seemed fitting tonight. She must assume you're strong enough to 'take care of me', or whatever."

I grimace, then laugh. "I didn't think I was quite the match for someone like you."

Cain studies me, his gaze slightly soft and his cheeks red again. The color is so lovely on him. "You could be."

My face must flush darker than ever, judging by the heat rushing to my cheeks. "I—what?"

Cain smirks when he realizes I'm nearly speechless, but before he gets the chance to say anything else, the doors are opening behind us. I push to my feet as my family comes through, my mother striding up to me without missing a beat.

"Come home, Daedalus," she says, her hand catching on my arm.

I know she's serious, and she must be angry, but instead of agreeing immediately, I pull my arm away and take a small step back, my attention still focused elsewhere.

"Yes, Mother. I'll meet you there." Before she has a chance to disagree, I turn back to my drinking companion for the evening. "It was good seeing you, Cain."

His smirk melts into a warm smile, and he nods politely. "It was good seeing you too, Daedalus."

That voice, the way it rumbles quietly between us—I cannot help but latch onto it, his earlier words on repeat in the forefront of my mind.

'You could be.'

What could that mean? What could he possibly be up to?

The magic wreathes around my body instantly, hiding me from view of anyone else—one of my favorite tricks I'd picked up over my younger years from my father—and I follow the elf quickly out of the manor's gate.

I stroll along through the darkness of the street, weaving in between lamp posts and through small crowds of people as they head home for the night. My eyes set intently on that cascade of crimson hair that flutters with the evening breeze.

That same old hunger I'd felt while training with Silas rises in my gut, one I'd never acted on but always thought of, an urge I always shoved down. Only this time felt... different. Cain felt different. Chasing him like this reminds me of prey, and I the looming predator he has no idea about.

Should I be giving into my urges like this? Likely not, but his words made me curious. *Horribly* curious, and in desperate need of answers.

You could be.

Does he want me to be a good match for him? Is he pitying me? Making fun of me? Why the sudden change in interest?

As I follow him through the surprisingly well-lit streets, to see just how Nemoure reacts around him, as if the city comes alive with each of his steps, swaying towards him like he is a flame keeping it warm. People leaning outside of clubs call out to him; one stunning Luceri man offers him a cigarette and lights it before he passes; others practically bow before his presence. Some judgmental looks are shared, but others he seems almost friendly with—or at the very least, cordial enough to offer a smile.

The lights wink off glittering jewelry and equally as bright outfits, but I barely pay any mind to them, focusing instead on the glowing end of his cigarette as he strolls past the dark storefronts.

Everything is so oddly beautiful through Cain Sidrelle's eyes.

He slips into a familiar-looking café titled Fauna, decorated in all sorts of Fae-styled décor—glowing butterflies and stars drawn on the outside over baby-blue and lavender paint, statues of fawns with bird wings, and a massive pair of trees on a short patio shimmering like the sun itself is painting its golden leaves. I pause for a moment to admire it all, inwardly marking it as a place I should come back to before stepping inside behind another elven man. It seems a cozy place, and one I am not surprised to find Cain in, when I think about it.

It only takes a quick glance around the small café to locate him, and I find him sat in a wooden booth against the wall, a familiar face grinning at him from across the table.

I take a moment to breathe in the varying scents throughout the room, making a quick note of coffee, hazelnut, and fresh bagels. Marion is dressed like he just came off a show—which, knowing him, might be the exact reason behind his glittering outfit and emerald-green fur coat. He slides Cain what I assume is a coffee, and that's when I carefully shift into the shadowed space behind their booth with my back to Cain's.

I wonder what his coffee order is. Maybe a latte? Maybe something simple?

"How was dinner?" Marion asks, smiling over at the other and breaking up my train of thought before I can get too lost in it. "Bearable?"

"Ugh, awkward as ever," Cain replies, and I can practically hear him rolling his eyes. "But I did get Daedalus alone for a moment, so that was fun. I got him to drink some of Minos's whiskey with me before we joined the table because I know damn well, he would've been an anxious mess otherwise if *I* was already uncomfortable."

Marion sips his coffee and hums, and I imagine him nodding along. "He drank with you? That's surprising, I don't think I've ever seen him drink."

"We *have* only seen him at school, Marion."

"True true," Marion says, laughing warmly. "That's nice, though. What was he wearing tonight? Anything good?"

Keeping my back to them is *killing* me, but judging by the tone of Marion's voice, he's definitely teasing him. I turn slightly to the side to see them out of the corner of my eye, smiling to myself at the sight of Cain's lightly reddened cheeks.

"Oh *gods,* yes. He was in this black button-up tonight, and it was just tight enough around the waist...I don't know, I would jump on him in a *heartbeat.*" Cain leans back, shaking his head, as my face turns hotter than the Hells themselves. "And he laughed tonight, Marion. He *laughed*! I couldn't believe it."

Marion's eyebrows raise as he takes another sip, leaving a smudge of green lipstick on the edge of the white lid. "*You* got him to laugh? That's crazy, and gods I can only imagine how bad you want to get on that. He's the talk of the town, in one way or another... do you think you're going to take him to the ball?"

That's why I followed him.

"He is... and it's not just his looks, you know. I'm curious about him, too. He can't just be hot, mysterious, *and* smart. There has to be more to him," Cain says, laughing. "I don't know. I'm figuring it out. And? Maybe. I'll see if he asks."

The ball? Oh, fuck.

"How did the rest of the dinner go?"

"Oh, just *wonderful*. My father attempted to intimidate Daedalus and my mother attempted to marry us, which his mother denied...so, that was fun. And annoying. We had fun drinking despite all that, though."

Their conversation trails into less exciting topics after that—other classmates they have opinions about, terrible outfits, their friend group, and Irsa—so I decidedly push away from my hiding spot and slip back through the entrance. The city outside is quieter now, weighed down by the night's possibilities and the conversation I just overheard.

I'd jump on him in a heartbeat.

Fuck, I'm going to hear that sentence until the end of time.

Unfortunately for me, I know I have to return to the manor—but knowing what I know now about Cain and I's seemingly budding friendship? I'm somewhat okay with that.

Somewhat.

7

— • —

A FEW weeks after the tense family dinner, the talk of a Sidrelle party has become the center of Whitestone's rumors. My classmates haven't stopped whispering about it—at least, the ones who share business classes with Cain and the richer sorts haven't—all giggling and muttering about getting to witness Minos and Cain in action, getting them interested in their business ideas or already-functioning possible investments.

To me, it sounds boring. Exhausting.

But, my curiosity won out, in the end.

After hours of training and pacing the length of my bedroom, I quietly open a shadow-wreathed portal, allowing the magic to pool in my palms, and slip through without a sound.

On the other side, the open gates leading up to the Sidrelle mansion stand high over my head, glinting in the pale moonlight bathing the warm-colored grounds in cool tones. People are everywhere, scattered across the stone walkway with champagne flutes in hand, all dressed in suits and dresses and clothes all too nice for a simpler event. I quickly step into my shadows and exhale as the magic consumes me, grateful to be out of sight. Comforted by the familiar feeling.

I don't bother lingering outside—instead, I weave through the outer crowds and find my way into the mansion, ducking past servants holding silver trays of appetizers and more fancy flutes. It's warmer inside, likely due to the amount of bodies spread all throughout the spaces I slip into. Chandeliers cast warm lighting over every inch of the rooms I pass through, some varying in size and number of jewels dangling from their rings, some decorated with diamonds and others with rubies. It smells pleasant, like cedar wood, smoke, and a mingling of perfumes that is surprisingly easy to breathe through.

My eyes flicker over every face, landing on a few familiar class-mates before finally falling on Cain in the center of the living room, standing beside his father and in front of what must be a full-sized painting of the Sidrelle family. Part of me wonders how many servants had to shove the room's furnishings into another area of the mansion solely to make room for the two men and all the people who want to talk to them. How long would it take to move it all? I distantly recall there being a couch, a loveseat, a chaise lounge, a table in between and one by the entrance to the hall on the right. None of it looked light, either. I can only imagine what it must have been like to move.

Like this, I can truly see the resemblance between Minos and Cain—not only for their shared color palette of red hair, eyes, and fair skin, but their similar face shape as well, with the same drawn-down eyebrows and haughty laugh echoing through the room. Tonight, Minos is dressed in his usual, entirely crimson suit, and Cain is in his vest and button-up, as I anticipated. One of Cain's hands cradles a shorter glass of amber-colored liquid, which he lightly knocks into Minos's matching one before they both take an equally long sip.

It's interesting, watching how they maneuver around each other. Both seem disinterested in their company, yet they manage to keep the attention of the people around them so easily. It's truly fascinating, and makes more sense as to why so many people murmur about them being so intimidating.

I certainly wouldn't want to be one of the people trying to offer my business to them, that's for sure.

An elven man leaves their range in a storm, aggravation rolling off of him in waves as he curses about 'those damned Sidrelles' and something along the lines of them 'missing opportunities'. I step away from his path of anger and ease myself against the back wall, surveying the people around me as they jostle to get closer to the Sidrelles. A woman dressed in fine red clothes bats her eyes at Minos, and I almost laugh at the way he dismisses her and moves onto the next. Almost like she's nothing to him. Some might find it concerning, the way people seem to revel at their attention, or how pleading they are to get their word on an investment. I never saw anything like this in Makor, not even over the Archmages.

They were respected, sure, but people never clamored for them the same way they do over Cain and Minos. So many of Nemoure's people begging for even a drop of their attention, to have their red, sharp-pupiled eyes land on them for even a second.

Nemoure truly is a different beast.

I let my eyes fall on Cain again, eyeing the glittering makeup on his high cheekbones for a moment, before he looks in my direction. It's nothing more than a glance, but I swear he sees me in that second, and my heart stops in my chest. The heat of his magic roams over me for the briefest second, then it's gone. Leaving me empty, and very nearly unfocused to the point of revealing myself. His sharp eyes roam over the people around me with a curious expression before falling back on a man in front of him, that passiveness returning to his face as swiftly as it left. I force myself to swallow and regain my composure, drifting further into the crowd curiously, trying to get closer without exposing my magic.

"Daedalus, where are you? You should be home," my mother's voice filters into my mind, followed by the drain of her magic on mine. The vastness of it, tugging at the threads of my own. *"Did you leave?"*

I pause and stand still against the wall, careful not to spread my shadows out too far. *"Yes, but I will be returning momentarily."*

My mother makes a sound akin to a 'tsk' in my head before she disappears, leaving my heart racing in the wake of her absence. The feeling of disappointment radiating from one singular noise almost squashes my confidence, turning my stomach over and over until I'm left swaying against the wall. I squeeze my eyes shut and open them again, and the instant I do, I meet Cain's gaze from across the room.

This time, there's no doubting he sees me, or at the very least, my magic. I quickly pick my way back through the crowd, stepping outside and into the coolness of the night air, aiming to get beyond the gates before he can catch me.

I'm not so lucky.

Cain's footsteps fall hard and sharp behind me as I reach the gates, stopping short as my shadows drift away from my form. "So, you were there. I thought so," he says as I turn back to face him, and though I expect irritation, I find light surprise instead. "Why are you here, Daedalus? I wouldn't think this is your thing."

"It isn't, truthfully," I reply, glancing over his shoulder at a few men who are paying too much attention to us. To him, more likely. "The simple answer is: I was curious."

"Curious?" He smiles, raising an eyebrow. "About what?"

You, I want to say.

I shrug one shoulder and swallow nervously, studying his drink. It's slightly lower than it was before, just enough to be noticeable. "Your party. Our classmates wouldn't stop talking about it."

Cain snorts, raising the glass to his lips and wrinkling his nose as he takes another sip. "Ugh. Right. They always do that. For some reason, they think just because we share classes, I'll be more likely to invest in their businesses." He gestures out to his side, rolling his eyes. "Most of their ideas suck, or their already existing businesses aren't worth my time or my money. It's annoying."

The way he talks to me like we're already friends warms my chest, and it's a fight to ignore the feeling of it. "Right," I say slowly, my eyes darting to one of the men again, who seems like he's attempting to compose himself to approach Cain. "I'll leave you to it. I should likely get home."

"Wait," he says, his hand catching my sleeve for a second, before he moves away a little too quick. Like he didn't mean to grab me at all. "Meet me at the coffee shop down the way. I'll sneak out of here, and we can talk some more."

I mull the idea over, my anxiety heightening slightly at the thought of dismissing my mother's remark that I should be home. My responsibility to do so almost outweighs it—until I fully take in the fact that opportunities like this don't come around often for someone like me. Not with someone like Cain, anyway. And why does it make my heart miss a beat? "Alright. I'll go there now, then."

He smiles and nods, stepping back toward the party. "Good." So confident.

"Good," I echo, a light smile on my lips. "See you soon."

After roughly fifteen minutes of debating on whether I should have gone home, or if Cain stood me up, I look up to the ringing of the café door and feel an immediate sense of relief at the sight of him. His cheeks are slightly flushed, whether from exertion or the alcohol he'd been drinking, I'm not sure. He looks around quickly before spotting me at my booth in the back corner, tucked perfectly away from anyone else—not that there's many others at this hour, only a few students from our college littering the tables, with books and papers.

I'm grateful to see him, because I don't think I can find any more shapes or angles in the furniture around this particular café. An orange velvet couch sits by a hearth on the left, at least six oak wooden tables stand on the hardwood floor behind it, booths rest against the back and right walls, and monstera and pothos plants hang or sway from pots in every corner or window. It smells like warm spices and fresh croissants, which apparently, this café specializes in.

According to murmurs in the college, most seem to really like their hazelnut croissant the most.

"You made it," I say through a breath as he walks over to me, red eyes peering at the paper cup between my hands. "I thought you weren't coming, for a moment."

"Yeah, sorry. I got held up. People wouldn't leave me alone," Cain replies, rolling his eyes. "What are you drinking?"

I glance down at my cup and back at him, noting the fact he hasn't sat down yet. Maybe he's not comfortable. "Cinnamon tea."

He nods, holding up one finger before turning quickly and walking over to the barista. I watch him curiously, my eyes running over the fine lines of his back, down his long legs, back up to his curls. He's truly a work of art, all scarlet swirls and porcelain skin. His body is neatly composed, reminiscent of a marble statue with his smoothly carved muscle and practically perfect posture. For some reason, it makes my throat dry to look at him this way.

A moment later, he turns back to me, an amused look on his face and a paper cup in his hands.

I'm not sure I like where this might be going.

"Were you checking me out, Daedalus Macabre?" he asks, pretty lips tugging into an even prettier smirk as he slides into the booth across from me. "You can be honest with me if you were."

My face heats up, but I ignore it, sipping my tea despite the fact it's still a little too hot. My first thought is to deny it, to tuck myself back behind the walls I've fought so hard to keep up. And I do keep them up a little, but part of my resolve cracks ever so slightly under his gaze. " What would you say if I said yes?"

Cain laughs, eyes glittering dangerously. "I'd say that's very brave of you, and that maybe I liked it."

Another rush of heat hits me, spreading all the way to the tips of my ears. I let out an uncertain laugh and look away toward the floor, shaking my head. "Good to know."

"I guess I should apologize in advance," he says with a snort, cupping his slender hands around his coffee cup. "I get interesting when I drink. And I've had two glasses of my father's bourbon, which is strong as shit. So... sorry if I seem too forward, or something."

"It's fine," I say quickly, maybe a little too quickly. "Maybe I liked it."

He smiles knowingly at my choice in words. "Okay, good."

My heart picks up speed, quickening in my chest, as I study his amused look. The moment is fleeting, but it feels different. Daring, almost. Maybe I shouldn't have said that out loud. Maybe I shouldn't have spoken at all. But I did, and that smile on his face says it was worth it.

Oh Gods.

"So, what are you studying in the college, Daedalus? I know we discussed you being a scientist and a mage at that dinner, but I wondered," Cain asks, interrupting my derailing thoughts before he sips at whatever drink he got. From what I can gather, his smells like cinnamon too. "I know we share a few classrooms, but those seem to be mostly study hall types."

Cinnamon floods my mouth as another drink of tea passes through, and I study the angles of his fingers, how they're wrapped around his cup. "Science and magic, primarily, even though I'm well versed in both. My mother wants to make sure I'm at the top of my abilities, so I studied both back in Makor as well. I'm mostly here for the magic."

He nods, leaning his chin on his hand. "What kind of science do you like to do?"

"Anything to do with experimenting. Creating something new, something different, making injectable potions or changes to a person. I've also helped my father in his morgue before, so bodies also fascinate me, in a way," I say, swallowing the threat of nerves wanting to rise up my throat for talking about myself like this. "My mother raised me in the science field as well, so I've inherited liking it, I suppose."

"So you weren't kidding about studying anatomy that night," he remarks, laughing lightly. That dangerous glimmer returns to his eye, one that I'm starting to recognize spells out trouble for me every time it appears, before he visibly shudders. "You've helped in the morgue before? Isn't that gross?"

A soft laugh leaves me at that, and I shake my head. "Not to me. Like I said, I'm fascinated by it."

Cain grimaces, swallowing hard enough for my eyes to track the movement in his soft throat. "Ew, Gods, sorry. I can't do that. Dead bodies weird me out."

"I would ask why, but I don't want to set you off this late at night," I say with another laugh, looking away from him. It's almost impossible to do so, with the sense of gravity his entire body has. Looking anywhere else is a hard thing to do, so I peer at him from the corner of my eye. "Why did you want to meet me tonight?"

His eyes dance between mine and somewhere lower, possibly my lips, before circling back up. "I don't know. You're so mysterious, I thought it'd be nice to talk to you more. We always get cut off."

I nod, lightly thumbing the edge of the black ring on my pointer finger, turning it against my skin. "Mysterious, hm?"

"Yeah," he says quickly, snorting. "You've got that whole tall, dark, and mysterious thing going for you. Did you not realize that? You don't talk to people, you're always on time whether it's leaving or arriving, you play the piano in the middle of the night... need I go on?"

My cheeks flush ever so slightly at that, and I can't tell if I like the fact that he's noticed so much about me or not. "I suppose I've never thought about it like that."

Cain leans back against the cushion behind him, smiling in an amused way. "Well, it's true. All of my friends think so. We've talked about it before."

"You've talked about me before?" I remark, fully turning my eyes back onto him as his cheeks turn a little more red than they already were. It doesn't surprise me that he has, not after I overheard his conversation with Marion about him 'wanting to get on me', essentially. Not a surprise, but amusing to know. Amusing to tease him about, despite that not totally being my nature. "That's intriguing."

"Not like that." He scoffs, but judging by the way he looks off toward the rest of the room, it is exactly like that. "Gods. Maybe I should've waited until I sobered up more before coming out."

Another little laugh leaves me as I follow his gaze, watching the barista as they walk to each plant with a small, silver watering can. It's strange how comfortable I feel with him, how I can almost let my guard down. I don't know how he does that to me. "Sure, Cain."

Cain's eyes narrow, but he doesn't say anything at first. He looks me over a time or two before sipping from his cup again, shaking his head in a way that seems to be more at himself than at me. "I mean it."

"And I believe you." A little smirk tugs on the corner of my mouth, one I can't hide. "One hundred percent."

I've never been playful like this. Not even with my ex in Makor.

"Don't be a dick," he retorts, but it comes out much less sharp than I originally anticipate it to. His face is nearly as red as his hair. "Anyway, should we head back for tonight? I'm honestly exhausted from today... if that's alright with you. We can talk more if you don't want to yet."

Though my heart says stay, my mind knows better. Especially if my mother's been watching over my shoulder. I haven't felt her presence during any of our conversations, but I know she's looked before without me recognizing it was her, even with my magic sensitivities. Nodding, I slowly slide out of the booth and stand up. "I would like to stay, but I should be getting home, too. We can talk more another time. I'll walk you home."

Cain nods, standing up beside me. "You don't have to, I can handle myself, you know."

I shrug, guiding him out of the café. "I know."

We walk onto the cobblestone in silence, with nothing but his pleased smile to tell me he secretly appreciates this gesture. I know he could handle more than himself—judging by the intensity of the fire I always feel from him—but it felt like the right thing to do, after such a pleasant conversation. Nemoure is quiet at this hour, humming with vague music from a club around the corner and distant shouts from a bar. No one else marks the street as we walk, no horses or carriages.

Not that I mind. I prefer it this way.

By the time we reach the mansion, I'm visibly exhausted, and so is he. Cain offers me a lazy smile as we pause by the tall gates, unsure of what to do as they slowly begin to open without a sound. It's almost impressive how quiet they are. "Well," he says, stepping toward the building. "I'll see you soon, right?"

"Yeah," I say with a smile of my own, fighting off a yawn. "Goodnight, Cain."

He hesitates for a moment, then nods. "Goodnight, Daedalus."

Despite not needing to, I watch him walk inside, then linger there until the gates close before me. He leaves me behind with a strange pang in my chest, breathing in the scent of roses until I finally decide to turn away from the mansion and start toward my home.

What an odd night.

8

FOR THE first time in my studies, my magic falters the instant I attempt to pull a spell out of it.

My heart races as I stare at my hand, desperately willing my shadows to appear, to form anything. Normally, this would never be an issue; the problem is, *I'm standing in front of a class.* I swallow hard and flex my fingers, inwardly following the burning trail of magic aching to be released from my palms. It never comes. Panic seizes my chest at the thought of being stifled, that maybe my training isn't paying off—

But then, Irsa snickers.

I lift my eyes from my hand to where he's seated in the back of the class, a table away from Cain. One of his hands is ever so slightly raised, a barely-visible strand of purple energy circling his fingertips. Instantly, I look to our professor, who has a look of patience so earnest, I almost have to avert my eyes.

"Go on, Daedalus. Don't be nervous," she says, gesturing forward. "I know you can do this."

"Yeah Daedalus, why aren't you doing anything?" Irsa replies, another snicker leaving his lips. "It's not like we have all day."

Professor Saturn eyes him, folding her arms over her chest. "Quiet, Irsa, or I will send you out of this classroom immediately."

I attempt to fight my nerves and glance back at his hand, following that trail of energy. Anger rips through the fear in me, searing hot as my magic grows larger under my skin, nearly becoming too large, my bones adjusting as if they too want to raze him to the ground. Rolling my neck out to avoid the slight tick that wants to come out, I allow my magic to pulse in my fingers, finally surging to my skin in a blast that fires through the room. The daylight vanishes in a wave of black, casting the entire area in pure shadows.

Gasps and murmurs flood from my classmates, and I swear under all of it, I hear warm surprise from Cain.

"Very impressive, Daedalus," Professor Saturn says from the darkness, followed by the proud clapping of her hands. "Are you able to return it to yourself?"

I nod, smiling in that brief moment of privacy, before allowing my magic to come back. It seeps into my skin like an old friend, settling into my veins and filling the empty spaces with the darkness that has always lingered too close. My eyes find Irsa again, watching how he shakes his hand out in an attempt to remove the smoky tendrils still floating around it. He isn't smiling anymore.

Good.

He glares at me, looking pointedly at the shadows moving around his hand. "Are you going to remove this too, Daedalus?"

Professor Saturn glances between us, and before she can say anything, I hold up a hand and let the wisps return to me in one swift motion. The distant scent of iron-rich blood reaches my nose the instant I do, mingling with a stranger smell of something that twists my stomach. Irsa curses low under his breath as I quickly walk to my seat, my next classmate taking their place at the front with a smile on their face.

Instead of watching their small display of magic, I turn my attention to the main book on my desk—one I borrowed from the secretive parts of the library, covering all sorts of Astral magic, and spells to learn from it. Before Asher mentioned his experiment, I never thought of using it. Never once had I imagined diving into that vein of magic, specifically because it's never taught to mages. It's somewhat forbidden, alongside blood magic, but the texts still exist all over the world, if you know where to look.

Honestly, I was impressed Whitestone's library had anything on it, even with it being the biggest one in Nemoure. I expected to have to go on a wild chase, to maybe find out what other cities like Makor or the Epicenter had in their own libraries.

It may be only one book, but it's a start.

I carefully flip it open, thumbing through the first part of the weathered pages. Essays upon essays fill the book, crammed to the brim with information on the Astral beasts and Eldritch beings that live amongst it—it honestly impresses me how many there are. People don't speak much about these creatures, or the Gods that hide in them. People try desperately not to talk about Mindweavers either, those tentacled humanoids that devour the mind in one easy bite, all because they've found their way onto our plane.

A slight shudder runs down my spine as I open the book up to the spells, taking in the various drawings of hands conjuring up Astral portals, small bolts colored in purples and stars, gravity spells only someone like my mother would know. My eyes wander with every page, barely breathing as they finally part to a wide spread about one particular spell. A blade. An Astral-formed weapon so destructive, no one has been able to truly wield it in a long, long time. If the book is correct, its practically torn from a fraction of the plane itself, stars and galaxies writhing among the surface of the sword, breaking weapons on impact and ripping blackened holes in the bodies of enemies.

Immediately, my brain flickers into action, imagining all the different ways I could possibly try to create this thing. How I would even access the Astral to get to it. It's exciting, sending a thrill down my spine at the thought of trying something so new.

The moment the class comes to an end, I hurry to my dorm, the book pressed firmly to my side. My excitement doesn't settle, still sending my mind in a looping spiral centered around this dangerous weapon. I quickly close myself inside and exhale, setting everything down on a table by the door before opening the book to that damning spell.

My veins thrum with energy as I call my darkness into my hands, willing it to life. I close my eyes and try to imagine the Astral, the void of it, the empty space filled with gods and races I've never seen. Being I've never been there, my mind tangles over images, attempting to recreate something I have never seen by myself. A small drop of sweat runs from my forehead as I call my magic forward, attempting to form the weapon with a yearning slight of hope in me.

Instead, the shadowed blade I've grown so familiar with takes shape, black wisps circling my hands like an old friend. I curse under my breath and shake my head, sending it away. Another attempt, the same. A third, nothing changes. Frustration surges into my chest, and in it, I cast my magic out at the room and sigh when it blots out the light.

Maybe someday, I'll succeed, and my mother will be proud.

Maybe then.

9

TWO MONTHS after the dinner, I'm sitting on a large and comfortable gray-blanketed bed—my bed, to be exact—with a bottle of peach flavored wine clasped in my right hand.

Despite knowing exactly what Morgana would say about it, I'm drinking anyway. It's a nice night, Cain Sidrelle himself is offering, and how could I say no to him? I don't think I would forgive myself if I ever did. Chances like these only come once in a lifetime for people like me.

I shake my head a little to clear my mind as Cain rambles over the mistake of sleeping with Irsa, talking about how short he lasted and how he deserves *"so much better"*, and I very nearly laugh.

He always seems to find a way to make me laugh, and I'm finding that I like it.

The numbness I've felt for years breaks, cracking like glass, splintering just enough to let bits of contentment through in that same way it did the last time I was with Cain. It's confusing, feeling this way. Is this what most people feel like? Something close to relaxation, allowing my shoulders and my guards to drop?

We're sitting only a few feet apart, our legs crisscrossed and our knees almost brushing, but not quite. I don't know if I've breathed since I noticed. The bottle passes between us every few minutes as we just sit there, contently talking.

Just talking.

What else could I do with him?

Almost hurriedly, I pass the bottle back to Cain, slipping my hand down the neck of it before our hands can do so much as touch, because I'm not quite sure I could handle it. This is the closest we've been in all of our conjoined time at Whitestone, and it feels far too personal.

The bottle leaves my hand, and Cain scoffs a moment later, swiping drops of pale pink wine from his lips with the back of his right hand. "It's annoying, you know—am I losing you?"

I lift my gaze from his mouth briefly, shaking my head. "No, sorry. I was lost in thought again."

Cain laughs, a little slow, a little warm. "It's fine, I figured that was the case."

I nod, taking the wine once he offers the bottle back to me, golden eyes glancing to the cream-colored ceiling. I know better than most about what Irsa is like, being he has yet to let up on me.

Ever since he noticed me talking to Cain the littlest bit, the man has been all over me—shoving me around, knocking my things over, outright being an asshole. It hasn't helped any of my recent moods, even *if* I had gotten good at ignoring him. He's an equation I don't want to figure out, one that's far too frustrating and not worth the work.

"Has he been giving you issues still?" Cain asks. His gaze feels like a burn at my throat. Hungry, in a way, that I don't mind.

I take another drink, relishing the sweetness of the peach flavor rolling over my tongue.

"It's been months, Cain, and he still hasn't stopped." I shake my head, handing the wine over and inwardly cursing when our fingertips brush. He doesn't move immediately, allowing our skin to remain in contact, but just when I think I could memorize the curve and point of his nails, he withdraws and drinks down a big gulp.

"I'm sorry. I'll talk to him," he says, offering me a smile. I barely notice it as I open and close my hand. My skin tingles, the feeling of his still lingering there on my fingers.

It makes me think about that uncomfortable dinner—both of our families too busy with their mild shows of power to bother being anything more than forcibly polite to one another. All that magic in one room, and yet it was Cain whose power drew me in. Cain who felt the most genuine.

Even then, in the face of both our families' embarrassments, Cain was so *kind* to me even then.

You could be.

Morgana had been so angry with me when I returned home that night—for avoiding her demands, for drinking, for Cain—that she trained me for twenty-four hours straight before finally letting me leave.

Yet surprisingly, I do not regret that night. How could I, when it led me here?

"What are you thinking about?" Cain's voice breaks me from the memory, his head tilting enough that I can see him out of the corner of my eye.

I glance to him and then the bottle, another laugh slipping from my lips. "I was remembering that dinner we had, with our parents. That strange power-play your family did," I say. "I know it was only two months ago, but it feels like it was yesterday."

Cain groans, dragging a hand over his face. "Gods, that was the *worst*. So glad we got out of there early."

I nod. "I agree."

"I mean, could you *believe* how uncomfortable that was? My parents about to fight, my mother attempting to marry me to you, ugh." Cain shudders, shaking his head.

Witnessing Minos and Celeste Sidrelle on the edge of a likely too-long-for-company argument had been a curious thing to me—especially since they all acted like nothing could touch them, nothing could shake them from their perfect stature. Nothing except for each other, apparently.

"Ah, not *ugh* at the idea of marrying you," he corrected quickly. "*Ugh* at the whole thing—you get it, right?"

"It was pretty bad," I agree, taking the bottle from him and drinking down another gulp. It loosens my shoulders a little more, easing me down from my former nerves, giving a pleasant warmth to my gut I can't seem to ignore.

Cain laughs, something wild and unrestrained, tipping his head back and causing his bright red curls to tumble down across his shoulders. It's impossible not to look at him like that—his smooth throat exposed in the low light of the room, the peek of his sharp collarbones past the champagne-colored silk shirt he has on. The sight makes my throat tighten, forcing me to tear my gaze away as I drum my fingers against my thigh, all to keep my mind off of it.

"It was! They love embarrassing us, right?" Cain suddenly exclaims, startling me.

We both quickly fall quiet to listen for any sounds out in the hall, eyeing his door and breathing out a sigh of relief when there's seemingly no sound of someone coming to quiet us down.

"Sorry, I guess this is hitting a little more than I expected." Cain laughs, waving the bottle at me and the room before taking a drink from it. He's entirely loosened up, not nearly as guarded or as tense as he always seems to be, and I like it. Part of me appreciates seeing him this way. *Maybe he thinks the same thing.*

We sit in an extended silence as the last of the bottle slowly trickles down our throats, our limbs loose enough for our knees to finally touch. I stare at the angle of his, at the folds and creases in the champagne silk of his pants, the way it shimmers in the light. I'm a fool, a hungry fool. My eyes wander with my thoughts, tracing patterns in him, the odd way his body is leaned back in our near-drunken state.

I imagine the way his legs might look in something other than silk sleep pants or uniformed slacks. Imagine him in dresses and skirts, the way he they might look in something much tighter where I could see the angles of his legs much clearer, far easier to gauge. Would he wear dresses that stop at his thighs, showing off everything else? Or, perhaps he would wear one of those dresses with the slit to show off one singular leg, just to tease?

I imagine him in a dress that flutters around his knees like flower petals, and in my mind's eye, I trace the arcs and circles it would carve through the air when he danced. Follow the fractals and swirls his hair would create when he spun around me, guiding us expertly across the dancefloor while the entire ball watches in jealousy and awe.

The ball...

The thought has me sitting upright with a jolt, my gasp a little more frantic than I mean it to be judging by the way Cain jumps in surprise at the sound. The alcohol really *has* loosened me up. "The ball! *Shit*. That's tomorrow, isn't it?"

Cain puts a hand over his chest, exhaling through a laugh. Quickly, I realize a moment too late that we hadn't been talking about anything even *close* to the ball—or anything at all, really—so my exclamation likely doesn't make sense to him.

"Gods, Daedalus—what in the Hells... Yes, it is." The amusement in his gaze melts into something sharper, more mischievous, as he leans towards me. "And, you know... I have no one to take me."

I freeze a little, looking at him—or well, more looking at his chest than his face because I can't hold his gaze right now. *Is he actually asking me to take him?*

Originally, I had no intention of going. Social events aren't usually my go-to, *especially* not one where I'd be expected to dance with someone I barely know. I don't like touching people, or having them touch me, so a ball sounded like one of my worst fears.

But he's obviously hinting, Daedalus. Oh, Gods.

I swallow, tracing a circle over the velvet of my pants. "Would you... like me to take you?"

Cain laughs, nodding with an amused smile on his face and leaning back on one hand. "Yes, I would. And, if you do, I could introduce you to some people, you know, get your name out there a little more."

I nod slowly, leaning back again, almost mirroring his current pose. Although being shown off to new people sounds terrifying, going with him makes it feel somewhat worth it. "I look forward to it, then. I wasn't going to go at all, originally."

His gaze moves elsewhere in the room, leaving me behind on some train of thought he must be chasing momentarily. "You'll pick me up tomorrow night, yes?"

I study the sharp line of his jaw, swallowing past the drunken temptation to follow the edge of it with my finger. "Of course."

Cain's red eyes slip back to me, curiously. "Sounds like a plan, then."

The following day, all I hear about is the ball. My classmates won't stop talking about it in hushed voices, some giggling as they describe their outfits to each other, a few even wondering who Cain might be going with. I'm sure I overheard Irsa proclaiming how he has a date no one knows, but no one really gave him any interest in response.

Every time I hear murmurs about the event, my mind wanders to my... date. My date. *That's* strange to say.

It's odd but exciting to think about how *I'm* going to be the one picking up Cain, looking at Cain, *dancing* with Cain—

I curse under my breath, shaking my head to clear my mind of the almost obsessive nature my thoughts were headed toward. They would only serve to distract me, and my nerves are distraction enough already. It is all I can do to steady the tremble in my hands before tugging my tailcoat jacket on over my black vest and matching shirt. The only part of my outfit that isn't dark are the silver skeletal hands pinned to my collar, a little something I picked out years ago but hadn't yet had the chance to use.

It's almost time.

I step past the servants that have been lingering at the edges of my room in case I needed any help, dismissing them with a smile before carefully walking downstairs and outside to the single rose bush we've had growing alongside the inner wall of the yard. Somehow, I've narrowly avoided running into my mother all day, which has made it easier for me to plan this outing. The flowers are a deep, velvet black that is almost blue in certain lighting, and had only recently begun to bloom—perfectly in time for this event, for me to bring one along.

Pinching the stem of a fully bloomed rose, avoiding the thorns with care, I check the petals for bruises or bites from insects. Each one is pushed apart, the center inspected, then I move on. I'm particular and thorough about it, humming a little under my breath as I look over the deep green leaves too. It needs to be perfect, if I'm to give it as a gift.

It's almost embarrassing, bringing one with me, but I know it's fitting to do for someone like Cain.

Will he even like it?

Horseshoed hooves clattering on the stone road outside my gate keeps me from worrying, making something close to a smile tug at my lips. The carriage I paid for is exactly what I hoped—a fancier type, deep red with a black metal frame. There are two small windows on either side, but it's clearly large enough that we could easily fit five more people in it. The Friesian horses pulling it are beautiful but intensely powerful in appearance, their jet-black bodies almost purple in the low lighting, wavy manes tumbling down the slopes of their muscled shoulders.

The driver, a brunette elven man in a flat cap and brown tweed jacket, smiles down at me before gesturing to the door. "Good evening!"

"Good evening." I offer him a tight smile before stepping inside, ducking my head to avoid hitting it against the roof.

Inside, it's just as plush as the exterior. Red, soft velvet seats, a carpeted flooring, not a speck of dust in sight. Leaning forward to the small slot for me to speak to the driver, I direct him to go to the Sidrelle mansion. He shudders at the name, though with fear or intrigue, I cannot tell. I'll never know if this man fears Cain and his family.

The man nods, and with a snap of the long leather reins, we continue down the road.

My leg bounces restlessly, unable to keep my nerves from exposing themselves in the motion of it. I let my mind drift, closing my eyes—what will Cain look like? What will he wear? What sort of divinity will he appear like tonight, in all the glory that he is? Will I even be able to speak when I see him?

My head snaps up as we draw to a halt at a random spot in the road. I lean forward to the slot, eyeing the driver with hope that he isn't plotting something, but he looks just as confused. Relieved, I watch the door as it shifts open, revealing the one person I could've went my entire night without seeing.

Irsa.

He leans in and eyes me, only irritation on his face. "Hello, Daedalus."

I lean back against the seat, hands tense as I press them down into plush velvet. "Irsa."

Now, he smiles, clasping his hands at his waist. "I have something to ask of you."

A snake of disgust rears its head inside me, flickering over my face. "Spit it out. I don't have time to waste talking to you."

His jaw clenches for a moment, the muscle visibly flickering under his skin. "Funny, your time actually matters to this ask of mine. I don't like this whole"—he waves a vague hand in my direction— "thing, that you think you have going with Cain. I don't like seeing him with someone like you. So, I ask that you cancel on him and go home, and we won't have any issues."

I scoff, eyebrows raising at him in disbelief. I've known that Irsa gets jealous of *anybody* who grows close to Cain, and that he obviously doesn't like me for reasons I don't and likely will never understand, but this is a whole new level.

He remains there, searching my expression with his bright eyes. He's trying to be threatening, no doubt, and he is failing miserably. "So, what do you say?"

My jaw clenches, my leg falls still. Everything in me goes quiet as I stare him down, letting something confident and angry take over my tongue. "Get out of my carriage and back to *your* date, Irsa, before you can't walk back there at all."

Irsa tilts his head and raises an eyebrow, leaning his shoulder into the doorway. "Are you threatening me now, Daedalus Macabre?"

I almost smile. *Almost.* "If you want me to *really* threaten you, I will. And, if you want me to show you which one of us is to be feared in this carriage, I can do that too. But other than that, I'm going to continue with my night."

He watches me for a moment before leaving the carriage, shutting the door hard enough to rattle it behind him. *Such a child.*

I knock on the wall once it's clear, letting out a relieved sigh as the driver continues on down the road. The sounds of hoofbeats, birds chirping, and people chatting as we pass lulls me into relaxation—might have, if not for the lingering anger at Irsa swirling with the nerves of meeting Cain.

One particular thought keeps circling back, over and over again: *What if he isn't coming with me after all?*

I try to shake it off as I glance out of the window, my leg starting to bounce again once we stop in front of a towering pair of black iron gates. Beyond it, the Sidrelle mansion lays in wait like it did those few months ago, looming and ever beautiful, equally as intimidating as the people living inside it.

I open the door to the carriage and watch the entrance nervously for Cain, tapping a foot on the floor, trying not to let my anxiety win. *What if Cain is ghosting me?* No, he wouldn't miss this event. *What if he lied about going with you?* That possible, unfortunately.

What if he's doing this to make fun of you there? What if he's just going to laugh at you, right in your face? What if Irsa got to him and convinced him no to go with me? What if—-

The moment my thoughts start to get a little too loud, the double doors swing inward, revealing Cain a step or two behind them. I shiver at the sight of him, eyeing his now obvious curves, shown off by the tightness of the black dress around his torso. It loosens around his calves, accentuated by the matching heels, and I nearly lose my breath over the slit cutting into the fabric to expose one of his long, slender legs. *I was right.* Ruby red sequins glitter in the low light from the lamps alongside the walkway on his hips, and I kick myself for getting lost in the sway of them as he walks closer.

His hair is down, exactly the way I've started to like it, which sounds strange to think about too. That there's a way *I* like Cain's hair. Somehow, that feels wrong.

His curls are more accentuated than usual, falling delicately over his back, partially tumbling over his left shoulder. I follow the path of them where they're pinned back by a black rose head on the right side, tucked behind his long, pointed ear and draping down behind him.

The makeup he wears is extravagant, but accentuates his sharp features nicely—deep red eyeshadow and black eyeliner that sweeps out in a long, neat line, adding another angle to his face for my mind to hum over. As he comes closer, I get a better glimpse of the lighter red glitter pressed over the eyeshadow, making his already crystalline, crimson eyes more dangerous for me to look at.

His dark painted lips curl in a smile as he pauses before me, gesturing to himself. "What do you think, Dae?"

The nickname halts any of my thoughts, forcing me to catch my tongue between my teeth so I don't say anything stupid. I study him a moment longer, searching for the right word—nothing as simple as 'pretty' can define the man in front of me. It would be more of an offense than a compliment, because anyone can say he just looks *pretty*.

"You... ah." *Shit*. My words are failing me.

Cain laughs, tilting his head at me. "I what?"

I shake my head, blushing in the face of his teasing. "You look... incredible. Ethereal, maybe."

Another chuckle leaves him as he smirks at me, poking a long, red-nailed finger into my chest and pushing me backward into the carriage again. "I'm glad you think so," he purrs, waving off a servant attempting to help him inside.

I nod, offering him the rose I'd brought before I can lose the nerve. "It feels silly, but I brought this for you."

His eyebrows raise, followed by a soft little glimmer in his eyes that makes my chest oddly warm. "That was sweet of you," he says as he takes the rose.

Forcing myself to look back at my hands, I let out an airy laugh. "I'm not exactly accustomed to situations like this... I thought it was right."

"Well, I appreciate it. This should be nice... I hope," Cain says with a slight grimace, lightly leaning back into the seat. "People are going to think it's crazy that we're going together, so there might be a lot of attention on us. Just saying."

I nod, looking at the window instead of him. "We should be the last two people going to a ball together, I feel like."

He laughs, shaking his head. "But we're here, aren't we?"

Another nod. "We are."

Cain's smile does something horrible to me when he has lipstick on. I trace the patterns of it in my mind, the different expressions I've seen him make, before he reaches over and takes my right hand in both of his. It frees me from my thoughts, bringing me back down to the planet with him, back into his center of gravity. "What are you doing?"

He traces my bone markings with a fingertip, from one end of my finger to the next, over my knuckles, down the back of my hand and across the veins beneath. "You have nice hands," is all he says.

I can't move. I'm surely frozen here, pinned in place by his touch and the weight of his gaze on me, stuck to this carriage's seat. An involuntary shiver races down my spine, skittering along with a flood of goosebumps. "Thank you."

A few long minutes of content quiet passes between us until we come to a halt alongside a row of other carriages, and when we both realize it, Cain smiles before releasing my hand from his. "Looks like we're here!"

I step out first, holding the door open for him. He smiles as he walks out beside me, leaning over and pressing a quick kiss to my cheek that has my heart absolutely *racing*. I don't think I'll ever be calm around him. I don't know how anyone *is*.

"Thank you, Dae," he murmurs, lightly tugging his dress down around his waist before looking over to the ballroom.

The building holding the ball is stunning—all white marble intricately carved with swirling golden pillars and smooth walls overlooking a view of the ocean behind. Bright light pours out through arched windows and the open doorway, outlining two guards at the entrance and a small crowd talking to one another in the courtyard outside. The scent of fruit from a vineyard they claimed to have to the left of the ballroom sweetens the air, hanging over the lingering smoke from the crowd's cigarettes or cigars.

From this distance, I catch glimpses of champagne glasses and fake smiles, of walls being put up to guard hearts and feelings. Nemoure is built on that sort of façade much more than Makor ever was.

Cain reaches over and loops an arm through mine, hooking at the elbow, as we walk into the courtyard—and instantly, I wish I was far less visible, as countless pairs of eyes land on us. I look over everyone in quick glances, trying to maintain *some* form of confidence due to who my date is, but it isn't easy at all. Cain makes it look effortless, while I have to inwardly fight to keep my eyes up from the ground.

Murmurs cross through the people surrounding us as we walk by, and I really should've known better than to be surprised. Most of the people *love* gossip in this city. The further we walk, the more people appear—glancing at us, standing by or sitting at cloth-covered tables tastefully placed around a well-kept wooden dancefloor, sipping wine or champagne or in some cases, even whiskey.

I must tense at the attention, because Cain glances up at me with a slight expression of concern.

"What, are you nervous?" He searches my gaze for a second, then flashes a polite but venomous smile at a woman as she passes us.

I shake my head, eyeing a waiter with a tray of glasses as he makes his way in our direction. "No, well, yes. I don't really like being looked at."

Cain smirks, following my gaze over the crowd. "Sorry, you *definitely* came with the wrong person then," he says with a laugh, and that air of confidence strikes me again. *I don't know how he does it.*

Plucking a pair of wine glasses from the tray as the man pauses in front of us, I shrug back at him. "I knew what I was getting myself into."

"Oh, did you?" He raises an eyebrow and takes a sip of the wine, making an odd face at it. "This must be aged well. It tastes like a brand I don't like all that much."

I take a sip of my own, inwardly hating the dryness of it. Red seems to be a favorite of my mother's, but I don't think it's one of mine. "I'm not a fan, truthfully. How do you know what brand it is?" I ask, peering at the glass. To me, it just looks like any other expensive red.

Cain laughs, slipping a little compact mirror from the inner edge of his dress and popping it open. "I collect all manner of wines. I typically know what the different brands taste like these days."

I force myself not to watch him check his lipstick before looking around, taking in the room instead, if only for something to distract me from the way he purses his lips.

The walls are the same white as outside, with matching pillars that appear to be even taller than the ones in the courtyard. Painted on the gold-lined ceiling are soft cherubs on clouds and gods pointing to one another, all pastel blues and warm tans and pearl whites. On the opposite side of the room, an opening to another patio or balcony is partially hidden by thin golden curtains, glittering in the light from the chandeliers. They flow lightly on a breeze I can't feel from this distance, but I imagine the warmth of it all the same.

"So... do you dance?" I ask, looking over at Cain once I hear the compact snap shut again, swirling the wine just to give myself something to do with my hand.

Cain raises an eyebrow at me, resting his free hand on his hip. "Oh, yes. Obviously, I wouldn't come to these things if I *somehow* didn't know what I was doing."

"So... we probably should then, right?" I smile nervously before glancing away from his somewhat sassy expression, studying the dancefloor. Most seem like couples with barely any space between them, familiarity in their smiles. Others are obviously newer to each other, laughing at the space between them and looking somewhat awkward with their hands.

I don't know which one to expect us to be.

Hopefully not the latter.

Cain nods, smirking playfully at me and polishing off what remains of his wine in one swift gulp. I do the same, ditching my clean glass and his lipstick-marked one on a nearby table as he tugs me toward an open space on the wooden floor.

Arm in arm, we step out together just as the previous song ends and slips into another, quickly falling into a smooth rhythm. One hand on Cain's hip and one in his hand. Two sets of feet, picking up speed with the song. We turn about easily, the gap between us closing as fast as the music.

Three moments with all my focus on Cain.

How his body moves with mine, how close he is. The dark curl of his lips and the brush of his hair against my hand where it traveled to his lower back. The press of his hand against my chest, the firm weight of him here, with me, grinning with something wild in his eyes.

I starve in this moment, the touch thrilling through me as the room starts to blur around us. I starve for that look, exhaling through the longing that claws through my ribcage.

I have to close my eyes to keep myself from doing something stupid, and when I open them again, it hits me just how many people are watching. Nearly everyone on the dancefloor has moved aside to stare, lips moving, jaws dropped, a hush of conversation rising under the music that I somehow don't feel nervous about. All of them focused on the two of us.

A match made in the Hells.

A duo that likely should never have met, but here we are, spinning together.

Like no one else matters.

And no one else does.

Cain is smiling at me, smiling like no one else ever has in my whole life, and if I was crazier, I might have kissed him. He's smiling at me, and there are no words I can possibly put together to describe the feeling it creates in my chest. Luckily for my dignity and self-control, the trance we hold over the crowd breaks as the music slows, and we do too, both unable to say anything as we exhale together.

His smile turns sly, laughing lightly. "I was a little worried I was going to have to teach you how to do this."

I shake my head, a little private smile of my own on my lips. "Fortunately, I was taught how to dance ages ago," I reply, turning gingerly across the floor in something closer to a waltz. "That, and part of my magical training is a form of dance, so I know it well."

Cain opens his mouth to reply, but a voice calling out his name cuts him off—much to my dismay; I'd have liked to know what he had to say—and we turn just in time to see Irsa practically dragging his date our way.

"Oh Cain," the man says with an overly flirtatious smile, "There you are!"

Irsa's partner is an elf I only recognize because Cain has mentioned him before, though never in a very positive light. Kira, I think his name was.

He's pretty enough, with long golden hair and brown eyes sharply lined in the same cobalt blue as his fancy suit, but he's all performance, rather than substance. I suppose that's why it's so hard to understand why Cain has ever been jealous of him. Kira wears a painted mask to make himself beautiful, but Cain has a natural beauty rivaled only by that of nature herself. What use is it to be jealous of someone like him?

"I know. It's nice to see you again, Kira." Cain directs his smile to Irsa's date, Kira, and there's that indirect poison he laces his politeness with. His body language is open and entertained as he loops an arm through mine again, but I know it's simply for an effect and not truth.

Kira huffs slightly, sipping wine from a glass decorated with golden leaves before nodding. "You as well."

I turn my attention away from the conversation with a quiet sigh, glancing around the room to look for familiar faces. Minos, Cain's father, entertaining a small group with laughter and what must be a celebratory toast. A few classmates dancing together or sitting at tables drinking. My mother—

My mother.

The former isn't shocking, given the social aspect of this event, and the location being in between the council buildings and the college. The latter, however, has my heart missing several beats in my chest.

"You know what all of this means, right?" Morgana's voice cuts into my head the moment I see her, sucking all the sound out of the room. She's leaning against a pillar by the door, an empty glass dangling in her hand, shifting as if she was swirling wine. Except for that little movement, everything about her is still. Tense, waiting to pounce, almost.

I decide against answering, swallowing my fear and returning my attention to Cain and the conversation with Irsa—finding it surprising when I realize it's only him and I still standing here. Irsa and Kira stand a couple of groups away, with the latter looking more pissed off than he was originally. *Shit, what did I miss?*

"What's wrong?" Cain says, red eyes searching the crowd before falling on my face.

I shake my head, studying the cut of his eyeliner and the shimmer on his cheekbones before finding my words. "My mother was talking to me. I apologize."

One of Cain's sharp eyebrows raises as I attempt to refocus, trying not to think about what this could mean. What *she* could mean by that. This night means so much to me; it's the closest I've felt to real freedom in ages.

I'm not going to let anyone ruin that.

What did I want to tell him about? Oh, right. "Ah, another thing. Irsa threatened me before I picked you up."

Cain blinks in surprise, though whether he's shocked at the sudden topic change or the admission, I'm not sure. "He did? I don't know what his damn issue is..." He huffs and frowns over at Irsa, his brow furrowed in a way that makes me want to smooth it out with my fingers. Before I've the chance to thoroughly embarrass myself by doing so, Cain turns back to me with a devious smile. "I have an idea. Follow me."

"Where are we going?" I ask, but he doesn't answer just takes my hand and tugs me away from the dancefloor, leading me back to the entrance. Outside, the cool night air is a welcome relief from the warmth of the ballroom. My mother is nowhere to be seen as we cross the courtyard to the carriages, stalking back and forth between the group of them until Cain finds what he seemingly wanted.

I study the one he stops at, looking over the royal purple wood and black metal frame questioningly. The drivers are nowhere to be seen, either. "What are we doing?"

Cain's smile becomes a grin, wild and intense. His eyes glitter with hidden embers, the irises nearly black in the low light when he looks at me. "We're going to make it *real* embarrassing to bring his date home. Do you have a knife on you?"

I make a perplexed face at him, laughing. "Um... no."

His confidence falters for a second as he pauses, looking back at the carriage. "Well, thank you for not bringing a knife with you, I guess. I thought about having my own on me—not to stab you with, obviously—"

"Wow. Thank you for clarifying," I remark, my tone dry but playful as I smile and fold my arms over my chest.

He laughs, shaking his head. "I didn't mean it like that."

A little laugh leaves me. "I know. Anyway... I *do* have a spell that creates a sort of shadow blade, if you'd like that."

Cain nods eagerly, holding out a hand with a devious smile on his lips as I reach behind me, calling for the shadow magic within my fingers. It hums and vibrates across my palm as it forms, becoming a wispy hilt and a sharp blade—I close my eyes as the spell takes shape, crawling out of some inner darkness within me. Once it feels solid in my hand, I bring it forward and settle it in Cain's hand, our fingertips nearly brushing when he closes his around the hilt.

He hums a vaguely familiar tune and steps over to the horses, brushing his free hand over the closest one's muzzle before slightly cutting into the leather harness keeping it tied to the carriage. "Keep an eye out, Dae, okay?"

I nod, more to myself than to him, turning my back to him and eyeing the ballroom. No one in the distant crowd is looking in our direction, and apparently, no one cared how fast we left. I'm sure most of them probably thought we were going to do something *much* different than vandalizing a carriage, come to think of it. Knowing Cain's history, they likely assumed he was dragging me from our too-close dance for something *far* more intimate than this.

Even thinking about the smallest *hint* of that makes me shiver.

The sharp, smoky scent of burning wood catches my attention, and I look back at Cain with my eyebrows raised just in time to see him very carefully burn through small spots of the wheels and the upper frame of the carriage's body.

It's not the first time I have seen him use his magic, but it is the first time I've been close enough to feel it sing through me like this, that bright little flame sending bursts of heat and embers skittering through my veins. I have always thought his magic as beautiful as he is, the sensation of it just as addictive. I wonder what it might feel like to touch it, to reach out and slip my fingers into the flames. Would they burn? Would he feel my touch through them as if I was caressing his own skin?

Somehow, he is managing to keep it very contained, but it still makes me rub my hands together a bit nervously. From the fear of getting caught, or the need to reach out and burn, I do not know.

"We *have* to be here when they leave," Cain says with another grin, before he ducks inside the carriage. "Oh, gross".

I tilt my head at the door, glancing back toward the ballroom to be sure we're still going to be alone. "What?"

He leans his head back out and grimaces. "You don't want to know."

I laugh a little, taking my blade from him once he passes it over and willing it away as he steps back outside. He tugs me over to our carriage, only two down in the row, and leans back against it to wait.

As we sit there, listening to the sighs and stomps of the horses and the distant orchestral music still playing, Cain tugs a cigarette from somewhere within the neckline of his dress and tucks it between his lips.

I must have made a confused face at him, because he raises an eyebrow at me and asks, "What?"

"Nothing, just... where were you keeping that? And the mirror from before?" I glance down at the open parts around his chest, finding nothing that would tell me where he could possibly be storing anything. No bumps, edges, or lumps in his outfit give it away.

He laughs, reaching a hand into the left side, where I just barely catch a glimpse of the rounded edge of the mirror pressing against the fabric before he brings out another cigarette. "Here. Marion and I added inside pockets to these dresses, so we could carry mirrors or lipstick or, well, these."

I nod as he lights a small flame on his fingertip, bringing it to the ends of our cigarettes. The smoke is a new feeling in my lungs as I hold it there, closing my eyes, focusing in on the distant music almost accidentally. My fingers tap along to the rhythm of it on my thigh, a lovely classical piece I could easily recreate on my piano at home or on the one in the library. If I can keep the notes in my head, if I can remember, maybe I'll try to—

Cain nudges me with his elbow, gesturing with his cigarette in the direction of the ballroom where Irsa and Kira have just exited and begun heading our way. I keep my mouth shut as we watch them start to step inside their carriage, fighting off a smirk at a disgusted scoff that filters out just before the door shuts.

A driver appears from the darkness and mounts his seat, taking the reins in his hands. There is a muffled word from Irsa, then the instant snapping of leather to urge the horses on. The carriage lurches with momentum, before sinking down into the dirt a moment later, groaning and creaking as the wood buckles in on itself, and Cain's chuckling becomes a full-on laugh.

Irsa does not notice us as he hurriedly stumbles out of the carriage once more, trying to stammer out an explanation for the mess to both the exasperated driver and his date, but Kira doesn't listen. He storms away, hands clenching tight at his sides, stalking back to the ballroom with anger writhing off him in waves.

Irsa's face is horribly red as he chases after him, desperately trying to calm the elf down while Cain's laughter breaks from its cage and follows them across the yard.

Cain links his arm through mine, still laughing as we put out our cigarettes and step into our carriage, sitting down on opposite sides. "Gods, that was amazing. I'm glad we did that."

I nod, tasting the remnants of somewhat-pleasant smoke on my tongue, resting over the even more distant wine we'd had. It's a nice enough taste, but as Cain absentmindedly wets his lips while grinning, it's hard not to imagine what it would taste like from his mouth.

I swallow, then nod. *Focus.* "I am, too."

He leans back against the plush seat, watching me almost curiously. "If you'd like, you could come to my dorm with me. I'm starving."

"I'm hungry too, honestly." I'm surprised I even noticed that I am. "And... I don't really want to go home right now, anyway." After everything that happened, I almost forgot about Morgana speaking to me in the middle of it all. Her cryptic message and the anxious confusion it left swirling in my gut.

I'm glad I didn't let her ruin it.

"Good, then. We'll make something at mine." Cain nods, nudging my knee with a heeled foot before he crosses his leg over the other.

I study it as the dress falls away, eyeing the angle of his knee and the folds of the fabric, swallowing past the dryness in my throat. "Yeah. Sounds good to me."

I pay our driver maybe a little too well upon arriving at the college, thanking him as Cain leads the way into the building and to his dorm. Our rooms are on the same floor, but I haven't known exactly which one belonged to him—surprisingly, he doesn't have any sort of big sign or marking with his name on it like the others. No flame, no red, no roses. Just the same metallic plaque with a number on it.

On the outside, the rooms are similar, but on the inside, Cain's is only a little bit different—the layout of his 'living' area beside the kitchen being much more modern compared to mine, with a sunken part of the floor filled by two long, built-in couches and a table in between. An arched window sits in the upper part of the opposite wall above two square windows, allowing in a flood of moonlight that makes it difficult for me to look at him, just like back in the library. And just like then, I can't help but look anyway.

The light highlights him beautifully, catching on the gems at his hips and torturing me all over again. It brightens the reds of him. It makes me wish for the feeling of him under my hands again, the sway and the heat of him as we danced.

"I'm going to change; I'll be right back," Cain states, his voice cutting through my longing as he strides toward what must be his bedroom and disappears behind a white door.

Once he leaves the room, I remove my tailcoat and the vest I wore, being sure to neatly fold and set them in a pile on one of the chairs at the island in the middle of the kitchen. Undressing any further is something unattainable, being Cain has not seen the multitude of scars littering my body, and that is a whole conversation I'm not ready to have yet. Not with Cain. One of his servants steps away from a small closet and smiles at me, offering to take my clothes, but I shake my head and thank them for it.

It stuns me to think some of the people here have servants in their dorms as well, but I suppose I can't judge *too* harshly.

I hum as I cross the room to the pair of towering bookshelves pressed against the left wall, curious about the books that line them. I've never asked Cain what kind of books he reads, or if he was even the reading type—so I take the moment alone to look them over. When the majority turn up to be business related, I sigh and step away from the shelves. Not my style, particularly.

How to start a business, how to maintain one, how to crush the competition, bigger businessmen's thorough essays on how they became as big as they did.

Nothing interesting in my eyes.

"What types of books do you read, Dae?" Cain's voice startles me, but it is a welcome surprise in the quiet.

I tuck my hands in my pockets to avoid rubbing them together, looking over to where he leans in the doorway, an amused and curious look in his eyes. He's wearing those champagne silks I've really started to like, all his makeup wiped off except for the littlest hints of mascara still clinging to his lashes. Somehow, he's just as stunning like this as he is all dressed up. "I tend to lean into darker themes. Horror, thrillers, Gothic poetry, things of that sort."

Cain laughs and nods, likely finding it an obvious answer as he waves me over to the kitchen, removing a platter covered in fruits, crackers, and dried meats from the counter and setting it before him. He starts to pour tea in a pair of red mugs, filling the air with the scent of raspberries and hibiscus.

"That shouldn't surprise me, I guess. Feel free to eat whatever you want, by the way," he says, gesturing toward the platter. "I need to get it out of here."

It's a struggle not to watch the elegance of his movements, but I make myself get a small plate of food as directed and walk to the couch to sit down.

Cain joins me a moment later, settling my mug on the table in front of me and sighing as he sits. "Thank you for taking me to the ball, Daedalus," he says, then places a small cherry on his tongue. "I really enjoyed it."

A yawn escapes me, which comes as a bit of a surprise, as I pick up my tea and press my palms against both sides of the mug. "I'm glad I went. With you, of course, but generally as well."

"I'm glad... Are you tired?" Cain sounds so *close.* His voice is low, slightly raspier than usual, and *gods* I want to look and see how close he is—but I can't bring myself to lift my gaze from the pink liquid inside my cup.

I nod, moving one hand to make a small, organized stack of cracker, meat, cheese—if only to give myself something to do with my hands. "I think the exhaustion is finally getting to me."

My habit of barely resting to study, train, or even write music, has definitely turned on me very quickly. I can't help it, though. It's been ingrained into me since I was much younger—somewhat out of stress, somewhat out of necessity—and I haven't let go of it since.

Cain shifts beside me, lightly humming in thought. "If you want to stay here tonight, I don't mind."

It feels odd to have that offered to me, being my dorm is only a few doors down the hall—but part of me *wants* to stay. I want to know what it is like to wake up to Cain Sidrelle in the morning. To anybody, really, but especially him.

"I think that would be nice."

Cain nods, leaning his head onto my shoulder. "Good."

We eat in quiet for a few minutes, sipping our tea in between bites and enjoying the silence. I don't know what to do with Cain touching me like this. I haven't known what to do the entire night, with him. His hair is soft where it brushes my neck, where it touches the corner of my jaw. I can almost imagine running a hand through it, if I was a more confident person.

He stands up after a moment and stretches, moving to carry his plate into the kitchen. "You can sleep in my bed with me, then," he says, casual and confident.

My jaw all but drops, and I open my mouth to speak, but nothing comes out for several moments. "Are you sure? I could sleep out here—"

Cain strides back over, pressing a finger to my lips. "I said what I said, Daedalus. Come with me."

As if he put a leash on me with that singular statement, I get up and put my dishes away, then follow him silently to his room. It's unsurprisingly made up by the same white walls, with two square windows lined by red curtains and a red carpet covering the floor instead of white tile. A large bed takes up the majority of the space, and there is a walk-in closet, a dresser with a mirror and some makeup on it up against the wall.

I watch him as he pushes back his blankets and crawls under them, nervously standing at the end of the bed. My hands rub over one another without me thinking much about it. "Are you sure about this?" I ask again, glancing back at the open doorway.

Cain pats the space beside him assertively, something warm glittering in his eyes. "Yes. Come over here."

I swallow and slide in beside him, unable to breathe as he takes my arm and pulls it over his waist once I finally lay down, shifting so his back is against my torso. Nothing in me moves. I don't even think my heart beats, and all my thoughts go quiet with the press of his warm body against mine.

My hunger for a kind touch, for something, *someone*, being this close, rumbles up from my guts. Starving, I pull him closer. I'd pull him into my ribcage if I could, tangle him up in my veins, drag him into the depths of me—

He glances over his shoulder at me, smiling. "Is this alright with you, Dae?"

My nerves are so high, it is a wonder my voice does not crack when I answer.. "Yes... yes. It is. This is fine."

Cain laughs, shaking his head before resting it down on the pillow again. "You don't have to be so nervous."

"I apologize. I'm not familiar with this, is all," I say, shifting against him a little and yawning as the comfort of the bed threatens to make me rest for once.

He chuckles, then settles into me a little more before I hear his breathing slow.

I make myself close my eyes, breathing in raspberries and roses until the night finally takes me.

10

— • —

I DON'T rest for nearly long enough, the exhaustion still clinging to me when I wake once more. Gravedust itches at the inner corner of my eyes, and I scrub it away before carefully pushing up and out of Cain's bed.

I glance back at him as I stretch—admiring how his bright red hair is mussed up about his head like a violent halo, his face softer than anything I've ever seen. I can't help taking a moment to admire how gentle his edges look with him this relaxed, before turning to face the room.

Stepping over to the desk nearby, I hunt down a piece of paper and a pen, writing a brief apology for having to leave early and setting it on the pillow beside Cain's own. It's nearly impossible to leave him, wishing I could simply settle back into bed within the cradle of his warmth, or that I could feel him pulling my hand over him again.

But, I know I have to go home. *Unfortunately.* Who knows how much worse things would be if I didn't.

Slowly, I make my way out of his room and eventually the college, wishing things could be different. Wishing *I* was different, so I didn't have to leave Cain alone in his room. It's foolish really—thinking I'm going to get away with that. No person leaves someone like him to sleep alone, if they have the chance.

But someone like me doesn't get someone like him. Someone like me doesn't get choices at all.

I watch myself in the rippling reflection of the courtyard's fountain and in shop windows as I pass them, trying to calm my rising nerves.

Knowing Morgana, she will still be awake at this hour and will be expecting me.

Somehow, she always knows.

I watch the stars glitter in the inky darkness far above my head as I pause at the manor's gates, resting a hand on the cold iron for a moment. Black paint breaks off in flecks as I trail my fingers over it, counting each tiny piece that falls away, counting the few constellations I catch glimpses of. The light pollution is almost too bad to see them deeper in Nemoure, but from here, I can see a few.

My mother will open the door any moment now, so all I have to do is count.

Stars, seconds, paint. Stars, minutes, paint.

The doors open before I can finish my counting, and, exactly as I predicted, Morgana stands on the other side. She towers above me as I approach, wearing her heels even at this hour, and I swear the brightness of her pink eye increases under the glare she gives me. One dark-nailed hand rests on the doorknob and the other at her side as she watches me approach, her eyebrow raising sharply in response to my very obvious hesitation.

I will always hate how small she makes me feel.

Gods, help me.

She turns sharply, her cloak snapping out behind her. "Come with me."

Morgana walks straight to the training room, as I expect, and I follow her as if she cast a spell over me. I hate her. I don't know how *not* to hate her. She was supposed to love me, to care for me, and she made me like this, she did this to me—

I sigh in slight relief at the sight of Silas standing in his usual place at the center of the room, hoping it's another usual night between us. He smiles at me and nods, shifting his weight from one foot to the other. "Good evening, Macabres. Will it be another session between me and Daedalus tonight?"

Morgana shakes her head curtly, stabbing a finger in the direction of the opposite wall. "No. Not tonight," she hisses, glaring him down. "You, stand over there and *watch*."

Her words are a snarl, fully saying 'I will hurt you if you interrupt me', making the hair on the back of my neck stand up as I watch Silas nod and cross the room silently. It's a very obvious threat. I should be running away right now—if I knew what was good for me.

My heart pounds as I swallow again, feeling my throat tighten as she calls her blade to her hand—a rich black longsword, detailed with deep red rubies and bits of silver around the hilt and swirling hand guard. It glints in the light as she carves it through the air to admire it, or herself in it, and then she turns to face me.

My hand shakes as I extend it, summoning my own longsword from the wall instead of my usual rapier.

Morgana swings her sword in an arc before looking to me, her eyes narrowing. "Come at me."

I nod, more to myself than to her, leaping and darting toward her—cursing when she catches me in a quick swing of her arm and nearly throws me across the room. "Wrong, Daedalus," she snaps, anger lacing her words.

My stomach turns as I force myself to face her again, snapping my blade upward to catch her own quick approach. The resounding *clang* vibrates through my core, and I swear, somewhere underneath it, I hear Silas gasp.

"You can do better than this, can't you?" she asks, her dark lips curling as she shoves me backward, leaving a small opening between us.

I don't allow her to get too far, closing the gap quickly and striking her blade out of her hand with a well-timed hit to the hilt. It clatters to the ground, remaining abandoned for only a moment. She smirks as I drive her back from her dropped weapon, chasing her across the room until she finally calls the sword back to her hand and slams it directly into my stomach. With my own momentum meeting hers, I reel back into one of the pillars behind me, grimacing as I cough and gasp for breath I really don't need.

My vision swims for a moment, barely allowing me enough time to get away from her next attack.

One swing and she knocks me off my feet; one swing and I catch her arm with the tip of my sword. If I dare to get so close, Morgana simply shoves me away telekinetically, and I dive at her again. The ferocity in which we train this time is much more intense than anything I've done with Silas—in a way, it feels sickening, and in another, it feels *good*. Oddly so, being her disappointment is thick in the air, unmistakable. But it feels good to be able to drive her back, to have *any* sign of frustrating her because of how well I'm doing.

I wince as she launches me across the floor with a fierce swing, my body shaking so hard it's likely visible. Colors dance around the edges of my vision, and all sound is so muffled now that I can only hear a high-pitched whine ringing in my ears—leaving me in an odd silence for a moment until, under that, Silas starts telling Morgana to stop. I don't know if she was approaching me again. I don't know anything, anymore.

"Get up, Daedalus," she states, and I drag myself to my feet.

Before me, beside her, stands Bren. He's a little older than when he first arrived, a little older than the last time I saw him, which seems like forever ago now being I've been keeping him away.

It isn't surprising, given that Witchbloods age faster than most races due to their Fae heritage. I stare at him for a moment before looking to Morgana, shaking my head.

"No," I reply simply, and she smiles in a way that doesn't reach her eyes.

"Yes, Daedalus. Once you can find the real version of Bren, you can be done. You're *supposed* to be like me. You can handle it."

Bren instantly morphs into ten different versions of himself, circling me in a way that makes me dizzy. I turn and face each one, trying to decipher which one is him by looks alone—but they're all the same. Identical. All wavering with his magic, glimmering and twisting with the fantasy of the Fae.

I shake my head, swallowing too hard. "I don't want to hurt him."

Morgana scoffs, her irritation growing. "Find the real Bren, Daedalus."

Fear spears through me as I lift my blade again, launching at the first Bren. A slight gasp ripples from every version of him, as if he didn't truly expect me to listen to her, and then he starts to *move.* Every Bren circles me, weaving in and out of my reach as I slice through illusion after illusion. My shadows writhe around my hands as I twist toward the next, spearing this Bren in the chest despite the terror that floods me over thinking it could truly be him. When it fizzles away to nothing, relief nearly makes my heart stop.

Panic makes my slices sharper, a little too frantic, as I lunge for the Bren in the center before me, and he disappears too. *Fuck.* This is taking too long. I should've found him by now. I whirl around again, facing the next version of him and thrusting out my sword.

It nicks across his cheekbone, and all of the variations of him sweep back into him.

Bren's red eyes stare up at me in surprise as he touches his cheek, his fingertips coming away bloodied as I sink to my knees.

"Very good, Daedalus," Morgana says, striding toward me. "Again."

"Morgana, stop," Silas says firmly, *unexpectedly,* and everything goes silent as I watch her turn to face him.

I blink at the floor, sitting on my hands and knees as I stare in muted fear at the deep red droplets forming on the tile. I must have overextended myself a bit, or she got my face in a hit earlier. I don't remember.

The sound finally comes back to me, allowing me to hear a scoff and then the sharp sound of Morgana's heels as she leaves the room with Bren at her side. Neither of us moves until they are out of earshot—but the moment she's gone, Silas rushes to my side and kneels down, putting a hand on my shoulder that I involuntarily flinch away from.

He moves his hand but doesn't move away from me. "Easy, it's just me, Daedalus."

Fury and an odd sadness tangle inside of me like a pit of snakes, coiling around my spine and settling somewhere between my chest and stomach. Everything aches, and I only truly acknowledge it as my gaze focuses on the blood before me.

"I know," I say, quiet. "I'm sorry."

Silas watches me push up to my feet, frowning. "Don't apologize, Daedalus. Are you going to be alright?"

I nod, wiping the blood from my nose with the back of my hand. "I'll be fine."

"You don't have to be, you know," he says, standing up beside me and thankfully making no move to keep me from leaving the room. I'm already starting for the door as he speaks, ready to hide in my bed and act like no one else exists.

I don't answer him as I leave, sighing to myself once I reach the hallway.

As I walk back to my room, I grimace as Bren's door creaks open, trying to ignore the frown on my younger brother's face as his red eyes land on me. He's catching on to too many things, and I can't make myself speak to him because of it. I swear he got older in just a few weeks.

"So, she did that?" Bren asks, gesturing to the blood on my face. His voice is lower. I never noticed that before. *Has he ever spoken to me, really?*

My room has never felt so far away.

I don't answer him, and he chases after me, catching my sleeve. "Daedalus, you can't just ignore me. Not after all of that."

My eyes burn for a moment, and I blink a time or two before looking down in his direction. Not at him, but somewhere past him. "This isn't a good time, Bren." *I have to ignore you, I'm sorry.*

His ruby eyes flare with anger, but he doesn't let go of my sleeve. "When will it ever be? You're never home, you don't talk to me—don't you think I could help you if you just talked to me?"

I can't talk to you. I know why you're here. You're just a test for me.

Something dark claws up through my warring fury and depression, ripping through them like they're nothing. I taste the bitterness of it, the vile burn of it on my tongue, the press of it beneath my skin.

The Rot laughs in my head, pacing the feeling through me like a clock.

"No, I don't think you could." I shake my head, pulling my arm away from him. "I don't think so at all."

Keeping Bren at an arm's length hurts like a thorn digging into my side, but it has to be done. I can't let him, or anyone, get too close because of *this* exact reason. If he got hurt, someone would ask questions. If I didn't get close to anyone... no one would ask anything. No one would get hurt. No one would know.

A shaky sigh rattles from me as I continue down the hall, leaving Bren to sit in the hurt *I* caused, finally reaching the door to my bedroom. Relief floods through me as I step into it, relishing the familiarity of my dark walls and pinned bats. The room almost seems to hug me as I cross the black rug, pausing to sit at my glossy grand piano. It plays on its own for a moment before I lay my hands over the keys, smiling at the cool surface of them, as welcoming as ever.

Morning arrives hours later in the form of thin sunlight shining on my floor, and I'm not surprised I barely got any rest. Despite feeling a strange peace from playing my newest piece all night, a less strange and more familiar numbness has decided to fill me up to the very brim, pushing at my seams and threatening to overflow.

Nearly on autopilot for the millionth time, I change into a velvet turtleneck and matching velvet pants, add chains to my waist and slip on a pair of platform boots before leaving my room.

As I walk down the stairs, my eyes wander over the various portraits of my family on the wall, wishing I didn't have to stop at my own every time I see it. I'm very young in it, somewhere between five and ten, and it almost angers me to look upon myself like that. How innocent I was then— it's difficult to imagine. The anger dissipates quickly, chased after by sadness at the fact that I don't look happy there, either.

Was I ever happy? What was I doing then, in this picture? There's a book in my lap, maybe it was science or fantasy or horror, or maybe I was calculating the angles of the pages if I turned them certain ways. I don't know. Maybe I was just staring at it because there was nothing else.

My father steps around the side of the stairs with Darrien at his side as I reach the bottom, and I almost smile at the sight of them.

I've never been quite sure of Darrien's place in the family, only that he went to college with my parents and Cain's father, but it has always been obvious that he is much closer to my father than Morgana. I don't remember when he arrived in the old manor—one day I walked downstairs and he was there, glowing like an angel cast upon us, guarding us.

Compared to the darkness of my family, Darrien stands out, always dressed in stark or creamy whites. Every bit of him is pale, from his skin to his hair. Even his eyes are pure, nearly shining like a beacon.

Mikhalis nods and smiles at me as we pass each other, and I welcomingly breathe in the mingled scents of their sandalwood and evergreen colognes as they continue up the stairs.

Bren has likely already left the manor, either having a class or wanting to get to the college early—ever since he aged far enough to be in Whitestone, Morgana decided to enroll him to pursue his illusions. I haven't known how to feel about it, sharing my space with him in a way that's no longer just at home. *Especially* after seeing how quickly some of Cain's friends took to him. Regardless of what reason he's not here for, I'm a bit glad for the walk alone.

Exhaustion feels like a gnawing thing, teeth sticking to my ribs and digging their way in.

The morning is as quiet as the night I had walked through on my return to the manor—a little dreary, with a bit of a sprinkle starting to fall on my hair and shoulders. I know I could open a portal to the college if I truly wanted to, but the rain's presence feels inviting, so I keep walking. The streets are populated by only a few people, most with black or colorful umbrellas hiding them away from the oncoming pour. Some are students, though it seems a majority of them are the typical shoppers I've seen walking around.

Maybe they're tourists. They're lucky, in that sense, not having to grow up in the clutter and politics of Nemoure. I've never been a tourist. I wonder what it's like. I wonder if they're happy with their money and their bags of things they'll eventually forget they bought.

I peer up at the top of Whitestone before heaving open one of the doors, ducking inside just as the rain starts to pick up. My hair and clothes are damp from the sprinkle I walked through, but a quick wave of my hand and a muttered spell dries them instantly.

Students hustle by me in groups and pairs, many stepping out of my way and casting me odd looks as I hurry past. My walk had taken longer than I'd have liked, so I have only just enough time to stop by my dorm room to grab my books before I'm off again to my first class of the day.

It's not until I get there, pausing just outside the door, that I remember Cain is going to be inside. With my mother's sudden training, I'd nearly forgotten about the ball entirely, and what happened after.

Would he be waiting for me? Would he be upset I left with only a note? Certainly he would ask questions, especially with my appearance—one glance in the mirror tells me how rough I currently look. *You look like shit, Daedalus, get yourself together, Daedalus, why do you look like that? Who hurt you, Daedalus? Why are you like this? You're better than this, Daedalus, I told you what would happen—*

I grimace, dragging a hand over my face before forcing myself to continue on regardless. I cannot afford to miss classes, not with my mother's anger already hanging over me like a guillotine.

Inside, the room itself is painted a soft blue, with long wooden desks resting over the white marble floor. It's peaceful, if you consider classes to be that way. Cain and Bren sit at opposite tables, the former writing down notes in the spot next to mine, and the latter staring at me instead of his book.

I don't look at either of them, moving toward my seat, but I can feel them—the eyes, the staring, the pokes and prods at my mental barriers. Too many, too loud.

It feels too strange seeing my brother here, so openly ready to learn and so agitated with me already.

Asher eyes me from his corner, catching my eye before I sit down, and I know I would not have even noticed him there if not for his heavy gaze. His magic reaches out to mine and I accept with a swift click, settling deep into the recesses of my hungering shadows with the cold and dark arms of his own.

"Are you alright?"

The question does not surprise me, though its asker does. While Asher has been friendly recently, I have never imagined he would care.

"Not very. I will be, though." I reply, and he gives me a slight nod. I expect him to push, to ask for more, but he simply turns back to his books, and the connection between us fizzles away.

"I thought you weren't coming in today," Bren says, his voice tense as it drags my attention away from Asher. I hadn't realized I arrived at my desk already, but there is Bren, leaning toward me with hushed whispers as I take my seat. "You looked... You looked like you wouldn't be, and I know you didn't sleep."

Cain looks over at me with a frown as I nearly drop my books onto the desk, setting his pen down. "Are you alright?"

When I glance over, there's an almost genuine form of concern on his face. It surprises me almost as much as the fact that he isn't in his usual button-up and vest, but instead a deep red sweater over his black slacks. Much more comfortable, compared to the business attire he always wears. Cashmere, maybe, no, it's cable-knit, that doesn't make sense...

I shrug, going through my ritual of spacing out my things and opening my book. "I'm fine."

"Stop lying to him and tell him the truth," Bren snaps, glaring over at me, or so I assume by the burning feeling that hits my skin before he looks away again.

My jaw clenches for a moment, tight enough to hurt, then I let it go. "There's nothing to tell," I reply, flipping the page I was reading to the next one without ever truly looking at the words. "And I'm not lying."

Cain looks between us as a deep rumble of thunder sounds from outside—distant but crawling over quickly. What glimpse I can catch through the windows of the darkening clouds beyond tells me I should be glad I left when I did, or else I would've been stuck in a downpour.

Bren opens his mouth to say something else, then shuts it at the sight of a few of our classmates streaming into the room. They are mostly some of Cain's friends—Marion, Louis, Jesse—and a few people I haven't really bothered to learn the names of, all walking straight to their tables. Our professor returns to the room behind the passing group a moment later, flashing a big smile at us as they take their place at front of the room.

I do not bother listening to whatever lecture he begins, instead opening my book to a chapter a few ahead of the class, continuing where I had left off in my notes. I never mean to get so much farther than the rest of them, but it's hard to help it when many of my sleepless nights are spent studying and reading, whether by stress, my mother's pushing, or my own choice.

A slight wince crosses my face as I shift in my seat, a blaze of aching pain shooting through me as a reminder of what happened the night before. Cain's fingers twitch around his pencil, and I glance over to find his eyes on me. For a moment I can't look away—trapped in an odd few seconds of staring, watching him watch me, wondering why he's looking at all. *Does he calculate angles like I do? Is he studying mine?*

He searches my face for a moment before looking back to his book, and I let out the breath I held onto during. There is an odd urge in me to explain to Cain what is happening back at home, but at the same time I don't want him that close. I don't want to see the pity in his eyes, or the concern, or the sadness it'll probably bring. I don't want any of it, but I want to tell him. *Why in the Hells do I want to tell him?*

Cain leans over to me, just close enough that our arms barely brush. "Would you like to get breakfast after this?" he asks, soft enough our professor won't notice.

I pause, thinking the option over in my head. Breakfast could be nice, as I haven't eaten anything in a day or so. And breakfast with Cain? The chance to get to know him further, to spend time with him outside of classes... I need that right now, I think. Need the breath of fresh air he offers me. The distraction of his presence and his smile and his conversation.

Eventually, after what must've been minutes of awkward silence, I nod. And *ah*, see? There's that smile.

The class passes by without further distraction, and I'm not at all surprised when Bren makes quick work of leaving without saying anything to either of us. I watch him go, noting the hint of anger in his posture before sighing to myself and neatly closing up books, stacking them particularly.

I look over at Cain as I tuck them under my arm, watching him do the same. "Where are we going?"

He watches some of our classmates leave before looking back at me, a slight smile on his lips. "There's a place I like to go down the street, if that's fine?"

I hesitate in following him through the door of the classroom, just for a second, then nod and give him a slight shrug in response. It doesn't matter to me where we go— the food is likely going to be good anywhere in the city, or so I assume, and he would know the better places more than most.

Cain nods back as we walk side by side to our dorms, leaving our books behind and continuing on out of Whitestone. The rain is calmer now, barely a misting over my skin, making the walk easier as we pass through puddles and over soaked cobblestone.

Cain looks at the buildings we pass, then to me. "I hope you like this place."

"I'm not really picky, so I don't see why I wouldn't," I reply with a shrug.

My eyes drop to our hands as his fingers brush across mine, wondering what they'd look like linked together—my tanned skin against his fair skin, the darkness of the bone markings beside the bright glint of his jewelry, each knuckle pressed together in rhythmic patterns, back to back...

As I'm about to see it for myself, he stops short and gestures to a small building to our left. "Here we are."

The diner, a one-story building composed of red bricks painted with two swans on a lily pad covered pond, is simply called 'The Swan's Diner'. Two square windows sit on either side of the doors, and through them, just past the window boxes of flowers, I can see people sitting together, smiling over orange juice and coffee. I study them for a moment as we walk closer, letting go of my nerves in a single exhale.

The warm scent of bacon and fresh toast fills the air when Cain opens one of the white doors for us, stepping in ahead of me and looking back over his shoulder.

"Welcome," he says with a dramatic sweep of his arm, "to the Swan's Diner."

He says it as if I should be impressed with something grand and important, but while the diner is quaint and cozy, it is just that—a diner.

"Do you know why it's named that?" he asks, and at first I think he's trying to make a jab at me.

I make a face at him, because of course I don't—but even if I did, I'd want him to explain anyway. I enjoy his voice, even moreso when he is speaking on things he enjoys. "Not a clue, no."

"Not a clue, no."

He laughs, wiping his boots on the mat inside the doorway. "The diner is owned by a pair of elven men, Valenci and Victor, who have been married for so long, they like to say they're married for life, like swans. So, the name became 'The Swan's Diner', which is simple, but fitting. I've always liked it."

A short, dwarven waitress greets us with a big smile and seats us at a booth next to one of the wide windows, asking Cain if he wants his coffee like usual. He nods, asking for a mug for me as well. The familiarity of the interaction creates a new warmth in my chest I don't recognize.

Instead of dwelling on the strange emotion, I look out at the rainy street, drumming my fingertips on the table. "You said you go here often? It is obvious by the waitress—she knows your order."

He nods, smiling in a less "public-persona" sort of way. "Marion and I started coming here a while back. Not sure why, actually. I think Marion had an older gentleman treat him to breakfast one day, so he told me about it. We've been coming here since."

I raise eyebrow at that comment, but there isn't much shock behind it. Mostly questioning, really. Marion is a singer, and more often than not, from the stories I overhear, is catered to by older men—or simply just *rich* men. Whether it was through his musical career or his performances at a club down the street from White-stone, he seems to do well for himself. He apparently has plenty of expensive outfits and items from them, and he goes on plenty of dates or trips that most people wouldn't be able to afford in their lifetime. He's rich already without them, but apparently, the richer types are attracted to the 'pretty singer, sugar baby' sort.

Cain seems perfectly happy to move on as he picks up one of the paper menus on the table before us, his eyes moving swiftly over each side. "What's your go-to breakfast food, Dae?" he asks, peering at me over the edge of it.

I hum, taking my own menu and scanning the options. "Steak is likely my overall favorite food, depending how it's made... so I suppose steak and eggs?"

The nickname he had started using on me comes as a sur-prise each time he says it, but I'm starting not to mind it at all. Something about it is comforting, in an odd way—something I've never felt before, and haven't been able to place.

He nods slowly, then lowers the menu and starts pouring cream into his coffee from little plastic containers. As he stirs, he watches me. I can feel the familiar burn of his gaze on my cheeks, searching, though I've no idea what for. "Can I ask you something?"

I narrow my eyes a little, glancing at him over the edge of the paper. "Perhaps... what is it?"

"Will you tell me what actually happened to you?"

I flinch, more visibly than I'd like, and drop my eyes to the scratched tabletop instantly. "I don't know if I can," I admit quietly.

Before Cain gets the chance to pry into what I mean, our waitress walks back with a pad of paper in hand, cutting our conversation short so we can order. Cain asks for a venison steak and eggs, medium rare, and I uncomfortably order the same, but as rare as can be. She offers Cain a few moments of small talk, her smile friendly and sweet, his kind and unhurried. The words are muffled in my ears, drowned out by the Rot whispering through my veins. Urging me to tell Cain everything, to dig my grave even deeper than it might already be. It asks for the pain of explaining, growling and rumbling about how pathetic it would be to admit to my mother's actions, to admit that she had done this, and I had let her.

I glance around nervously, wondering if everyone else in the room could hear it too if they listen hard enough. I pluck up my coffee and sip it, attempting to distract myself from the murmuring in my ear, from the way my hands threaten to shake and my breath promises to quicken.

Cain must catch my paranoid glances, shooting the rest of the room a dagger-filled glare, as if it was something around us making me so nervous. "What's up?"

I shake my head with a sigh, closing my eyes for a moment. "Nothing, I'm sorry. I'm on edge lately, I suppose. I can tell you some time, it's just a lot," I say, slow. "And I mean, a *lot*."

He nods and lifts his coffee to his mouth, studying my steak when our plates are settled in front of us a second later. My stomach growls as I breathe in rosemary and pepper, watching a thin trail of blood as it joins the juice from the meat. I likely would've asked for it to not be cooked at all, but not many people knew what I am and that also isn't very morally acceptable, last I checked.

"You really like it like that?" Cain asks, cutting a piece from his own.

I surprise myself with a laugh, nodding at him. "Yes, why?"

He shakes his head, smiling in an amused sort of way. "No reason. Surprised, I guess."

We eat in calm silence afterward, despite the feeling of wanting to crawl out of my own skin from the presence of the Rot still lingering behind my eyes, in my fingertips, prickling beneath my teeth. ***Stab your hand, Daedalus. Put the knife in it,*** it whispers. ***It would be fun! You'd have fun. Are you too afraid? Are you a*** **coward?** ***Failure, boy.***

"Did you want me to tell you now?" I ask, desperate for a distraction, even if it means returning to our earlier conversation. "About what happened, I mean?"

"Oh, no, not here. Not with so many ears about." Cain's smile is tight for a moment, before he takes another sip of coffee and sets the mug down. "Though, I *have* been meaning to ask you, what's your favorite book? You mentioned horror?"

That's an easier topic. "It's called *Nocturna*. It's primarily horror, involving eldritch beings."

His eyebrows raise, tilting his head curiously. "Oh really? I'll have to read it sometime."

I must make a face in surprise, because Cain laughs.

"Sorry," I start, laughing too. "It caught me off guard that you'd actually want to read it... I do have an extra copy, if you'd like me to bring it sometime."

He nods. "I think I'd like that."

While I still remember the conversation, I know I'll have to pull the book out and set it with my clothes and books for the next day, because there is a very real chance that Morgana will take the memory of today from me. That, or she'll make our conversation look like a bad experience, so I stay away from Cain even more. The thought makes my stomach turn as I swallow another piece of steak, forcing it down.

Sometimes I wonder why I still listen to her, but it's so hard not to when she has so much control over *everything*.

"What is your home life like?" I ask, trying to distract myself from the way my head wants to tick again. "I know you've loosely mentioned your mother is an issue, but I wasn't sure."

Cain hums, eyeing me before swallowing his current bite. "It's...tense, at times. My father is not often home due to the counsel meetings, or his own business ventures. My mother is religious, and more often than not trying to find someone to marry me, because she thinks I need someone to care for me. I'll tell you why I think she does that some other time. Again, without so many ears." He smiles a little, looking at the rest of the room for a moment. "The mansion is quiet, unless my parents get in one of their arguments or if we're having one of our parties. Truthfully, it's not as bad as it could be."

It doesn't feel like the full truth, but I won't say that.

"I see," I say simply, nodding. "Mine is quiet, as well, typically. The manor isn't very loud, not unless I'm training."

"Training," he muses, sipping at his coffee. "I don't think I've ever really trained for anything."

A light laugh leaves me, shrugging my shoulders. "I do it often, under my mother's rule."

Cain nods, and the conversation fades out as we both continue to eat. It seems harsh to get a real conversation out of him in such a public place, but I understand why—the people of Nemoure are known to be nosy, always having their fingers in someone else's business or gossiping. Talking about such a deep topic out here is dangerous to do, especially when it's someone as high-up as him.

We finish eating a little while later, quickly paying and leaving a nice tip beside our stacked plates before walking back out into the dreary weather. I peer up at the gray clouds above our heads, eyeing how the shades of them range from dark to near white, and Cain paints a bright red lipstick over his lips with the same compact mirror I saw at the ball.

He smiles at me as he snaps it shut, returning it to his pocket. "I do have another class unfortunately, so I'll see you around."

His hand brushes across my forearm, brief and gentle, as if he considered resting it there and decided against it, fingertips touching my wrist just above my sleeve before he walks away from me. The touch lingers for much longer than it should, feeling like it seared a spot on my skin.

"Ah, goodbye for now, then," I call to his back, and he waves.

Cain moves fast, much faster than I can keep up with. Not his walking speed, of course—but the speed in which he goes from being sweet to being completely business, walking with a confidence I will only ever be able to imagine having as he strolls down the street.

I watch him, wishing for that quick bit of attention to fall on me again. I don't know why I want it, but the thought suddenly makes me realize I'm just like everyone else in this city, vying for a drop of Cain Sidrelle.

I sigh, turn my back to him, and start for the manor.

Instead of going to the front door of the manor and bringing attention to myself, I call a portal forward directly into my room, smiling as the spell travels with a wave of goosebumps down my arm. It forms like a pool at my fingertips, expanding into a black, raven-edged rip in the air—like candlewax dripping on the back of my hand, warm at first and cold the next.

I step through it and onto the carpeted floor of my bedroom, moving to take out my usual black-on-black outfit for the following day. As I set *Nocturna* on top of the pile, Bren's voice raises from down the hall, and I immediately recognize it as a warning that *she* is coming to me, likely with my brother in tow. A burst of fear freezes me in place, staring at the door with my hands still on the book.

Three sharp knocks ring out from my door, and I instantly want to vomit.

I swallow the urge down, stepping away from my pile. "Yes?"

The door swings open hard enough that it crashes into the wall, opening wide enough that I catch a glimpse of Bren standing behind the towering shape of my mother before she closes the door behind her.

All of a sudden, I am fifteen again and so small, and staring at her like a deer in headlights as she reaches out to take hold of me.

I stumble backward, nearly tripping over myself. "No, Mother, please."

All of the feelings of being a child under the crushing weight of her grasp rush back into me as she gingerly takes hold of my head. I know my pleading falls on deaf ears, as she easily follows my backward step, her mismatched eyes crystal sharp. I think about struggling for a moment, wanting to fight back, but then my mind starts to feel fuzzy, awash with static—slowly going blank, all the sound fading out around me.

After a long moment, tears roll down my face.

And then I'm back, hating that I know what she did because she *let* me know.

She'd taken something from me again. But what?

Morgana doesn't smile at me, doesn't say a word, taking my hand and tugging me through the halls leading to the training room. I stumble, finding myself a little sluggish, rubbing my temples to try and get myself back together before we begin this, but I can't. She lets go of me only once the door closes behind us, drawing her sword and pointing it at me the same way she did last time.

I call my rapier to my hand, rubbing my temple with one hand again. I don't feel right. "Why do we have to do this?"

I blink, and she appears in front of me, blade crashing against my rapier. "Because you continue to disobey me, that's why," she states, lunging forward again, aiming to knock me over. There almost isn't enough time to get out of the way. "And, because you're supposed to be getting better at fighting like me, Daedalus. You know why I'm doing this, right?"

I look around for a split second, realizing that Silas is nowhere to be seen, and my previous dread returns full force. "No, I don't. Where... where's Silas?"

Morgana rolls her eyes at me, lip curling in disgust. "Not here right now. Focus, will you? You need to be in top shape, Daedalus. I need you to become like me, you know this."

My mother lunges at me again, her magic nearly launching me from where I stand—a gasp echoing throughout the room as I fly backward and barely manage to land on my feet. I drop to one knee briefly, trying to get my bearings, before I throw myself back at her. We meet in the middle, the sound of our blades ringing out, her anger rippling off her in waves.

Tears run down my cheeks again, having continued from when I started crying in my room. "I'm sorry, Mother, okay? I'm sorry." I do not know what I'm apologizing for.

Morgana slashes again, glaring down at me as she shoves me a few feet away with the sword itself. "I don't want to keep doing this, Daedalus."

Her hand thrusts forward to telekinetically shove me, causing me to trip over myself and fall. Disappointment sweeps through me for the lack of my typical grace, but I'm *tired*. So tired, and my body aches to the point that it's starting to shake more visibly than before.

I don't bother trying to get up as Morgana steps over to me, pointing the tip of her sword at my throat. For a moment, I wonder if she'd really do it. If I was in her position, I would. "You've been disappointing me lately. Do better."

Tears continue to fall, wetting my cheeks and dripping onto the floor beneath me.

I lay there as she leaves, staring at the ceiling and letting my mind drift to where Silas could possibly be as the tears slowly roll down the sides of my face. My trainer is rarely ever out of the training room, to the point that I started to assume he must rest in here. It's very unlikely for him to have left—so Morgana must have had something to do with it, as usual. Maybe she banished him, maybe she killed him. I'm not sure if I'll ever find out.

She should've stabbed you. It would've been so fun.

The Rot had been excited when she pointed her sword at me, so close to my skin. It wanted to feel a new sensation, a new experience. So many times I've had moments like this, where I wish I could cut it out of me, but I'm not even sure if that is a possibility.

I close my eyes, sighing as I imagine resting here on the floor. Except I can't, for the fact that it doesn't feel safe—though nothing does in this house anymore, not since Morgana had started all of this.

My heart aches like the day I realized she never truly loved me, and only wanted a copy of herself. Laying beside that ache is a void of nothing, reaching out with darkened arms to swallow the organ inside it.

If I lay here long enough, maybe it'll take me away entirely.

A few footsteps sound from the doorway, followed by a gasp as they pause. They pick up again as whoever they belong to rushes to my side. I glance over through a blur of tears I no longer feel, blinking in surprise at the sight of my father kneeling down beside me. "Dad?"

"Daedalus, oh god. You're alright. Okay..." Mikhalis looks around the room before looking back at me, likely searching for Silas. His eyebrows furrow, searching me next, trying to discern his own answers before he asks anything. He must be where I get it from. "Where's Silas?"

I shake my head, closing my eyes again. "I don't know. He's gone."

A long sigh leaves him, no longer certain of anything. "I'm sorry this keeps happening."

"Why can't you help me?" I whisper.

Mikhalis shifts, sitting down on the floor. "I want to, desperately, Daedalus. But I barely have my magic anymore. Your mother cut me short one day when I attempted to stop her from... taking something when we were younger and it hasn't been the same since. She would stop me before I could do anything."

I look back to him, focusing my eyes on the 'X' shaped scar beside his left eye, how it carves across his cheekbone. It's easy to wonder if it was left behind by my mother in that moment he mentioned, or by a battle, or a monster. Well, I guess two of those things are the same, really.

As I look at him, in some strange, sudden way, I'm hit with the feeling that I don't belong. Not here, not in the college. Anywhere.

It guts me, leaving me with no reason to get myself off this floor. "I don't think I can be here anymore," I say, so soft it barely even echoes.

Mikhalis' frown deepens as he stands up, reaching a calloused hand down to me. "I'm sorry, my son. I am, truly. Please get up." He sounds like he's pleading with me. "I'll try to distract her, alright? Go get some rest, you need it."

I take his hand and let him pull me up, wiping drying tears from my cheeks with the back of my hand. My father hugs me for a moment, and I barely feel it, only recognizing he touched me at all when the absence of it threatens to make me cry again.

Walking to my room feels like it takes forever, nearly dragging myself into it and to my pile of clothes within. I frown at the copy of *Nocturna* lying on top—*why did I put that there?* I don't remember ever touching it, at least not today. As I'm picking it up to put it back, something deep in me says *no, stop, keep it.* Something that isn't the Rot. Something that halts me in my tracks, and I let it.

Don't stay here.

I nod to myself, picking up the clothes and weakly opening a portal again, wincing at the way it sputters and hisses with my lack of energy. It lasts long enough for me to stumble through it and into my dorm room, then closes with an angry crackle at my back.

Gods, my mother did this to me.

My own mother.

Weren't they supposed to be good to their children?

11

— · —

AS I'M walking toward my bed, a whisper of familiar magic resonates in my veins. Cold, but not the same chill of dread. Simply the shiver of the Astral, vast and empty, full of possibility.

"Can I come in?" Asher's voice leaks into my mind, careful and searching, as if he can sense my pain from the other side of the door.

From what little I know of him, Asher and I are very similar. He has a considerable appreciation for science and experimentation, we both have shared long amounts of time between laboratories and syringes and scalpels. Not together yet, but hopefully someday. He studies near as much as I do, always keeping his nose buried in books or notes or both. I haven't been able to speak with him much, but I've gleaned little bits of information about him through others in our classes or through simply studying him—and he seems to be the best person for me to keep close, if I really needed someone.

I take a deep breath, readying my exhaustion for his presence. *"Yes."*

The door eases open carefully as I sit down on the edge of my bed, looking him over when he steps inside and shuts it behind him. He's dressed in an entirely black outfit, from his tight-fitting, long-sleeved shirt and pants, to the cloak hugging his shoulders and falling down to his knees. I don't think I've ever seen him in anything else, truthfully.

Just gives us another reason to be similar.

His tan skin has a particular warmth to it today that I didn't notice in the classroom, making his vibrant purple irises stand out more than usual. "Hi, Daedalus."

"Hello," I reply, softly. I don't have the energy to be any louder.

Asher runs a hand through his tousled black hair as he studies me, giving me a long look that makes my hair stand on end. "Are you alright? You don't look... great."

Why does everyone feel the need to ask me that? "I'm surviving, yes."

He laughs, stopping a few feet in front of me. There's something different about his body language that intrigues me, something to do with the feeling of his magic still twining with my own, swimming in the air around us. The fact he hasn't let go of it yet makes me curious, but at the same time a little hesitant.

"Why did you want to see me?" I ask, pushing that connection a little bit further. Shadows and darkness, mingling together...

He smiles when he notices, folding his arms over his chest, causing a few new folds in the cloak and his sleeves that my eyes trace over instantly. "I want to be better friends, so I wanted to come to you while it's still night. And, I thought we could experiment something together."

I study him again, really taking him in. Little scars crisscross his skin, ones I never truly noticed in the classroom or the few times I've seen him in the hallway. Once, I thought they were stitches, but not so much anymore. I can't tell if he's breathing. Is his heart beating? There's a sound similar to it, somewhere in him. "Go on."

"I've always had this... thing, I wanted to try with someone. Something that's equal parts magic and equal parts mental connection, but I haven't met anyone I thought I could trust enough to do it. I guess this is also where I should tell you I'm not *really* a *kai.*"

Kai. A race of elves known to live in dark places, typically underground in caves, or in the plane of Night itself.

My eyebrows raise, almost involuntarily. "You're not?"

He shakes his head, laughing. "No. I know you won't say anything, so I had to tell you, because I can sense you aren't truly what you say, either."

I almost flinch, hearing raven chatter in my head. "I won't say anything, as long as you don't."

Asher's hands knit together in front of him, a tangle of his fingers I get lost in watching for a moment. "I haven't yet, have I?

That's why I wanted to approach you about this. To be closer, and to share this thing with you, if you would let me."

My exhaustion almost seems to slip away as I watch him step toward me, tensing a little at his approach. If it wasn't considered an experiment of some sort, I may have declined right away—but my curiosity is getting the better of me. My own want for knowledge and the intrigue at what he's claiming won't let me turn it down. "Alright, I accept, then," I say, watching him.

He nods, stepping forward until his thighs brush against my knees. It's almost easy to forget his shorter height until he stands right before me like this. I watch him as he carefully raises his hands to my cheeks, pressing his palms against my skin despite the flinch I can't hide, his skin chilled against my own.

His forehead meets mine, pressing us together for a long moment that I almost back away from, until his magic fully reaches for my own.

I suck in a sharp breath, allowing the intrusion on my magic. I push mine back out to him, meeting his in an embrace that feels far more like we're tangling together, my shadows twining thoroughly with the tendrils of his own. Purple and black mist writhe together, soaking up the air around us and flooding me into a new vision—one where I'm not exhausted, one where we're perched on a gray rock in what must be the Astral instead of my bedroom. It churns around us, purple and pink and dark. Thousands of stars cross the sky, glittering in welcome, and our magic clings to every movement, every breath.

At first, I don't see Asher with me. I turn around, surprised when my gaze lands on his elven shape peering over the edge of the rock and into the darkness below. His skin is no longer tan, but shades of purple similar to the color of his irises, almost seeming to shift with the air around us. I swear I catch a glimpse of tentacles peeking out from under his cloak, but the vision only lasts a moment before it thrusts us back into my dorm room.

The feeling of the connection is intense—our magic coils in a way that's nearly sensual, even though the act of what we're doing lacks anything of the sort. Asher's cold palms turn warm against the heat of my skin, and in my hunger for knowing what exactly he's doing with this, I push my magic into them. I let it scale across his hands, sinking into his wrists where gnarled veins should be, and he exhales. Just once, but enough to tell me it's what he wants.

He pushes back, sending an electric wave down the length of my throat where his fingertips nearly brush. What hides inside me claws at my ribcage to be let out, grabbing at the strands he sends through me, speaking like raven calls in our combined minds. A shiver passes through him, and I swear the temperature around us drops a few degrees as it does.

I don't speak, though I want to.

That vision of the Astral returns, but this time he has his forehead against mine in it as well. Every breath smells of peppermint until my magic surges into the space again, bringing with it a wave of rain before thunder.

Flashes of the Astral and the stars within it go by my vision in sparks, followed by glimpses of what I assume is Asher in a monstrous form with others that look like him on massive ships. An elven person reaches into the sky and screams before there's a blinding light. Asher recoils, dropping to the deck of the ship and hiding his blazing eyes as the light burns as bright as the sun itself.

Asher laughs, breathy and shaky, and it's hard for me not to follow with my own. I don't think he knows what I saw.

"What?" I ask, and my voice almost echoes in the space.

"This is more than what I expected it to be. Far more than what I calculated it to be," he answers with a quiet chuckle.

I don't move away, but I peer at the now obvious tentacles shifting under the cloak. "Why did you choose me for this?"

Asher hums, a low vibration that I feel in my chest, one that makes the beast purr in me. "I knew you would be the most capable of understanding it, and where it comes from."

As he speaks, everything clicks—the strange, squirming hunger in his magic that reaches for my mind is eldritch, one of the easiest forms of it I can decipher. I've never known why, but it's been that way since I was young. That, and the creature I am, it's all connected.

That's why he chose me. It makes sense now.

The thought connects us fully in a single breath, twining together like the veins to a heart, like the cords to a rope. His heartbeat thrums in time with my own, my hunger meets his. All in a single second, we are one, and we want for nothing more than this. I taste saltwater and smoke. Blood and vanilla. It's all one equal flood, spreading through my entire body eagerly.

Then, it crumbles away as we part from each other in an easy disconnect, caused by him leaning back from me.

I stare at him, feeling exhilarated and exhausted all at once, struggling to breathe normally.

All this did was make me want to attempt that spell again, that blade.

He stares back, likely feeling the same. "It seems I was right," he says through an exhale. "Thank you for running this very... kind of personal, experiment with me."

"You're welcome... it was fascinating." I smile, because my words are absolutely the truth. Whatever this was showed me a lot about him, this strange meeting of the minds. Hopefully, it didn't show him too much about me.

Asher brushes off his cloak as he backs away, and I almost immediately miss the strange connection we had. "I'll leave you alone now, though. I hope we'll talk more?" he says with a pleasant smile. My body feels electric.

I nod, and for once, I actually mean it. For once, I'll hold myself to talking to someone more. "For sure."

He smiles over his shoulder at me before walking to my door, giving the wall a light pat as he opens and closes the door behind him.

The instant I'm alone, with the magic of the Astral still clinging thick to my skin, I pull out the book again. Anxiety brews in my chest as I flip to the weapon's section again, knowing I very well could fail like I did the first time—but I don't *want* that to be the case this time. I *want* to successfully pull it out, to finally have something to show for all of this training. My heart pounds as I gaze down at the drawing of it, stepping back from the edge of the table and holding my hands out.

Shadows instantly weep from my palms like wax, dripping off my fingers and pooling into the air. The connection to the Astral sings in my veins, and I force my focus into it, trying to twine it with my darkness. I close my eyes and exhale thinly, clenching my jaw tight as my mind stretches in attempt to recreate something I only have the smallest connection to.

And in my hand, an obsidian hilt forms, but the blade isn't right. The blade is still my own, wreathing with the tendrils of my magic, not the glittering stars it should be. I cast my glare of disappointment up to the ceiling, cursing the way my magic feels fulfilling but not yet *enough.* Just a little more, and maybe it would've worked.

I glance down at the book and back at the weapon, studying the hilt. Somehow, I managed that correctly—but nothing else. *Fuck.*

The frustration wells up in me again, enough to cast the blade away and slam the book shut.

Soon enough, I'll master this damn spell. I have to now.

There is no other choice.

12

I SETTLE MYSELF on Whitestone's rooftop an hour later, taking the time to admire the city around me. Just a moment to myself.

Just a moment, a singular breath of time to organize my messy thoughts about Morgana and my memories, Cain and his too-soft bed, and whatever strange intimacy I shared with Asher.

As I'm pulling my knees up to my chest and resting my chin on top of them, I watch the lights from a club somewhere down the street glowing through on open door. Small bodies are silhouetted against pinks and purples, almost hypnotic among the usual golds and whites that the rest of the buildings have. My mind drifts as I watch them change to red and blue, wondering what it must be like inside—probably hot, reeking of alcohol, no place to get away from anybody. Bodies on bodies, smudged makeup, people making out or throwing up in the bathroom, probably always in pairs. It's always twos. Always.

A light breeze coasts across my skin and onward into the night, easing me further into the peace I've created for myself.

That is, until I hear the faintest creak of the window below opening further, and what sounds like boots against the stone wall.

At first, I expect it to be Irsa, come to make me feel worse or looking for someone else entirely—but I'm instantly relieved and confused when it turns out to be Cain in his usual white shirt and black slacks. He looks at me with equal surprise, glancing back down behind him.

"What are you doing up here?" he asks, hesitating in his climb.

I shrug, looking back over the lights of the city. I prefer it at this hour, all golden. "Watching. It's nice sometimes."

Cain nods, sitting beside me wordlessly, no more than a few inches apart. "What are you watching?"

"The club down the street, but other than that, nothing. I like finding different shapes, analyzing different angles." I say, shifting as my eyes land on a triangular window on a skyscraper a street over, studying the rectangular ones beneath it. Countless windows, all the way down where I can't see them on the street-level.

"Your mind is so interesting," Cain says, and I scoff.

"How so?" I glance to him and away again, back to the colored lights.

He laughs, pulling a small carton of cigarettes from his pocket and offering me one. "I don't know how to explain it. You just seem... fifty steps ahead of everyone else, sometimes."

I hesitate at his offer, at first—it's not like we haven't smoked together before—but end up taking it just so I have something to distract my hands from moving too much. "I'm not sure I know what you mean."

A small flame snaps to life at the end of his finger as he tucks the cigarette between his lips. He uses it to light the tip, before holding it out to mine a moment later. We fall silent to breathe in and let out mutual clouds of smoke, and then he smiles. "It's hard to put it into words, Dae. You're always finding something different, like shapes or angles of things. You look like you're studying things when you look at them, even if you don't mean to."

Wow, he really has been paying attention.

I laugh quietly, shrugging a shoulder. "I can't help it, I guess."

Another small silence, and then he looks over at me again. "I finished the book."

I can hear the smile in his voice without looking, but my confusion keeps me from enjoying it. "The book?"

Cain leans back as I look at him, tilting his head all pretty like. This is one of those moments where I expect him to move too fast for me again. "Yeah, the book. Nocturna, remember? You lent me it. It was creepy for sure, and not really my sort of genre... but I think I liked it more than I expected." I nod, smiling more to myself than at him, and he sighs. "Can I... ask you something, Daedalus?"

Please don't break my heart.

He looks away as I shift hesitantly, as if unsure he should ask at all. "Yes, I suppose," I reply, slow and unsteady.

Cain shifts and exhales, ruby eyes returning to the city beyond. The lights brighten him up, reflecting in his eyes like fireworks as he seemingly considers his words. "What's been happening to you, lately? You've been distant, and you look worse every day, no offense. Bren talked to me one night, said there were things you want to tell me, and I need you to tell me the truth," he states, startlingly firm. "Please, be honest."

That's what I thought.

I can't hide a flinch as flashes of the past few trainings blow by in my head, and I sit so my legs are crisscrossed instead of pulled up to my chest.

Do I want to tell him? Of course I do. I have wanted to tell him for days—weeks even. But there has been a part of me too afraid of what might come from it. Would Cain be upset? Would he be furious at what Morgana has done? Or would he agree with her? Take her side and insist that the training is for my own good? Then again... would he even care at all?

I can almost hear his voice in my head, the scoff on his lips, the confusion on his brow as he says, *"What, that's it?"* I'm not sure I could handle it if he did.

Worse though, is the fear that he would see me as weak. That he would hear what she does to me, hear what I let her do, and think differently of me afterwards. Like I am this fragile thing that cannot take care of itself.

Still, he has asked, and I have found lately that there is very little I can deny Cain Sidrelle.

"I... fine. Yes, very well. I will tell you the truth." I take a breath to fortify the nerves skittering underneath my skin, clenching my fists in my lap once, twice, a third time before releasing them. "Morgana, my mother, has recently taken over training me instead of my typical trainer, though I hesitate to call it 'training' nowadays... more like torture. Between my studying and her endless lessons, I haven't been sleeping very well. That and—"

I pause here, the nerves flaring and itching at my veins, The Rot giggling somewhere in my chest. Cain isn't the first person to see my bruises and cuts. He isn't even the first to know how exactly my mother treats me. But this... this is something I have barely allowed even myself to know. To admit.

"She takes away my memories." The words are blurted out before I can stop them, and I even grimace at myself because of it. "Sorry, that was a lot more than I meant to say."

Cain shakes his head, his eyes wide and unblinking. "Holy shit," he breathes.

"Yeah," I say, sighing out smoke. "Yeah."

From this vantage point, it is almost possible to see the wider sprawl of this side of Nemoure—from the closer rich side to the lesser middle-class area beyond it. Lights wink out from shops and homes, in windows of apartments nearly level with us. The Macabre manor is out of sight, but I can easily see where the Sidrelle's mansion is, or at least the very top of its roof. A vague echo of pounding music barely reaches us as someone somewhere below opens the inner door to the club, and then everything falls silent once more.

Cain doesn't say anything else for a while, unnerving, but understandable. A moment later, he tilts his head, not looking away from the lights, and sends a thin stream of smoke into the night. "What do you mean exactly, by her taking away your memories?"

Another shrug as I do the same, emptying the smoke from my lungs from a deeper drag than I intended to take. "It's exactly what it sounds like. She uses a spell, and either shapes them or takes them away. I never knew it until recently."

He shakes his head, blinking wide in disbelief. "I know my mother is a crazy bitch, but... damn. Thank the Gods she doesn't do that—she likes to call me crazy and take away my assets, but at least it isn't my memories," he says, almost a mutter. "She may be terrible in her own way, but I've always kept my memories."

"Why would she call you crazy?"

Cain shakes his head, pinching the bridge of his nose. "I had what she likes to call a 'psychotic break' or something, because she made something bad happen, and I went off the deep end a bit. But it's not because I'm crazy! I mean, I guess if I was, it'd be from my father, I don't know. All I know is I shouldn't have been locked in my damn mansion for two years. It's…Hard to explain. She tried to marry me to someone, and he was shitty. Really shitty. I blocked out a lot of it."

He leans over and rests his head on my shoulder, and the moment feels so soft, so fragile, that I'm once again reminded of how easily this man could break my heart if he wanted to. "I don't think you're crazy, Cain," I say.

Cain laughs in a way that makes me unsure if it's out of relief or because he genuinely appreciates the statement, then turns his head to look in my direction. His hair tickles my cheek, little red curls brushing over my skin. "Thanks, Dae. I try."

We go quiet after that, looking on toward the horizon and finishing our cigarettes in peace. He surprisingly doesn't pull out another one, even as he sits upright again, turning to face me with a slightly more intense energy than before. "You know… we could own this city if we wanted to."

"You think so?" I ask, amusement licking through me as he springs to his feet and throws his arms out to either side of him.

He laughs, wild and rough. "We could! Between my expertise in business and yours in magic and science, we absolutely could. We could run this fucking place, Dae! People already can't say no to me, can you imagine if I *owned the fucking city*?!"

I smile, unable to keep it away with how contagious his energy is. "Nobody would be able to mess with me like Irsa does, if that were the case."

Cain nods eagerly, grinning at me. "Exactly! We could be better than the damn king himself."

He's definitely thought about this before, if his passion about it has anything to say. It's easy to picture him on Nemoure's council beside his father, his face painted on screens or buildings as the face of the city, the sharp-toned golden boy. They already love his fashion, his businesses, his parties. He's well-loved in the spotlight already, handling investments and sometimes even direction from the king, if I've heard correctly. Some of it is inherited from Minos, sure, but he's worked hard to get himself his status.

I would be at his side, sure—but he'd be the icon of our work, the speaker, the wink to the public eye.

I could almost dream of it.

"You know..." Cain pauses as he sits back down, this time leaning right up to my side and pointing out over a certain section of buildings near the shore. "I'm going to make a casino, right there. It's going to be amazing."

Clearing my throat a little, I follow the direction he's pointing to an emptier space in the rich end, one that must be waiting for him to start building. "Is that what you've been working on?"

He looks over at me, so close I can almost feel the warmth radiating off him. So close, I can pick out every little bright red fleck to his irises. "Yeah. I made the plans for it a while ago, actually." He turns his gaze back out at it. "I'm really excited about it."

"How much progress have you made?" I ask, tilting my head to the side, only to give myself a few inches of room between us. Only to breathe, so I don't think of kissing those pretty lips of his.

"The blueprints are done, and I had a meeting with the right people to start building it. I haven't really told anyone besides Marion what it's going to be, so... don't tell anyone."

I laugh at that, this one feeling much more real than the last. "Cain, I don't talk to people."

Cain shrugs, a playful grin spreading across his lips. "Fair point."

The longer this easy conversation goes, the more I feel like I'm hanging on by a thread. It's so easy with him. *Everything* is so easy with him—it almost feels like I can breathe, like I can forget the darkness lingering at home, in my mind, in my *bones*. Like I can pretend it's just the two of us against the world.

It terrifies me how much I want it to be true.

"Dae...Are you going to be alright?" he murmurs as he rests his head on my shoulder again, and I shrug. *How can I be, with everything going on back home?* I could lie, but I know he'll see right through me and call me out. Or worse, he'd believe me, and I don't need him doing that either.

"I don't know. Probably. Maybe. I can't say for sure." I say, sighing and smoothing my hands down my thighs nervously. "I wish I could lie to you."

He nods, tickling the side of my neck with his hair. "Well... you know, if it would maybe cheer you up a little... Louis is having a party tomorrow night, and I'd really appreciate it if you came with me."

I tense, pulling back to look at him. "Cain. You *know* that's not my scene."

Cain smiles at me, shaking his head. There's something soft about the expression that takes down my walls a little, making me even more unsure if he's being nice just to play with me or not. "I know, but it *would* be nice."

I grimace and shake my head at him, pinching the bridge of my nose. The topic change isn't surprising, being I'm starting to realize how Cain isn't much of a feeling's person. Not very touchy-feely, barely going into his own emotions, let alone other people's. When he opens up, it's a wonderful thing, but it feels difficult to get him to that point.

I guess we're the same in that regard.

He pushes at my arm playfully and pouts, looking at me with big, bright, pleading eyes. "C'monnnnn Dae, it would be fun!"

Groaning, I shake my head again. "Cain—"

"Daedalus." Firm, and I like it.

Knowing I'm not winning this battle, I laugh out a sigh. "....Fine."

Cain crows triumphantly, standing up and reaching a hand out to me. "Good! You can come get me then. On another note, we should probably go in."

I nod, taking his outstretched hand, because I don't think I would have had the strength to get up on my own. "Yeah, you're probably right."

While Cain steps down to the window again, I hesitate to look back at the view. One of these days, I'll have to come up here to see the sunrise—I can picture it perfectly, painting the sky in the same bright pastels as my old city, the sun vibrant as it pours over the polished surfaces of the buildings all around me. I wonder if it's brighter here, or if it'd be easier to see depending on where you were in the city as it rose.

"Dae, are you coming?" Cain asks as he looks up from the window, pulling me from my thoughts.

I quickly turn toward him, nodding. "Yes, my apologies."

His laughter reaches me even as he backs further into the library so I can climb in beside him, filling my chest with warmth. As I step inside and close the window behind me, he smiles as he stops beside the piano.

"That was kind of nice, you know. We should do that more often."

I nod, scanning the room for anyone else, then let my gaze fall back on him when it turns up empty. "I agree."

Cain drums his fingers over the glossy surface of the piano, his eyes on the fallboard that hides the keys. "You play this, don't you?"

Hesitantly, I nod again. "Yes, why?"

"Oh, no reason. Sometimes I swear I can hear piano music being played from my dorm, so I wondered…" Cain trails off slowly, seemingly in thought for a second. "I thought I was hearing shit for a while, because I'd wake up in the middle of the night and hear it. Then, I assumed it was just dreams or someone playing it from their dorm. I don't know why I never thought it was down here."

For once, it isn't me being the one to disappear into my own mind. "What were you thinking about?"

He shakes his head, smiling warmly at me. "Nothing really. Maybe you could play for me some time."

He leaves it at that, and I don't prod him as I follow him out the door and into the hall beyond. Walking back to our dorms feels nice, far more relaxed this time, and I hate that I have to fight the urge to take Cain's hand again—I so badly want to link my fingers between his, to feel the warmth of another person, to try and make note of his pulse in his wrist. I imagine pressing the pad of my thumb into his skin, counting the beat, feeling it reach out to me. Calling for my skin the way mine does his.

I don't touch him, and before I know it, he's gone behind his door and I'm left to my thoughts.

The need chases after my heels even once I'm alone, settled in for the night by the window, attempting to study. The idea of his heartbeat spins around my mind, sure that if I just knew how it felt, I could make it into a beat behind a song. A metronomic beat

I could compose around, perhaps. *Would that be weird? Gods, I'm probably being weird...*

It takes up so much of my mind that I don't even notice I'm drifting into sleep until I wake up face down in my books.

I rub my cheek as it peels off the page I was reading, scoffing at myself and readjusting my glasses over my nose as I force myself upright. Closing my notebooks and the book I accidentally rested in, I find myself replaying the night again in my mind. Cain's laughter, his smiles, his pout.

A pout that somehow led to Cain *somehow* managing to get me to agree to the party tonight. *Shit.*

I'm not particularly prepared for it, but if there is one thing I can count on, it's that Bren will likely be there. My brother is seemingly becoming a bit of a party fiend since meeting Cain's group, or so I've heard rumors of—almost perfectly fitting in with Louis despite how terrified he was of strangers at first. To a point, it angers me that he can so freely have so many friends, while I am scolded and erased whenever I try.

But, I am starting to understand that Morgana wants me to be mad. She *wants* me to do something about it.

The thoughts of my mother only make my exhaustion weigh heavier on my chest, and for a moment, I regret not following Cain to his room, or inviting him into mine. Despite having grown accustomed to being alone over the years, being around Cain so much makes it feel near impossible to be by myself with my thoughts. It's a lot like swimming in the ocean, but the waves keep pulling you under and under and under with no reprieve for air.

At least I only have one class today.

13

Glancing at the clock on my wall, I decide there's enough time to go to the manor and get an outfit for the party, despite the fear that comes with the thought of going there. Moments like this, I truly curse myself for not bringing more to the college than I did. I suck in a breath and hold it in my lungs as I open the portal again—smiling at the familiar magic, the coolness of it surging through my veins like fresh water. For a moment, I sit there and feel it, *really* feel it. The trickle of it crawling through the scars on my arms and into my palms. The hum at my fingertips, dripping like wax onto my floor. The taste of smoke at the back of my throat.

A shudder passes through me as I step into my room, walking to my closet and frowning as I decide what to wear. This sort of event is so far out of my comfort zone, that I'm not even sure what in my wardrobe would fit. Would it be formal like the ball? Or would it be more like the clubs I see glimpses of in the city? All flowing and revealing clothing? I certainly had nothing like that to wear...

Before I get the chance to wind myself into a panic, there is a light knock on my door. I freeze momentarily and finally let the air out from my lungs, watching the doorway for a second. Neither of my parents knock that way, so it is either a servant with a lucky guess only person in the house that might actually be able to help me.

I shift a little uncomfortably, studying the shadow under my door, trying to recognize its caster by the shapes and angles alone. "Hello?"

"It's me!" Bren calls, cheery as ever. "Can I come in?"

It's a surprise that he's home right now, but a welcome one. What doesn't surprise me, is the fact he sensed me—his Fae heritage often makes his magic heightened, meaning he can sense any one of us returning to the manor with only a breath.

Relief floods through me, lowering the tension in my shoulders despite knowing it'll return soon. It never leaves for long. "Yes, come in, Bren."

He steps in quickly, shutting the door behind him and facing me, eyes bright and sharp. His Fae energy swirls around his body in a visible cloud, smelling of citrus and lavender, tempting my magic to seep out from my fingers to meet the chaos of it. "I hear you're going to Louis' party, yeah?"

I sigh and nod, trying to ignore the strange feeling in my chest at how *normal* he's trying to be. "I suppose I am, yes," I say, slightly tense. "Why do you ask?"

"Let me help you find an outfit then. You can't wear your usual stuff." Bren strides up to me and opens my closet wider, starting to rummage through the clothes inside without hesitation.

Frowning, I watch the way his hands dive in and out of the hanging garments. He's surprisingly thorough in his hunt. "Why not?"

"You're too formal," he answers in an amused way, flashing a smile at me before turning back to his self-appointed task.

I don't ask him what he means by that, because I know damn *well* what he means. Silence fills the room between us, only broken up by my piano starting to play on its own. I suddenly feel like crying all at once, completely out of my control. "Bren." *Why are you helping me? We aren't right. None of this is right.*

He doesn't look at me as he tugs out a few different shirts, eyeing me and then putting them back. "Yeah?"

My throat feels thick, impossible to swallow through. "I don't understand—"

"Listen, Daedalus. I know things aren't great, and I know that's probably what you're about to talk about, but I don't care. I might not understand why you don't like me, or why things are the way they are, but... Just let this be normal, please? I just want to act like this is normal for us."

I watch as his throat moves with an obviously forced swallow, and then he pulls out a silk turtleneck with a teardrop cut-out over the chest that I honestly forgot I even owned. He holds it up to me, giving me a strained smile. "How about this?"

"Sure, yeah. That's fine." I nod, unable to look at him.

"This works? Wow. I must be a genius." His laugh comes out sad, and it breaks my heart.

I nod again, approvingly, as he sets it on one of the armchairs nearby with a matching pair of silk pants.

Bren moves quickly around my room, as if it's easier for him to keep his emotions back if he keeps moving. We're a lot alike in that regard. "What do you have for shoes?" he asks, clasping his hands at his waist.

I raise an eyebrow and gesture to the selection of different pairs of boots sitting by my closet—most being combat styled, one with more of a platform to them, the last pair knee-high. All black, and varying states of matte or glossy.

Bren studies each set closely, shaking his head at the first few before stopping at the platform pair. "How well can you move in these?"

Frowning, I study them too. "Fine, why?"

Another forced smile flashes across his lips as he picks them up, holding them out to me. "Well, knowing Cain, you're likely going to end up dancing... that's why."

I groan a little at the idea of dancing with Cain again—not because I didn't like it last time, but because I liked it *too much*. Being touch-starved is hard when all the other person wants is to be as close as possible when they dance with you, which most people probably do, but I'm not familiar with it. Any of it.

"Daedalus?" Bren draws my attention back to him, and I still can't bring myself to look in his eyes.

"Yes, what?"

"You're acting like it's the end of the world, have fun, okay?" Bren returns to my closet for a moment, stepping back out with a black belt, two sets of chains to attach to it, and a silver skull-shaped ring. "That should be awesome. Cain's not gonna know what hit him. What do you think?"

I roll my eyes, letting out an airy laugh. "Whatever you say, Bren. Thank you for helping me, though."

He grins at me, flickering his favorite illusion of the six spider eyes over his forehead. "It's what I do!"

It comes out way too thin, forcing the cheeriness he has with everyone else for me before he leaves my room.

I hate hearing him like that.

I step away from the clothes and over to my piano, trailing my fingertips across the keys. The ache to play it again, to finish all my newly composed songs, is stronger than anything. To sit down and let the melodies draw from my heart, to crash my anger into something new—it sounds lovely right now, but I can't.

You don't have time, Daedalus. Keep moving.

Shaking my head, I reopen my portal once again and leave the room behind with my clothes in hand.

My class about the finer points of arcana goes by in a flash, and before I can really process what I'm about to do, I'm stepping through a portal onto the pale walkway of the Sidrelle mansion. This time, I chose not to bring a fancy carriage or anything, and I really hope Cain doesn't mind—it's just me and a spell to teleport us there. Just me. Just us.

Gods. I exhale thinly and hesitate in my steps upon seeing a golden-yellow skinned man with blonde hair, swept-back black horns, and a long tail speaking with Cain by the entrance.

The man is dressed in a pale gold, see-through shirt that shimmers in the light, highlighting every muscle he has as if he is a god or a finely-carved statue. His pants are a shade darker than the shirt, and billow out at the ankles—showing off a pair of gold boots that just barely cover what I swear are scales on his skin. Gold jewelry drips off him from every angle, and I can't help but grimace at the print of a red lipstick kiss on his cheek.

Jealousy is a bitter being, and I'm quick to learn that. Over and over again.

Cain looks beautiful as always, wearing an entirely champagne-colored jumpsuit that glitters, a matching bag dangling from his elbow and a pair of dark sunglasses concealing his bright eyes. His hair is a wave of red curls down his back and over his shoulder, which means this event must be much more relaxed than I expect. The print of lipstick on the man's cheek matches the vibrant shade on Cain's lips, which he seems to be taking a moment to touch up before he notices me waiting, standing there helplessly.

Instead of looking at the two of them, I look toward the rose garden in the back of the mansion, working to unclench my jaw. They have countless different colors tucked amongst neatly trimmed bushes, and it makes me wonder if they are the cause for Cain's usual rose scent, or if it's something he chooses to wear. From what I've gathered, the garden is apparently massive, with hedges in between the flower bushes and a fountain somewhere in the center. Fit for parties, some would say.

Cain smiles at the man before strolling over to me, the sound of his heels causing me to flinch ever so slightly. "You ready?" he asks, one perfectly shaped eyebrow raising above the edge of his sunglasses.

I huff a little, nodding. The jealousy won't leave me alone. "I've been, are you?"

His other eyebrow joins the first, and he smirks a little. "We're going to have *so* much fun, Dae."

It's not that I don't *want* to believe Cain, but I certainly don't. Parties aren't my thing in any shape or form, so I haven't been looking forward to it—or at least, not the whole loud-music-surrounded-by-people part of it. *Especially* since the people who will likely be there are probably the type to stare, and I hate *that* more than anything.

Maybe I need to stop going places with Cain.

"Dae? Hello? I'm talking to you." Cain waves a hand in front of my face, studying me as he puts his hands on his hips. "Where did you go this time?"

I startle slightly, looking back at him. "I'm sorry, what were you saying?"

He smiles, tapping a red-nailed finger against the open cutout of my shirt, right above the marking of my sternum on my skin. "I *was* teasing you about how much skin you're showing off."

"This is about as much as anyone will see, if I have anything to say about it," I mutter, shaking my head and reaching a hand out to start calling the portal spell forward again.

When I glance back at him, a smirk starts to form on his face. A wide one. "I'm sure I could change your mind about that."

A furious blush rushes to my cheeks all the way to the tips of my ears, making me shoot a quick glare at him before directing it back to the portal. The spell falters under my skin, sputtering with electric sparks momentarily before I can focus long enough to bring it back, exhaling out my embarrassment.

"Don't distract me," I tell him with a shaky laugh, coaxing the shadowed arcana into the air before us.

Cain shakes his head and starts to snicker, which turns into a loud bit of laughter rougher than anything I usually hear from him. A lot like his father's, which I've only heard a time or two. "We *so* have to get you a drink when we get there. You need to loosen up a bit. Also, let me make the portal, since you don't exactly know where we're going."

I swat at his arm lightly with one hand, shaking my head as Cain swiftly makes an ember-ringed portal for us and leads me into what must be Louis' yard. His magic kisses me as I pass through it, lapping at my skin with the heat of live fire and promises, distracting me for a split second. I've never had the opportunity to know what his portals feel like, and I sort of enjoy it. No, I *really* enjoy it. It is bright and wild against my darkness, fanning my hunger with sparks. *Interesting.*

The mansion we walk up to is made up of smooth white stone, with well-taken care of shrubs lining the front walls, each one dotted with lavender flowers. Music pours from inside, loud enough to rattle my damn brain, and I preemptively rub one of my temples at the sound of it. A few people stand outside on the vibrant green lawn, chatting with brightly colored drinks in hand, but it's obvious the full party hasn't moved out here yet.

Cain leads me the entire way, happily greeting Marion, who stands just inside the door. His long blonde hair falls in waves down his back, laying over an emerald green, nude-illusion style dress with matching heels and makeup that brightens his warm brown eyes. It's almost hard to look at him with how the patterns of the illusion fall on his skin— framing his hips and swirling up over his chest, hinting around his legs in a way that's intentional to show off his ass—so I purposefully keep my eyes anywhere else in the room.

Marion smiles at me slyly, lifting his drink to his lips. "Hi, Dae."

He practically *purrs* it, and I hate the way I feel myself blushing again.

I would eat him too, if I had the chance.

But I don't want him. Not enough.

I nod at him and nervously rub the back of my neck as I follow along behind Cain to where everyone has left their bags, watching him leave his behind before we slip through the slight crowd to get to the drink table. Cain smiles at me before snapping his fingers at the pale, elven servant beside the table, requesting some kind of colorful cocktail that I don't even try to catch the name of. The music is so loud in here, I can barely hear myself think.

While Cain waits, I pour myself a shot without looking at the alcohol type and swallow it in one go. It burns on the way down, lingering in my throat a moment after the liquid is gone and turning my stomach hot. He laughs and grins at me, then follows suit—shooting from the same bottle I took from, with much less of a reaction.

God, why do people like this stuff?

I grimace a little and have the servant make me something with whiskey, then step away once Cain seems ready. We stand together nearby until Louis appears from the dancefloor, wearing a white mesh crop top and white pants, matching his pale hair and pink eyes. The shirt shows off the lean muscle of his torso, invitingly so, but I don't look long enough for him to notice. He extends his hands out to Cain, and when I realize he's taking the offer, I instantly tense.

Cain leaves his drink, and more importantly *me,* behind.

Which, of course he can have fun. I'm happy he's having fun. I just don't know what to do by myself here, and I'm terrified of being alone in this place.

The fear threatens to swallow me up for a moment, and I swiftly drink down the dark liquid I was given to push it back. Whiskey makes a warm path down my throat and into my stomach, soothing me slightly as I glance around, gripping my glass a little tighter. Booming music pounds in my chest, vibrating right down to my very core—at least *that* I can appreciate. The beat of it keeps my mind afloat with every sip of my drink, calming me ever so slightly, but not *enough.*

I almost don't notice when Marion steps up beside me, sipping a cocktail that is nearly as bright as Cain's. "I would ask you to dance, but I know I'm not your type," he says in a teasing way, nearly yelling to be heard over the music. I must make a face, because he holds up his hands and laughs. "I'm messing with you. Besides, I'm waiting for Jesse to show up, so you have nothing to worry about."

His brown eyes sweep over the crowd as he speaks, obviously searching, and I watch him as I try to hide a displeased grimace. I don't know him well, but Jesse is nice enough, from what I recall. Bright marigold colored skin, golden blonde hair, radiates light, makes each room he walks in at least twenty degrees warmer. He's a Fae creature of summer, purely embodying the sun, with a big personality and a big body to match.

The problem comes with who usually tags along at his side. Julian, a vampire who Cain seemed intrigued by in the past—or so I had overheard him mention to Marion once a while ago. It made me have an automatic dislike for him, but I know it's only the jealousy talking. Blonde hair, red eyes, pale skin, apparently much older than he looks. He's not a bad guy, but I'm not a fan.

A slight sigh leaves me as I look around, grateful when Marion excitedly trots off through the crowd and collects Jesse from the doorway. I scan the crowd and find Cain again, watching the sway of his hips as he dances with Louis, struggling to swallow my next sip when he looks in my direction and promptly turns around to press his ass against his friend.

He's a horribly tempting siren as he watches me watch him, and I know he's aware of what he's doing.

Entirely aware.

My body pulses with foreign desires as he bends down low, still staring me down, almost like Louis isn't right there with his hands on his hips. The entire room feels hotter by about ninety-something degrees gazing at him. He purposefully arches his back ever so slightly, and it takes everything in me not to walk over there and—

And what? Embarrass myself?

"Fuck, what is happening to me?" I mutter under my breath.

Thankfully, Cain strides through the crowd a moment later as if he heard what I was thinking, smiling brightly at me as I hand off his cocktail.

"Thanks for watching my drink," he purrs, leaning close enough to be heard without yelling. His proximity threatens to break the tightrope of my restraint. "I appreciate it."

I shake my head, forcing the last swallow down. "I wasn't exactly, but you're welcome. That was quite the show, you know."

"You liked that?" Cain smirks, gazing up at me through his damn long eyelashes. "Why don't you come out there with me, then?"

I try to protest, but he doesn't hear it, making me leave my glass behind and tugging me by the hand onto the dancefloor—which I'm sure is just an opened-up living room with the furniture pushed back out of the way. It's even warmer over here than it was when I was watching him, among the close bodies and heavy breaths and *people*.

My body shudders at the thought of being so close to anyone else, but then Cain is right there against me, red eyes glittering deviously in the low lighting of the fairy lights and neon strobes Louis had hung up around the room.

He takes my mind away from it instantly, leaving me breathless in the process—the sight of him under these colors sends my brain in a thousand directions, to the point where it is getting difficult to focus. *He's so close. Fuck, what am I doing? Gods. He's beautiful.*

"What's going through that head of yours, Macabre?" Cain murmurs, voice lower and raspier than I've ever heard it before, leaning forward to talk right into my ear so I can hear him at all under the next song.

An electric shock races down my spine, forcing my gaze to the ceiling. "Nothing, nothing at all," I respond just as low, and he chuckles before shifting back to gaze up at me.

He leans forward and smiles slyly, close enough I can smell the sweetness of the alcohol on his breath. "Liar."

Cain takes my hands and directs them to his hips, and I freeze as he rolls them into me, just a bit, just enough to *feel*. My heart pounds away in my chest, hands locked in place except for my thumbs petting the slightest circles over the silky fabric of his outfit.

He smirks at me before snatching two shots from a passing servant's tray, handing one to me as he takes his own. I drink it at the same speed, finding that I'll definitely be needing more if I'm *ever* going to keep up with any of this—and it burns down into my stomach, lingering around my tongue and coating my mouth in the taste of raspberries.

"Dae... Loosen up, I'm not going to bite you." Cain breaks my concentration on his body and the shot, his voice warm.

Gods help me.

I want him so horribly, so tangibly, that I'm afraid he might know by looking at me. It's probably all over my face, all over my body, all hunger and need and desire.

It is impossible, this wanting, and yet I'm still so *hungry* with it.

A breathless laugh leaves me, studying the curl of his eyelashes before glancing away again. "I'm sorry, I'm trying, I mean it," I reply, shaking my head at him.

He nods and closes any tiny remaining gap there might have been between us, red eyes still looking straight at mine. It's almost like he's looking right into me, not even *at* me. His hips roll into me again, flashing pure temptation through every limb, making my hands tighten where they've finally fallen still against him.

I close my eyes, unable to look at him for a second. Just a second, a mini break to keep me from losing myself in his gaze. "Don't laugh at me, Cain."

Another laugh, amused. "I'm not laughing at you, I promise. You're funny," he says, red lips curling into a cat-like smile.

"What do you mean?" I ask, gaze dropping to his lips next. A slight shimmer highlights the curve in the top of them, catching my eye for far longer than needed. *Maybe it's the alcohol.* "I don't think I said anything."

Cain shakes his head at me, smiling almost secretively. "You just need to *relax*, have some fun, y'know?"

I'm relaxed. I'm so relaxed.

I shake my head again but find myself smiling. Fun is never something I've been allowed before, but like this, I feel like I can allow it for tonight. Maybe I could let myself be free, if that is even a possibility. And who cares if she watches? I sure don't, or, well, I probably would if I didn't have alcohol in me. I'd care a lot, but I don't right now. All I care about is Cain, and the drinks he keeps grabbing for us.

And keeping him close.

Cain catches us two more shots and smiles when he notices me watching him drink his own, staring at the movement of his throat. The expanse of it, scarless and perfect. *What would it feel like to bite, there?* I wonder. To sink my teeth into the soft flesh, to taste his blood, to hear his sigh of bliss as he sank into devouring oblivion.

The moment is swiftly interrupted by an unwelcome tap on my shoulder, which I startle at—causing a new wave of irritation to strike through my core that Cain giggles over, as I direct my look at my infuriating distraction.

"What?" I snap, glaring down Julian as he attempts to smile at me.

His red eyes glow bright in the lighting around us, his hands politely linked together as he looks only at Cain. "Hey, uh... you.

Do you mind if I steal Cain from you, for a little bit?" he asks, as kind as can be.

I snort, feeling oddly confident, feeling the least bit entertained with the vampire and his smile. *I do mind. Back off.* "Yes, actually, I do."

Julian's dark eyebrows raise, and he nods, extending both hands in front of him in mock surrender. "No problem, no problem."

As he walks away, I catch the sound of Marion laughing from somewhere nearby, followed by the deeper laugh of Jesse beside him underneath the music. "That was amazing, Daedalus!" he calls, and it's almost a struggle to find them both for a second.

I look over my shoulder in time to see Jesse nodding eagerly in agreement. "Yeah, I've never seen him get shut down so fast before," he says, his grin practically radiating sunlight. It's damn infectious, is what it is. "That was hilarious."

I shrug, hands tensing slightly on Cain's hips. "Well, I *did* mind," I say mostly to him, shaking my head. I know it is likely something of an ego boost for him to have someone keep him like that, but I don't care. I can't imagine separating from him right now.

The hours and songs begin to blend together after Julian's interruption, and it isn't long before everyone starts to pass out. Some sprawl across chairs, some even in the grass of the lawn outside, where a majority of the party ended up a while ago. A few people had even ended up in the doorway to the mansion itself—which we quickly found our way into a giggle fit over as we traipse over them, finding an empty chair in the yard and dropping into it.

Cain slumps against my shoulder in a chair pulled as closely as possible to mine, looking at me through heavily lidded eyes. "This was so fun, Dae," he murmurs, sounding lazy and barely awake.

I smile equally as lazily, studying his expression through a haze. "You going to pass out first?"

He giggles and nods, leaning upward and pressing a kiss to the corner of my lips. "Probably."

I *know* I'm blushing horribly, but I try to act like I don't notice as he presses another to the edge of my jaw, sinking lower as he shifts back against my shoulder. His lips are soft when they touch the side of my neck, causing my breath to leave me in a shudder I can't quite contain.

"What are you doing, Cain?" I ask, almost out of breath.

Another giggle as he settles against me again, yawning. "Noth-inngggg."

As I shake my head, he falls asleep—and I, frozen in place, join him a moment later.

I jolt awake the following morning to glaring sunshine, grimacing as I sit up with a considerable headache.

No one around is moving yet, not that I mind. I glance over at Cain, who is still curled up in the chair beside me, and I fight the urge to reach over and pet his long red curls by turning away from him. A few feet away, Marion is passed out on top of a sprawled-out

Jesse, and as I look further around the yard, I spot Bren and Louis tangled up like a pair of cats in the grass.

As I'm taking the view in, a small grumble sounds from Cain—and as I look back to him, I'm surprised to find him climbing into my lap and curling up once more.

"Cain?" I almost whisper, stifling a soft laugh as he responds with a quiet 'mm?', meaning he definitely isn't fully awake. Instead of moving, I settle deeper into the chair and study how soft he looks, like that day when I had woken up beside him. Before I can stop myself, I brush some of the hair out of his face, watching a faint flush of pink rise to his cheeks.

Gods, I'm in trouble.

14

Long after the party cleared and our apparent hangovers passed as well, Cain reminds me about a social event in the city we're meant to attend as we return to our dorms. Another one of my least favorite types, of course, being it likely means mixing with business types and people who are all too formal for the wrong reasons.

I decide on a black button-up under a corset vest, black slacks and a matching belt—and as I'm starting to slip on the vest, someone knocks at my door. A trio of thumps, likely hitting the wood at the knuckle.

"Come in!" I call, forcing my usually quiet voice loud enough for him to hear. I know it's Cain. It always is.

Cain walks in, shutting the door quietly behind him as he crosses over to me. "Hi, Dae," he greets with a smile, and I practically *feel* his appreciative look roll over me.

I look back toward the rest of my outfit waiting on the armchair in front of me, exhaling slowly. "Hi... Can you tighten this for me?"

He strides over gracefully, humming under his breath. "Of course I can."

His hands run over my hips and sides thoughtfully, freezing me in place and sending a shiver down my spine that burns where his hands had touched. My gaze finds its way to the elf's lips, stuck looking over my shoulder at him, biting my own a little in thought as he laughs.

There is a tinge of pink to his cheeks, and as I notice it, I also notice how his red eyes darken when they look to my lips and back up at me. Something aching burns in his irises, and it impresses me that I can even hold his gaze for so long with him looking like that.

I swear I'm going to crumble instantly as I tear my eyes away, grateful to be relieved of their crimson intensity.

Wincing slightly as Cain pulls the strings of my corset as tight as he can, I wait patiently for him to tie it before grabbing a tailcoat I set out on one of the chairs nearby. As I turn around, my heart catches in my throat upon seeing what he's wearing—a glittery, low-cut red dress that hugs every inch of him and shows off his right leg from a slit in the fabric, much like the one he wore to the ball. He has another black rose neatly pinned in his hair, matching the darkness of the smoky makeup around his eyes.

I stare at him in awe, shaking my head. "Wow," I murmur, absolutely breathless. *When doesn't he make me this way?*

Cain laughs, smiling at me. "What a way with words you have, Daedalus," he remarks.

"Sorry, I..." I laugh too, quiet and on a rush of breath. "You're stunning. Intimidating, maybe. But...stunning. Like a rose, or a ruby. Or, more specifically, like the type of sunset people stop and admire—shit, I'm rambling, aren't I? Was that all corny?"

His eyes twinkle with something mischievous as he watches me, sighing what I think is fondly. "Not at all, Dae. I like hearing what you think."

I nod, almost unable to take my eyes off him—though I quickly force myself to turn and face the door with an arm extended out to him so we aren't late. Cain loops his arm through it, an amused smile on his deep-red painted lips, and walks contentedly alongside me as we leave the college and start down the street.

It's a beautiful evening; the sun is setting and painting the city in oranges and reds, the barely visible stars are starting to peek out high above us, the breeze is a perfect mix of cool in the already warm air. All of it is comfortable, keeping me content for the moment.

People part for us easily as we approach the tall, gray stone building. There isn't much in the face of a lawn outside, instead having strips of grass on either side of the pathways to the courtyard that are covered by purple-flowered bushes. Long, arched windows sit in pairs on either side of the doorway, showing off the edges of royal blue curtains and the crowd within—I promptly grimace at the sight of my mother and father, sitting at a table up against the wall, both looking unamused in their solitude.

Cain looks over at me after smiling thinly at a pair of women, raising an eyebrow. "What's that look for? You're not regretting this already, are you?" he says softly, attempting to follow my look.

I shake my head, taking a deep breath and letting it out through my nose. "No, I just saw my parents. I'm nervous, I suppose," I say just as quietly, relieved when it doesn't seem like they've noticed me yet.

He squeezes my arm with his and smiles, glancing around us as we start to walk through the doorway. "I won't leave you, alright?"

I nod as we enter the room, my senses instantly flooded with the sounds of voices, laughter, glasses clinking together, and a hint of music playing underneath it all. Cain doesn't let me go, and I more than appreciate it, even as Cain's mother, Celeste, directly approaches us. She tows along an older elven man who seems far out of Cain's age range, and Cain tenses beside me at the sight of them. Ever so slightly, like he's trying not to be obvious about it.

Celeste smiles big and bright, dark eyes glancing between us. "Hello Cain! This man here would be perfect for you, don't you think? He has successful businesses, plenty of money to take care of you with—"

"No thanks, I don't need any more suitors, Celeste," Cain cuts her off easily, plucking a pair of champagne flutes from a passing tray and handing one to me.

The woman's sudden arrival, and the realization of what she's doing, surprises me a bit. Cain had told me his mother was bad, but I hadn't realized she was *this* bad.

"What? Why?" she questions, resting a hand on her hip and leaning her weight into it. "He would greatly benefit our family, you know."

Cain smirks and sips his champagne, giving her a lazy shrug. "I decided I'm going to marry Daedalus, instead."

I choke on my next sip, side-eyeing him quickly as he pulls me in closer.

"You're *what*?" Celeste says slowly, the other man slipping away from the group once her focus is directed onto her son. She turns to glance at Minos, who seems pleasantly distracted talking to a group of men in suits—her gaze swiftly becomes pointed, almost a glare, and I can only assume by the slight movement of Minos's head that he is rolling his eyes at whatever she's messaging him. A moment later, he strides over through the crowd with an entertained, but slightly lazy, smirk on his face, already snickering.

At the sound of it, Cain laughs too, causing them both to devolve into that raspy and low, nearing maniacal, sound.

"Cain, my favorite son." Minos struggles to stifle another bout of laughter, shaking his head. "I am here to tell you, as requested of me, that you can't marry anyone. At all. Ever."

Cain's face breaks into an amused smile, leaning into me a bit as he studies his father. Celeste seems less than pleased with the outcome, pushing Minos's shoulder slightly.

"No one?" he echoes, faking confusion. "Or no one, if she doesn't have a hand in it?"

"No one," Minos agrees, choking back another laugh.

Cain shrugs, giving them an exaggeratedly dramatic shrug and sigh. "*Fine*. I'm sure I'll live without ever marrying someone."

Both father and son burst into a raucous round of laughter, and I quickly realize that it likely isn't going to stop for a while once Celeste exasperatedly stalks away from us.

As I glance around, I catch a glimpse of the cold and angry gaze of my mother in the crowd, and the alcohol in my stomach immediately turns sour. My hands rub together nervously as Minos slips away from us again, trying not to make it obvious that my anxiety is heightening just by *seeing* her.

"Are you alright?" Cain asks softly, leaning in close to be heard. "Is she doing something?"

"Not exactly," I reply, shaking my head. "She's only looking."

He eyes her direction, surprisingly fierce. "*Great*."

A few of the businessmen who had been having some sort of drinking game nearby walk over to us, asking Cain to join them for a round or two. Each one of them are dressed in black suits, some with hats or cigars and some without. I can't help but realize that these are exactly the type of people Cain fits in with—Nemoure's vibrant Upper Circle looks good on him. He glances at me to make sure I'll be alright, only leaving once I nod, despite knowing it is a lie. I won't be alright, but if there's one thing I *don't* want to do, it's stop him from having fun.

Even *if* my anxiety grows louder with every step he takes away from me.

Cain doesn't go far, still visible in the crowd, but the distance makes it feel like we're miles apart. I shift my weight nervously from one foot to the other, tensing at a tap on my shoulder—I already have an idea of who it is, but indecision between a stranger and my mother forces me to face who it is regardless.

My mother has a storm in her eyes when I briefly meet them, and it makes me want to disappear into the floor. "Hello."

She doesn't answer, sipping her wine and watching Cain just over my shoulder. My stomach twists again, causing an uncertain urge to want to leave my champagne somewhere else.

Why isn't she answering me?

"He's... *interesting*," Morgana states after a long moment, coldly. That way she speaks, I'd heard it before—years ago, a brief memory when she was speaking to another woman in the manor. It hits me in a flash, from when I was much younger, walking through the halls and pausing at a slightly opened door. I remember their silhouettes laying across the wall, her hand rising toward the woman's throat and my father sounding furious. She had spoken in that same tone to get my father to sit down and be *quiet.*

It was a threat, that was to be known.

I vaguely remember an explosion of magic, and my father's angered expression as I hurried on down the hall.

"Right." I force the word out, hand tensing on my glass.

"You continue to disobey me, Daedalus. When will you listen to me again? After all, you know I know what's best for you," she says, her tone laced with anger but somehow completely empty. Devoid of light, of emotion. Her dark lips curl into a sickly smile that doesn't meet her eyes, a hand moving to lightly hold my chin for a brief second. "If only you listened, you likely wouldn't be here, alone. Uncomfortable. Do you truly belong in this crowd, my son?"

My world shatters like a mirror in front of me, everything splintering in shards, her words icy knives stabbing into my head and heart. I want to curl in on myself, become smaller so she can't hurt me. *Is she wrong? I don't know anymore. I don't belong here, I'm not like them—*

"Please leave me alone." I jerk my chin out of her hand and look at the floor instead, hoping it will open and swallow me up. Hoping, *desperately.*

"You'll see, trust me," she replies, shrugging as she turns, her casual expression a mask for the crowd. I can feel her seething under it, burning like a wildfire deep in her chest, threatening to burn me.

Morgana steps away, and I immediately leave my glass on the nearest table, weaving through the crowd and leaving the room. I find the bathroom down the hall and pace in front of the sinks for a moment before bracing myself against one, hands gripping the sides so tight I swear I could snap it in half. Panic starts to settle in, swimming through my stomach and taking over every piece of rational thought I might've had left. The room feels too small, *much* too small, as if it's truly closing in around me.

My hands go to my head, tangling in my hair as the urge to scream rises from deep in my chest. Maybe it would cure me—to scream loud enough that it would echo in these halls for years. Maybe I could walk back into that room if I did, even if they knew it was me who made the sound.

Everything in me feels so small, curled up and hiding with its hands over its ears like the child I once was. Even my heart starts rabbiting away in my chest, a relentless hammering on my ribcage as it too is desperate to escape me.

I am awful. Disgusting. She's right, what am I doing here? They all know I don't belong. I never have; I never will. Why did I come here? They're probably all making fun of me because of her. They know how terrible I am. They know. They know. They know. I should jump off this building, make a scene out of it.

It's quiet in the room, but I feel so *loud*.

I swallow the want to cry, trying to get myself back together by practicing deep breathing, but it doesn't settle me fast enough. The door creaks open, and I'm sure it must look like I'm hyperventilating to whoever walks in, but why would they care? They shouldn't—

A hand falls on my lower back, startling me.

I'm rotten, and he knows it.

"Easy, Dae. It's me. Is everything okay?" Cain rubs my back slightly, watching me nod and shake my head all at once. "What's wrong?"

I grip the sink tighter, turning my knuckles pale. "My mother, I-I can't do this."

"What did she do?" Cain's voice lowers, a dangerous tone I've never heard him use before. It almost reminds me his father, all that intimidation he uses to keep people in line. "Did she hurt you?"

""No. No she just—gods, it's stupid. She just spoke to me.T hat's all she did. That's all she ever has to do," I murmur, trying to keep myself calm. Trying with all my might. My next breath leaves shakier than the last, fighting me along the way.

Cain shakes his head, exhaling thinly through his nose. His anger is palpable, almost reverberating through the entire room as he looks me over, big enough for me to feel the ripple of flames over my skin as his magic surges with it. "What did she say?"

I will never be like you. She knows.

"I'll be right back, okay?" Cain murmurs when I shake my head a little frantically and stay silent, rubbing my back gently before leaving the room.

You really are the worst. What are you even doing here? You disgusting creature. What are you worth, really?

"Shut up, shut up, shut up," I whisper, lightly pounding my hands against the sink before standing upright again. I can't even look in the mirror, because the rotten feeling inside of me is too overwhelming, and I know all too well that seeing myself would make me do something terrible. It's how it always is. I panic, see myself falling apart, and self-destruct. It's a repeated cycle that never seems to end.

After a passing moment of my pacing, the door opens again to reveal Cain with a soft smile on his face. "She's gone, you're okay," he says softly, walking over and extending a hand to me. "Is it okay if I ask what you're thinking right now?"

I shakily take his hand in mine, twining our fingers together in the same way I imagined just days ago, letting them fall between our hips as I close my eyes. "When she speaks to me like that... I fall back into old cycles. Bad ones. Telling myself all sorts of shitty things, things I used to hurt myself over when I was younger. I... don't want to repeat it."

Cain frowns, leaning over and kissing me on the cheek. "I'm sorry, Dae... I don't think you're any of the things you're telling yourself, okay? I'm not good at this kind of stuff, but genuinely, I mean it. You're one of the best people I know. I care about you."

I shift my weight from one foot to the other, looking at the floor. It is nearly impossible to believe him, to take in what he's saying. What proof is there, besides Cain always saying he was right about everything? *What a joke.* "Thank you, I... need to hear that more. It's hard to believe you," I mutter, closing my eyes.

Cain nods, rubbing his thumb over the back of my hand where our fingers are still tangled together. His lips part a time or two before he sighs, looking to me with an almost somber expression. "If it makes you feel any better, I can sort of understand where you're coming from," he pauses, looking at himself in the mirror. "I don't really know how to explain it, but I feel insecure too. A lot, actually. Mainly because my paranoia gets really, really out of hand—I'm not sure if it came from Celeste or Minos, but... I'm not sure where I'm trying to go with this."

He laughs a little, but it comes out quiet and a little uneasy as he gestures vaguely in the air. It's obvious he's never talked about this with another person, or at least not in a setting like this.

Instead of letting him sit in an awkward quiet, I nod. "My paranoia is really bad too. I get what you mean."

Cain smiles at me, something soft. "I'm glad we understand each other, then."

We don't stay at the event much longer after our conversation in the bathroom, mainly more for my comfort than anything. As we walk down the street, our hands linked together without either of us fully realizing, I finally feel my mind settle. It calms with the touch of his skin and the press of his ring against my fingers, working as a steady reminder, pretty gold digging just under my knuckle.

Cain glances over at me, sighing and rubbing his arm with his right hand. "Hey, Dae, can I tell you about something? It belongs to our conversation earlier."

I watch his bright eyes follow a carriage as it passes us, studying the sudden nervousness in his body language before nodding.

"When I was talking about my paranoia, I said I wasn't sure where I got it from, right? Well, I guess I kind of lied. I got it from my mother—but not in a genetic way. She's always been fixated on sending me off with suitors, even back when we lived overseas." Cain gestures exasperatedly into the open air, huffing. "Back then, she had me matched up with this older elf. She drugged me in an attempt to get me to go along with it, and even when I tried to reach out to my old friend group for help...some of them didn't believe me. I was a party person over there too, but not like I am here—anyway, the guy ended up stalking me at one point, and it was honestly terrifying. I guess that made me this way."

His voice falters just enough for me to frown, squeezing his hand lightly. "I'm sorry that happened. Is he... still around?" I ask, gazing anywhere but him, so as not to chase him away.

For some reason, it feels as if he catches me looking, he might run.

"No," he says quietly. "He's not."

"Is he—I mean, did you—?"

He laughs quietly, continuing to look away from me. "Oh, gods no. I didn't do it. I paid someone."

"I see," I murmur, nodding.

Cain nods too, turning to face me so quickly it makes me stop short in my tracks. "I'm only sharing this with you because I trust you. And because, I guess, I want you to know you aren't alone in having to deal with shitty stuff, okay?"

I nod again, looking down at the cobblestone. "Okay."

He leans over and kisses my cheek, then continues to lead me in the direction of the college.

15

— · —

I HAVEN'T been home in weeks. *Weeks.* A few since the last social event, a few since I stepped foot in the manor. It's hard, knowing I can barely even *think* of the place without feeling some sort of dread in my chest.

I inhale slowly, deciding I'm not tired enough to lay down and rest—so I push away from my little table and leave my room, heading in the direction of the library.

No one else is up and about at this hour, making the whole dorm room floor quiet, much to my relief. No sounds come from under doors except faint giggles or the turn of a page, the shadows laying still over the floor as they reach toward me.

Instead of rushing past the locked doors, I pause to call on my magic and let it envelope me, becoming one with the surrounding darkness. It coats every limb, every breath, silencing my steps and rendering me practically invisible to the naked eye. The last time I used it, I was following Cain into Nemoure.

Now, I'm simply using it so no one catches me out this late.

The library is even quieter than the halls as I step inside, the smell of books rushing to meet me like an old friend. I breathe it in welcomingly, closing my eyes for a second to feel for anyone else's energy—and when I don't pick up anything, I continue into the room and let my shadows drop. I carefully make my way across the patterned carpet to the grand piano, uncovering the keys and lightly running my fingers over them. Every time I stand here, it feels like an invitation, as if the piano itself is alive and *wants* me to play my songs.

The seat welcomes me as always, and I quickly begin to play one of my unfinished compositions. It is coming together nicely, though I know all too well that I have to keep practicing it, or else it won't come together at all. My hands race up the keyboard, filling the air with something somber, full of emotion. Even the higher notes in the song sound sad, wilting, falling over themselves—

"Go to *bed* already!"

I freeze at the sound of a yell from outside, standing up and frowning as I walk over to the window. It's cracked open just enough to let a small breeze in, easily hidden from a distance, so whoever sat above me wouldn't be caught. Pushing it further with one hand, I peer at the city beyond, tilting my head up slightly in the direction of where the voice came from. "I apologize for interrupting your... time," I say, attempting at an offer of peace. "I didn't feel anyone else in here."

A startled sniff, then a sad laugh. "Sorry, I didn't know it was you."

Cain. Of course.

I frown, looking up at the edge of the roof. "Who else would be playing the piano at this hour?" I ask.

He sighs, and I imagine him shaking his head. "I guess I wasn't thinking about it."

With a burst of forced courage, I climb out from the window and up beside Cain, sitting down and listening to him sniff beside me. He doesn't move, keeping his face hidden against his knees even as I settle onto the rough roof. I don't say anything, and neither does he.

Sad silence settles between us.

I study him, exhaling softly. This is Cain, completely undone—hair spilling out of its usual ponytail, curls mussed down his back. His white shirt is unbuttoned most of the way and haphazardly tucked into his dark pants, marred by a single splash of what must be red wine. Seeing him this way unsettles something in me, so I force myself to look away and back over the city, allowing him his time to calm down.

After a little while, Cain shifts over and rests his head on my shoulder, looking down below us. "I always feel like if I jumped, I'd be fine. I don't know why," he murmurs, exhaling. "If I stepped off the roof, I could just call on something and fly away. I'd just be fine."

It's an odd statement, but he doesn't sound sad about it. It just comes out like it's truth for him—he would be fine, and that's just the way it is. *How many times have I been up here, contemplating the same thing, but knowing it wouldn't be fine for me?*

I nod, glancing down at the winding streets below, slightly unsettled by the topic at hand. "Are you alright?"

Can sighs, then nods. "Yes. No, I don't know. My mother has been trying to label me as sick, like she did before when I freaked out about what she was causing. She keeps trying to get people on her side."

I frown a little deeper, watching the twinkle of a few pink lights on the horizon. "What happened?"

"I had a full-blown fight with her. She has this idea, and claims I need to be 'helped'. What I told you about that suitor, if you remember right—I blew up after that. Off the walls. Ever since, she's been super intense and wanting someone to 'take care of me' or keep my things away from me because I 'need help'," he says with a sniff, a little angrier this time. I can practically *hear* him rolling his eyes.

"I'm sorry," I murmur, because there isn't much else I can think of to say. My mother is crazy too, but she doesn't want to help me. She wants to make me exactly like her, and that's it. *What if I turned out as the image she had in mind? Would I be like I am now, or a carbon copy of her?*

Focus.

Cain doesn't respond, but nods against my shoulder, another sniffle following.

If there is one thing I've learned about Cain Sidrelle, it's that he's stronger than people give him credit for. Something like this will be temporary in his eyes, because of how quickly and swiftly he moves along, and because of how he won't let anyone else know he's bothered by something. Tomorrow, he'll be scheming with Marion over how to disrupt his mother's plans, or he'll be plotting something for his business and that will distract him enough. He'll be sad now, but by this time tomorrow, something new will take root inside of this frustration.

He fascinates me, in that way.

The moment passes in quiet, and eventually we both sit upright and look at each other. I look more at Cain's chest because I can't handle looking him in the eyes, but we stay here anyway, still as statues. My hands fidget nervously in my lap; Cain's are calm against his own. The only sounds are the gentle breeze and the vague clanking of armor down below from the city's guards—peaceful, despite the slight somber overtone to everything else.

Looking at each other, with a brief glance to connect our gazes before it is broken again.

"Why don't you look at me?" Cain asks softly, slightly above a whisper.

I shake my head, shrugging. "I don't look at anybody. I don't know why."

I'm scared you'll see me for who I really am, and your beauty kills me.

Cain shakes his head, laughing. It's soft, almost fond. "Can you be honest with me?"

I tense, letting out a breathy laugh of my own as I look to him once more, trying to hold his gaze for longer than a second. "You have very intimidating eyes. They show me a lot more than your whole being does. It scares me to know you see through me sometimes," I say, pausing to swallow uncertainly and to think over my following words. "And, I'm also sure that your beauty will be the death of me."

Cain's laugh stumbles out this time, a flush of pink spreading over his cheeks as he shakes his head, standing up. I wait a moment before doing the same, unsure if I said something wrong—only to be caught off guard by him catching me by the hand. Neither of us move any further, looking over the city.

It reminds me of our conversation about taking it over, so no one could ever question us again.

The thought is almost too good to be true.

He turns to me and smiles, taking a small step closer. Then another, and another. Cain only stops when we're a few inches apart, and I don't dare to breathe.

His other hand reaches up to cup my cheek, brushing his thumb over the scar Silas gave me, his eyelashes falling low over his eyes. They look impossibly dark like this, with pinpricks of pure red dotted amongst them from the city lights below, and I cannot help but stare because I don't know what else to do, searching for words and finding none that could possibly explain what I want to say. He fills my lungs; he drowns me in him.

"What is it, Dae?" he murmurs, and I shake my head.

Somehow, the spell between us isn't broken.

"Can I show you something?" I ask, stepping backward slightly, just enough to be able to use my hands.

Cain nods, watching me as I move my hands between us. My magic, black and shadowed, swirls into the air—devouring us in one motion, dragging us into a perfect night without the city, just pitch darkness. I hear his sigh only a breath's away as I let it take my emotions into the black, an uncertain heartbeat echoing around us. "Do you feel it?"

"I do." He's still close, good. "Can I add something?"

"Yes." My darkness, cold and wanting, floods with heat the moment the word leaves my lips. His magic, roiling red flames, surges into the air—casting us both in a crimson light as it tangles up in mine, roaring and spitting embers into the dark. I struggle for words again as he moves it into my own, pulling and reaching, calling out to the deepest reaches of me.

We're connected, if only for a moment.

He looks at me and smiles before closing his eyes, and when I close mine, something opens through our combined magic. I see us on the roof, the moment before this, lit by the city. Cain's hand crossing my scar, his eyes meeting mine.

He kisses me in this vision, and I *feel* it. My lips turn warm with the imagined press of his, tasting of wine and salted tears and red velvet cake. The scent of roses and fire fills my every breath, and though I don't want to inhale, I do, desperately. His hand still cups my cheek, the other reaching around to card into my hair, tentatively exploring. I freeze in it until I bring my own hands up to cup his jaw, holding him there, pulling him into me with a small motion.

The vision vanishes with a blink, but our magic is still there. Holding the feeling of that moment in the air, allowing the intimacy of it to linger.

Cain smiles, searching my face. "What did you think of that?" he asks, low and soft.

I laugh breathily, searching him right back. He feels genuine, he *looks* genuine— "I... want that. I don't want it to just be magic."

I need it. I need you.

He steps forward, the same pace of stepping until we're only inches apart once more. My hands grab for him, desperate to find some purchase in his shirt or on his waist as his own fall on my cheeks, dragging me forward. I meet him somewhere in the middle, messy and hopeful, pressing my lips to his and finding his taste to be exactly as the vision had depicted it. His body leans into mine as our magic surges and twines together, my dark filling with the crackle of his fire, my hunger meeting his. I kiss him like there's nothing else in the world for me to taste ever again, anchoring my body to his.

He kisses me just as eagerly, just as slowly, and everything falls right into place. We take our time with it, hands shakily exploring until they find some uncertain purchase on his hips and his on my chest.

Eventually, Cain leans back to catch his breath, resting his forehead against my own and breaking the magic around us.

I sigh softly, slowly releasing him from my grasp. I don't know what to say to him, if there's anything I *could* say.

"I liked that," he murmurs before I can, then withdraws from me completely. "Should we go back in?"

I nod, forcing myself to swallow as our magic fades, returning us into the glow of the city. He looks beautiful, even if he's slightly tear-stained. "I think we should."

Cain smiles, carefully climbing down and ducking back into the room. I watch the lights glitter for a moment longer before joining him, slipping through the window and shutting it behind me, rubbing the feeling of the rough stones off my palms by pressing them against my thighs.

As he leads me out of the library and down the hall, he makes a curious little humming sound. Something in thought, I'm sure.

"You know, we could stay together. Here. There's no sense going back if it would be a shitty outcome for both of us," he says, glancing over at me. "Neither of us have to go home."

I look at him in surprise, weighing the options. Going to the manor is no longer one, unless I want to have another near-death moment with my mother. Staying here with him is much more attainable, especially with the taste and remembered touch of him still lingering on my mouth. "I think that's a good idea... Would you like to come to my room, for the night?"

Cain's eyes twinkle dangerously as he smiles, stepping past me. "I'd like that."

We stop outside of Cain's dorm so he can collect whatever he might want for the night, or for however long he decides to stay with me for, before going to my own. It isn't a surprise to see him in a champagne silk robe with two dark wine bottles under his arm, but for some reason the sight makes me struggle to form words. His hair spills out around him, no longer in a ponytail, and *Gods,* he's so damn pretty, even with the cry-messy makeup still on his face and the slight tinge of sadness in his expression. I don't understand it. I can't figure out how someone can look like him. *I want to know what's beneath it. I want to see him—*

He smiles at my staring, raising an eyebrow at me. "What, cat got your tongue, Daedalus?"

The slight view of Cain's collarbones and pale chest, hidden by the robe, is killing me.

"No.... no. Let's go," I answer in a hurry, turning on my heel and walking down the hall to my own dorm, my cheeks and ears hot. All I can think to call this unknown feeling in me is *hunger*—I want to devour Cain until there is nothing left for anyone else to look at, I want to sink my teeth into him and never let go.

When did I become such a carnal thing?

I catch a glimpse of Louis poking his head out of his room at the sound of us passing by, his light eyebrows raising sharply at the sight before him. It probably gave him the wrong impression, thanks to Cain's outfit and what he's holding, but I don't care. Honestly, I'm not even sure how he heard us, being we have been walking down the hall as stealthily as possible. Maybe it was a clink of the wine bottles, or maybe he heard doors opening and closing. I don't know. It hardly matters, as he ducks away just as quickly.

I let Cain into the room first and close the door behind us, watching as he expertly pops one of the corks from a bottle and starts to rummage through the cupboards for glasses. Despite not being much of a wine drinker, I have a pair of red glasses that have designs of cathedral windows along their sides, and swords carved around the stem—they're both from a set that is difficult to find now, and I get this odd sense of pleasure seeing the face of approval he makes when he takes them out. I brought them from home, without my mother knowing.

Cain glances around the room before pouring us both a glass, likely looking for a servant I don't have, then tilts his own in front of his face to eye the designs. "These are pretty rare, aren't they?"

"Yes they are… and thank you. Is this one of your 'fancy' wines?" I purposefully use light air quotes around the word fancy, trying to hold back a smile.

Cain snorts, shooting me a look that is quickly followed by a smirk. "Yes, it's one of my 'fancy' wines, Dae. Why should I settle for anything less?"

The cockiness in his voice quickly washes away with a deep sigh as he steps closer to me, carding a hand lightly through my dark hair. I freeze in place, flinching the tiniest bit at his touch, watching his smirk fade. "You're so soft," he murmurs, pinching the gray streak in my hair between his fingers. "You know, for an elf, you shouldn't be graying this early."

I watch his hand, leaning back against the counter and shaking my head a little. "I'm not an elf, and it's not from age."

He tilts his head at me, letting my hair go. "You aren't? What are you then?" he asks, curiosity lighting his eyes.

"I'm a dhampir, Cain. Similar to a vampire, but not quite." I take a drink of the wine, surprised by the sweeter taste of it. Cherry, maybe hints of vanilla, flood over the drier alcohol bite. "Some might say I'm a little scarier than an elf."

His eyes light up, a devious but curious sparkle in them as his hand lowers, fingertips brushing across my lips—likely thinking of the sharpened teeth that lay behind them. "Oh *really*? That's interesting."

I shrug. "I suppose."

"So, do you drink blood?"

Another shrug. "I *can*, but I don't choose to most of the time. Some dhampirs eat it solely, but a lot of us eat other things."

Cain pauses before finishing his glass, pouring himself another almost immediately. "What do *you* eat, then?"

Another drink of wine, followed by a slight exhale. "Ah, well... there's a reason I like steak as rare as possible. Every once in a while, I get a craving for raw meat," I explain, laughing a little as Cain visibly cringes. "What was that for?"

He shudders again, shaking his head. "I couldn't imagine that. Textures."

I shake my head at him, pausing to finish my glass before setting it in the sink. "It's not as bad as you think, but I get it."

Cain finishes his glass after me, eyeing the bottle for a moment before decidedly leaving it alone. He yawns, walking over and leaning his head on my shoulder—something so casual and soft and *familiar,* it makes my heart flip inside my chest. "Should we go to bed?"

I nod, lightly taking his fingers in my hand and leading him to my room. It feels beyond intimate, taking him there, bringing him to my bed. He looks around with a little smile on his face, taking in the dark walls as if they were more familiar than they really were, then slides into my bed. It's so easy, so *comfortable*, that I could almost let myself imagine us doing this more often. I can *almost* picture him walking into my room like it's his own, all confident and taking over the bed with me.

Knowing that probably can't happen hurts a little.

Cain tosses his robe aside and snuggles up to me, his bare back against my torso. I hope for a moment that my clothes are soft enough for him, that they don't bother him, before very carefully laying my arm over his ribs.

He twines his fingers into mine and yawns, and we swiftly fall asleep.

...

Daylight leans into my room for a peek at us, strolling across my floor in between my curtains. As I move to sit up, I hesitate at the feeling of Cain's head on my shoulder, and despite how much I would like to get out of bed, I can't make myself disturb him. A soft sigh leaves me, tensing when I hear my door carefully open in the living room. There is only one other person who has the key to my room—despite everything, Bren—so I cross my fingers and hope to hell that it's only him.

"Daedalus, are you coming to class?" Bren's voice drifts into my head as he leans his head into the doorway, raising an eyebrow upon seeing Cain beside me. His red eyes glance to Cain's robe on the floor, then back to me. *"Wait, did you two—"*

I make an exasperated face at him, shaking my head. He'd never understand what happened last night even if I tried to explain it. *"No, Bren. What do you want?"*

"I asked you already, are you coming to class?" He says, making a face back at me and folding his arms over his chest.

"I can't move right now, I don't know when he'll be awake." I glance to Cain with only my eyes as he makes a soft sound, shifting and resting his head on my chest—then shoot my brother a look that means 'go before he gets up', and Bren quickly scurries from the doorway and back out of the room.

As I close my eyes, willing to admit defeat to not getting up, a different voice slowly slips into my head. *"Hey, Daedalus, I'm going to help you out."* Louis. His magic is strangely sensual, tinged with the color purple and a taste of smoke.

I'll ask Cain about that later.

My door closes quietly, leaving us in silence. *"How so?"*

"Do you have a servant in there?" he asks, and I make a face at the ceiling. *Why do so many of them have a servant in their rooms?*

"No."

"What—Okay. Well, I'm going to send you one of mine. Cain will always wake up to coffee, and if you bring it to him in bed, he'll be very happy and like you even more," Louis explains, and my eyebrows raise at the implication.

I admit defeat for the second, maybe third, time, sighing softly. *"Fine, my door shouldn't be locked, since Bren stopped by."*

"I know. I'm with him."

It takes a few minutes, but a soft knock sounds from the door—followed by a short, brunette elven man walking in and smiling at me, setting a platter on the table beside the bed before stepping out with a little bow. Once the door is closed again, I use a small wisp of shadow to make sure it's locked, then lightly nudge Cain.

"Mm?" Cain's red eyes slowly blink open, looking up at me lazily. I could look at this face, this moment of softness on him, for a long time.

Instead, I gesture to the coffee beside me, watching him smile as it brightens his face. "There's coffee, if you want some," I say, smiling a little nervously.

"Oh, thank you." Cain sits up with a soft yawn, sweeping some of his red curls from his face and reaching over once I sit up to start pouring.

I give him a little nod, sitting back with my mug so he can reach across me. "There's sugar and cream too, if you need that sort of thing."

Cain nods, mixing both into his mug before carefully sitting up again. He takes a slow sip—one I give him a questioning look for, because I know just how hot it is based off the heat flowing through the walls of my mug. "What are you doing?"

"What?" he asks, giving me a funny look right back.

I press my palms to either side of my own cup, the heat of the liquid within leaving hot spots on them. "Isn't that scalding?"

He shrugs. "It doesn't bother me."

We sit silence for a moment until Cain climbs out of bed and stands up, stretching carefully so he doesn't spill his coffee. I look over as he does and immediately turn away from him, my face turning countless shades of red at the sight of his slender body—though I know even if I look away that he'll still be able to tell. Cain is in the littlest amount of underwear possible, something I don't get a good look at beyond red lace, and I honestly don't know how I didn't notice last night.

"Oh, shit—sorry, Dae." Cain laughs loudly, sipping his coffee again.

I shake my head a little quickly, staring at the floor on the opposite side of the bed. "I... it's fine. I just didn't expect that."

He snickers as he picks his robe from off the floor, and I swear he bends over in my sight completely on purpose. "I didn't mean to catch you off guard. I thought you realized what I was wearing last night," he says, and the amusement in his tone is godsdamned frustrating.

I pinch the bridge of my nose with one hand, letting out a thin breath before drinking some of my coffee. Although it's hot, it's not intolerable. "It's fine."

"You sure you're going to be okay?" Cain asks, sly, as he sits down on the edge of the bed again.

He ducks as I swat at him in a desperate attempt to get him to stop talking. "Yes! Yes, I'll be fine. You know, I *did* have a class this morning."

"What about it?" He raises an eyebrow at the way I say it, tilting his head to one side.

Why does he have to be so pretty? "I couldn't go to it, because *someone* was laying on me."

"I'm *sorry*, you're very comfy." Cain shrugs, laughing. "You didn't move, so I didn't get up."

I shake my head at him, setting my coffee down so I can stand up and stretch—listening to the sound of my vertebrae realigning as I do so. A river of cracks run down my back and from my arms, and something in me aches to escape because of them.

Cain grimaces at me, looking me over. "Good *lord*, Dae. Doesn't that hurt?"

"I guess my back does hurt most of the time," I remark with a shrug, knowing it is definitely due to my not-so-perfect posture. Being a pianist and being constantly curled up over books or notebooks doesn't do me any favors, though I don't overly mind. Sure, my back aches, but I'm familiar with it.

"You should get a massage," Cain says, and when I shake my head almost instantly, he frowns. "Why not?"

Another drink of my coffee, then I eye him. "Cain, I don't like being touched, *especially* not by strangers. Why would I want to do that?"

"It feels so good, though!"

I laugh a little, finishing my coffee and re-adjusting the few buttons on my shirt that had come undone overnight before standing up and setting my empty mug on the tray next to us. As I open my mouth to say something else, an unnerving feeling creeps around somewhere deep inside of me. It stirs like a spark, jolting to life in my gut and swiftly blooming into something worse around my sternum. Something goes cold in the college, storming on the wind.

I recognize it quickly, looking toward my door.

I let my guard down.

Morgana knows.

16

A FLOOD of panic rushes through my body, making me wrap my arms around myself in some hope of protection. "Cain, I really hate to say this but you have to go to your dorm. I think... I think Morgana is here."

Cain's eyes widen, darting to the door and then back to me. "What do you mean she's here? Daedalus, are you going to be safe?"

I shake my head, curling in on myself. "I don't know. Just please—I'll find you again. Just go."

The fear takes over so quickly that I can only mouth apologies to Cain as he steps out and hurries down the hall. Swallowing, I struggle to make myself breathe so I can focus on her presence—on the cold dread of it, the swamp of fear, the drowning ocean of anxiety. My hands shake as they press into my sides, searching. Searching close, searching far.

Her energy, her *magic*, swallows me up like a black hole as my door snaps open and Morgana lets herself in, mismatched eyes blindingly angry as she looks around. She studies my walls, my table, my unmade bed.

"Daedalus," she snarls, voice thin as ice. "I didn't think I'd have to actually come *here* to speak to you, but seeing as you won't come home all of a sudden, I had to *chase* you. Do you know what that's like?"

Why do you hate me so much?

I want to ask terribly. I want her answer.

She storms toward me, closing the door behind her. I don't know how she managed to get past the Dean or the counselors with her acting like this. "You should be in a *class* right now, Daedalus Macabre. And what *have* you been doing—hanging out with some boy and day-drinking?!"

"He's not *some* boy," I say thinly, instantly regretting it.

Morgana's glare worsens at that, a scoff turning into an angry laugh. "You act as if I *care*, Daedalus. You should be better than this!"

The words sting like a snake bite, forcing me to fight off the wave of emotion they cause. I'm getting choked up, and *God* am I tired of nearly crying in front of her every damn time I've seen her lately. "Morgana, please—"

"*No.* You've run out of chances, Daedalus." She sweeps across the floor and takes my head in her hands, holding harshly enough that I can't move away—until I suddenly realize I can stop her. She gave me the power to stop this from happening, all because of her training and my own studying. She *forced* me to have the power to stop her, because she wants me to be like her.

As my mind starts to go blank, I reach through the fog and place my fingertips against the inside of her wrist, searching for her pulse.

I don't find it. I don't feel *anything* when I try, but I cast the spell anyway.

It surges through me like a lightning bolt, shooting from my shoulder into my wrist, flowing in spider web-like rivers to my fingers. My shadows meet her own in an aggressive collision, crashing against each other in a way that should very well throw me off my feet. The electricity makes me shudder, connecting with something deep in her—and for a moment, I see the haunt inside my own mother. Her blackened heart surrounded by nothing but a void, never beating.

My mind rushes back into itself as I step away, nearly tripping over a chair in the process.

It worked.

Though I wasn't sure if I would be able to stop her with that particular spell, it *worked*.

Morgana looks at her hands before they clench into tight fists, her breathing turning fast and heavy with her anger. "You have disobeyed me for the *last* time, Daedalus. The next time you come home, you better bring your best."

Then she rips open a portal in the center of my room, steps through it, and vanishes from sight.

Falling backward into the couch, I crumple before I can even stop to think and start sobbing into my hands. I can't help it, the way it wrenches out of me—everything hurts when she becomes that way. There is no way there won't be a horrible training session waiting back home for me if I return, or worse.

I won't go back, not yet. At least, not right now.

I force myself onto my feet and stare at where she'd stood, putting my glasses back on and attempting to wipe at my eyes. The chest-aching sobs make it a practically useless thing, but I try anyway. I wipe and wipe and wipe, continuing to come away with the backs of my hands wet and my cheeks never drying.

Something I do know, is I want Cain. I don't know why, but it feels as if he could protect me from this feeling in me. He will hold me and never let go.

Why do I need him like this?

In a moment, without thinking much about it, I dash out of my room and hurry down the hall to Cain's. I knock quickly, trying to stop crying before the door actually opens, but it isn't happening. One of the servants in an entirely red outfit answers my knocking with a stern look on their face, explaining that Cain is in a bath so I should come back later.

I shake my head, wrapping my arms around myself. "Please let me in. I need to see him."

They grimace, glancing back inside, then sigh and nod. "Fine, but behave yourself. Master Cain will not be pleased with me for allowing someone in."

I hurry past them and sit on the couch, willing myself to calm down, but nothing is working. My body still feels so small, so afraid. *Why did I bother coming here like this?* Part of me doesn't want Cain knowing this side of me. Maybe I should just go, maybe I shouldn't be here. *Why did I think he would help? That doesn't make sense.*

As I'm shakily standing again, the bathroom door opens, revealing Cain in his usual business-ready outfit.

"Hi—oh, Dae..." His voice is raspier than usual as he walks over, a little slowly, almost tentative at the sight of me.

My knees falter and I sink back onto the couch, looking at him through the blur of tears. "I'm sorry, I... I don't know why I came to you. I thought—I didn't know where else to go."

"You're fine, it's alright," he murmurs, crossing the room and taking my hands, directing a look over his shoulder at the few servants he had in the room. "Can one of you get him some tea please?"

I hold onto his hands like they're anchors, trying to steady myself.

"What happened?" Cain eyes me, keeping his voice quiet.

I swallow, sniffing. "I don't even know. I think she wanted to go after my memories again, and I... stopped her."

His eyes go wide, looking me over for a moment. "You *stopped* her?"

"Yes, there's... there's this spell I know that will stop anything. Any spells, most magic—I know it, and I used it. She didn't like it—it actually made her angrier!" The laugh that follows comes out a little wild as I run a hand through my hair, looking at him wide-eyed. "And, to top it all off, she threatened me. She told me when I came home next, I better bring my best."

Before he can say anything, one of the servants returns with a mug of chamomile tea, as well as a silver tray with cream and sugar. Cain shoots them another look, and they swiftly start making my cup without me even needing to ask. I cup it between my palms, grateful for the heat against my skin as it calms my wild emotions for even a second.

"Would you like to do something together today? Get this off your mind a little?" Cain asks, looking at me with a hint of concern in his gaze. "There's always Laia, that town I told you I would hunt in with my friends. I think you'd like it there, it's a little spooky."

I let out a cry-laugh, shaking my head. "Do you think I'd like it because *I'm* spooky?"

He smiles, laughing with me. "Yes, Dae. In a good way, obviously."

I smile a little too, wiping my eyes as I recall his stories of Laia. Cain always mentioned his two friends, Aymar and Jamie, with a visible love for the former over the latter, and how he'd learned how to hunt because of them. The two have always sounded like an interesting duo to be around— Jamie being a somewhat rowdy half-elf with short dark brown hair and matching eyes, and Aymar being some kind of elven-merfolk hybrid with deep brown skin and teal patches, fins, and long brown hair. Cain also told me about their pet fox, Cinnamon, and how quickly they let Cain live with them when things were going downhill at home.

They sounded kind and caring every time he spoke of them, and it always makes my heart feel strange.

There is also the fact that Cain speaks so fondly of Aymar, or at the very least, seems softer with him than anybody else. That never bothered me before, but it feels strange now that I feel for him the way I do. Not that I'd ever tell him that, though.

A soft sigh leaves me, and I nod, taking a second to sip the tea cautiously. "I think that would be nice," I murmur, grateful for the floral and sweet taste of the liquid as it washes away the salt of my crying.

Cain beams, squeezing my hands lightly and standing up. "We could get lunch there. Aymar and Jamie showed me a nice place, so I already know where we could go."

"Thank you for... caring like this, I suppose," I say softly before he can fully remove his hands from mine, looking up at him.

He laughs, nodding and letting me go. "Of course, Dae. Let's go then."

Only once I finish my cup of tea and manage to pull myself mostly together, Cain has the same servant who greeted me before call us a carriage so we don't have to walk all the way there. It would be a few hours, or so he says, and neither of us have the energy for that. Not even with the cool afternoon air or the gentle autumn sun.

I don't mind the quiet between us as we settle into our seats inside the red-painted carriage, watching the city slowly fade out of view a moment later and become browning fields and reddening forests. Briefly, I glance over to Cain and smile a little at the sight of him framed by all the shifting Autumn colors, watching the trees pass by behind him—the reds of the leaves hold nothing to him, no matter how vibrant some of them are.

He glances over and catches me looking, bringing a smile to his lips. "What?"

I shake my head, leaning into the velvet seat. "Nothing. I'm admiring the colors." A lie, and maybe not a very good one, but he doesn't question it.

Cain laughs, resting his hand over my knee and leaving it there before looking back out through the window. I stare at it for a little while, following the curve of his knuckles and sharp fingernails, then pick it up and gingerly turn it over. He watches me from the corner of his eye as I study his palm, tracing the lines and creases of it, following them to the hint of blue veins beneath the skin of his wrist nearly hidden by his sleeve.

"What are you doing, Dae?" he asks, and I shrug.

"I simply like studying."

An hour of quiet between passes by with more of my tracing, and I only look away from his hand when the carriage comes to an easy stop. Outside, Laia looks exactly as Cain described it—slightly creepy, with buildings painted in darker tones or made from stone or brick, gardens that have faded and died off, and worn-down dirt or grass paths that seemingly either lead into town or into the darkened forest beyond. Houses and shops huddle close together among the thickets of evergreen trees surrounding them, most obviously lived-in or at least visited, though a few of the structures appear abandoned—like the singular church sitting down the beaten path.

As we step out, thanking our driver, Cain starts to lead me down the broken cobblestone street to the place he'd loosely mentioned. It's a quaint little building called 'The Fawn Tavern'—likely given the name by the stone statues of fairy-winged fawns outside in the yellowed grass lawn. It almost reminds me of 'Fauna' in Nemoure, with their matching Fae aesthetics, though this place is much darker compared to the café back in the city. The building itself is constructed in wood, with a dark shingled roof, and very few windows to sneak glances into. My nerves creep up again as we walk inside, peering at the rug under our feet to the bar on the left side of the room, then over to the tables of people on the opposite side.

The atmosphere of the place is welcoming, at least.

A rickety, flat wooden stage hides against the wall across from the table Cain brings me to, and as I study it, I easily imagine the types who probably play here. Likely loud, boisterous and gesturing with mugs of beer in their hands, maybe even pirates. Big guys with beards, dwarven sorts—

"Hey guys!" A cheerful voice breaks through my thoughts, quickly followed by the sound of a chair dragging across the floor to our table. I glance to my right, finding a man who must be Jamie—if Cain's descriptions were truthful—straddling the chair, making the man not far behind him Aymar by reason of deduction. He's exactly as Cain described him, with a few more scars and a deeper teal breaking up his warm brown skin than I previously pictured. It's a lot like vitiligo, only blue-toned rather than fair, like I've seen before.

Aymar waves to Cain and smiles at me, but I don't return it—only a nod, as I study the glinting scales on his cheekbones that frame the fins on either side of his face.

"Hi, you two," Cain greets them, surprisingly fondly. "Daedalus, this is Aymar and Jamie. Aymar and Jamie, this is Daedalus. I know you've both heard about each other, but I figured I should introduce you."

"Nice to meet you," Jamie says in my direction, and I offer him a slight smile in return.

I have never really been comfortable with small talk, nor do I usually participate in the conversations of people I'm not well acquainted with, so it's of no surprise to me when my focus begins to wander as soon as Jamie asks Cain about his recent business adventures. I find my gaze meandering around the room like a visitor at a particularly curious museum, intrigued by the various displays of taxidermy decorating the tavern—deer heads mounted on the wall, a full bear in the corner, a raccoon peering down at me from its perch above the doorway. They were surprisingly good executions of the animals. The forms must have been perfectly sized, or whoever did them is just that talented, which is impressive for a low-key place like this.

"Are you two going to be here for the music?" Jamie asks, a wide grin on his face as I force my attention back to the conversation at hand.

Cain looks across the table to me, tilting his head slightly before looking back to him. "I'm sure we will be, actually. Is it good tonight?"

Aymar laughs, smiling at him warmly. "It's always good, Cain." His lifting accent catches my attention; a type I've only ever heard from people who arrived in Nemoure from the northern-most continent, Shoth, which is apparently over-run by pirates and smaller in size when compared to Vira.

His energy is intriguing too, all summer warmth mingling with the chaos of the Fae I recognize from Bren's own. He makes me curious, though not enough to ask.

"So, what's been up with you two?" Jamie leans his arms against the top of the chair, a devious look in his eye. "Got anything good going on?"

"Well, both of our mothers suck, so neither of us are going home, there's that," Cain says with a shrug, and Aymar frowns at him. *Definitely* concerned.

Jamie eyes him before resting his chin on his arms, humming in thought. "Have either of you heard about... normal families that don't suck?"

It's definitely a joke, but I can't help being somewhat serious about it. "No."

"Nope," Cain adds, laughing as the waiter carries over two glasses of water.

Aymar shakes his head at him, leaning back on his heels, acting as if the fins on either side of his face aren't twitching and giving away his thoughts. Jamie glances up at him, a slight frown on his face before he looks back to us and studies our faces, searching for something hidden. I don't appreciate it, not from people I hardly know—I barely tolerate the poking and prodding from people I do know—so I don't bother stopping the displeased scowl that cuts across my face in warning.

As soon as Cain sees it, he whistles and lets out a laugh. "I have *never* seen you make that face before, Dae," he says, and I shrug.

Thankfully, Jamie's scrutinizing gaze moves on, and Cain doesn't pry on what just happened. Unfortunately, there is only so much a small tavern like this can distract me, and my mind keeps trailing back to Morgana—furious in the middle of my room, snarling out words I could only wish she never said out loud.

Why would I go home now, if there is something like that waiting for me?

With a soft sigh, I try to refocus on my tablemates, watching the three of them talk without paying much mind to the topic of conversation

It's something I like doing sometimes—watching from the middle of a conversation. It's what I usually do in the face of Cain's friend group or in the classrooms—finding the little things they don't realize they are truly saying, seeing how they respond to certain things being said. Little, barely noticeable twinges in a typically normal conversation. Sometimes it lies in their expressions, or their hands moving, a simple shift in their positioning. It tells me things about people they usually want to hide, helps me predict and account for what they might say or do next.

I've started to be able to tell when Cain gets pissed off and doesn't want to show it—usually when Irsa is spouting his unneeded comments about his mental state—or when something makes him close down on the conversation. His silent anger lights up his eyes with embers, the muscle in his jaw twitches, his hands clench tight or tap a pen harshly against a notebook.

Him closing himself off is different, though. He casts his eyes down to whatever is below him, whether it be a desk or the ground, and his gaze turns unfocused. His eyebrows furrow, he bites the inside of his cheek.

I don't know if he knows I can tell.

I, despite catching on to their amusement in talking about hunting, find myself shutting down the same way with the three of them, unsure of myself—though smiling when I realize that Cain's hand now rests over my own as they talk. It is such a small, *small* gesture, but something in me feels calmer and more grounded because of it.

Warmth blossoms in me like a rose, filling my entire chest.

"Are you two still staying?" Aymar asks as he looks toward the stage, which Cain then looks to me for confirmation.

"What do you think?" he says softly, brushing his thumb over my knuckles. "Are you feeling alright enough to stay?"

I hum, thinking it over before nodding, a little smile on my face as he smiles back at me. "I think so."

He looks over to Jamie, rubbing his thumb over my knuckles. "There's your answer. Looks like we can introduce Dae to what happens when the music starts!"

A frown crosses my face as I look over at him, slightly tilting my head. "What does that mean?"

Cain laughs, eyeing the other two. It's oddly secretive. "You'll see. It's fun."

A moment later, I catch a glimpse of movement out of the corner of my eye—a group of bards currently taking the stage, including a towering half-orcish man with olive green skin and black hair that is tied back in a ponytail but still falls to his thighs, an obviously excited forest elf with warm tan skin and bright green eyes, and two other fair-skinned and ginger-haired elven men who appear to be twins. I study them for a long while before turning back to the others, listening to the tuning of a lute and violin behind me, all discorded notes before they finally come into harmony.

As the music starts up, something very bright and almost joyful, people start to get up from their tables and dance. Jamie gets up, flashing a big smile at the both of us, and drags Aymar out with him into the crowd. The air in the tavern suddenly feels much more alive, full of contentment and laughter that I can still hear over the song playing. I watch as the crowd forms, startling when Cain grabs my hand and tugs me out of my seat.

"Come on Dae, let's join them!" he says with a bright smile, and my own smile becomes all the bigger because of it. He looks beautiful, all relaxed without the pressures of our city weighing on him.

Gods, I want to tell him that.

Aymar and Jamie drew this side of him to the surface with such an ease, and I'm not sure if it is because they are naturally calm and fun, or if it really is the lack of pressure on him in Laia. Whatever it is, I'm grateful for the chance to be able to witness this, all of it.

I allow myself to be pulled along, following Cain's steps because I really have no idea what kind of dancing is happening here—and then I quickly realize everyone is passing their partners around.

Oh *Gods.*

Panic takes over for two seconds, making me stumble as I get my bearings on the people surrounding us. Instead of walking away from the dancefloor and sitting back down, I make myself shake off my obvious new nerves—loosening up enough to find myself with Jamie, a stranger, *many* strangers, and then back to Cain again. The energy of the place consumes me, making it impossible not to smile as Cain starts laughing. He looks so soft, so *bright*, not nearly as sharp as he is back in Nemoure, and I can't help but stare with what must be a stupid-looking, happy expression on my face.

"What, Dae?" Cain asks, blinking up at me.

I meet his gaze willingly, perhaps for the first time in our whole friendship, laughing a little. "Sorry if I was staring, it's just... You're glowing."

A trace of red blooms across Cain's cheeks, vibrant on his pale skin. The laugh that leaves him turns sheepish, and it makes my heart miss a beat. When did my heart decide that it was *this* one it wanted? Even The Rot wants to know, wants to *feel* what it is like to crave someone who I thought was once unattainable.

Well, now it knows.

"Sorry, I had to tell you..." I trail off a little nervously, becoming sheepish myself. My own blush forms on my face as Cain shakes his head, waving a hand at me almost dismissively to get me to stop talking.

"It's fine, Dae, don't worry. I just wasn't expecting that at all," he answers after a moment, lips curling into an amused smile. "I like it when you say things like that."

I turn my head away to hide the deepening redness on my face, hearing Cain chuckle a little, and everything in me aches in this moment. I want so *badly* that it almost isn't fair—hell, kissing him sounds perfect right now but I can't bring myself to do it. It would be so easy, cupping his cheek and reeling him in. I could try not to feel as desperate as the first time.

I look at him again, and damn it, I can't do it.

After a few hours, we start walking back to the carriage with my arm looped around Cain's shoulders and one of his around my waist, listening to his giggle filling the air. All four of us had a few drinks during the time we shared, and when I glance over my shoulder at the tavern, I catch Aymar and Jamie leaving quite the same way. Aymar spots me looking and waves, a big smile on his face, and I return the favor because his energy is so damn infectious.

Once we hop inside the carriage, Cain leans his head on my shoulder and sighs in a long way, leaving no space between us. "You know, I really like you, Dae."

"Why?" I ask, unable to stop it from slipping out.

He shrugs a shoulder, closing his eyes. "I don't know, you make me feel... not bad. You're comfy. I like how I feel with you."

I shake my head and smile to myself, looking off at the colorful sunset through the trees. It's hard to see in full until the forests become wide fields again, but it is beautiful, showing off vibrant reds, oranges, golden yellows, and traces of pink. "I like how I feel with you, too."

Sitting here, looking at the sky next to Cain Sidrelle of all people—

It feels unreal, but I'm almost at peace.

The city creeps back up on us before I know it, washing away the stretches of nature I was starting to like out there. Carriages pass by us on the opposite side of the street, carrying entertained voices from within, and I let myself study the few people walking past us as we go. All elves, casting quick glances in our direction before continuing on unbothered, likely heading back home or to their inn room for the night.

Listening to the horse's hooves echoing on the stone, I glance at Cain and sigh as the peace in me turns to a knowledge I wish I didn't have.

I know what I must do, and I hate it.

I have to go home.

17

—·—

RETURNING TO Whitestone makes the gravity of the situation cling to me, weighing heavy on my chest. Not knowing what the trip back to the manor is going to look like bothers me beyond words, but I force it from my mind for the moment so I can focus on Cain as we lay down together in his dorm. I don't want him to know that I'm thinking about going back. I *can't* let him know.

Cain moves so his head is resting on my hip, taking over my mind and driving me mad in a way that forces me to look up at the ceiling instead of him. A light tracing of fingertips crosses my opposite hip, warm on the exposed bit of skin from the way I stretched out. Those once-foreign desires become real all over again, blooming hot and violent in my chest, circling my sternum. I can barely breathe through the ever-so-gentle touches he keeps brushing over my skin.

He hums, pushing the edge of my turtleneck farther up my stomach. "So, these are all over your body?" He asks, and when I glance down, he's admiring the bone patterns printed on my skin.

His finger traces the edge of the pelvis marking, and a shiver races down my spine.

"Yes," I breathe, shuddering as Cain leans closer, almost touching his lips to the trail of hair leading below my slacks. Pure fire lances through me, pooling in my hips. "I'm the only one who got them that way."

"Interesting," he murmurs, his breath hot against my skin as he brings his face even closer to me. My hands tense as my heartbeat catches in my throat, struggling to even glance down again, because I know that what I would see there will take me out on the spot. Cain shifts so he's positioned more solidly between my legs, running his hand up my stomach and letting it settle on my chest, over my knocking heart. It tries to climb out of me and into his palm, reaching desperately, and he smiles as if he can tell.

"Can I see?" Cain asks, voice low and husky.

I nod, unable to stop myself from agreeing, my usual nerves nowhere to be found.

It must be the lingering alcohol.

At my nod, Cain's hand runs back down the length of my torso and pushes my shirt up further to see the entire ribcage marking over my chest, tracing it in intrigue before bringing his hands down to my pants again. Every touch feels like electricity going through my body—something so new but so familiar, something I haven't allowed myself in so long. I watch in a daze as Cain unbuttons my slacks and slips them down to my ankles, swallowing as hard as I can as he all but *devours* me with his eyes.

He meets my gaze, pupils in hungry slits. "Is this okay?"

I nod again, hating how I can't find any words to respond to him.

Fingertips drag searing paths down my thighs at my confirmation, following the tattoo-like marking of the femur, patella, tibia. As his hands come back up, his palms press fully to my thighs, dragging a gasp from my lips—one that makes Cain smile at me, all coy and sly as he hooks his fingertips under the edge of my boxers.

"This too?" he murmurs, voice somehow even lower.

My heart is racing, unable to take my eyes off of him, my hands knotted in the blankets to keep myself from floating away into space. Cain has a gravitational pull like no other, and I want to get lost in his atmosphere so *badly*.

"Yes," I whisper, like a hymn, like a prayer.

Cool air crosses my hips as Cain slips the boxers to my ankles as well, and being so exposed in front of him instantly makes my face burn up. It has been a long, *long* time since someone has seen me naked, and the realization is abrupt. Fear tries to crawl into my throat, but it's easily pushed aside as his hands traverse the insides of my thighs, forcing any thoughts out of my head.

"Wow," he murmurs, strangely awed.

Awed by me? Impossible.

I clench my jaw as his fingertips trail further over the pelvis marking, circling the edges of it. His red eyes have never looked so dark, flaming colors burning around his pupils as his eyes meet mine. The charged air between us grows heavier, and a moment later that charged gaze begins to roam my skin again. I can feel it like a physical presence, like his fingertips are following along even though they have not moved from my hips. His eyes carve through my chest, my ribs, my belly, before finally landing on the embarrassing erection sitting between us.

My lips part and still as I watch the peek of Cain's teeth sink into his lip, shuddering at the ideas immediately flooding my mind. "Cain," I croak, strangled by need. "Don't look at me like that."

I can barely get the words to come out, to get my voice to work at all. My mouth is drier than a desert, and his name is the only thing I can find to say, especially with his fingertips pressed into the space where my thighs start and what is aching between them begin.

"Like what?" he replies, husky and hungry, and it makes me spiral.

I need this. More than anything, I need this. Need him. The distraction he offers, the attention he lays upon me. I'm desperate for it in a way I cannot remember being for anything else. "Your fucking eyes, Cain, I can't."

"What is it, Dae?" Cain asks, reaching back to push my clothes to the floor, precariously settling himself down between my legs again, head on my hip once more. He looks comfortable, spread out on his stomach before me. My entire body shivers, but not from the coolness of the room. All because of Cain, Cain, *Cain.*

"I... I don't know," I say softly, laughing on a breath. "I need something, *anything.*"

Fingertips tracing circles on my hip again, but ever closer, making me tip my head back to get a sense of control. "Is there something you want?" Cain's voice is almost taunting, and I swear I'm going to break something if he keeps talking to me like that. His breath gets closer, hot against the base of my cock, the heat of it so close that I can't stand it.

It is *horrible* how much this man gets to me.

"Whatever you want to do, please do it. Take what you want from me." I hate how feverish the words come out, how *pleading,* and I'm unable to look down at him as Cain laughs—a low chuckle that spells out nothing but trouble. My entire body tenses as he readjusts again, suddenly followed by a heat I didn't know was possible.

The heat of Cain's tongue, running over me, making me so weak that I'm sure that if I would have fallen over instantly if I was standing. He teases me easily, sweeping up my length and around, drawing what is almost a whine from my mouth.

Cain smirks before taking me in fully, drawing me into his throat and keeping me there, swirling his tongue around the edges of veins, pulling me into his gravity. I push my hips up into him, asking for more, groaning when he starts bobbing his head slowly.

I can't help the sounds that he drags from me, clamping a hand over my mouth in an attempt to keep quiet. It's been so long that everything feels amplified—every sweep of his tongue electric as I push my hips up into his mouth for more, more, *more*.

All I want is Cain, all I want when I look down at him is to see how pretty he looks with his lips wrapped around me, how his eyelashes curl against his cheeks.

Cain looks up at me as he travels upward again, teasing my tip for a moment before removing his mouth entirely, stroking me instead. "What are you thinking, Dae?"

I whimper as he slows his hand down painfully, dragging it up and down. "I... you feel good, Cain."

"And what else?" He smiles as he leans over, licking along a vein and running his tongue all the way to my head again.

"You look beautiful on me," I reply through clenched teeth, and he chuckles, nodding his approval. "I want to feel what it's like to truly have you on me. Skin to skin. Nothing else."

He sucks me down into his throat again, working me apart with his tongue until I drop a hand to his head, clenching my fingers in his red curls. I hold him there, chasing the heels of my orgasm as it gets ever closer, whining when he moans around me and the vibration nearly does me in.

His tongue strokes over one particular spot that has me thrusting into his mouth eagerly, and I can't stop myself from shuddering as a tear weeps from his eye. It's so beautiful. *He's* so beautiful.

I don't have time to warn him before I'm crashing over the edge, spilling into his throat.

Cain keeps his mouth on me for a moment, swallowing, before he sits up and chuckles. "That was a lot, Dae."

My face is hot, I can tell. "I...I know. Sorry, I meant to warn you—"

He laughs, shaking his head. "Don't worry about it, I liked it."

Oh this man. He will drive me insane, I know it.

Sitting up, I grab him by his shirt and flip us around, pushing him backward where I was previously laying. I waste little time in stripping him of his slacks and boxers, petting down his pale thighs as he coasts a pretty hand down to his obvious erection, smiling at me all decadent.

I watch as his hand moves past it and lower, swallowing past the dryness in my throat. "What are you doing, Cain?"

"I thought you might like to watch," he answers, shifting to reach over to a drawer under his bedside table before turning back to me.

I stare as he coats his fingers in lubricant, following their descent until he presses them into himself, and I'm hard again before I know it. He smiles hungrily at me, tilting his head back and moaning when he curls them in just right.

My body *aches*. I want to be inside him; I want to touch him. It's almost impossible to sit here and simply *watch*, but I force myself to be patient. My eyes trace the angles of his hand down to the knuckles, the curl of his pale veins under his skin. I force myself to watch the thrust of his fingers, the arch of his wrist—until I physically can't take it anymore, leaning forward to stroke our lengths together in one hand, just as feverish as before.

His laugh entwines with a moan as he continues touching himself, looking up at me in a haze. "Can't keep your hands off me, can you?" he purrs, playful but equally as strangled as I sounded before.

I shake my head, grinding my hips into his. "No, I can't. I never will, if I have the choice."

He removes his hand and tilts his head at me, looking like some fiery devil come to make a ruin of me. "Then fuck me."

The order zips through me like a bolt of lightning, and I am sliding into him before I realize I've even moved. He's so warm, so tight, that the moan that punches out of me nearly cracks into another pitiful whine when I'm fully seated inside him. I have to stop and rest my forehead against his just to get my bearings, to get my lungs to remember how breathing works.

We sit there for a moment, adjusting to each other, before I start to set a pace—one that quickly slips out of hand, one that becomes faster and desperate and *starving* before I can stop it.

Cain claws at my back, calling my name in unholy cries that have me begging at the altar of him, worshipping every inch of pale skin. The pleasure of him is sinful, but I am more than glad to sin if it means I get to be the one thing that Cain Sidrelle moans to.

Cain's moaning of my name nearly becomes prayer by the third round.

I don't want to hear anybody else say it like that.

Hours later, with both of us dressed again, I lay back on the bed with Cain. He rests his head on my chest as he carefully takes my arm and lifts it to his lips, kissing across my sleeve-covered skin. So gentle, so *careful*. I'm shaking by the time he reaches the open expanse of the inside of my wrist.

I visibly shudder more than once, causing Cain to look up at me with a soft frown. "What is it, Dae?" He asks, his lips soft as they brush against me with his words.

A slight shrug as I look away from him. "I suppose my arms are sensitive, now," I reply, sighing.

"Why?" He frowns, sitting up on his elbow to see my face better. Like he's searching me, searching for unspoken answers that I can't give.

"Because I ruined them," I answer, almost too quietly, before sitting up and moving to the edge of the bed.

"Where are you going?" Cain asks.

The high of countless orgasms has started to wear off, bringing back what I need to do front and center. Clutching my arms over my chest, I stare at his bookshelf across the room and study the spines, desperate to find something to say that isn't going to sound pathetic. I know Cain is looking at me. I can feel his gaze as I always do, warm and heavy on my skin, like a favorite sweater. Perhaps that's why I know he is there even with how silently he moves, how I feel him before he touches my back, circling around my side to gingerly pull my hands apart.

"What's wrong?" he murmurs, a strange look in his eye. More than worry, but not quite panic. I can't place it.

I shake my head, closing my eyes so I don't get focused on figuring out his expression. "I really like what happened but... I don't know what I'm feeling right now. Not because of you, because of her."

Cain studies me from head to toe, but if he finds what he's looking for, I cannot tell, "Well, what do you feel?"

"Terrible. I *am* terrible, and so... angry."

"Dae, we could do *so* many things to make this city ours. To get rid of the people we hate, including her," Cain says slowly, watching me shake my head again. "And, I don't think you're terrible."

I smile faintly. "That's sweet of you." A moment of quiet, then I force myself to make up my mind. "Cain, I... I have to go home tonight. I don't want to feel like this anymore, or deal with it anymore."

"What?! Why? That's such a bad idea, Dae!" Cain exclaims, putting his hands on my shoulders and giving me a little shake, staring up at me.

I don't look back, but I know how wide his eyes are right now.

"I know it is. I need to get this over with, whatever it is. I can't keep running away from her," I murmur, my throat tightening the longer the sentence goes on—so I eventually close my mouth and swallow the words down. "I'm sorry."

He squeezes my shoulders a little tighter, shaking me again. "Dae. What if... what if she *kills* you?"

"I'm not going to allow that."

Is this what it feels like to have someone worry for you? For your safety? The thought makes me feel strange, but then again, everything with Cain does. All things I have never felt before, all things that are new and special.

And there is a very real chance I'm about to flush it all down the drain.

Instead of just sitting there, I tug Cain into me and pull him further onto the bed, allowing him to use my chest as a pillow.

Neither of us speak.

No one bothers us, no one comes knocking on the door.

And I'm grateful for that.

When I wake again, Cain is already up and pacing in the center of the room. Moonlight streams in through the window, lighting his form each time he passes it, casting him in slightly eerie, pale light. I watch him momentarily, studying the quick way he moves—four steps down, quick turn on the heel, four steps up, quick turn on the heel. He worries at his lower lip uncertainly, the anxiety on him palpable even from here.

I yawn, sitting up slowly. "Cain?"

His head snaps up in an instant, and he is in front of me as soon as I stand up, red eyes wide and wet with unfallen tears. "Dae, you don't *have* to do this, right?"

I tear my gaze from him and sigh, folding my arms over my chest. "Cain—"

"Dae, *please*. I have a bad feeling about this," Cain whispers, and his pleading breaks my heart.

"I'm sorry, I am. You'll never know how sorry I am, but I have to make this right again." I turn away from him, ripping open a black-edged portal into my room at the manor. The shadows weep from it, and from me, as I take a step forward, letting them lick at my skin, letting them pull me in only to pause as an unbidden thought slips into my mind.

I can't leave him.

As I'm about to step through, Cain catches me by the hand and kisses me like the whole world depends on it. Like everything is falling down around us—and Hells, maybe it is. So I kiss him back, the sound of the piano playing in my room surrounding us.

Desperation makes me cling to him, though my hands are gentle where they cup his face. He holds me just as desperately, the arms around my waist keeping me against him as close as he can.

I allow myself to feel every single thing in this moment, every single thing for *him*.

There is passion here, for every week, day, hour, minute, *second* that we haven't kissed. My heart pounds in my chest, my hands seeking purchase on Cain's hips and shoulders, unable to keep them still. He is a magnet and I'm a stray piece of metal, floating through the sky.

A tear runs down my cheek, before I quickly wipe it away.

But then he is gone. Or rather—I am gone, a hand grabbing at the back of my shirt and yanking me through the open portal before I've a chance to even utter his name.

She need not say anything for me to know it's Morgana. I would know her anger anywhere. I can taste it in the magic writhing around us, feel it in the familiar way she drags me out of my bedroom and down the hall to the training room.

It's horribly empty again, with no sign of Silas anywhere. I still don't know what happened to him, but I am wise enough to know that Morgana would never tell me if I asked, and that I would not like the answer if she did.

For a long moment I think the house is empty, the only sound in the silence being the thundering beat of my heart. Then the distant sound of Darrien and Mikhalis talking to Bren rings out from the floor below, their laughter echoing up the stairs as she shuts the door behind us.

So, this is how it's going to happen.

Unknown to everyone else.

I snap my rapier into my hand as Morgana charges at me, barely giving me any time to move out of her way. The sound of our blades crashing together echoes around the room, feeling louder than the sole sound of my heartbeat pounding away in my ears. She swings again, catching my upper arm with the tip of her blade, and I just manage to catch her side even though I nearly drop my weapon from the sharp sting of the wound.

This fight is beyond different.

Morgana casts a gravity spell somewhere behind me, dragging me backward with a thunderous rumble as I lose my footing and slip into it. The wall I crash into makes my head spin momentarily before I regain my composure—extending a hand to will an explosive spell into it, before quickly deciding against the idea so I don't burn the manor down with us. Magic burns in my palm as it fizzles out, thankfully simmering in my veins, lying in wait instead of firing off anyway.

The sharp twang of my blade hitting the ground snaps me out of her fog just as she charges forward, and I have only a single breath to jolt out of her reach, her blade mere inches away from my throat.

It then hits me what's happening, and why this fight feels wrong. Morgana has never been a kind trainer, and not once has she ever gone easy on me, but still, this is different. Because now...

She's trying to kill me.

Out of pure instinct, I forgo my rapier entirely and reach a hand toward the ceiling—calling from the depths of my magic to summon a glowing, inky sword composed of what could only be described as a glimpse into space, and I inhale deeply as it trembles through my hand like an earthquake.

My veins blacken with the magic, nearly hidden under a veil of shadows as they wreath around me, surging up into the form of my almost-forbidden weapon. The obsidian hilt fits neatly in my palm, ice cold and shimmering with stars, swirling around my fingers to protect me from impact.

I curse under my breath as I bring it down to block her charge with it, exhaling thinly as her own blade begins to crumble, making her rip it away before it can shatter entirely. Steel pieces clatter to the floor as they break from the force of my weapon, and I catch a glimpse of them reflecting the light before purple energy begins to form in her hand.

Another spell is shot at me, though this time I manage to push through and overcome the vise-like grip of it, stalking toward her.

There is a strange look in her eyes I have never seen before—not fear, but something almost like it, something shocked and unsettled.

Good, I cannot help but think, something predatory grinning within me, baring its teeth. I'm not going to be her prey any longer.

"You shouldn't be strong enough to use that blade!" Morgana hisses, her mismatched eyes narrowed and her fingers tightening around her own weapon.

I can't help but laugh as I swing it forward, pointing it at her and peering down the length of the swirling galaxies within. Her face warps from the energy of the blade, twisting and writhing through the space of it.

I shake my head at her, watching her sword closely. "You always underestimated me."

She swings in a perfect arc the moment I finish speaking, slicing into my side and opening herself up to get a deep gash across her chest. It still isn't enough to take her down, and it angers me that it isn't. In my frustration, she leaps again and carves a hand through the air—creating a blinding white circle air, electric bolts of light tearing free and shooting in my direction.

I catch two of them in my sword, hit home in my stomach, hip, and thigh—forcing me down onto one knee with a pained grunt. I swear and spit out a bit of blood as Morgana laughs. The sound echoes too loud in the otherwise empty room, before it cracks and breaks as I extend my hand and reach for her with my magic. My fingers curl into a cruel fist as her skin turns pitch black from her hands to her shoulders, her veins like dark snakes just below the surface. The spell surges from my sternum and sinks into her like fangs, spewing darkened venom into the very matter of her body.

She staggers backward, coughing, as I rise to my feet and crack my neck, but still she does not give in.

We meet in the middle once more, blade to blade, hers beginning to crack even further with the pressure. One of her hands wrenches away from the hilt of her sword to physically shove at me, and I don't manage to stop her in time as she casts a necromantic spell that I recognize instantly.

One that could reduce someone to nothing but ashes.

The feeling of it coursing through me instantly sends stars dancing through my vision, something akin to a fist clamping around my heart making my hand grasp for any sort of purchase on my chest. It tears a gasp from me as I stumble into one of the pillars in the room, trying to get past it and bring myself together again.

If only I had a moment to use that spell on her in return, but I know I'll never get that chance.

She'll never let me.

As we meet again, Cain crosses my mind—his warmth, his smile, the way the lights reflect in the rubies of his eyes. The laugh he lets out when it is only the two of us. How carefully he touched me earlier today, and how he didn't look at me judgingly when I was naked in front of him. His magic, his violent fire.

I can't lose. I can't lose. I can't lose.

Morgana has enough time to stab me again, a time or two, through me responding to the spell. My strength is starting to wane the longer I fight her, and with one blocked swing of her blade, she forces me down onto my knee again. Though it's becoming increasingly difficult to stop her swings, I manage to push my sword up against hers and smile as it explodes—scattering pieces across the floor, crashing in between us.

This has to be my chance, I can see the end of this fight slowly dawning on me—

Morgana calls forth a shadowed version of her sword and stabs down at me, becoming unhinged in the motions. Her face is horridly emotionless, brutally cold as she jabs the wreathing darkness toward either side of my body. She kicks me onto my back with the toe of her heeled boot, and I have to do everything I can to keep her from actually stabbing me again, twisting back and forth with every plunge and point.

She swings upward in a wide arc, opening herself up to me, and my world slows down.

My chance. My *only* chance.

I thrust the sword upward, closing my eyes as I do until a splatter of hot blood hits my hands, chest, and face. A dull yet blazing pain radiates from my stomach in the same moment, blooming in its violence, mixing her cold and vast darkness with my own.

When I open them again, my blade protrudes through her chest, and there is no glow to her eyes anymore.

The shadow blade she held, embedded to the hilt in my stomach, vanishes—her eyes no longer bright—and my blood-soaked hands shake tremendously.

I cast away my blade and maneuver her body onto the floor beside me, carefully sitting up on my knees as the taste of metallic iron races over my tongue. A once welcome flavor, but not now. My hand presses over the shadowed wound in my stomach as I sit up on my knees, staring down at her, trying to see if there is any hint of breath left—and there is, barely. Blood runs from her dark lips, and as I reach out, to do what I'm not sure, Morgana weakly wraps her hands around my throat and tightens her grip.

A gasp leaves me, and I instinctively do the same to her, tighter, tighter, tighter still, until her throat caves and breaks under my fingertips.

She stops breathing, and I stare again.

My hands are covered in her blood, and I don't know what to do about it. The only thing I can hear is my heartbeat pounding away, adrenaline cooling in my veins as I study her empty, dead face. Not a moment later, my body seemingly catches up—starting to shake so badly I can barely move.

The fact that she is truly dead really dawns on me all at once. Sure, this is what I wanted, but actually doing it is something different entirely.

What the fuck have I done?

My stomach turns as I press my hand into it more, hating the slickness of my own blood on my palm mixing with hers. "*Fuck,* what do I do, what do I do, what do I do?" I mutter, panic rising up like an ocean wave, cresting higher in my chest. "What in the world do I *do*?"

The vague sounds of footsteps on the floor ring out from behind me, followed by a gasp that echoes in the silence.

I can't tear my eyes away, not even as I recognize the warm vanilla scent of Darrien's cologne when he moves closer, letting out a shout that sounds muffled to my ears—likely calling for Mikhalis. His hands fall on my shoulders, turning me away from my mother's ghoulish face and making me look at him.

Even as he makes me stand and move away from it, I can't stop looking.

"Daedalus, hey, look at me, look at me," Darrien's voice breaks through to me clear as day, like the sun in the clouds. "You're okay, you're okay."

I shake my head, almost frantic, and he cups my face in his hands.

I never even realized I started crying until the moment his skin makes contact with the hot trails on my cheeks.

He gingerly takes my hands, leading me further from the body and outside into the hall, never letting go. Mikhalis always said he was gentle, but I never fully believed it until now. "Let's go get you cleaned up, alright? Everything will be fine."

The moment we step into the bathroom, Darrien makes quick work of cleaning my hands, my face, even my glasses. No matter how clean my hands get, all I see are the stains of blood marking them—my palms, my fingers, constantly covered. I can't speak or do so much as *think*, even as Darrien removes my turtleneck and begins to heal my wounds, his magic like a warm ray of sunlight over the void in me.

I wonder if the Macabre family is destined to destroy itself from the inside out. Are we all made into weapons, created for magic, created for tests? Are we all just experiments, made to be broken? I imagine my mother killing her mother, standing over her. I wonder if she stared the same way I did, if she cared. Did she enjoy the blood? Did she enjoy how her magic was used to do it? Was I made solely for this?

What else could I have done?

A sharp, near frantic set of knocks echoes from downstairs, jolting me out of my thoughts, causing both of us to look toward the door as the sound of the main doors creaking open follows. Then, a pair of hurrying footsteps echoing up the stairwell, almost at a sprint.

The door opens quickly, revealing a wild-eyed Cain on the other side.

"Dae, oh *god,* you're okay," Cain whispers as he rushes over, over to where Darrien sat me down on the edge of the tub, perching next to me like he belongs there.

Am I okay? None of me can truly feel anything, and the fact of what happened is becoming even harder to believe.

My eyes stay on my hands, on the floor, anything but the faces around me.

"What happened?" Cain asks, more to Darrien.

"He—"

"I killed her," I say, quiet, cutting him off.

Cain's hand goes to his mouth, more in thought than in shock, looking between us. "We can't let anyone find out about this," he says, eyes glancing toward the hall at the sound of a door opening and closing in quick succession.

I close my eyes, my body shuddering as I let out a deep sigh. "They'll find out no matter what, Cain. Even *if* we try to hide it, they'll know."

I hadn't exactly thought of what could happen to me until now. They executed people for this type of thing in this city, unless whoever it was had the power to escape it. And that was the exact thing they'd be sure I *didn't* have.

What if it happened? What if they did kill me?

Why are there so many 'what if's' in my life?

A sob breaks free from my chest, unable to hold it back any longer, the first of many yet to come. Have I always been doomed?

Was there nothing, or nobody, that could have helped me somewhere along the way? Cain tried, sure. So did Darrien. And yet, here I am.

Doomed to die. Doomed to fulfill an unexpected prophecy of the Macabre lineage's failure.

Cain's fingers comb through my hair in an attempt to calm me, gently petting. "I'll stay here with you, we don't have to go anywhere, we can ... stay, okay?" he says, and somehow, I feel like he's more telling himself than me.

Everything is going to hell so fast. Morgana is dead, and it should've been easier for me. *Why isn't it ever easier?*

Cain leans his head on my shoulder and continues petting through my hair, moving his hand down to rub my back after a moment. No one says a word until I stop crying, sitting upright with tears still streaming down my face. I'm horribly empty, like a yawning void cracked open its jaws inside of me, swallowing any emotion I might've had as it did.

I can't even close my eyes, because all I see is her.

Bren and Mikhalis come to the door, and I can't bring myself to look at either of them. My father is likely grateful that one of us had finally done it, but now we all know consequences are going to catch up to us. We all know there's no hiding, no running, no proving it to anyone. They want someone to make an example out of. They don't want people to know they can simply kill the powerful people, and still continue on.

There's simply horrifying acceptance.

I don't want to accept this.

It is terrifying to think that I could easily be executed tomorrow.

They could have me arrested in no time.

Bren isn't looking at me, isn't looking at *anyone*, but I know it's because it's probably hard to right now. Nobody knows what to say, or do, in this situation.

It isn't until Cain stands up and takes my hand, squeezing it in attempt to focus my gaze on him, that the silence is broken. "You should lay down, Dae," he states, tugging me to my feet.

I nod numbly, allowing him to lead me from the room.

With Cain's hand in mine, we walk to my room in the trembling, apprehensive quiet of the manor. Unable to focus, or think, I make it to my bed and lay down, staring at the ceiling. Cain's head gently falls on my shoulder, his red eyes focusing on the window on the opposite side of the room, one hand tracing small circles over my stomach.

"What do you think is going to happen to me?" I whisper, and the tracing pauses for a moment.

"I don't know, Dae. But," Cain sits up, looking over at me, "I do know I will fight tooth and nail if anything does."

I don't know what I feel from that, but it causes a little twinge in my chest. Something breaks through the emptiness in my gut, and I realize, beyond the numbness coating me, I'm *afraid*. I'm terrified of what is to come, if *anything* is to come. At the very least, I know there will be no rest tonight, not even a shred. I'll be sitting here studying my ceiling for hours and hours, counting the seconds as they pass.

How could I even think of doing anything but laying here with Cain, or crying, or screaming?

"We'll be okay, okay?" Cain murmurs, closing his eyes tightly before looking back to me.

I shake my head, exhaling shakily. "How can you be so sure?"

He shrugs, a soft but long sigh leaving him. We fall into silence again, the only sound filling the air being the quiet piano playing nearby. Neither of us move, except for Cain's hand petting small circles now on my chest, trying to keep me calm.

As the piano changes songs for the fourth time, I rise from my bed and move to look out of my window, watching what I can see of the streets below for any sign of the city guards. It seems quiet out there at this hour—the streetlamps beginning to turn on, people disappearing into shops or other buildings across the way. Barely anything moves, though I know it's likely due to the oncoming cold of winter. The nights have grown chillier; the pretty colors of autumn have drifted away into browns and yellows and crunching leaves underfoot.

Winter, with its threat of snowfall, looms over the city with heavy clouds and biting cold breezes.

Barely anyone in this city likes being out in the cold.

Cain joins me at my side, one hand on my lower back, looking off at the city beyond. "Winter's almost here, yeah?" he says, almost to himself.

I nod, swallowing the lump in my throat. "It is."

"Maybe it would be a good day for hot chocolate tomorrow, or coffee, and we can walk around the city. Just us, in warm coats with comfy drinks." He smiles, but I can't bring myself to return it.

"That sounds nice," I whisper, and tears run down my cheeks again. I can almost imagine it, walking the streets with a steaming paper cup in hand, at his side.

Maybe we'd laugh over the way our breath ghosts in front of our faces, or we'd kick through piles of browned leaves as we stepped into shops. I almost let myself believe that it'll happen.

Almost.

His touch is comforting, something solid to lean against—and Gods do I need something to hold me up right now, because I don't think I can do it myself anymore. Everything is so still; even the night itself is still. Barely a breeze runs through the trees, almost as if the world knows what I did and can't stop holding its breath.

It is almost eerie.

And then, Mikhalis calls for me, as well as Darrien, and my blood turns cold.

Another call, a moment later.

"Fuck, Daedalus, that—that sounds important," Cain whispers, and I nod slowly as I swallow down the returning threat of tears ready to fall once more.

I turn and kiss Cain with all the feeling I can muster, before I walk to my door and step out into the hallway.

The voices ring clearly up the stairs.

Guards.

My heart drops into the floor and I almost wish I could join it, curled up under the marble. I move on autopilot as I carefully walk down the stairs, wishing I could have had more time to be with Cain, to be with my family—but that isn't an option anymore. Someone had let them know Morgana is dead, someone inside the house. Fear and shock spiral into me at once, an icy knife stabbing into my sternum.

I knew it was coming, but I didn't know it would be like this. I didn't *think* they would get here so fast.

And now that they are, I'm terrified.

The guards aren't telling Mikhalis who exposed us as I walk in front of them, icy breeze drifting in through the door, my eyes falling on their stark silver armor. My mind whirls, warped with confusion and anger as I stare at their helmeted faces. Immediately, I wheel around to face my shell-shocked family, our handful of servants behind them.

"Which one of you told them? Which one of you?" I shout, voice cracking with desperation and fury. Darrien and Mikhalis both shake their heads, attempting to extend their hands out to me, causing me to recoil and curl in on myself. My arms wrap around my chest protectively, barely keeping me together.

"One of you *had* to tell them." I direct my snarl in the direction of the servants, wishing one of them would just say *yes* so I could have someone to point my fear at.

Shriek shakes her head at me, but I know better than to accuse her. She'd never do this to me, but the others *would*. So many of them were so close to my mother that it was disgusting. I glower at them as they shrink back, my magic threatening to pool in my hands and break free from me, wanting to explode.

I consider the idea—throwing something down at my feet, blowing up everything in the vicinity, sending the Macabre family to be written about in papers about its 'tragic downfall'. There would be nothing left but remnants of the manor and the guards' armor.

They would write about me, and it would always be depressing.

I can't bring myself to do it, crumbling like an old brick wall and dropping to my knees, no longer able to hold myself up. The head guard—a blonde, elven man with fair skin and green eyes—sets his steel helmet back on and moves to me, grabbing me by the wrists. I don't hear what he's saying, but I'm sure it's along the lines of "You're being arrested for the murder of Morgana Macabre," with something about rights that I supposedly have.

In my desperation, I attempt to plead that it was only self-defense, this isn't right, but none of them are listening. Words fly from my lips in a panicked struggle to get them to hear me, but they just pull me to my feet without any hesitation.

The cuffs they place on my wrists glow the instant they touch me, clicking shut as the head guard turns me toward the door. I attempt to cast something, *anything,* and the metal sears across my skin. No escape. No chance to message anyone, no chance to blow this entire group to pieces out of my own desperation.

Cain snarls threats at them, but the group doesn't pay too much mind as they shove me through the door and onto the street. Even if they respected him, they all have to do this. They have to arrest me, no matter their feelings about the Sidrelles.

They have to take me away, to put me somewhere no one will find me.

I barely notice the people staring as we walk by, allowing myself to be pushed along the long cobblestone streets, hating the cold as it sinks deep into my bones. Fear at what is to come worms further into me, playing tag with the overbearing sadness that has been drowning me since it happened.

The jailhouse isn't very close to my home, so it takes us a while to actually arrive, but when we do, I look up and study the stone building, breathing out icy steam. The gray-brick walls are lined with small windows, which are mostly open squares with bars to keep anyone from getting the wrong idea. My anxiety rises with every step, filling me with a dread so foreign yet so familiar, I can barely make myself move.

Inside, it has a decently sized pocket to the right for the guards, and past that, walls of cells. Some empty, some not. Those who stand inside some of them clamor against their bars, watching the group pass by, a few even asking who the 'new guy' is. The head guard pushes me into what must be my cell—a surprisingly clean room with a mattress that isn't much of anything, no lights, and one slit of a window on the back wall. Nothing kind, nothing sweet.

Sinking into the farthest corner from the bars leading out into the hall, I drop to the floor and turn my head into the cold stone, giving up.

What else is there to do? No one will save me.

Across from me, a golden scaled, bipedal draconic man makes his way up to the bars and leans on them, watching me. "Hey kid," he says, voice gruff and low. "You'll be alright."

I look over at him, shaking my head before staring at the floor. The man sighs, shaking his head in return. His glittering body is covered by a brown, battered tunic and pants that match, nothing fancy, except for the torn royal purple cloak hanging from his shoulders. I can easily picture him in armor, and it makes me wonder why he isn't wearing any already.

"What are ya even here for?" he asks, huffing out a thin cloud of smoke through his nostrils.

I sigh, closing my eyes. "I killed my mother."

The dragon lets out a surprised laugh, watching me. "Ah, shit. Well... I'm not sure what they'll do to ya. What's your name, kid?"

"Daedalus."

"Calus. Nice to meet ya, Daedalus," the dragon answers, and I shrug.

The corner seems to be the safest place for me, not even the rickety mattress that will likely be uncomfortable. I hate the lingering scent of rose on my clothes, wishing it wasn't there and my heart wasn't shattering like glass at the slightest smell of it. Loneliness clogs my mind, replaying the images of what Cain and I could be doing today over and over—drinking hot chocolate or hot coffees, holding hands to keep our fingers warm, breaking out our heavier coats for the oncoming winter for the first time. Laughing, maybe sharing a kiss or two, if I was so lucky.

I open my eyes again in hopes that maybe this is all just a bad dream—that somehow, I'm in bed and not on the floor of a bitter-cold cell. My hands pinch my upper arms in a desperate search for proof that this is just a horrible nightmare, but all I come up with is a sharp pain on my skin and nothing more.

Oh, how I ache for the man the rose perfume belongs to, wishing he was here to comfort me.

But he isn't, and no one else is going to be, besides my memories.

18

NOTHING CHANGES for a day or two, aside from allowing myself to open up to Calus more, until the guards finally come for me.

People on the streets walk alongside the group of armored men, me being pushed along in the center, shouting in anger, shouting at *me*. Everyone in the city knows what is happening, and I hate that I know most of the citizens will be there to watch it.

It stings that no one will help me out of this. No one will understand why I had to kill her, no one will know because I had to keep it hidden. Morgana Macabre hid me and what she did to me, and no one *saw*. No one *knew*. No one *bothered*.

The day is bitter cold, the first snow beginning to fall as I pass the already forming crowd, whose yells and angered cries go unheard under the deafening muffle overtaking my hearing. Everything sounds drowned out, completely underwater, as I'm walked onto that wooden stage.

My eyes find Calus and the others I never met in the back of the crowd, still handcuffed and watched by guards—but there to see me as an *example.* We have grown only slightly closer in the two days I'd been left to crumble in the jailhouse—having interesting conversations about what landed the draconic man there, my life and what my mother was like, why I killed her. We talked about love and our matching lack of it; I told him about Cain; we talked about anything that could possibly happen in the coming days.

There *has* to be something after this. I'm not done yet.

So much left to do, to see, to *say.*

I can't be done yet. This can't be my end, right?

There's a brief moment, as I look around, where I'm sure I see Irsa in the crowd, and it ignites fury in the empty sea of my gut. If it truly *was* him, likely smirking as he thought he won over me, I know I'll find him. One day, I'll come back for him no matter how long it takes, and that is a damn promise.

My heart stutters when my gaze lands on someone else, my flame, my heart in a person's body—

Cain, pushing to the front of the crowd as the guards around me start to give their speech.

Cain, shouting angrily, threatening, doing anything he can until the guards have to physically restrain him. He thrashes against them, struggling against their grip and snarling when they don't immediately let him go.

Cain, looking back to his father, Minos, in a moment of desperation, and Minos shaking his head as if he too, were disappointed by the outcome of it all.

I try casting a spell, a simple message to tell Cain I'll be alright, but the handcuffs burn on my wrists and stop it short. The magic withers before it can ever escape, and that is when I realize there is truly no hope, not like I shouldn't have known. So, instead of watching him, I tip my head back and stare up at the snowflakes falling—feeling them melting on my cheeks, watching them leave behind little drops of water on my glasses.

Cain screams at me to do *something, anything*, but I can't. There isn't a damn thing I can do, and I'm truly coming to terms with it. I've never felt so useless before.

For a moment, I close my eyes, thinking over all that I'd gone through for the sake of the woman that is getting me killed anyway. Thinking of Morgana, carving me like marble into who I am now, feeding me the Rot—who is overjoyed to know what this is going to feel like. The woman who had taken away so much of my memory, altering me to the point it made me kill her.

Mikhalis, who had his magic broken by her, to the point he couldn't help me, despite wanting to so badly.

Darrien, who helped take care of me, who seemed closer to my father than Morgana herself. He is here too; I can feel him somewhere in the crowd.

Bren, my mischievous sibling who had become a fiend for partying quickly after meeting Cain's friends. The one who didn't have to be watched, guarded, kept away from people. The one I kept at arm's length because I knew she just wanted to test me with him.

Asher, the one person besides Cain who actually befriended me. My gaze finds him in the crowd, dressed in his usual black, purple magic warping around the hand he has resting over his mouth. I know he's probably trying to think of a way out of this. I know his mind is probably whirling, calculating all the different ways this could go, and mostly coming to one outcome.

I shake my head when our eyes meet, before looking away.

Back to Cain, drawn to him always.

I can feel my heart breaking in my chest at the disheveled sight of him. His hair is a mane of wild curls around his face, down his back, his shirt unbuttoned halfway. There is pure chaos boiling in his eyes, sparks spitting from his lips as he snarls at the guards holding him.

Cain, the first person I ever wanted, the first thing I felt I could hold onto without fear. The first person to truly acknowledge me, to not be afraid of what I am.

The first person to care about what was happening to me, the first to kiss me in so many years, the first to dance beside me and show everyone what it was like to be a match doomed to fall apart on the first try.

Cain and his cries that fell to the wind, a desperate plea better left unheard.

Tears burn in my eyes, so I force my gaze to the sky above again. It is almost peaceful, if I focus on the snowflakes instead of what is actually happening—if I just focus on the sounds of the flakes falling and sticking to my clothes and the dirt, instead of the sounds of the guards swearing as they struggle to keep their grip on Cain. They can't hold him *and* the prisoners behind him, I know that all too well.

Still, they are certainly doing a damn good job of it, despite knowing that whatever happens here means Cain will never be silent over this. He'll riot.

Or, he'll forget you entirely.

The rope is dropped, and despite knowing this isn't an issue with breathing, it will likely still snap my neck. And I'm just *accepting* that, waiting for it to come because there isn't anything else, and I can't fight them like I want to.

If the cuffs weren't holding me back, I would've been casting all sorts of spells to get out of this.

This really can't be it. I can't end this here. I need to tell Cain everything. I need him to know. How will he know what I felt? How will he know I can't stop this myself? How will he know *anything*?

I sigh, feeling my shirt growing damp from the snowfall. It is beginning to stick more, not that I have to worry. The cold of the air bites at my hands, cheeks, and ears—giving me something to focus on other than the rope's rough edges now touching my skin.

I wish I had more time.

One last look to Cain, who is only staring at me with tears streaming from those ruby red eyes.

"I'll come back for you. I really did love you," I mouth, and Cain screams.

The last thing I see of him is flames bursting from his lips, covering the guards and the ground around him.

I take one final look around at every face that shouts in support of my coming death, at every man standing at my sides. Then, back up to the sky, willing the snowflakes to fall a little harder, so Cain doesn't have to see what comes next.

As the first snow falls in the city of Nemoure, Daedalus Macabre is executed for killing his mother, and everything changes.

Part

TWO

19

—·—

FOR A moment, I'm floating over my physical form. Conscious, but not enough that I can do anything.

I'm staring at myself, watching the color flood back into my skin, eyeing the thickening grays in my hair. *Look at me against the red velvet, look at my skeleton marked skin.*

Darkness encroaches on my vision as I attempt to take one last look around me, but I can't. I'm stuck staring at this meaningless thing six feet in the ground—and there is something horridly claustrophobic about it that I try not to focus on as thick shadows begin to writhe around me. It's sudden, like gravity had been turned on, before I plunge into the darkness below.

A gasp rips out of me, and my eyes fly open.

I'm alive.

Daedalus Macabre, me, laying in a grave, alive again.

I fight to remember something, *anything*, and the memory of magic strikes me first like a bolt of lightning. It vibrates in my veins as my eyes dart around at the red velvet, the lid above keeping me in complete darkness. With the littlest amount of space I have to move, I call that blade from the void again, watching the stars within its inky depths twinkle in warm welcome before I thrust it through the top of the casket, and into the earth itself.

I cough on dirt as I rip the soil away from me, forcing myself up, breaking from the hole in the ground. My hands clawing at the earth, fighting for a grip; dragging my body from what had once entombed it, willing my blade away the moment I feel fresh air and the soft grass around my grave.

The desperation to be free calms, only once I'm above the edge of the hole, somewhat blinded by sunlight.

I shudder as the feeling of being alive again rolls through my body, brushing the dirt from my clothes and carefully lifting my legs from the dirt, slowly standing. It's aching—but at the same time, it's new and fresh and enticing. My body is odd, all long limbs and pointed bones, and it hurts, every muscle slowly unwinding from themselves.

I'm perfectly empty, in this strange, dusty place between a cruel life and a crueler death.

A long stretch comes next, every bone in me cracking as I reach toward the sky, reveling in the sensation of it. Smiling the littlest bit, I peer up at the open blue expanse above before crouching down to push the cool dirt back over my grave, eyeing the head-stone. *My* headstone. *Ugh.* A fancy statue of a weeping angel leans over it, along with my name, dates, and a quote about me being a beloved son.

As fast as I look it over, a flood of memories pours into my head, causing me to reel back from the headstone and stagger away, hands pressed against my temples.

Memories of people, of angered voices, the distant snap of a rope. Flames roaring into life.

A family I don't know, faces flashing by.

The memories slow their assault on my mind as I gingerly kneel in front of the grave again, letting my skeleton-marked hand rest over it for a long minute before standing and looking to the grave beside it. A pair of them, the second less fancy than my own, sitting in a secluded space in a grove of trees spaced out well from the rest of what must be a full cemetery.

From this distance, I catch glimpses of dozens of headstones crisscrossing the grass outside the grove I currently stand in, all different shapes and sizes. Statues of angels, crosses, some even decorated with flowers, larger mausoleums.

Did anyone bring me flowers?

Shaking my head, I drop my gaze to the second grave. It has a much simpler headstone—a standard stone cross—standing at half the height of mine, engraved with the words:

"MORGANA MACABRE

MOTHER, WIFE, ARCHMAGE"

Another rush of memories, snapping back into me hard enough that I physically recoil once again. Flashes of hands on my head, blood on my hands, the sound of blades crashing together.

I grip my head in my hands for a moment, attempting to shake it off, but the images of the blood linger longer than they should. My hands are slick with it again, coating my fingers and palms, dripping down my wrists. I'm stuck in a tile room and the walls are closing in and all I taste is iron and dust—

I force my eyes open with a gasp, staring at my dirt-marked hands and breathing a new sigh of relief.

A shudder passes through me as I start leaving the cemetery, crossing the yellow-green grass to a worn wrought-iron gate that complains as if it is rarely opened. As I walk along the dirt path leading up to it, I drink in the landscape around me—freshly green trees, singing birds, flowers starting to bud on bushes, it has to be spring. The air is still cool, which I breathe in with a new appreciation, even as I remember I don't need to and sigh it back out.

Everything feels so strange. I still feel like myself, but I can tell I definitely changed, and it is probably the type of change I can never take back.

I feel like a phoenix rising from the ashes of my old self, new and waiting to be made into whatever I want.

This phoenix can be whatever *I* want it to be—not the one created by the ghost of a memory, by someone I once called mother, parent, *killer.*

The recall of my name and the glint of pink eyes, the whispers in a woman's voice telling me to never let the people who turned on me feel free. That someday, I may be as she hoped. I would be a threat to anyone who opposed me, same as she. She tells me to be a weapon, to use the magic I had spent so long on for *worse.*

I don't want to be her.

My hands shake as I walk along the carriage and horse-worn path for a while, admiring the unchanging green and yellow landscape, until a pond partially covered in pale green lily pads comes into view on my left. A lone doe scrambles away from me on the opposite side, and I don't really blame her for it. If I saw someone fresh from the grave, I'd likely run too.

I smooth my palms down my dusty black slacks and lean over the water, peering at myself in the clear, sunlit ripples. My eyes are a soft gold, my hair dark but grayer than that one streak I vaguely remember having, my skin somehow still a warm tan. I'm wearing a black tailcoat over a velvet turtleneck, black pinstriped pants, and knee-high boots—and the thought that I had been buried in this, somehow *living* in this outfit for however long, hurts my head.

My heart beats once, unsteady, and it startles me.

Closing my eyes, I dip my fingers into the water to remember how it feels, startling for the second time at the bitter cold of it. My hand jerks back reflexively, and I laugh a little at myself, taking one last look at my wavering reflection before continuing on my way. Of course, I have little idea as to where I'm headed—all I know is that I need to get away from the cemetery, because it didn't feel right unless I was lying in a grave that no longer belongs to me.

After what could have been hours of traveling, I spot the edges of a shoddy town, seeming run-down closest to me, but nicer the farther it stretches. I walk closer, warily keeping my eyes out for signs of other life, and it immediately feels like a place I wouldn't ever want to live in. Windows on the buildings are cracked or hidden by wooden boards, bricks break off from their formations in chunks, vines threaten to swallow walls and doorways. Nothing about it smells wonderful either, tainted by what I assume are rotting flowers, something sickly sweet clinging to every breath.

The buildings coming into view are mostly constructed from wood and stone, but the materials aren't the quality I once knew—the structures themselves short and stocky, rough and uneven, nothing compared to what little I can recall of Nemoure's skyscrapers. Those were tall, so many of them similar or the same in height, all covered in bright lights and glossy windows. This place feels almost like it's trying to stay hidden behind the forest beyond it, as if the buildings are stuck in a permanent crouch. There's nothing to show off here, nothing to be proud of.

The brief memory of Nemoure and its glittering buildings makes me slow my steps and glance around in mute wonder. That place betrayed me, I know inwardly, and yet—why can't I remember it well enough if it did? Why can't I recall any of the people? I shake my head, gaze wandering to a small cemetery across the road, my breath sucking in sharp. My body instinctively starts to shiver as I watch a small group of people in dark clothing begin to heave dirt over an open hole in front of them, very quickly feeling sick to my stomach.

Who buried me? Who had to pack me into the dirt?

A rumbling voice answers in my head. *Your own family, Daedalus.*

"What?" I whisper aloud, surprised at the sound of it.

I swear it chuckles, before it speaks again. *Your family buried you, Daedalus. And someone else.*

"What—who are you?" I look around, searching for anyone who might be looking back in my direction, but no one is even paying me any mind. I'm not sure anyone has even noticed I'm standing here, lost and confused.

Your Rot.

Hugging my arms around myself, I shake my head and continue to walk. My Rot. The words stick in me like barbs, uncertain and prodding, turning up the stones of my mind to show me what the Rot is. A taste of ash fills my mouth, a remembered ball of shadow tumbling down my throat. I glance down at my left hand, watching the skeletal markings writhe with the swirling darkness of it and grimacing when I realize what it is.

The symbiote didn't die with me, then. How unfortunate...but, *why?*

People shuffle about around me, keeping to themselves with their hands tightly in their pockets or in bags they hold close to their bodies. That intrigues me too, giving me something else to focus on and washing away the sick feeling in my gut with curiosity. Everyone in Nemoure, from what I can remember, walked around without a care for themselves or their things, because they never had to worry about danger a day in their life, but these people are different. Something here scares them enough to hurry past alleyways, to hug their belongings.

Patting myself down, I find that I don't have to worry like they do, because I don't have any belongings anywhere on me.

I lift my hands in front of my face, turning them over and back again. There is still a hint of dirt on the edges of my sleeves that I keep desperately trying to ignore, so I can act like I *didn't* come straight out of the ground not that long ago. Everything is still so new, though, and I find myself staring at my hands for a long while, trailing over the dark veins under the skin of my wrist and snaking across the backs of my fingers.

My single heartbeat startles me again, and I drop my hands to my chest just to feel it thump beneath them.

A woman eyes me as she slips into a darkened alley, disappearing from sight. The people can probably tell I don't belong here, not *anywhere* around here, and it makes the itch to leave skitter over my bones. Oddly threatening, even if none of them will fully look me in the eye.

I tuck my hands in the pockets of my pants and hum as I walk, eyeing the broken shapes in the buildings around me. Mostly square windows, slightly rectangular bricks and stone slabs. Rectangular paper posters haphazardly tacked to wooden fence posts or boards. It's all rectangles, how odd. Ninety-degree angles, for the most part.

The soft sound of a cello crying through the air from an open window gives me a reason to pay attention again, looking up at a second-story room looming above me. I try to imagine who might be playing—perhaps a woman or a young man or someone in between, dressed in white and black clothing, maybe with ginger hair. Maybe they have makeup on, and they're staring at music on a page, or their eyes are closed entirely. Their body sways like the breeze with every pull of the bow, and I *feel* the ache of it within me.

An ache of remembrance, tugging at my fingers.

I rub the fingertips of my left hand together, smiling at the obvious callouses still leaving them rough and solid. Though I never had a cello of my own, I still played in college—*what college?*—but that was few and far between. I did love it, I remember that, nearly as much as I loved playing my piano.

I tap my fingers in time with their song, following each beat and measure, wishing I could play with them. If there was a piano here, perhaps I would remember more...

With a soft sigh, I silently thank the person above me who has no idea I'm listening for their song, nor how much it has settled the strange, almost-living thing inside me again.

The hoof-printed dirt road widens out into a thick forest after another mile, leading into the shadows of towering trees that I gratefully slip into. Dread no longer nips at my heels as I pass into it, steadily leaving behind the concern of being followed the further it takes me, but I don't mind.

I still don't know where I'm going, or what I want to do.

My magic stirs to life inside me again, purring in my veins and deep inside my chest—but it isn't just *in* me. It's all around me, as if I'm a bee in a hive of pure arcana, surrounded by honeycombs layered with enchantment.

My breath catches, and I glance back uncertainly, but the town is somewhere on the other side of the trees, too far to feel now. It isn't from there, but something closer. Something *big*, something reaching back to me, something wanting my attention.

Whatever it is probes at my temples, searching for me as I search for it. I reach out a hand along the street, passing over pricking thorns and smooth leaves to my right, pushing tendrils of shadow from my fingertips into the air.

The forest reaches back, flooding with too many whispers to sort out as I walk onward.

Come, it whispers. *Come.*

20

MORNING turns to evening faster than I can keep track of, following me further into the town at the forests command with dusky hues of twilight purples and pinks. The stars glittering faintly in the indigo blues at the uppermost portion of the sky are the only thing familiar to me, keeping me walking, leading me forward as the path changes from packed dirt to neat cobblestone. It isn't Nemoure, not by a long shot—the buildings are too close, too dark, not tall enough—but it's something *new*.

It's something I can work with, for now.

On either side of the road, black lampposts topped with trios of swirling, metal-framed golden lights slowly start to brighten as the sun sets further, standing tall beside shops and what smells like a bakery and a tavern. My eyes catch on velvet clothing and silver jewelry, pointed teeth in a big smile, lipstick a little too close to the shade of blood. Dresses in shades of dark purples, reds and blues. Crosses are worn more for fashion than for religion—or so it seems, judging by the few I catch hanging from long, pretty necks.

My heart beats once, reminding me of my hunger as a dark-skinned woman catches my attention, her eyes bright as she wipes a smear of red from her lip with her thumb and licks it off. For a moment, I could have sworn she was an old friend of mine—a vampiric woman named Azizi, who lives worlds away it seems—but she doesn't have her ruby eyes, or that familiar sense of darkness that we sort of shared. She smiles at her androgynous friend, playful and almost a little too intimate for me, and I turn away from the feeling.

The buildings themselves are made up of gray stone, with darker gray-to-black shingles and perched gargoyles on their roofs, connected by thin pathways leading onto separate streets. Most windows are arched—except for those in the various clothing storefronts with their much wider ones to show off the clothed mannequins within—some having pretty, swirled frames at the top to give them a dark sort of elegance I find myself *very* attracted to. Pointed iron fences frame a large cathedral and yards along the walkway, all painted black and slightly rusted from weather and standard wear.

I drag my fingertips over a chunk of flaking paint, watching it drift to the stone below before continuing.

Under the sounds of nighttime birds and insects, piano music plays in the distance—luring me onward like a siren song. I walk without much thought, simply letting the music guide my feet, until it brings me to the closed gate of a large black manor.

The forest, fog-thick and dark, whispers about me as I put my hand against the cool iron.

Someone is back.

He's finally here.

He's alone.

Macabre.

The wrought-iron fences stand still as I push on the gate, smiling a little as it groans open. It welcomes me onto the stone pathway before the black-stone manor, pulling me in like a fish on a hook before it creaks closed again behind me—forcing me to meet the looming expanse of the building. It and the gargoyles sitting hungrily above the roof watch unblinkingly, staring for a long time.

You Should Not Enter. You Should Not Be Welcome.

Dark double doors heave open at the entrance, exposing a low-lit hallway decorated with paintings of people and churning landscapes.

You Should Not Be Welcome, But You Are.

I approach slowly, eyeing the fog as it creeps away from the untamed rose bushes clinging to the inner walls of the fences. The manor shudders as I step onto the wooden floors, pausing to admire the different paintings—startling when one blinks and the next shifts as if the ocean itself were alive, staring at them in muted awe. It feels as lonely as my old home did, clinging with shadows and a strange sort of want I can't place from a *building.*

The blood-red painted walls make me miss the cream whites of a building far away in my memory, just for a moment.

My fingertips brush along the wall, passing over smooth paint and the decorated edges of frames, and something reaches back out to me. Not fully magic, but an essence of it—an ages old brush with a spell, still alive enough to hum across my skin. It pulls a black tendril of my own magic from my palm for only a second, vanishing as fast as it arrived and leaving me to watch the coiling snake of shadow.

I thought it left me, for a little while.

The manor breathes, I swear. Or is it just my head? I rub my temple and focus on the walls, watching for movement as closely as I can.

Macabre, the forest whispers from behind the closed windows. *Welcome back home.*

It knows me. This town, this manor, this forest—it knows me, or at least, it knows my family name. The thought pushes me forward, makes me walk into what appears to be a dusty living room made up of a dark green velvet couch and loveseat duo, a brick fireplace, and a wooden coffee table with fancy carved legs in between them. Bookshelves hug the opposite walls, all dark oak, all polished beneath the layers of bent spines and dog-eared pages. The scent of the room is something like a freshly blown-out candle and old books, soothing my senses as I take it in one piece of furniture at a time.

A song played on a piano drifts to me from upstairs, calling me to it as I brush my fingertips through the dust layering the front cover of a closed book on the bookshelf, keeping myself distracted from immediately hurrying to the instrument. My exploration moves easily from the living room to the kitchen, finding an equally unclean marble counter against the back walls with ample room in between the stove, oven, and round table. A refrigerator stands tall in the right corner, pressed neatly against wooden cupboards that must have dishes of some sort.

My assumptions about the dishes is proven correct by a quick cursory glance, which I'm slightly thankful for.

The manor creaks, shifting a painting in the next hallway to get my attention. I step cautiously toward it, eyeing the way it flows and waves until I stand directly in front of the wall it's hung on—a dark ocean behind a man with short black hair wearing a gray suit facing away from me; it churns with an unfelt breeze as he points further down the way. His head never turns to show me his face, but I imagine he must have been handsome, whoever he is.

If he was even real, anyway.

I warily follow his brief pointing to a heavy wooden door, pleasantly surprised when the lock on it doesn't take five minutes to go through countless mechanisms, as some places might. It heaves and groans, opening up to a spiral stone staircase, perfectly smooth along the walls and only slightly cracked on a few steps that I notice as I start to walk down. The hum of piano music floors above me fades into a quiet only broken by the echoing of my footsteps on stone, almost rhythmic.

Every room I pass through has a different smell to it beyond the living room—the kitchen smells faintly of basil and cilantro, the stairwell is entirely musty dirt, the unfinished laboratory I walk into trailing with lingering chemicals and something metallic under it all. My senses whirl with the change in every breath, making me pause in the doorway just for a second to get familiar with it.

I tap my fingers on the side of my thigh, first in rhythm with my footsteps, then to a song I swear I hear playing.

It's colder here, in between the stone walls, as I admire the room before me. Black-topped tables stand in threes on either side of a much longer table, mostly bare except for a few beakers, tools, and sets of vials. The center table appears more important from a distance, with gears on the legs likely for adjusting its height or the angle that it sits at, if I can assume anything about it. Along the back wall, a door leads into separate rooms with wide glass windows in front of them, where the odd white-green lighting seems to be coming from.

Goosebumps crawl along my arms as I step further inside, leaving the stairwell behind me. The room is heavy, like it is weighed down by the things it might have witnessed over the years, and yet, all I know is that I'm about make it witness even more. This place feels made for me, made to be inhabited by someone specifically with my family name.

My experimental revenge can happen here, in between these four walls. The idea thrills me. Not the deaths sure to come, but the fact that I can experiment again, warp flesh and bone to my liking? It's exciting. I haven't done something of the sort since I was very young, after the morning dove incident.

I've killed once before, I remember now, in bitter spurts and flickers. My mother's face. A man tied to a table. My scalpel splitting him open, his blood the richest red under ghostly white lighting.

You were so young then, Daedalus. That shouldn't have happened, something in my mind whispers, quickly washed away by static.

Footsteps sound from behind me, and I startle at the sight of Cain in the doorway, leaning languidly against the wall. He isn't wearing what I expect him to—a white shirt with long, flowing sleeves and a deep 'V' exposing most of his chest, high-waist black slacks and knee-high brown leather boots. His red hair isn't in a ponytail, but spilling in big waves and curls over his shoulders and down his back, and I swear there's red makeup around his devilish eyes.

"What are you doing here?" I ask, stepping toward him as his red lips turn up in a handsome smile.

Cain doesn't move, folding his arms over his chest. "What do you mean? I've been waiting for you."

I take in the room again, rubbing my eyes when it doesn't look right for a moment. It tips and tilts, shifting unevenly as I attempt to keep myself upright in the face of him. I don't smell his roses, I thought I would. "You've been waiting for me?" I can barely get my voice above a whisper.

He laughs, all vibrancy. "Of course, Daedalus, I miss you."

Not 'I *missed* you'. I *miss* you.

I shake my head, watching him as he approaches me and tensing when he moves to put his arms around my neck. The room is even colder with him here. "You miss me?"

Cain nods, peering at me through his long, dark eyelashes before he leans forward to my ear. "I miss you so much," he whispers. Soft, without breath to grace my skin.

I blink, and he's gone. There's no trace of him. The room stops shifting, and I exhale shakily as I stare at the space he was standing in.

And before I know it, tears start running down my face.

21

—·—

WITH A coffee in hand, I stroll into the living area by the main door, eyeing the open books laying on the table in front of the couch. It's hard to shake off that lingering feeling from seeing Cain, that strange hope and sadness mixed into one, but I have to, for now. To look at the notes I spotted briefly, before. I hadn't taken them in much yesterday—everything was new to me, and I was more focused on what this place was rather than what it had in it—but I know there was definitely something about ascending, whatever form it may be.

Ascending. A word with many meanings, but one that carries over throughout most: immortality.

I've never considered the idea of gaining immortality in such a sense, not even with the power it brings or the attention those who obtain it are given or the worshipping—but I've changed. Or at least, my fears have become new and unwelcome, and now I find myself intrigued, desperate. The memory of my death, of being dead, of clawing myself out of my own grave—I don't want it. I never want to experience it ever again.

If I can manage this with the power I have…

I shouldn't get too hopeful.

Looking back at the tabletop before me, I cup my mug tightly and eye the papers. The word '*ASCENSION*' is neatly scrawled in a calligraphic font across the top of a page in the biggest book of the three, followed by paragraphs of information about it and the different types there are. Pages of messy notes are crammed in between each section, some clipped with small metal paperclips to hold them in place, some simply placed with the hopes of them staying.

I scan them loosely, dragging my fingertip over the letters and smiling at the small trenches left behind where the pen had pressed into the page before taking the words in—godhood, becoming a lich or a dragon, true vampires and the immortal-turned-dhampir-turned-immortal-again. It's fascinating, all of it, though the warning about ascension never being an easy process makes me slightly nervous.

'Godhood is the most usual and quite possibly the easiest form of ascension—mortals assuming they have power beyond their reach or craving whatever being a god may mean to them, done with magic or channeling the power of a legendary item. Dhampirs who once were an immortal being of some sort will have an easier time with this, as it would only call for an extreme form of spell-binding to get them their power back.

Becoming a lich or a dragon, however, is typically frowned upon due to the level of intensity one must go through to get there. A lich involves tying the soul to an item, which is very nearly impossible if you aren't sure what it is that is needed to be done, and is a grueling process that can harm the mind and body.

A dragon, however, involves swallowing pieces of the kind you are trying to become. This is never an easy feat, due to the fact that it is often frowned upon for markets to carry dragon parts—whether it be scales, claws, shreds of wings, or teeth. In my research, however, there are black markets that carry this sort of item. Not easily obtainable of course, but they have them. There are other less-known sources for becoming a dragon, but even I haven't fully discovered those yet.'

Taking a deep breath, I look over the notes in the torn-out pages stuffed into the main book, trying to match the handwriting to any I'd seen before in my past studies. It's familiar—neat and swirling in most sentences, tumbling in others where the words tend to collide with one another, making it very particular compared to other scripts I've seen. Those are almost always robotically compiled, each letter perfectly curled so it is clearly legible.

This scientist or researcher seems to care less about the readability, and more about the content, which I prefer.

'Some researchers will say that ascension takes countless amounts of souls, or a very powerful item to allow the person to ascend. In my own personal research, some of it does, yes—but most of it has to do with magic. Very powerful people—mostly sorcerers, archmages,

and scholars—have made the connection to ascending through spells, from what little I've found, Ascending always takes a portion of the person away, even if it fails.

Apparently, failure is more of an option than getting far enough to reach the greatest heights.'

A grimace crosses my face as I lean back into the couch, peering up at the ceiling. If I tried to ascend in one way or another to escape the possibility of death, what would happen if I failed? Is there any way to fail without harm? Probably not, I can easily assume that. Am I mad for even considering it? That's definite, but how will I keep myself from ending up in a grave again?

I drag my hands over my face and groan, then lean forward to take another sip of my coffee.

'I have been studying ascension for decades of my life, trying to figure out how to manage achieving the greatest thing any mortal can possibly do. It seems that any form of it can be done with magic as I said above—mostly godhood, and sometimes lichdom if the body has the ability to hold the necromantic/necrotic powers they wield. Becoming a lich seems it may be the easier to attain, though messing about with one's soul is a dangerous sport. Be wary, reader, for you may lose more than you want if you attempt this.'

Underneath the last paragraph is a familiar signature, one I wouldn't ever have recognized if I hadn't studied for the majority of my life. It comes back to me in a rush, paragraphs of calligraphy printed in college books or handwritten notes I found in crevices in the oldest parts of the libraries, all ended with two letters.

-F.M

Feloren Macabre. A powerful, vampiric mage in my family line who was said to have blue skin and flame-colored hair, who wrote many of the books I found my magic in.

According to the stories, Feloren was always chasing their obvious ability for magic—doing whatever they could in the process to wield it better, including the various elements and types that were deemed "forbidden"—and then one day, they disappeared. There was an explosion and a great roaring from a valley not far from the village of Eclipse on Lur'ala, and then they were gone. It is said the earth there has been charred ever since.

This must be their manor, then. No wonder the forest welcomed me home.

I run my fingertips over their signature for a moment, shaking my head as I look at the room around me. It would make sense if it was theirs, judging by the magic imbedded in *everything* and the fact that the manor itself has a connection to the Astral without combusting. They must have hidden out here to study Ascension closer, and then only left to do it.

The manor's magic aches again, spitting sparks from the hearth in a fashion all too similar to crying.

My coffee's bitterness makes me sit back again, hooking my ankle on top of my knee as I look at the ceiling. Even despite Feloren's clear warnings, I still want to do it. I can't die again. I don't *want* to die again, not ever, especially not when I have to face the memory of it at least once every waking moment.

I have to reach that untouchable peak. No matter what it takes.

Something cold washes over me, erasing the warmth of the fire in my bones and replacing it with pure ice. My body shivers with a mix of dread and adrenaline, making my hands tremble badly enough that it forces me to put my coffee down and rub them together, looking around the room in concern. A dark shadow passes over the ceiling, followed by the intensity of being watched by something—or someone—that shouldn't be allowed in this realm.

My slow heart picks up speed, knocking hard against my ribcage.

I feel the moment its eye opens, large and oppressive as it stares down at me, freezing me to my spot on the couch. The feeling is oddly reminiscent of my mother's watchful eyes, chilling and dreadful. Black tendrils snake across the pale ceiling, slowly reaching down the walls and finding their unsteady place on the floor.

It reaches toward me, and I can't make myself move as a voice drags itself from somewhere far beyond here. *"Hello, Daedalus."* Its voice is a growl, bubbling and rough, almost echoing in the space around me.

I swallow, teeth chattering as I focus on the still-glowing hearth. "How do you know my name? Why are you here?"

The entity hums, and the tension of it watching me fades for a brief moment. *"I've known you for some time, Daedalus. You want to ascend, do you not?"*

"I never did before, but I do now, yes." I watch the fire sputter, almost choking against the entity's presence. Sparks spit from it, scattering in the air and amongst the still-vibrant embers.

"I can help you, Daedalus. Make a deal with me, and I can give you that power in the snap of a finger." A sharp snap follows, forcing a shudder down my spine.

"What are you?" I ask, and it makes a sound akin to a sigh.

"I am called Kalenopus. You are one of many who are yet to meet me."

Kalenopus. Eldritch in nature, meaning it's more dangerous than most. A being I don't know, but one that almost feels familiar at the same time. It makes my skin crawl to even *imagine* working with something like this—and for a moment, I picture saying yes. I imagine what I would lose of myself if I did, or what would change about my person to show that it's working with me. Maybe my eyes would be black, or my veins would be more prominent on my face. Maybe my skin would disappear.

I shake my head, pulling my thoughts back together. I've been alone all my life. I made myself this strong, I made myself have this much power with little assistance from my mother or anybody else—the thought of giving something of my own up to another presence just so I can have the easy way almost disgusts me.

I keep my gaze level on the hearth, deciding against looking at the entity. "No."

It reels, withdrawing the tendrils from where they've slowly crept over the floor. *"What do you mean, no?"*

"No, I won't make a deal with you. I don't want power, I want immortality—and I want to do it myself. I've done everything myself already." I watch the tendrils continue to pull away from me, shadows sliding up the wall and back into the blackened spot on the ceiling.

It hums again, pulling back into the eye above me. *"You are different than the rest of those I've come to, Daedalus Macabre."*

My stomach turns at the sound of my name in its voice, and then it leaves without any other words. I shiver for minutes after, forcing myself to take thin breaths through my nose as I stare at the still-spitting flames, lightly hugging myself around my chest.

I'm going to do this on my own. I don't need anything else's help.

22

— · —

I DON'T remember the last time I've ever studied so hard.

My back aches as I sit upright from Feloren's notebook, making myself move for what feels like—what *must* be—the first time in hours. After *Kalenopus* left, I waited a while for the chill to leave me before diving back in, and every minute since has been *so* worth it.

Feloren wrote, in great detail, their thought processes on the magic behind each path of ascension. Their personal favorite was the way of the dragon, whereas mine is lichdom, but we both agree that godhood is the easiest to obtain. If only I could've met them before they disappeared... I'm sure we would've gotten along great.

Or, well, at least *I* think so.

Truthfully, I'm shocked the manor is still standing, after their vanishing. Upon finding it, I expected *someone* to still be here—but based on the disarray and discarded notes, the dust and haunting spirits, no one was come back in years. Feloren specifically, hasn't returned in years. It's no wonder the place feels so *sad*.

'The magical means to godhood seems simple enough—a powerful mage simply needs to gather the entirety of their magic, wound as tight as a stitch, and press it inside themselves. Now, it may sound too easy, but this is where the true test is. Making the magic behave as it presses inside them is part of the problem, and the other? Making the body allow *it. Many mortals will succumb to it, going mad or showing physical signs of their mistake.*

Some mortals will die trying to achieve it, but many will simply bear the scars of their failure for life. Facing the enormity of one's magic completely out in the open is one of the hardest things to do...but the strongest of minds may persist.'

Deep breath in, deep breath out.

"It's simple enough, right?" I ask in the direction of the manor, and the books snap shut in front of me.

The fire spits out a handful of embers, crackling its disagreement.

I frown, shaking my head. "You'll hold me while I try?"

This time, the manor itself hums. I startle as the fire turns blue, glowing brighter than before as the magic pulsating from every stone starts to wisp through the air.

It whispers *"Be careful of your ambition,"* in my ear before falling silent again.

I stand up, moving into the center of the room as blue sparks flicker in and out of the air around me, coating my every breath with nothing but pure *power.* My breath catches as I card a hand through them, and they pass over like silk across my skin—and then I decidedly bring my hands together, calling the essence of me in between my palms. Black lightning crackles from gathering pools against my skin, bursting between my fingers, jolting over my arms.

The manor whispers, *"Be aware, Daedalus.*

My magic unweaves from my ribcage like thin threads from a spool, pouring into my hands, turning the room around me pitch dark. I stop breathing again in my focus, watching as the blue flickers continue to dance around my shadows, twining with the blackness of my void. Black and bright blue come together in a writhing form, starting from the floor and rising until it stands as tall as me—and it's wearing my face. A magic-made version of me, copying my hand movements.

Me, with an obsidian crown of sharp points, in dark draping robes. Me, with golden eyes crystallized in their sockets. Me, with a veil hanging from my head and over the length of my hair.

The room vanishes from sight, becoming nothing but darkness. It swallows me and the form, bringing us to a perfectly empty space—a black room made of nothing but us, rippling water beneath our feet, and an oval-shaped mirror.

When I step closer, it follows.

I stare at myself through the mirror, at the other me with the unafraid gaze and confident stance. He peers at me not with judgement, but instead, recognition—reaching a hand out to the glass from his side of the mirror.

His hand is entirely bone, pale white and clearly defined as he points a finger toward me. The air swells with possibility, becoming thick with anticipation, thick with this moment of us reaching for each other. I swear time itself stops with the deep, distant ticking of a clock as I slowly reach for him, for *me*.

Tick tock, tick tock, tick tock.

Behind him, a strange silhouette forms—tall, nearly too tall to see at first. My eyes jolt to the shape of it, to the multiple heads and empty eye sockets of a crow-skull head, to the saliva curling from the wolf's head's lips beside it. Everything in this space falls short, the sound of a clock reverberating through my bones as I stare up at it. Somehow, the creature is familiar.

Look familiar, Daedalus? My Rot whispers in my ear, and a wisp of shadow spiral around the beast's hand.

"No," I reply, hoarse, though I know it's a damn lie.

It's you. What you truly are.

There's a split second where our gazes meet before everything shifts, and the mirror fractures.

The glass cracks further, breaking in ragged rings, becoming an intricate web. I reel away from myself as it fills the entire space of the frame—shouting when it suddenly explodes into thousands of glittering pieces. Glass cuts away at my skin, scraping at my temples, burning in my brain. Bones snap and realign; muscles expand and shrink and stretch too far. My jaw unhinges twice before settling into its place. My own magic shatters, taking any thought I had with it, taking *me* with it. I think I scream as I watch myself vanish, tipping over backward and falling into the blackened waters at my feet.

Possibility yanks out from under me as I burst from the water, sitting upright on the floor of the manor.

My chest heaves with desperate breaths, putting a hand over it as I glance around the room.

I attempt to make my blade from the ether, just as a test, and it appears in my hand as it always does.

You killed me, Daedalus, my mind screams. *You killed me and look what you got. You have nothing to show for it, not even godhood. Have you always failed? Do you know what you are yet?*

"Oh, no," I whisper to the manor, and the manor sighs back.

"I told you," it says, almost sadly.

I definitely failed, and my mind is all the worse for it. Oh well, fine. Maybe godhood didn't work—I'll become a lich. I'll become a lich and that will be what does it for me, that will be what saves me. I will be untouchable.

My heart ticks slowly as I drum my fingertips on the floor, recalling every face I saw that day. Elven men, elven women, a few Luceri as well. The guards and their silver armor. Though I don't exactly want full revenge, there's one man in particular I can think of—the guard who took me away that night, and executed me days later. He's the only one I want to track down, to show him what happens when someone returns from the dead.

Anger burns like an inferno in my gut, new and exciting. It pushes me up from the floor, making me walk as I grab Feloren's notes from the table. Anger becomes rage, and I almost feel disgusted by it as it storms around in my otherwise still veins, shivering with the dread it brings along next. I don't like the way this anger makes me feel. It's harsh, urging me for violence, too big for my akin. Another slow heartbeat, drumming uneasily with my tumultuous emotions, that are far too big for me to understand. Contradictory in ways I can't place, can't sort out in the frazzled spaces of my head.

I find a large, brown leather bag and cram the notes in it, alongside spellcasting books and other items that could come in handy. I'm not sure where I'm going to go, but I *think* I'm going to Nemoure.

I'm going to Nemoure, as soon as I can wrap up my work.

My hands rub together, trying to ease a new wave of anxiety as I pause by the door, resting my forehead against the wall. "Wish me luck, please."

The manor warms at my touch, and I swear I feel it hug me back.

"Wait," it says. *"Tell us about something you remember. Someone. Anything."*

I step away from the door and smile a little, closing my eyes to draw something up for it. My mind floods with misshapen memories—different pieces from different times, like someone with a blurred-out face who had blue hair, and someone who is crystal clear to me now. He was blurry a while ago when I thought of him over my breakfast, his features all warped and hazy so I couldn't place who he was.

But now, as I force my scattered mind to pull together, it paints him perfectly in my mind.

Cain smiling at me from across a diner table, laughing at something I said.

Cain blushing over wine.

Cain holding my hand on a rooftop, beaming at me.

Cain Sidrelle.

I tell the manor about him, all that I can remember. I go through every memory, every moment my mind allows me to recall, describing his beauty for it. Every brush of his flaming hair, every smile and bat of his eyes, the sway of his hips. The shape of his smile.

The manor, if it could smile, does. *You sound like you miss him.*

"I only just remembered him, and yet I feel as if I've been missing him for my whole life," I reply, putting my palm against the wall. "I need to find him."

Don't leave yet, Daedalus, it replies, and the magic embraces me again. *Finish your work.*

23

I DON'T know how many days it has been since I walked out of my grave and into the manor, because time moves different in the Astral and when I'm studying than it does in the material world. Even so, early spring continues to bloom outside my windows—mostly in pastels, with the random vibrant bush of flowers sprouting in between, standing out against the green grasses and budding trees.

A mourning dove calls, sending flickers of memories through my mind—all times where I seem smaller, more unsure, gazing through a silver birdcage at a tan and white bird. A masculine hand falls on the smaller me's shoulder in one of them, guiding me away and telling me in a low voice how it is all mine to keep. Then, I was confused as to why I was given a mourning dove of all things and not something like a crow.

Now, I think I understand—my father knew me better than I knew myself in those younger days. He gave it to me as a symbol, I think. A living symbol of the sadness I wore, of the grief little me carried even then.

I stop short as my head aches, flooding with new images of the bird with a bloodstained chest. All the downy, tan feathers running reds and pinks; and my hands beneath it, cradling extended wings and a limp neck. A pair of much colder hands on my shoulders, slimmer ones with sharper nails, guiding me down a hallway as I stare at the bird's forever closed eyes.

It was meant to happen, her even icier voice says.

My breath leaves in a shudder, full of uncertainty, as I make myself walk again. Why did it die? I can't remember. All I can see is a void in my chest and more limbs than I had before.

I don't know what it is, what I am, but I know the bird died and *Gods, I need to focus.*

"Daedalus!" an excited voice calls from the stairs, as if someone's coming down to see me. "Come look!"

I exhale as I drift toward the call, walking up to the stairwell and gasping at the sight of Cain there, wearing a beautiful red dress. It clings to every curve, every dip in his body, showing off one leg and hiding the other from sight. He beams at me with reddened lips, tilting his head curiously as he approaches. "Do you like it?"

"I do," I reply slowly, mouth moving to form too many uncertain words. "I missed your beauty, my Gods."

His laugh is beautiful on my ears. "Of course you did. Everyone misses it when they've been gone for so long."

He reaches out to touch me, but his hands never make the contact. My heart wrenches as he vanishes in a blink, his last words echoing in the back of my mind.

The piano music upstairs sounds far more somber as I walk back up into the kitchen, trying to see past the blurriness of the tears in my eyes. Seeing Cain in any form nearly brought me to my knees, and he wasn't even real—which only proves to me that I need to get to Nemoure *soon*. I need to see him, all of him, and not only in my memories or in visions that my messy mind conjures just to torture me.

And *why* did I see him? Is it my own failures coming back to haunt me? Or is it simply the yearning, bubbling up in my chest and growing too big for me to contain? New nerves well in my chest at the thought that I could be going mad, either due to my failed experiment, or my return altogether. What would Cain do if I came back, crazy and irrational?

What would Cain think if he knew I was seeing visions of him?

But what if he forgot about me? What if I go there, and he doesn't even know who I am?

I don't know how long it's been since... everything. I barely know how long it's been since I crawled out of my grave and into these unfamiliar lands.

I lean back against the door to the lab after I close it behind me, slumping down and dropping my weight into it. My chest aches as I look up at the ceiling, shaking my head, trying not to think of the fact that he might not even want to see me if I show up. Trying *desperately* not to imagine the fact that he probably moved on. Hell, he could be in a relationship with someone and not even care that I'm back for him.

For him. Ha. I'm still as desperate as always.

Anxiety claws up my spine and settles deep in my gut, making my breathing turn quick, uncertain of my own thoughts. My hand falls over my heart as it threatens to break, closing my eyes for a long moment.

Maybe we should know what that feels like. The familiar voice of the Rot, my rot, echoes inside my head.

"I don't want to know that heartbreak," I reply, quietly, honestly.

It laughs, or something like it. ***I do.***

I huff out a breath through my nose as my jaw clenches, working tight and loose over and over again. "I thought you would've died with me, you know."

Another laugh, rumbling and guttural. ***I'm the reason you came back.***

My stomach and my heart drop into the floor, freezing me in place momentarily. I never really questioned the '*why*'s or the '*how*'s—I simply accepted the fact that I stood again, that I breathed and my heart beat and I was no longer in the ground. I never thought about the Rot. I never considered it to be strong enough to even *do* something of that sort.

I shudder, deciding against answering it as I push away from the basement door.

I'm going to my old city.

The words are solid, formed easily and with as much conviction as I can manage.

I'm going to my old city.

As I walk through the kitchen, I call my magic into my hands and let it spill from them like candlewax dripping from a flame, forming the shivering shadows of spirits from the paintings down the hall. They crawl free from the decorative frames, wrenching their bodies from them before hovering over my floors. I smile, feeling the thrill of my calling running through my veins, electric and magnetic and leaving me almost pleased.

"Would you mind cleaning up the manor? I'm leaving and I may return with company," I tell them, and they wordlessly drift away into the next rooms.

I don't know if they're actual phantoms of this manor, or if they're my magic. Either way, I'm content with them.

The shadows twine around my fingers before vanishing into my wrist as I pass through the rooms, walking quickly through the main door and out into the yard. I swear the manor watches me, leaning over the path to see me closer—but every time I look back at it, it stands still and unmoving. My new home, as curious as I am.

It feels strange to call that... a *home*.

The realization makes me pause in front of the gate, lightly brushing the paint with my fingertips as I consider the thought. I can still recall the manor I lived in before, the one with the family members I can only half remember, but it was never a home to me. I know I never called it that; not with the dangers or the weight it left on my shoulders, not with the shame it filled me with, not with the hatred.

Home was a word I left out of my vocabulary as often as I could. A sour word I had no use for.

Frogs and insects chirp around me as I look back at the building, letting a little smile cross my face before I push open the crying gate and leave the yard. Outside, the town is quiet—still lit by the golden light of the streetlamps and the flickering candles in shop windows, but the streets are mostly still compared to their liveliness earlier.

It's a little more comforting this way, so I don't feel that odd pressure of *everyone is watching me* or *do I belong here.* This place isn't Nemoure, but I can't seem to shake that ages-old concern.

With every breath, the air becomes richer with the scent of alcohol—likely beer or bourbon, with touches of wine, flowers, and freshly baked bread. Sometimes, the scents overlap. Sometimes, I catch one at a time. The flowers in particular—roses, creeping phlox hanging over stone walls, peonies—they catch my attention more than the others, giving me a reason to pause and smell them just for the fact that I *can.*

I even stop outside a now closed bakery just to breathe in the lingering sweet scent of sugary frosting, solely because I'm alive. I'm alive and it feels... *good*, to know these smells again. Good in a way that has something akin to happiness bubbling just beyond the surface of my anxiety.

Very few people pass by me with their arms around each other or their hands intertwined, some staggering from a tavern and laughing as their friend nearly tips over. My heart aches for that connection, wishing for the happiness on their faces to be mirrored on my own.

But instead, I'm walking by myself in the hopes of finding someone who probably forgot I existed.

Gods, I need to stop reminiscing.

I force a deep breath through my nose to keep a small wave of tears away, exhaling it back out as I leave the main stretch of town through the entrance opposite to the one I arrived in before. Horses snort as they pass me, their shoed hooves echoing off the stone before I catch pieces of the conversations happening within the carriages they pull. A woman giggling, a man chuckling low. Glasses clinking together. A symphony of drunken, musical laughter spilling from another.

Someone says, "Ooh look, we've reached Eerie!" and it makes me pause.

Eerie. How fitting a name for a town like this. How I never discovered its name sooner is baffling to me.

The stone path turns to dirt after a while, cutting through a stretch of the whispering forest that continues to speak my name. *Daedalus*, it says. *Macabre. You're here. Where are you going? Come back.*

"I'll come back," I murmur, more to myself than the trees. "I have nowhere else to go."

Laughter falls away on the breeze, drifting into grasshopper clicks and owl calls the farther I get from the forest. A field of long, yellowed grasses extends on my right, reaching out to brush against the back of my hand as I admire the stretch of it for a moment, noting the perked head of a doe peering back at me amongst the brush. Splinters of memories prod into my mind again at the sight of her—an animal body splayed before me, blood on my hands, so much hunger—but they're gone before I can stop to think about them.

My stomach growls, and I try to push the gnawing feeling of it aside.

No one else walks the road, and no other carriages come trotting my way, leaving me to the peaceful night. Leaving me to look up at the waxing moon and its stars, smiling at their sparkling in the blackness above. I miss my comfort in the manor. I miss the space beyond it, despite the fact that the cold reminded me all too much of my death. It's *good* there. It's patient.

I sigh softly, only looking back down at the sound of slow-walking horse hooves on dirt and the grind of wheels crawling over the ground. A single, glossy black carriage with golden details being pulled by a gorgeous black horse moves steadily down the road, assumedly not in any sort of hurry judging by the easy pace. The driver appears elven, wearing a black tailcoat and vest beneath it, with a white button-up shirt and dark slacks. His blonde hair is slicked back from his face, but I can't discern most of his features from here.

He's chuckling at something the people inside are saying, but I can only figure that out by the sound.

Pale curtains hide the carriage's inhabitants from me, but not their conversation. As they draw closer, the sound of three masculine voices laughing loudly over something business related rings out, filling the otherwise quiet night. At first, I don't think anything of them. To me, they're just three men on their way to or past Eerie. They're probably nobles or rich businessmen or gamblers who just made it big. Maybe they're crime lords.

Or maybe, *I know them.*

My stomach turns as I recognize one of the voices—deep, a little huskier now than before, but authoritative and slightly cold. Tolland. The guard who came to get me the night where everything went wrong, the guard who assisted in my prompt execution only a few days later.

Something in me snaps like a rope under too much tension, and before I know it, my magic surges through my body. I blink, and I'm no longer standing on the road, materializing in thrashing shadows before the three of them, slightly hunched against the roof of the carriage.

My body moves without my permission when I lay eyes on his armorless body, meeting his bright eyes as they widen. The noblemen beside him stutter, staring at each other before staring at him, ignoring the fact that there's wine on their shirts and their glasses might be emptied by the shake of their hands alone. His fair skin turns shades paler as he gawks at me, shaking his head.

"You aren't real," he says, uncertain of his own words. "There's no way you're standing here right now. You're *dead.*"

The noblemen both nod in agreement, unable to take their eyes away from me.

My lips tug into an uneven smile, only for a brief second. "I *did* say I'd be back."

"It's been ten years; there's no goddamn way you're here. It isn't possible!" the man I don't recognize exclaims, trying to wipe some of the wine from his blue satin shirt with a handkerchief and frowning when he realizes it isn't working.

My hand flexes, the magic flowing from the singular beat of my heart down into my fingers, forming a pitch-black blade the length of my arm.

I don't look at him, even though I know he's also probably on my list, only at Tolland. Ten years almost floors me for a minute, but my mind doesn't make the connection, not with the storm circling it.

He swallows visibly, shaking his head again. "You should have stayed dead, Macabre. Your family is a curse on Nemoure, a *blight*, even. Everything was fine until all of you appeared in the city, like a shadow on the edges of the upper city. You *haunted* all of us, for no reason other than someone needed power and fucked the right person for it."

I see him standing beside me on the gallows, inexpressive as he reads from a slightly worn piece of paper. I see him pushing me into my cell, face hidden by a helmet.

The splinters of my memory and my anger meet as one, colliding viciously into unsettled fury, turning me into a volcano of movement. I don't see anything. I just know I move and one of the men shouts, or at least I think he does. The sound only lasts for a moment.

My vision is nothing but a blur of red. I think the carriage stops, but I don't really know. A pinprick of pain in my side threatens to break the fog, but it isn't enough to pull me back together. Glass shatters, something wet sprays over my arm.

Everything stops moving, and all I hear is my own rough breathing in my ears.

That was fun, Daedalus, the Rot says as I resurface, coming back in control of myself.

I blink a time or two, leaning back from the mess before me. The two noblemen lay half slumped between the floor and their seats, deep red patches blooming over their brightly colored shirts and spilling onto the smooth floor, staring wide-eyed into nothing with blood staining their parted lips. Somehow, their driver is sprawled at my feet— one hand reaching out of the door for the unhelpful night beyond, a large wound exposed through the fabric of his clothes.

"Holy shit," I whisper to myself, looking back at Tolland.

He's the worst, with uneven slices crisscrossing his torso and throat, deep enough I swear I can see bone and the glint of muscle under the crimson blood. His jaw hangs loose from his head, forever gaping at nothing with his big, wide eyes, blank and staring at the floor, searching for help that wouldn't come. There's a dagger on the floor between his feet, but it looks as if he never got the chance to use it, unless the blood on it is mine and not any of the others'.

The metallic, iron scent of blood fills my nose, my lungs. Every breath is *red*, every blink. It's so thick in the air that I can nearly taste it, making my fangs ache as I stare down at the bodies before me—and if I wasn't in better control of myself, I likely would have had a taste. A spray of it marks the skin of my hands, almost enough to throw me into another lapse of panic, but I swipe them off on my slacks so I can focus.

Just for a moment. I need just enough time to get out of here.

I climb over the driver's stiffening corpse, forcing him backwards into the body of the carriage and shutting the door. The horse is somehow calm, turning his large head at peer at me over his shoulder and giving me a moment to *really* look at him—towering in height, maybe 18 hands, with pitch-black hair that's almost purple in the moonlight and a wavy mane tumbling past his shoulder. His tail falls in matching elegant waves, nearly touching the ground his feathery, hair-covered hooves rest on.

I *probably* have room for a horse. Probably. Somewhere.

His nostrils flare at me as I reach my hand over, lightly scratching his velvet-soft muzzle before pulling myself up into the driver's seat. It isn't very comfortable, acting more like a simple and solid wooden platform to perch on than something to really *sit* into, but it works for now. I'm amazed no one has come down the road by now, not a single carriage or lone person walking, not another person on horseback.

I'm thankful for it all the same, but it feels strange.

I reach forward and gather up the reins, running the pad of my thumb over a crease in the leather, where they have obviously been bent for a long time. The horse picks up an easy walk without much of a command, quickly turning into a nice trot as I snap the reins over his rear, moving smooth and steady. I *feel* the force of his hoofbeats, thumping like a heavy drumbeat deep in my chest.

My fingertips tap to the beat of his pace, counting each step as a measure on sheet music. I imagine a piano keyboard, maybe even the strings of a cello making familiar callouses on my skin, and the music flows into my head easily. Uneven at first, but swiftly becoming a song I am itching to write down. It nearly becomes a waltz before I change my mind, curving it into something soft and melancholy, then back into something a little quicker.

I find myself smiling as we trot into the forest and further into Eerie, listening to his hoofbeats as they become sharper on the stone. There must be metal shoes on them, if the distinct ring of it tells me anything.

A few drunk elves I saw earlier shout as I pass, but I'm not really sure if they're calling out to me or if they're shouting just because they can.

I don't stop to find out. I push the stallion onward, my hands shaking as they clench the smooth leather, hoping the bite of them will keep me centered for the moment as we move down the road. My mind focuses on the music of his hooves, trying desperately to think of anything other than the fact that my hands have blood on them, and it's *staining, and it will never go away and I will never escape what I did to my mother—*

A deep breath rattles in my chest as I shake my head, trying to free the train of thought before it anchors itself to my mind. I just have to get home.

We pull to an easy stops outside of the manor, and instead of hopping down to open the gate, I make a shadowed version of my hand to do it for me. It breaks free from my own with the subtlest spark of magic in my palm, floating forward with a simple flick of my wrist and moving with my own motions as I make a fist and yank toward myself. The iron cries as it tugs outward toward the carriage, allowing me enough room to walk the horse onto the path ahead of me and further into my gray and gloomy yard.

The moon peeks over the tops of the trees beyond my fenced-in yard, casting slivers of pale light on me as we walk to the back of the building after closing the gate behind us. To my surprise, a small barn sits in the back toward the left edge, one that I'm sure hasn't been used for countless years. Hopefully, I won't find animal bones or any sort of monster inside it—who knows what could have made its home there after all this time. Who knows what chose to inhabit this property, from science or nature.

You're back, the forest says as the fog creeps in, crawling over my gate and around my feet as I step down to untie the stallion from the carriage.

I smile, a little strained. "I told you I would be."

The forest hums, a little breeze blowing through the leaves. It says nothing else.

I pet a hand down the stallion's neck, palm pressed to the softness of his hair. "I wonder what they called you before."

He huffs out a breath, warm against my skin as he noses my arm.

"I think I'll call you Nightshade," I tell him, gingerly taking hold of the long reins and bunching them in my hand so I can lead him to the barn.

The stallion towers over me, but I don't mind, even with the power of his hoofbeats making the ground tremble slightly. I walk uncertainly over the yard and pause at the dark wooden barn door, eyeing the swirling details carved into it for a second before glancing up at him and pulling it open with one hand—only to be surprised by the lack of *anything* within.

A rush of bats flies over our heads, squeaking as they dart away into the darkness of the woods, and I find myself grateful that Nightshade doesn't panic at the suddenness of their arrival.

I peek inside the barn warily, finding four vacant stalls, dust and cobwebs everywhere. One stall must have been where the animal's food was kept, judging by the remnants of hay and burlap bags of grain left scattered on the floor. A bag of brushes is left discarded nearby, tipped over and spilling, as if whoever was here before left in a hurry. Mice scatter from underfoot as I walk the horse into one of the stalls, taking the bridle off last once he stops to look around.

I spend a little more energy just to conjure him a decent amount of grain and hay, then lock up his stall for the night.

"Goodnight, Nightshade," I say over my shoulder, listening to his snorts and huffs for a moment.

He doesn't reply, and I don't expect him to.

Time to face what lies within the carriage.

Time to become a scientist again.

24

FOR A moment, I feel like I'm back in the old manor, standing in the laboratory with my mother again.

It's like seeing myself through a lens—smaller, much smaller, with tubes and syringes sticking out of my arms or sticking into them. My mother's scratched out face as she leans closer, directing magic into me, her hands covered in violent purple and black arcana as she coaxes something through my veins. I know I cried then, but she always shushed me.

"Don't cry, Daedalus. You'll understand someday," she'd say, never looking up to wipe my tears away.

Little me didn't understand because little me didn't know how to be a person yet.

Her lab was always dimly lit, the darkness in the corners hugging close, something watching over us. Something—no, now that I think of it, *someone. Kalenopus,* I think, because in that memory, the feeling is the same as what I felt when it approached me in the manor. Little me didn't recognize it because I was too focused on what she was doing, but I know I always felt it.

My lab is silent as I place the first body down on the long table in the center, cutting away the torn fabric of Tolland's shirt with a pair of scissors from a tray beside me. It falls away easily, exposing the slices I gave him, showing their blackened edges from the shadow magic I used to make the blade. I hum low under my breath—the tune from the cellist in that rundown area of Eerie I walked through—pausing to snap on a pair of latex gloves and lifting a slim knife next.

Little me fights as his mother lowers him into a tube, something wide enough to hold his entire body.

Little me coughs as he breaks free from a tube, head bursting over purple liquid, dragging himself onto the stone floor of a glass-walled room as his body convulses without his permission.

Cutting Tolland's torso is a simple process—one neat slice down the sternum, one across the stomach to open him up—exposing bright organs beneath that have since gone still and cold. I pin his skin back with wide metal clips, running a gloved fingertip over the arch of his ribcage, the surface of it slick with chilled blood. Most of him is still in good condition, with very few of the parts within damaged by my rage-consumed attack.

His heart, dark and quiet beneath the bones, comes away easily when I cut it out of him.

Little me stares at the dead bird in his hands, and my vision flashes back and forth between pale feathers and bloodied, red muscle.

Little me cries for help as his body coils in on itself, bursting with new appendages and feathers and a void in his chest.

I put a hand over my chest, pausing to stare at the heart for a while longer as the memory of my childhood plays in the corner of my mind. Something surges along with a singular heartbeat, something more like power than a part of my actual body.

Setting the heart down, I walk to a worn-down cabinet in the corner and remove a box of sealed bags from it, then return to Tolland's side. My breath leaves shakily from my lips as I pick the heart back up, turning it over in the pale light, eyeing the rippling veins and valves. It isn't *perfect*, but I can probably hold onto it in case I ever need it down the road.

I place it in a bag and seal it tight, then set it in the freezer as the first to be kept.

Tolland's jaw continues to hang loose, his head turned slightly to the side, as I continue poking around in his guts. I find a decent liver not *too* damaged from alcohol and decent kidneys, then decide to leave the rest within him instead of pulling his intestines or his stomach out.

I follow the same process with the next nobleman, cutting away his shirt and then into his chest. He bled out far less than Tolland did, so I quickly scramble to find needles and tubes to siphon what is left of his life's ichor into bags for reasons that simply come down to *what if's*. His already pale skin becomes gray and pallid as the blood drains steadily, thankfully coming out untainted by the touch of death, still deep red despite how cold it is.

Little me stares at the torso of a man on the lab floor, at the blood surrounding his broken body. His six hands are clawed and black, and there's blood in his mouth—no, mouths. He is a monster. He has finally done what his blurry mother wanted.

My hands stop moving again as I stare at the man's wide lungs, shaking my head. Through death, I forgot what I truly am. Because of *Cain*, I forgot what I am. Under my skin lays a creature, the root of my hunger and the root of my magic, the one thing I had chosen to push out of my mind for *years*. The thing my mother *made* me.

And then it clicks, all at once—she wanted me to use that form in my trainings. She was so angry with me because I wouldn't, and because I wouldn't, that meant her work was going to waste. No wonder she seemed to like me better when I was younger, when I was pliable and confused.

The knife in my hand taps in a frustrated rhythm against the man's ribs, becoming a waltz to distract myself from the sickening realization. My heart aches, but I continue working.

I cut away a few more organs once the blood finishes draining from him, sealing them with my magic and placing them in my freezer. Something in me feels strangely small, as if that little me is who stands here right now, staring into the abyss of the body I've laid out. Salt in the old wound, that must be it. Remembering is my price to pay for everything I've done.

Don't you hate yourself, Daedalus? Don't you hate what you did, now that you can barely remember me or anything else? Doesn't it just make you furious that I was right all along, that you were destined to do nothing but fail after you failed me? You will always fail to keep the things you want the most. You will always fail because you failed to listen to me. Me, your mother, the one thing to make you right, and yet you decided to go against me.

"Stop," I hiss through clenched teeth, shaking my head as I heave up the final body.

The Rot is cold in my head when it speaks again, this time in its own voice, rather than my mother's. ***Failed, failure, you hate yourself. I know you do. I hear you, Daedalus.***

"Shut *up.*" My hand tightens around the hilt of the knife, a new, vile anger coursing through my veins that tangles with the emptiness in my gut.

The man on my table says nothing, staring up at the ceiling, looking for a help that won't come.

Someone strolls around from my left side, someone I nearly startle at the sight of. Cain, in his white button-up and red vest, yawns as he leans an arm against my experiment table, watching me over the man's permanently frightened face. "Daedalus, when are you coming to bed?"

Disgusting, you're disgusting, you won't keep him either. He'll see your hatred. He'll see you.

"Shut UP!" The words leave as a snarl, directing the tip of the knife into the back of my left hand where the Rot's shadows tangle with my skeletal marks. Blood weeps from the wound, leaking out through my glove, but I don't feel the bloom of pain I know must have followed as I look at Cain.

He frowns at me, sympathetic or pitying, I don't know. "Please come to bed, I want you to lay with me."

I nod, pulling the knife back and wincing when the Rot laughs at me before it vanishes. "Soon, love. Soon."

Cain nods and strolls away, vanishing from sight and leaving me with myself, my bleeding hand, and the bodies. Only when I don't smell the roses I expect, do I remember he isn't real and I still have to find him.

I stab the knife into the wood of the table and slump down, allowing myself to cry this time. I allow the cries to become sobs, aching in my chest, tearing from me in painful waves that make me unable to stand again. Tears soak my cheeks and force me to remove my glasses with one hand, hating the blaze of pain in my hand and hating the sickness I feel at myself for even letting Cain go this long without knowing I'm back.

This time, I truly need to go find him. I need him by my side.

I don't bother finishing up with the last man, deciding instead to start hauling each body one by one upstairs and through the back door in my kitchen. Moments like this, I'm grateful for the extra strength given to me by my dhampir lineage—that way I can carry the weight of their increasingly heavy bodies as they continue to stiffen with the throes of death. Dragging them up the stairs is the hardest part, having to loop my arms under theirs and pull them backwards rather than simply tugging them along.

Sadness weaves into the piano music upstairs as I drag each one, finding a shovel leaning up against the backside of the manor after leaving the bodies in a pile at the back of the yard, closest to the forest. Its whispers become indiscernible as they overlap one another, trying to talk too fast for me to keep up as I start digging into the dirt. I heave pile after pile, tossing it to the side of the hole, hoping to get as much out of the way as possible before sunlight breaks the darkness of night.

After what feels like years, the hole is deep enough for the three men, and I am covered in dirt and blood and viscera.

It takes a moment to shove them in, and I cannot help but grimace at the sound of bones cracking when they hit the bottom of the hole. Tolland's head rests at an even worse angle from his fall, his jaw twisted to the side unnaturally, his body bent and broken.

The noblemen fall face-down, their bodies positioned crookedly over the head guard's.

I stare at them and their faraway gazes for a long while, feeling sick and disgusting, before I start throwing the dirt back over them with the hopes of forgetting they ever existed.

Then, I make a list of steps:

25

—·—

1. Go inside and clean up. Shower. Scrub everything off of my skin until it burns.

2. Dress in something nice.

3. Go to Nemoure and find Cain, for real this time.

FINDING Nemoure is easier after I bought a map from the little general store on the main stretch of Eerie.

If only I had walked the opposite way from my grave, I likely would've found it sooner. None of this would have happened if I had simply walked in the other direction.

As strange as it is to see the skyscrapers that never seem to change, I'm almost excited. Nightshade tosses his head as we walk through the streets leading into the Upper Circle, passing by groups of elven people who gawk at me over brightly colored drinks or shopping bags.

Everyone here is far different than those I've seen in Eerie—they're dressed in much brighter outfits with less velvet and lace, more slim-fitting and tight to show off whatever it is they feel the need to be appreciated for or to show off the fact that they're *skinny.*

I ignore their wide eyes as I lean over Nightshade's neck, rubbing my hand up and down the length of it to ease his obviously ruffled nerves. Their stares make anxiety creep up in me, threading through the old insecurities I had from this place and dredging them back up from wherever they had been buried before.

Ugh. I'm only back here for Cain, I remind myself. I don't have to stay in this place of fake smiles and faker personalities. I can leave anytime.

Just keep reminding yourself of that. You don't have to stay here.

Dropping my hand against my thigh, I tap a strange new melody over it as we walk in the direction of the outer beach side—heading toward the rumored new casino I only know of due to a blonde high-elven woman in a bright blue outfit shouting about losing the majority of her money in "that damned casino and it's rigged machines!" I watch her kick at a bit of loose stone on the road, shaking my head as she crosses her arms over her chest and huffs with all the exasperation of a child.

She takes hold of her chunky pearl necklace, and I *swear* she's about to rip it off for a moment, but she seemingly gives up the thought and storms away.

The scent of salted ocean air wafts through the buildings as we walk on the road beside the sands, catching on my tongue with every breath. I study the roll of the clear ocean waves, finding that I oddly missed it from my time away. White foam clings to the tops of them as they sweep in, spreading strands of bright green seaweed and silky kelp onto the pale white sand, taking very few pieces back with it as it turns out again. The waves roll in and out, a pleasant sound over the whispers in my mind that I've grown accustomed to back at the manor.

My gaze strolls from the beach to the large pirate ships docked only a mile down, then across the road to a massive, glossy building with stripes of rectangular glass windows I know probably aren't seen from the inside. It's nearly as tall as the skyscrapers themselves, with bright red lighting casting in beams up into the air and glowing from the inside. A long scarlet carpet stretches from the arched main entrance and onto a stone patio, cutting off at the steps leading up to it.

A younger human man in a red and white suit rushes up to me, smiling wide and holding out his hands for my reins. "I can tie your horse around the corner for you, sir! He'll be well taken care of."

I nod hesitantly, then swing myself over Nightshade's back and onto the stone surrounding the steps. My legs ache from my time spent in the saddle, spreading a new wave of soreness from my feet up my spine. "Thank you."

He nods, taking Nightshade from me and starting for an area around the right side of the building. "Of course, sir! Have a great time."

Two guards standing on either side of the door side-eye me as I pass, but neither make any motion to stop my progress. The room beyond the doors is painted in multiple shades of red—dark on the walls, crimson velvet couches and chairs to the right over a black tile floor, private rooms hidden by glittering curtains in ruby.

Wide chandeliers hang over the sitting area and the gaming area to the left, and one incredible in size rests over my head, covering the walkway in shimmering gold light. From a quick look over, it's covered in rubies and dripping with diamonds, casting shimmering patterns on the floor and red carpet beneath it. Fake fire dances everywhere I look, even in the glass-walled corners, and the servers are seemingly dressed as incubi and devils.

I find I like it, perhaps moreso than I expected, but I suppose it makes sense considering the casino's owner. It is very like Cain to make a place look like a layer of the Hells.

I continue past the main area, stepping through a wide hallway lined by bars and restaurants on either side, trying not to feel disgusted with how close I have to brush to other people as I slip my way through the thick crowd. A mix of alcohol, cigarettes, cigars, and cheap perfumes fill the air, clogging my ability to smell anything else beneath it all as I attempt to squeeze through.

More people shoot looks at me for getting close to them—or worse, because they might recognize me or my markings—but I try to ignore the anxiety it fills me with. That, coupled with the booming music and jingling game machines and people shouting, is all quickly becoming too much.

How do people enjoy casinos?

A man with tan skin, angled-back horns, and long emerald-green hair starts to passes me by with a clipboard in hand, looking over briefly to cast me a quick smile and nothing else. Purely business. His entire body drips with golden jewelry, from his horns to his neck, even his hands—marking him as a richer sort—though the pure white suit he wears would be proof enough to those with an eye for such things.

Curious and a little bit hesitant, I wave him over. "You wouldn't happen to know Cain Sidrelle, would you?" I ask, wringing my hands together at my waist.

"Yes, of course. How could you not?" the man replies, swishing an arrow-pointed tail behind him as he looks me over in one swift glance. His vibrant eyes narrow but light up at the same time, suspicious and intrigued. The response is expected—Cain was far too well-known before we liked each other, and I can't imagine that would've changed at all over the years.

I can't help but smile despite the questions in his gaze, looking around us. "This is his casino, right? Where might he be?"

He studies me again, eyeing a golden watch on his wrist. "Ah, yes this is his casino. It's been running for about a year and a half now. How did you not know?"

He's definitely suspicious. Shit.

"I've been out of town for a long time," I manage, watching as he looks over my black turtleneck and corset vest, down to my black slacks and the chains hanging from my waist. It makes me nervous, wanting to crawl out of my skin. "I haven't seen him in a while."

The man glances at his clipboard for a moment, checking something off with a swift dash of his pen before leveling me with a surprisingly firm look. "And you are? I hope you know, if you're lying to me or trying to pull something, I'm his business partner, and I *will* have you taken out of here."

"Daedalus Macabre," I answer easily enough. "Any chance I can meet with him? I'm not trying to do anything sneaky, I swear. I... I just want to see him, nothing else." Impatience grips me over how tedious the questions are, but if this man knows who and where Cain is, it has to be done. Still, it makes me rub my hands together, trying to ignore the urge to move any more than that. Trying not to be twitchy, even though it's all my body wants to do after acknowledging what lies beneath it.

The man's body freezes, visibly tensing for a second as he stares at me. "That doesn't make sense," he states, seeming unable to catch himself before the words slip out.

Oh.

"How do you figure... Salvador?" I ask slowly, my gaze tracing over the name tag pinned to the pocket of his suit.

Salvador almost flinches at the sound of his name, running a hand back through his hair and pacing for a whole two steps before he turns to face me again. "Ah, nothing. I... nothing. I misspoke." He lets out an uncomfortable laugh, bringing a hand up to one of his pointed ears to what must be an earpiece. "I'll let the guards know to let you through."

My smile must brighten more than I mean it to but I can't bring myself to care, quickly thanking him as I continue along the carpet in the direction of the elevators. The edges of the machine are wrapped in burnished golden swirls with rubies embedded in the corners, and the door itself is a matching, shimmering gold. My gaze follows the waves that line the door as I wait for it to open, watching a few people drunkenly tumble out of it before quickly shuffling my way inside and pressing the button to close the door.

Of course, the inside of the elevator is a bright red.

As the door finally slides shut, I am met with the shocked expression on my own face, reflected back at me by the metal surface of the door. A new wave of anxiety takes over, warring with myself about the strange slenderness of my body and the stretched length of it, the odd scarecrow-like way I look. An ages-old fear, but one that still clings to me like sinew clings to bone.

What if he doesn't like it anymore?

Gods, focus.

I roll my eyes at myself and pull a ribbon from my pocket to tie half my hair up, leaving the rest to fall as it usually would. Once it's mostly out of my face, I fold my arms over my chest and focus on the hum of the elevator as it fluctuates between floors—sometimes the only thing I can hear, other times vanishing slowly under the sound of a deep bass rattling through the floors.

The higher I go, the less I can hear the elevator's mechanics, until that bone-shaking music is the only thing permeating the thin red walls around me.

Am I getting close to the top floor, or is it still just the other layers passing by?

My nervousness is promptly answered when the doors part easily, gliding open and exposing the dark gray floor beneath the roof, the music much louder here than it had been coming up. I step out warily, looking down the hall to my right before finding the pair of glass doors that must lead upstairs, slowly approaching the men waiting for me.

Two large, orcish guards stand on either side, eyeing me over their dark sunglasses as they motion me to a stop when I approach. Their olive-green skin tone is almost warped by the neon lights coming from the area beyond the doors, turning them odd shades of almost-purple and pink.

The one on the left looks down at me, folding his arms over his chest firmly. "Who are you, and how did you get up here, sir?"

I swallow, glancing between them and hating the fact that I can't see their eyes, trying not to focus on the sizable tusks protruding from the right one's lower lip. "Daedalus Macabre, Salvador said he'd send a message up here about me."

They glance at one another, back at me, then at the doors.

The man on the right nods somewhat slowly, pushing the door he guards open to me. "He's right. Go on, don't cause any trouble."

For a moment, I almost expect there to be an issue, for this all to be some strange sort of test, but they wave me through without another word and I don't waste the opportunity by hesitating.

I hurry up the remaining steps to the roof and look around, admiring the neon-lit pool that takes up the majority of the space, the equally-as-bright bar, the barely-to-mostly-dressed people. My gaze scours everyone, on the hunt for a shock of red hair and coming up empty despite my attempts. The music is even louder here than downstairs, something bass-filled that vibrates deep in my chest, adding to the slight overwhelm that has been building beneath my skin since I arrived at this ostentatious place.

Someone passes me a colorful drink, one that is most definitely not my style, but I take it anyway just to have *something* to hold onto.

I catch a glimpse of someone familiar—*god, what was his name again?*—Marion, that was it. Cain's best friend. He's in a deep, peacock-green dress that clings to his slender, tan body, every shift and turn showing a flash of a more neon green shimmering beneath. His makeup is impeccable, sharp around his brown eyes with matching green lipstick on his grinning lips, and he's looking up at a surprisingly curvy, blonde elven woman I don't recognize.

Not his type, from what little I remember, but I don't think it's that sort of interaction. Friendly and platonic, for sure.

I look around again, hoping to spot Cain in the crowd before messaging Marion, but I don't find him.

With a deep breath, I give in and focus on the man only a handful of feet before me. My magic reaches out to his, connecting in a way that feels the same as the Astral did when I stood in it for only a brief moment with Asher, wrapping cool waves of energy between us. *"Hi, Marion."*

He jumps visibly, glancing around the area before looking back to his friend. *"Um... hello?"* His voice is pleasant in my head, concerned but soft, just as I recall it being.

I sip the drink I've yet to try, wrinkling my nose a little at the sweetness of it. *"Where's Cain?"*

Marion frowns, shaking his head at the woman as she too, starts to look around. *"Remind me, who is this?"*

"Don't tell me you forgot what my voice sounds like," I reply, almost amused, but it comes out a little more tense than I mean it to due to my nerves. *Don't piss him off.*

"There's no way—This isn't... Daedalus?" he asks, scanning the crowd for the source of my voice. The way he says my name tugs on my heart. It's almost sad, almost hopeful.

More "almosts".

I shift a bit further among the throngs of people, weaving in and out of the shadows they leave behind to make sure I'm not immediately picked out by him or the friend he's with. *"It is."*

Marion nearly drops his drink, bringing a well-manicured hand to his forehead before turning on his heel and starting in the opposite direction of the bar, slipping through the crowd with effortless grace. *"Daedalus, it's been 10 years. How the hell are you here?"*

Gods, that confirmation jars me every time. *"You don't want that answer."*

Marion doesn't reply, so I slip through the darkness between people laughing and dancing to follow him, discarding the overly sweet drink somewhere behind me. He's quick, but I keep my eyes on the glow of his bright blonde hair, following the remnant tug of his magic as it slowly frees itself from mine.

A moment later, he pushes through a group of men who easily move for him, exposing Cain in all his glorious beauty. His entire outfit is sleek—from his high ponytail of red waves to the black satin dress pouring over his curves like an oil spill. It cuts deep over his chest, exposing his pale collarbones and the long gold and pearl necklace he wears. Drawing my eyes back to his face before they can fall any lower, I take a breath to admire the way his makeup clings dark and smoky around his intense eyes, his lips the exact color of blood and glistening as if he'd recently reapplied whatever gloss he used to tint them that way.

A smudge of the shade marks the cigarette he's currently tucking between his lips, and I watch as all of the men around him extend a lighter in one hand to light it.

All that previous wanting I had comes slamming back into me so hard, I lose my concentration on keeping myself in the shadows.

Something about Cain has changed since my passing—from the ferocious air of confidence to the anger in his eyes. Even at a party he should be enjoying, something about him seems cold and business-sharp, unwilling to be anything else with the people currently surrounding him.

Marion looks pale as he rushes up to Cain, brown eyes finally falling on me before he looks to Cain, who removes the cigarette from his mouth likely to question his friend's expression. I can't get myself to look away, to do *anything* but stand here and watch, frozen in place all because my desperation for this man is far too big for my body.

And then he looks up, eyes locking on mine despite the crowd.

For a moment, he just looks through me, confusion and surprise warring in his gaze. It almost hurts, because no matter how long it has been, no matter how much he has changed, I would recognize Cain by sight alone. By scent and touch and the sound of his oh-so-beautiful heartbeat. No matter what senses are stolen from me, I will always know him.

Then comes the recognition. The flash of pain.

As one of the men steps towards him in what looks like concern, the elf's drink drops and shatters loudly on the floor. The music all but swallows the sound, but those nearby enough to hear it fall quiet as their eyes follow the noise, eager and nosey for a hint of drama.

Cain stands beneath their scrutiny and curiosity for only a second before he spins around and vanishes down a small flight of stairs just behind him.

I'm moving before I even realize it, darting through the crowd after him, following Cain carefully around a corner and through two black glass doors before anyone else can. It opens into a beautiful, wide penthouse—both the marble floor and the smooth walls a stark shade of pale cream that makes his golden decorations and red furniture stand out far more.

I follow him right into what appears to be a living room, judging by the deep red couch set into a rectangular pit in the center of the floor. It's a little reminiscent of what I can remember about his college dorm in Whitestone, and even though I can barely take my eyes off of Cain, I still allow a moment to admire the craftsmanship of the room around us.

"Go away," Cain snaps, and I tense at the crisp tone to his voice.

"I can't do that, I'm sorry," I murmur, and he freezes before slowly turning on one of his red heels to face me.

He searches my face for a split second, his eyes flashing through countless emotions before settling on anger—his pupils turning to thin slits, almost invisible in the deep red of his irises. "Whoever you are, pretending to be someone who is fucking *dead* to fuck with me is a total dick move."

He steps closer as he snarls, stabbing a sharp fingernail into my chest as he glares up at me.

He still smells like roses. Standing this close to me, I take note of everything, painting him clearly in my mind, memorizing him. I trace the sharpness of his eyes, his long lashes that nearly reach his brow, his sharp cheekbones I ache to press my palms against, his soft lips I want so badly to drag the pad of my thumb across. My want for him haunts the very air between us, coating every second we stand here staring at each other.

I swear I can feel Cain's exhalation barely brush across my scarred throat, shaky and as uncertain as I am right now. His teeth sink into his lower lip, and he shakes his head again—pausing only for his gaze to linger on my neck for a moment too long before darting up to meet my eyes, then away again.

Disbelief rolls off of him in sheets, so much so I'm losing the confidence I had in reassuring him.

"Cain, I'm not faking it," I say slowly, taking the elf's hand in mine and guiding it down from where it rests on my chest. "It's really me."

"No, that's..." He pauses, slapping my hand away. "That's not possible. I saw you *die* ten years ago. How—*why* are you here? This isn't right. I must be hallucinating," Cain says quickly, laughing in a breezy way as he steps back, crossing the marble floor to an island in the kitchen area. His eyes turn from angry to a little wild, a little more unsettled than I'm familiar with on him. Wide enough to show the whites of them clearly, like a deer caught in a snare. "Maybe my mother was right. I need fucking medication or *something*. I've officially fucking lost it."

I suppose I shouldn't be surprised at how quickly Cain jumped to that conclusion. There is a part of me that knew it would go like this, knew that, even ten years later, Cain's mother would hang over his head just as my mother still hangs over mine.

"Cain, you aren't hallucinating.' I step toward him, cautiously, only stopping when he shoots a sharp look in my direction. "I'm here. I'm real."

"*No.* I already told you, that's not possible. Daedalus Macabre died ten years ago. You can't tell me you're now here somehow," Cain spits, the viciousness I rarely saw in him rearing its head again. I always knew it'd be slightly terrifying to be on this side of Cain's anger, even just the painful embers he gives me now, and I was right. I can't imagine how he would look at his angriest. I'm not sure I could handle it.

"There's no way it's really you. You're just some shitty person trying to get back at me or something. Who are you, really? An ex? A jealous noble?" As I go to respond, he stalks forward and puts a finger to my lips. "Don't speak until I tell you to. What the hell are you doing here? Speak."

I shift a little uncomfortably, glancing at his hand and then his face again. "I came for you. After my memories returned, I just... I wanted to see you again. It's truly me."

Cain narrows his eyes again, throwing his hands out on either side of him. "Tell me one Godsdamned thing that only the real Daedalus Macabre would know about me. *Now.*"

The broken pieces of my mind whip into motion, crashing together all the different little fragments of conversations, of secrets shared over wine or on the rooftop of the college. I roll my neck back and forth to ease the urge to twitch as I think it over, finally pinpointing one for him. "You were locked away by your mother for two years and she took your assets during that time. You've been on the outs with her ever since, and you were fighting with her before we kissed on Whitestone's roof. That was the first time we had done anything like that."

The longer I look at him, the more the fire in his eyes starts to dwindle and fizzle out.

"I don't understand," Cain whispers, his voice turning shaky. His resolve starts to crumble before my eyes, his shoulders hunching as his fury dissipates. "I... what..."

I don't touch him, standing there, waiting as tears start to form in his eyes. I've never seen him so fragile, or so lost for words. I'm not sure what to do, how to help. "I promise, it's really me," I say quietly. *Hopefully.*

"Daedalus... what the *hell*." Cain asks, blinking so the tears don't fall. He either isn't trying to show it, or he doesn't want to mess up his makeup, or both. Either way, I hate seeing it.

Cain looks at me hard, as if staring me down might give him answers to questions neither of us know how to truly ask. I can't say I blame him, but the look feels somewhere between heavy and a knife cutting into me, and I can't figure out which half is worse.

"I'm supposed to be having a party with my friends, and now you're here... and I don't know what to do about it," Cain gesturing around the room before dropping his hands to his sides in what I can only assume is surrender. "I've changed, you know. I'm more important in this city than ever."

I consider holding my hands out to him, but with the way Cain's voice sounds, I don't think it's the best idea. "I can tell. I'm not surprised, truthfully."

He steps away from me again, running a hand through his hair, seemingly deciding to keep his eyes off me.

My mouth opens to try and say *anything*, wanting so badly to reassure him.

But what could I possibly say now?

Cain turns his back to me, and my heart wrenches as his shoulders begin to shake.

"Can I touch you?" I ask, only moving once he nods.

Cautiously, I reach out to gently grasp his hips, carefully pulling him into me. I don't know if this is the right move. I don't know if *anything* is the right move anymore—I just know that if I withdrew, who knew if Cain would allow me to touch him again.

"You don't know how much I missed you," Cain murmurs, finally turning around to face me again. He steps closer, until my hands slide past his hips to wrap loosely around his waist, then buries himself into a hug in my grasp. "You don't know what I've done since then."

The feeling of him, right here, warm and soft, is overwhelming.

"I've missed you terribly." I reach forward, lightly brushing a few strands of hair from his face once he looks up at me. "And, I've done some things since then, too. I'm not worried about that."

Cain leans his head into my touch and exhales shakily, a hint of a smile on his lips. "This doesn't feel real...How long have you been back?" he asks, and he sounds almost *hopeful*.

I grimace, glancing away from him. "I've been back for a little over a month, I think. I had some things to take care of, and some memories to recall before I could come see you."

"You waited a whole month to come see me?" he asks, soft and so, so small.

He looks like the pinnacle of elegance, the pinnacle of beauty, the thing to sate my appetite. I'm the wick burning under his flame, he's the wildfire in the forest of me.

Ten years didn't change the way my heart tries to break out of my ribcage every time I see him.

"I came back for you," I whisper, close to his lips, but not close enough.

He laughs, teary-eyed and a little breathless, resting a hand on my chest. "I've been waiting."

Something unspoken hangs in the space between us, filling the silence without anything needing to be added. Cain shifts and looks into my eyes, and when I make myself not look away like I always would before, a smile blooms across his face again.

In this moment, I'm certain my want for him is leaving bloody trails in my footsteps. In this moment, I am gutted, stripped bare.

How terrible it is to be known like this. How terrible it is to be seen by him, to be witnessed, to be *wanted.* It's strange, all of it.

I blink, and all of a sudden Cain's lips are on mine, deep and messy and absolutely perfect. I don't even care that his lipstick is staining my mouth. He's here, and I'm with him, and I finally *have* him. I taste the lingering sweetness of black cherry and tequila and smoke on his tongue, chasing the feeling of him as he presses me close to him, so close I can't escape even if I tried.

Something in me says I shouldn't be doing this, but Cain is *here,* and Cain wants me, and—

And hells, I need this too.

At some point he starts moving us backward toward his couch, and once the back of his thighs touch it, he pauses, pulling back to create some space between us. I miss the touch of his skin immediately, but he doesn't make me wait long.

He doesn't make me wait, because he slaps me. *Hard.*

I recoil in surprise, putting my hand over my cheek as I look back at him. The pain is distinct, emptying my mind of my racing thoughts for once—and then he does it one more time when I tentatively drop my hand. The second isn't as hard, but just as jarring as the first.

Cain doesn't look angry, though, when I stare at him in disbelief. He just smiles. "That's for leaving me, you asshole."

He grabs me again, pulling me with him so we fall over onto the couch, one of his legs hooking up onto my hip. I shiver as his hands snake under my shirt, pressing his sharp fingernails into my back—a playful move, but I am so *hungry.* Hungry enough that even when Cain pulls away and runs kisses down my throat, I do nothing to stop him. Nothing to slow him down, no matter how much I want to savor this.

His lips are so careful over the scar circling my throat, that it nearly brings me to tears.

"What do you want to happen right now?" I ask him breathily, and he shrugs.

"Why don't you tell me?" he replies, cool and sharp.

I tilt my head ever so slightly, studying his expression. My hunger reflects back at me in the reds of his irises, colored vibrant with *want* and *need* and...*hope.* He's as hopeful as I am right now.

Oh.

It takes me a moment to process what exactly he wants, pulling together the threads of my mind to make up a scenario in my head. "Well, love...depending on how you want this to go, I'd say I want to touch you, I want to remember how you feel. If that's not the direction you want this to go in, we could meet at the bar for a drink. We'll talk—for a long, long time."

He hums, eyeing me. "And what if I said I like both options?"

I smile, chuckling a little as his expressions turns a little devious. "Then we do one first, and the other after."

Cain pushes me back upright, sinking to his knees, perched and poised on the floor. "I like your first option, then. What else do you like, Daedalus?"

"Well..." I swallow, watching him closely. The feeling of authority almost feels backward, compared to the first time we did something like this—from what I can recall of it, anyway. "Use your mouth on me, then, and I'll give you the pleasure you want. We can have a discussion about what we like after. I don't want to waste any more time."

He reaches for my pants without hesitation, quickly starting to unbutton them as he eyes me. Something twinkles in his gaze, something I *know* I've never seen before.

"Yes, Sir."

The honorific is obviously playful, but it strikes something deep in me that has me cupping his jaw, smoothing my thumb over his smeared lipstick. "Good. I like that."

Cain releases me from my boxers a moment later, taking my hardening length in his hand to give it an easy stroke and smiling when I let go of his mouth. He doesn't give me long to think about how I almost put my thumb to work on his tongue, ducking his head to drag my cock across it instead, bringing me into the heat of his mouth with ease.

I can see the way his lipstick quickly starts staining my skin, and it hits me that I likely have it *everywhere*. My lips, my neck—but I love it. I love it because it's Cain's, and I wouldn't trade that for the world.

My hands tangle in his hair to keep myself steady, and my head tips back as the low sounds of pleasure begin spilling from my mouth, quickly devoured by the music up above. He moans around me, drawing me in further, holding me in the back of his throat.

I shiver when he glances up at me, his eyes heavy with lust, low-lidded and gorgeous.

"Fuck, Cain," I groan, and he smiles around me before going back to work. "You're divine. Absolutely divine."

His tongue curls around veins, pressing harder in certain spots, giving me more attention in others. I moan for him, hell, I *whimper* for him, fisting my hand in his hair and using it to hold him in place as I pull him down to the base. Foul prayer, that's what this is. His head bent down to me, moaning reverently to someone who was almost a God.

I keep him there until his mascara runs the slightest bit, then allow him to continue his motions.

Everything about this is so perfect, even the way Cain leans back and wipes his face with the back of his hand when I crash over the edge a second later, leaving faint red streaks on his pale skin. For a brief moment, I almost feel bad about ruining his beautiful makeup, but at the same time, I like seeing him this way, so the feeling doesn't last.

Leaning down, picking Cain up and setting him on the couch, I kiss him again. My hands play across his skin, tugging away his clothes eagerly, touching him in all the ways I desired to so long ago. His body glows under the suite's lights, calling me to him like he's a lighthouse and I'm a ship lost at sea. I am so hungry, murmuring sweet nothings into his skin as my fingers explore him, worshipping his beauty, yet again my altar. Drinking in his sweet rose scent, listening to him repeat my name over—

And over—

And *over*.

"Oh *Gods*," he gasps, throwing his head back into the cushions.

"Don't say their name. Only mine," I reply in a rumble, sinking deeper and deeper into the oblivion that is his pleasure.

I thrust into him, and he tangles his fingers in my hair, pulling me down to kiss him again and again. I've dreamt of kissing him thousands of times, but these last few make every bit of my imagination far more worth it than the rest. Soft and slow, hard and needy, the kind that alcohol likes to make gentle and sloppy. Every kiss I have with him in this moment is better than all of them. Every kiss I have *for real* is better than anything I could dream up.

My hands press into the couch on either side of his head, giving me some sort of balance as I pick up an easy pace—one that has him moaning eagerly against my mouth, clawing up my back. I drive deep into him, wanting to be connected, anchored to him so I don't float away.

I fuck him exactly as he wants, wielding my desire as something moldable, showing him just how much I'm here for him. He makes it so easy to fall into his gravity, centering himself in my world like I'm a comet, pulling me down to his earth.

I let him pull me. I let him drag me down under.

26

— · —

ONCE WE finally finish up, not that I truly want to, I admire Cain as he readjusts his dress and starts to fix his makeup. He doesn't get to all of it, deciding instead to pull a cigarette out from the table and tuck it between his lips, smiling when I flicker a little flame to life over my finger and hold it over to him. The action, though reversed from the last time, feels so...familiar. Heartbreakingly familiar.

"You've changed a lot, huh?" he asks, eyeing me over his shoulder as he takes a drag. It's more of a murmur, but I hear him all the same.

"I suppose I have," I reply, straightening out my clothes as I sit up, hips and arm still pressed against Cain's. I don't think I can bring myself to pull away from him ever again. The fact that I'm even here with him right now is amazing, and I continuously have to tell myself not to give my leg or arm a pinch to *really* make sure it's real.

After a moment, he leans his head back against the couch, tilting it toward me with a curious expression on his face. *Cigarette smoke*

396

and roses. What a beautiful thing. "So... if you don't mind me asking, how did you get back?"

Obviously, I knew the question would come up—but I never thought of the pointed, uncomfortable feeling it would give me when it did.

It's the elephant in the room, the one question everyone wants to ask. Not why, not when, always *how.* My miraculous return doesn't make sense, and I know that, but the knowledge doesn't make the question easier to handle.

My heart sounds a little too loud in my ears, and I squeeze my eyes shut, imagining the shadows of the red velvet, the claustrophobic knowledge of being trapped.

All I can smell for a moment is dirt, dirt, dirt.

"I woke up in my grave. I don't know how, or why, I just did," I start, pressing my hands into the couch cushions to keep them from shaking. My head twitches to the side, a monstrous tic of mine, and I just as quickly roll my neck out to make it less noticeable. "I carved my way out with a blade spell, and started walking away from the cemetery. Nothing more than that, really."

Cain nods slowly, turning his head to look up at the ceiling again. He seems to chew on that for a moment, shifting slightly so he can prop a leg over my thigh, blowing another cloud of smoke toward the ceiling. "Have you been up to anything interesting, since you waited a month to come see me?"

I nod, tracing a finger over his knee. "I have, yes. I've been making a new home, creating things in a lab, and a few other things."

He raises an eyebrow, laughing. "Are those other things a secret?"

I don't tell him about the bodies in my yard, or the organs in my freezer.

"For now, yes. Do you think we should go back upstairs?" I look up at the ceiling, wondering what his friends must be thinking. What *Marion* must be thinking. I'm surprised he hasn't come down here yet, truthfully. Out of his entire group, he is the only one I'd truly be afraid of—he's not afraid to attack people for Cain, or so I heard through stories Asher used to tell me.

If Cain is thrown by the sudden topic change, he doesn't show it, just shrugs and leans further into me. "I don't know if I want to, anymore. Though I will admit, I like your drink idea."

I make a clicking sound in thought, something akin to a raven, from deep in my throat—which he imitates a moment later, but a little higher.

It strikes something dark in my core, calling out to the monster in me that wants him as badly as I do. "I'd like that," I say after a moment, forcing the words from my mouth so the other part of me doesn't come out. "Where should we go, then?"

He rubs his palm over my knee, sending a wave of goosebumps through my whole body, before moving to stand "Let's clean up quick, and I'll take you to my favorite bar. I don't want to go back to that party, I'd rather focus on you, honestly."

He crushes out his cigarette in an ash tray on the table, then starts walking down a hall only a few feet away. Standing up, I follow his lead as we walk to his bathroom, which is surprising in its size. The bathtub is more of a Jacuzzi, with two showerheads side by side on the wall above it, and even the sink is wider than any I've seen before. A mirror hangs behind it, the same width as the counter, making it easy for Cain to lean over and check his face for anymore messy makeup.

I watch him for a moment, exhaling softly. "Why would you rather focus on me?"

He makes a face in the mirror, giving me a look that means 'are you actually asking me that?' before he reapplies his lipstick again. "I haven't had you for ten years, and you want to ask me why?"

"I guess you're right." I frown, looking back toward the door. It's still hard to believe sometimes that Cain would choose me over anything, much less a party with his friends. Eager for something else to fill the silence, a thought quickly snaps into my mind, and I jolt slightly. "Oh, I forgot! I have a horse outside. I suppose I should take him with us, in case I end up going home after our outing."

"You have a horse?" Cain leans back from the mirror and laughs, smoothing his dress out with his palms. I can't stop watching every little motion, focusing on the way the muscles of his arms shift with the movement, eyeing the angle to his knuckles. It almost makes me feel normal, if only for a second.

"I do."

His smile warms slightly as he looks over at me, then he bends over to grab a small packet of wipes from a drawer under the sink. "Shit, Dae, I almost forgot to get the makeup off you! You look...interesting."

I raise an eyebrow, leaning in to peer at myself in the mirror and startling at my reflection. Even though part of my surprise is over the fact that I'm seeing myself—one, without my hair in my face, and two, I'm really here—most of it is about how much of his lipstick is painted on my skin. Red smudges stain my mouth, my jaw, my throat, smearing more in some places than others. I know there's more under my turtleneck, but I'm not willing to look.

His laugh comes out a little more bubbly, nothing like the raucous thing I can just barely remember, and he reaches over to take my hand in his as he wipes off my face.

The shock of our skin coming together again is enough to make me crumble, staring down at where our hands overlap and where they simply press together. It's as familiar as putting butter on toast—his fingers easily slipping through mine, our palms passing heat between each other, my sleeve brushing his wrist. I stop simply to look at the difference between my own roughened hand and the slender slope of his. It could make me emotional, if I'm not careful.

"What, Dae?" Cain is watching me, curious instead of cold, far unlike the way he was looking at the men upstairs earlier.

I shake my head, letting out an airy laugh. "Nothing. Lead the way."

He tosses the red-marked makeup wipe and tugs me from the penthouse, giving the guards a sharp nod before walking to the elevator. The moment the doors close, he pulls my hands over to his hips, drawing his body up close to mine. It's torture, standing here and holding him like this. I don't dare pull away.

"I'd kiss you again if I didn't *just* get the lipstick off your mouth," he murmurs, flashing a flirty smile at me that borders on seductive.

It almost snaps the leash I have on my restraint. Almost. "I'd let you if it wasn't for that same reason."

Cain smirks, playfully removing himself from my grasp as the elevator chimes, leaving me wishing for the heat of him in my hands again. *Craving* it. Being separated from him now feels painful, a physical ache that doesn't have a cure until his skin is on mine again. I feel whole when he touches me and split apart when he doesn't.

Fuck. I didn't think it would be this bad.

I follow him without a word, tucking my hands in my pockets to keep them from reaching for him. Waves of people walk up to us, attempting to talk to Cain and failing—it's almost impressive how he brushes them off or completely ignores them, checking his nails instead of looking at them, shouldering on his cold, business persona.

It's almost frightening, the way that mask looks so much like his father. The few times I saw Minos, he was always like that. Cold, calculated, speaking with the perfected sense of someone who knew your weakness and was barely disguising the fact that he learned it. A handsome devil, he was, and probably still is. He's likely worse now, if time has done so much to Cain.

The most powerful men in the continent of Vira are Minos and his son, that's a sure fact.

Cain walks down the street and into a neat black and electric-blue painted building only a little way past his casino, barely allowing me a moment to even get a look at it. The neon sign hanging above the door says something about THE TWISTED DRAGON in a matching blue to the outside, and I think I catch a glimpse of a winged serpent curling around it before we're ducking through the doors and it's out of my sight.

Inside, the low music and the shifting lights cast us in a dreamy haze—all blues and sparkling golds—making it hard to focus on anything but the elf before me as he walks me through a dancing crowd and stops at a glossy bar. His makeup is even darker in this lighting, making the seductive way his long eyelashes are lowered more intense, and when he meets my gaze, the colors swim in the pools of his irises like koi fish. I don't look away despite my urges to, and he smiles.

"I ordered you something with bourbon, is that okay?" he asks as he leans closer, resting a hand over my arm. The touch thrills through me, making the hair on the back of my neck stand on end.

"I don't know a lot about alcohol, but I'm sure I'll like it, thank you," I say close to his ear, smiling back at him before surveying the crowd farther behind us. High above their heads, large silver birdcages hang from the ceiling, and I swear I catch a glimpse of bodies moving within. "This wasn't the type of bar I expected you to take me to, by the way."

Cain laughs, following my gaze up toward the cages and back to the dancefloor, looking somewhere past it. "Right, sorry. This is Helios's club—you saw me with him before a party at Louis's house. The golden man who you probably thought was a Luceri?"

Closing my eyes, I try to picture who he's talking about, pushing through the splinters of my mind to drag his face to the surface. It takes a minute, but he eventually appears, glittering and being kissed by Cain on the cheek in front of his mansion. Ages-old jealousy strikes through me for a second. "Ah...right. I barely remember."

He doesn't answer right away, taking our drinks and passing mine over. I can't tell if the glittering liquid is *actually* black, or if the lighting is making it that way, but I don't mind. It smells sweet, somewhere between licorice and black cherry with the smooth bite of alcohol beneath.

All in all, I hope it isn't as sweet as the drink I tried on the casino's roof.

"Follow me," he states, taking my hand in his again and pulling me back through the dancefloor. We weave past multiple comfortable-looking sitting areas and neat tables all filled with people, crossing a small glittering platform to get to the back wall, I have to keep myself from stopping short when he ducks through a sheer curtain decorated with silver stars and into the room beyond it.

The entire back wall is made up of them—these curtained rooms—except this one's frame is ornately decorated with a swirling, flowery design that makes it stand out from the rest.

Cain closes a thin black door behind us as I step past him, taking in the seemingly private room. Compared to the blues in the outer area, this cove is lit by reds and hints of golds, making it feel closer and almost hungrier. The music is quieter here—more bass than anything else, still humming through the walls, adding a layer of sensuality I wasn't prepared for. Two long couches connected at the corners sit up against the wall over the black-carpeted floor, as well as a circular glossy table with a metal pole reaching from it to the ceiling. I imagine the ways people have danced there for a brief moment, before turning my attention back to Cain as he sits down languidly.

"Private room?" I ask, and he nods.

"Yeah, my personal one. Before you ask, I worked for Helios for a little bit. He treated me really well a few years after everything happened, and coming here was an outlet to escape myself for a while."

His gaze travels somewhere else in the room, and I immediately feel guilty for asking.

"It was also an outlet to escape Irsa, because Helios won't allow him in here, thank the Gods," he adds, shaking his head and crossing one long leg over the other. "I had fun doing it for a while, especially because he'd keep me up in one of those cages and make sure I was well tended to. My price to get any dances or anything of that sort was very, very high between his wants and my own."

Hearing Irsa's name again bites into me, shooting a burst of anger through my body like a flare in the night. "I'm glad you had fun. What did you do when you worked here?"

Cain smiles, patting the space on the couch next to him with one hand, eyeing me curiously as I step over to him. "I danced, primarily. We all offered lap dances and standard things of that sort, but anything further was a high charge—Helios didn't announce that on our menus, for our safety, but we were allowed to tell customers if we liked them enough. I even had a guy pay me once just to talk for a while."

Ha. Almost feels like what I'm doing.

Though I've never been well-versed in this line of work, I take a moment to imagine him dancing for someone who likely didn't appreciate him the way he should've been. Would he take to the pole across the room, or would he dance on them, telling them how they weren't worthy enough to touch him?

A strange wave of jealousy riles up inside me, knowing that other people could see him that way while I was trapped too far underground to experience it. To experience *him,* even if that might not have been the version of Cain I wanted to see.

I push the jealousy back down, reminding myself that *I'm* even lucky he's showing me his true self.

My gaze traces the shape of glittering hexagons on the wall from the golden lights, watching as they move easily across it. He takes my free hand and pulls it over to him, placing it palm-down on his knee where the dress falls just short enough for our skin to meet again. A shiver runs down my spine as I sip the drink he got for me, nodding a little in approval at the easy taste of it.

"Do you still come back here?" I ask, moving the tip of my pointer finger in a circle over his kneecap.

Cain swallows a sip of his cocktail, watching my hand. "I do, sometimes. Not nearly as often as I did before, especially with the casino being made... Do you remember touching me like this? We were in a carriage, and you kept doing that or something like it."

My hand twitches against him for a second before I settle it, closing my eyes to picture the moment he's describing. It comes back in pieces— it wasn't his knee that time, it was his palm. I kept following the creases of it, over and over again. "I do. It was your hand."

He smiles, nodding more to himself than to me as he gazes down at my fingers. "You know...you seem a little twitchier than before, Dae."

I follow the angle of his leg crossed over the other, where it meets with my hand on his knee. He's always been easy to follow like that, always forming new angles for me to look at whether it was from the folds in his clothes or the position he sat in.

"Ah, right. Something happened to me when I came back...something became more alive in me, I suppose. I also found an abandoned manor that was previously owned by a scientist mage, and I made a mistake there not long after I woke up, dabbled in places I shouldn't have. I'm alright. Just...not the same as before."

His hand lays over where mine rests on his knee, overlapping our fingers before he slips them together, simply holding on to me. It's as if he's done it for years, not only a few hours. So easy, so familiar. "That's okay. I didn't expect you to be the same." He pauses, and I hear the words without him saying them.

I didn't expect you to come back at all.

"I know," I whisper, and he closes his eyes. His breath hitches in his chest for a second, then we fall into silence. It fills with unspoken words, apologies and pleadings and cries in the night that will never be said or heard by anyone but ourselves.

My hands shake, making the ice in my glass clink against it.

Desperate to change the subject, I give his knee a light squeeze and look around the room. "I'd like it if you came to my manor. I could show you my lab, and I would treat you to a day you deserve."

He smiles, and it's a little tight. "I'd like that, too."

Cain moves to lean his head on my shoulder, and the silence is cast over us again. This time, I let it—not feeling as desperate to fix what lingers like I was a moment ago. He sighs, long and fully emptying, and I do the same.

"Hey, Dae?" he murmurs, and I glance over at him.

"Yes?"

"I just need you to know something, if we continue...whatever this is. You can't fix me, okay?" He sits up again, putting his glass down on the table and turning so he can take both of my hands in his. Something tells me this is far more vulnerable than he's ever been with someone in a long time. "Every time someone gets closer to me, they think they can, or they want to try. So, I'm putting it out on the table that I don't need you to try."

What?

My eyebrows raise at that, and I study his expression, finding him entirely serious. "What is there to fix?"

Cain lets out a light laugh, standing up. "Thank you. I don't know why I wanted to say that to you, I knew you'd be fine. We can go now, if you want."

27

—·—

CAIN'S eyebrows raise when his gaze lands on Nightshade, taking in the impressive height of him as I pull myself up onto his back. He gingerly pets his neck and down his shoulder before looking at me, then at the hand I extend down to him. "You have to be kidding."

I make a face at him, shaking my head. "Not at all, why?"

He laughs, looking the horse over one more time before reaching up to take my hand. "You never said the horse was *huge*, Dae. Also, I'm wearing a dress."

Oh, right.

This time it's my turn to laugh, sliding back down off Nightshade's back and onto the stone beside him. Knowing Cain is right, I reach a hand into the space before us and let my magic spill into my palm, expanding between my fingertips like webbing and forming a black portal for us to step through. It hums as it tears open, warping the air around it in the same way heat waves do. "There we go."

Cain stops, looking between it and me for a moment, a playful wariness in his eyes.. "I trust you, Dae, but if this somehow leads me to a trap—"

I peek at the hazy trees past the surface of the portal, then shake my head at him. "It's not a trap, Cain. Just my manor."

I don't blame him for being cautious.

He takes a deep breath before stepping through, and I follow behind with my stallion in tow. The trees whisper as soon as they see the three of us, talking over themselves, barely making sense. They want to know who my guest is, they want to *see* him, curious as to why he's here. They're happy I'm back. They're so, so curious.

I try my best to ignore them as we walk Nightshade to the barn, returning him to his stall before going to the door of my home. Inside, it smells far less like dust and old air, meaning the spirits I called did their job well—the entry hallway and living room beyond smell strongly of vanilla and citrus, mixing pleasantly when I breathe it in. Portraits watch us as we pass by the hallway, and I can tell when Cain notices because he hurries by one in particular depicting a spectral woman covered by a red veil.

"What the hell are these paintings, Dae?" he asks, and I swear he shivers as he hurries into the living room.

I shrug, smiling over at him. "They were here when I arrived, truthfully. I like them."

He shudders again, exhaling thinly as we walk past the velvet furniture and into the kitchen. So far, the manor looks gleaming and new in its gothic allure, and it makes me much happier to bring Cain here. It's so much *prettier* without the thick cobwebs and the layers of years-old dust clinging to everything, or so I think. I'm more than glad he didn't see how it was before.

I stop outside of the lab door, pulling it open and starting down a few of the stone stairs within. "Are you ready?"

Cain looks past me at the shadows hugging the stairwell, then slowly nods. "I think so?"

The temperature drops bit by bit as we descend, not touching once until he eventually reaches down to take my hand in his. I let him keep it until we reach the main room of my laboratory—which I'm immediately glad to see is entirely bloodless, compared to the way I'd last left it. I may have forgotten to clean it up. May have.

He squeezes my hand slightly as he looks around, and I hold onto him until he decides to release me from his grasp.

I would've held onto him for longer, if he needed it.

Clapping my hands twice, the green lights flicker on and cast the dark tables and their tools on top of them in an eerie, almost ominous glow. Notebooks with handfuls of notes, including Feloren's, are strewn everywhere alongside them, and Cain hesitantly strides over to take a peek at one. I don't mind, at least not entirely. Notes and science of this sort should be shared...probably.

Cain looks up from the notes after a second, surveying the room curiously, his eyes latching on to a glass partition leading to another room.. "What do you do in there?"

I look over, following his gaze. "That is one of the rooms where I do my experimenting. Live experiments, anyway."

"What are you currently working on?" Cain asks, drumming his fingertips over the notebook.

Flickers of organs and a bloodied ribcage, then my mind falls silent.

"I was considering making injectable adrenaline, essentially. I attempted it years ago, and the recipe took me about a week to get right when I still had easy access to a lab like this. Works well if you're a fighter—your muscles expand, and you become larger, angrier. So far, it doesn't last very long. I've never had much of a chance to try it out, at least not on anything besides myself," I explain, leaning back on my heels.

That was one of my first experiments, and one that I never truly finished, far away in my first home.

Cain's head tilts slightly to the side, leaning his hip against the counter. "What made you want to make it?"

A soft hum, looking up toward the ceiling as I mull the question over. "Well, I wanted to make plenty of things when I was younger. I suppose I inherited that from my mother." A grimacing pause. "I always had ideas, but never the time to see them through, or my mind would only focus on shapes and angles and not the equations

I needed to use to make what I wanted to. A little frustrating at times, but…I don't know. The idea of making something someone could use in fights like that seemed intriguing, if it would affect the body the way I expected it to."

He nods, his gaze traveling over my body in a scorching path as he steps over to me, close enough for me to feel the heat of his proximity again. "Would you want to try it on me?"

The question catches me by surprise, but the idea is exciting. Having someone who isn't me or to try to use my concoctions on sounds intriguing—so I give him an amused nod and reach for one of the empty syringes nearby. "If there's anything you want to take off, I suggest you do it now, or else you might rip it off in there."

Forcing my eyes away is a considerable feat, but I manage to, collecting a few vials from around the room. In one beaker, I mix a crushed Bitter White flower, a few drops of Ashen Pulp left behind by whoever lived here before me, and powdered rose thorns—touching a droplet of my magic to the rim of the glass and smiling when it begins to bubble and turn silver.

Cain watches me curiously, setting his dress in a neat pile on the tabletop. "What is all of that?"

I stick the needle's end into the liquid, admiring the way it flows into the glass part of the syringe. "Bitter White to advance the process, powdered rose thorns for an added boost, Ashen Pulp is the primary source for the adrenaline. It's typically used for harm, but mixed with these ingredients, the toxic part of it is reduced to about nothing. It becomes more of a steroid in this case. Bitter White can also be used in cases of reviving, or so I learned from a book years ago."

He nods, following me as I tuck a notebook under my arm and lead him into one of the glass-walled rooms. "You're so interesting," he remarks, and the slight blush on his cheeks tells me he probably didn't mean to blurt it out.

I laugh, unable to keep it back any longer. "Sure I am, Cain. Now, this might sting."

Cain's shoulders tense as I raise the syringe to the space between his neck and shoulder, considering the option of pricking him there. It would work, but the effects wouldn't last long enough for me to really write down my results... arm it will be, then. I lower my hand to his arm, turning it over so the milky expanse of his smooth forearm is exposed to me, then ease the needle into the flat of his inner elbow.

I have just enough time to back out of the room and close the door before the concoction hits Cain like a missile. His eyes light up with pure rage, the reds of them becoming increasingly violent and intense, roiling with an inner flame I can feel the heat of through the glass.

My hand moves quick to jot down every detail, admiring him as his fire blazes, coursing over his skin. It scorches the ground he stands on as he slams his hands into the wall, blowing clouds of smoke between his sharpened teeth.

It's hard not to stare at him. He's beautiful in this unnatural form of fury, snarling at the glass between us as I step closer out of curiosity. The heat of him fans me through the glass, striking in waves as he hits the wall again, aiming down at me.

To him, I'm an enemy, something to take apart.

To me, he's a violent angel, ruining me one step at a time.

Cain's hair fans out around him, forming a wild mane that cascades over his shoulders and down his back as he lunges at me, once, twice. I grin as I watch, shuddering with excitement, writing down another thread about his behavior.

The Rot rumbles, distant since the moment I stabbed my hand. **You should tell Asher.**

Asher. I had completely forgotten him since my time back above ground. *What a friend I am.*

Without much of a lead-in, I push my magic out to him, hunting for his presence. My shadows grasp and tug at anything that feels right but none of it does—at least, not until I catch a thread of his twisted darkness hanging somewhere in the air between myself and Nemoure.

"Asher, hi. I'm back. I'm so sorry I never messaged. You should see this experiment I'm performing right now, though."

The connection is immediate, clicking together a few gears in my mind that haven't worked in a long time. I swear I hear his sigh through my head. *"Fuck, Daedalus?! I thought Marion was going crazy when he told me he saw you on Cain's roof. It's so good to hear from you... What are you doing?"*

I smile up at Cain as the fire roils in his irises, colors dancing throughout the bloody pools of them. *"I made an injectable sort of adrenaline, in its early stages. I'm currently allowing Cain to be my test subject, speaking of which."*

Cain slumps back down to the floor a second later, his flames dying down beyond a few sparks leaving his lips. His presence becomes far quieter as he eyes me through the glass, his chest rising and falling in quick movements as he struggles to catch his breath.

Asher laughs in my head, mostly in disbelief and partly in amusement. *"Cain really let you do that?"*

I trace the flush to his cheeks and the slight smear to his lipstick before walking to the door, slowly opening it to step inside the room with him. *"He did."*

"What did you feel, Cain?" I ask, tapping the end of my pen against the page I made for him.

"That's amazing. He doesn't let anybody do that," Asher remarks in my head, and I can't help but smile at the implication that I'm somehow special to Cain.

Cain holds up a finger to signal to ask for a moment, as he struggles to catch his breath. "I felt angry, like I never have before. I couldn't control myself, even when I saw you—I wanted to *kill* you." He shakes his head, inhaling deeply and blowing it back out through his nose, touched lightly by dark smoke. "There was nothing in me that was thinking rationally. I just knew I had to get to you somehow."

"The anger was interesting to watch, to be honest. I knew it was going to happen, mainly because I was the same way when I tried it on myself. I had to lock myself in my lab so I could try it the first few times...I want it to last longer, though."

Cain takes my hand when I extend it to him, his body trembling for a moment. "I see. That was cool, though. I enjoyed it."

"Good! I'm glad you had a good time. Are you hungry at all now?" I ask, giving him a quick once-over and writing down that he seemingly had no permanent effects following the enlarging. If he stayed that way, I would've felt bad. "I was fairly hungry the first few times."

I can't help but want to treat Cain to the absolute best I can offer, even if I don't currently have much to my name after my return. I have plenty of ideas—making him dinner, taking him out to the garden with wine or champagne, making a platter of things to dip in chocolate. All things I would have done before, if Morgana hadn't been in my way.

"I'm starving, actually," he says, pulling me from my thoughts.

I funnel the spirit spell from before out of my hands and aim it upstairs, calling them to make dinner for us. Steaks, vegetables, wine if I have any. I don't get a response, but I hear them shuffling about overhead.

As we start to head back up the stairs, I run my hands back through my hair before lightly rubbing them together in front of me. The motion is interrupted by something dark on my palms, dripping from my fingers in steady rivers, soaking me to the bone.

Blood.

I jolt back and pause my ascent, staring at my hands with wide eyes. A flash of the training room, a flash of my mother. One of my hands rise to go to my head, but I can't touch anything on myself, because the blood seems so *real* that I can't see anything else. Memories fly by in ruinous flickers, crashing into my vision so violently, I can barely make myself move.

"Dae? Dae, hey, what's going on?" Cain asks as he leans into view, reaching out and touching my fingertips with his own.

My mind spins around the fact that my hands are stained, my hands are cruel and somehow Cain allows me to touch him anyway. I feel sick. I *am* sick. The room suddenly feels too close, the urge to scream in frustration climbing up in my throat as the walls box me in, shutting out everything else. Anxiety swells in my gut all at once, overtaking my body before I even have the chance to answer him.

"Dae?" he asks again, soft and concerned. It echoes around in the crowded space of my damaged mind, but I can't get out. I can't escape the visions of blood and her ruined face, her hands around my throat in a vice grip, the panicked emptiness I felt afterward.

Don't you hate what you did to me? You ruined everything. Everything.

Help, I want to say; but nothing comes out of my mouth but a raven's low chatter. *Now is not the time to go nonverbal, Daedalus. Come* on, come on—

My body quiets into one shaking void the instant I realize my face is pressed against Cain's chest, flooding my senses with the scent of roses and smoke. "Easy, Dae, you're okay," he murmurs, petting back my hair. I don't know when he grabbed me. I'm frozen in place, unsure really of what to do next, blinking as I stare at my hands. The blood is staining my skin, sinking in further and further.

"What's going on?" Cain asks softly, but I can't get my mouth to form any words.

He keeps me there, my back against the wall and my head against his chest, now pressing a bit harder so I don't have to see my hands. One of Cain's hands pets down my back, the other running through my hair, easing me into a quiet so deep it makes the whole manor seem still. All that comes out again is another raven sound, one he imitates back to me.

A shiver races down my spine at that, one ignited by intrigue from something he doesn't know about.

After a long moment, I summon the strength to stand upright again, eyeing the strand of my hair Cain is holding between two fingers.

"I'm glad your gray is still here, Dae. It looks good on you," he says in a soft attempt at distracting me, and I allow it to.

I smile a little, shaking my head. At first, when I open my mouth to speak, the monster's sounds spill out. I almost roll my eyes at it, before forcing the words through. "Thank you, I think," I answer with some effort, and he nods.

One of the spirits messages me a moment later, letting me know dinner is about ready, so I steady myself and continue up the stairs with Cain behind me. Scents of rosemary and garlic flood my nose as we get closer to the lab's door, making my stomach growl louder than it ever has. Clinking metal and the pop of a cork rings out as I step out into the room, holding the door open for Cain before shutting it tight behind us.

Two dishes of venison, roasted vegetables, and baked potatoes coated in butter sit steaming on the wooden table. My servant-like spirits waver in and out of sight as they finish bringing silverware to the table, adding a glass of probably years-aged red wine to the setup before they disappear entirely, leaving us alone.

I pull out Cain's chair for him and smile as he sits, moving to my own across the table from him. "This looks nice, thankfully. I wasn't sure what I would be able to make up."

Down the hall, the piano that never seems to quiet continues to play a soft nocturne, echoing softly throughout the manor. Cain surveys the food before lifting up his wine glass, eyeing the direction of the sound. "It does look nice...You have a piano that's always playing?"

I laugh, nodding in return. "Of course, I do. Why are you surprised?"

He shakes his head, smiling softly at me. "I'm not, totally. It actually makes me happy to know you still play."

Cutting into my venison and eating a piece as I study Cain, the want to sink my teeth into him and never let go strikes me. It is an old urge now, one I've never had about another person, despite what I am—but something about Cain makes me want to. I could bite into his neck, the muscle between it and his shoulder, maybe even his thigh. Hells, I would even take the inside of his forearm if I had to...

Maybe it's because I want to mark him, leave *something* of me behind so he can't forget me.

"What?" Cain's voice tugs me back to him, bringing along the realization that I *have* been staring at him for a little too long.

I shake my head, refocusing on my food. "Nothing, sorry."

"Don't be sorry, you know I like being looked at. I just wasn't sure *why* you were looking at me so intensely."

"Mm. No reason," I remark with a shrug, taking another bite. Not that Cain wouldn't *like* to hear all about what I'm thinking, but I figure it generally isn't the best dinner topic.

He squints at me a little before continuing to eat, shaking his head in response. "C'mon, tell me."

As I sip my wine, I hum at him. Amused, almost, that he would make me tell him—though I don't know why I'm surprised. "I was...thinking about how I want to bite you. I don't know why. I've never had that feeling over a person before you."

Cain's eyebrows raise, his hand falling still after stabbing his fork into a piece of asparagus. A hunger lights up in his eyes, curious and intrigued. "Oh, really?"

Nodding, I drag a piece of my steak through a puddle of sauce, creating a triangle with it for a moment before eating it. "Yes...Perhaps we could try it, if you would like. For now, though, let's keep eating so I don't get distracted. Tell me, what else have I missed?"

He smirks, nodding. "I'd like that, Dae. And for that question: obviously, I built the casino and it's doing very well. My parents finally got a divorce after my father attempted to burn the mansion down with my mother in it; Irsa has still been annoying me *but* he did get engaged to someone else, so that's a plus." Cain smiles, pausing to take a bite out of his potato. "I also have someone working under me to handle the loan part of my business, and I enrolled him in Whitestone. So, there's that as well."

The brief mention of Irsa again makes my hand clench around my silverware, fury hot in my gut. He was one of the few I want revenge on the most, for all of the hell he had caused besides supporting my execution. I can vividly recall seeing the smirk on his face when I was standing on the gallows, and it makes my jaw clench tight enough that my teeth ache.

"Whoa, Dae, are you alright?" Cain asks, pausing with the rim of his glass to his lips.

"Fine, I apologize. I have a lot of anger in me since my return," I admit, sighing quietly as Cain reaches a hand over and lays it on top of mine. He doesn't say anything, simply letting his hand do the talking for him.

I don't mind. I don't mind one bit.

Once we finish eating, I make Cain a portal back to the casino and walk through it alongside him, his fingers tangled in mine. As much as I wanted him to stay in the manor for the rest of the night, he has work to do before we see each other again.

Unfortunate, but I don't mind.

He stops me in front of the red carpet leading into the building, looking up at me with this content expression on his face. "Today was nice, Dae. I really missed you."

I smile at him, bringing the back of his hand up to my lips. "I want you to come back in a day or two, so I can treat you to something. A day you deserve, and perhaps we can discuss what we talked about over dinner."

Cain's eyes twinkle again as he smiles slyly, watching me kiss his hand. "I think we can more than discuss that."

He moves his hand to cup my face instead, leaning up to kiss me.

That kiss feels like temptation, and I starve for him when he parts from me, watching him as he walks away.

I think I will always be starving for him.

28

—·—

A FEW DAYS pass before Cain arrives at the manor again, wearing a red cloak that reminds me of a specific tale I heard when I was younger. Little Red showing up to the Wolf's home. *How funny. How fitting.* My heart pounds at the sight of him—followed by a swift wash of anxiety over what I have prepared, quickly making me rub my hands together to try and ease it, palm to palm.

I force my mind on his cloak, biting the inside of my cheek. I'm the wolf in disguise, waiting for him. Hunting him down, I might even say, if it wasn't *him* showing up at *my* doorstep.

"Hello, Cain," I greet him warmly as he steps inside, watching the way the fabric drifts around his legs.

What if he hates it, Daedalus? What if he's just pitying you?

"Hello, Dae." He smiles up at me, leaning forward to kiss me on the cheek. "What's your plan?"

"Ah. I have some things set up for you, if you would follow me."

I lead the way down the hall, pausing at the door of a room I've started to leave mostly empty, except for a cushioned table and a small piano I don't have much use for. Inside, an elven masseuse from the main stretch of Eerie stands by a table covered in the softest furs I could buy, as well as a crimson silk robe and a small black box.

She smiles at us both, rolling up the sleeves of her shirt and exposing floral tattoos on her gray-skinned forearms before looking to Cain and back at me. "So this is him, hm?" she asks, her bright eyes twinkling with intrigue.

I nod, glancing between them momentarily. "Yes, it is… Cain, meet Elira. I had her come to stay for the entire day, so you can have as many massages as you'd like. First off though, you are scheduled a full body massage. There's a new robe for you, and do be sure to check the little box."

Cain's face turns soft as I explain, a bright smile on his face. "This is amazing already," he says with a slight laugh, walking over to the box and opening it. The necklace inside is made up of a golden chain with a ruby and emerald rose pendant, one that took me far too long to find. A fashion store owned by a vampire dressed in royal blues named Elric had it, and it was too perfect to leave behind. It glitters in the low light as he turns the box back and forth, each little crystal sparkling.

He looks back at me after a long moment, something sweet in his expression. "This is beautiful, thank you, Daedalus."

I nod, sheepishly looking away from him again. "Don't thank me yet, there's more to come."

"There is?" Cain asks, his eyebrows raising as he tilts his head, nearly bird-like.

"Of course, you'll see. Go get your massage first."

As he takes the new robe behind the curtains Elira set up on the other side of the room, I carefully sit myself down at the piano across from the table and begin to play one of my softer compositions. I never had the chance to *really* play for him like I wanted to. It was always something I thought of, something that caught in my head and never truly slipped out even after the ten years. He's heard me before, sure, but that was different. Not as intimate, not as personal.

I want him to *hear* my feelings about him, too.

When Cain steps back out, I'm sure I feel his eyes on me—and I imagine the look on his face to be gentle, maybe loving, if I'm so lucky.

A soft smile finds its way on my face as I slip into the rhythm of the music, my hands scaling gingerly over the smooth faces of the keys. It's easy to lose myself in it, though it always has been.

What a dream it is, to have Cain Sidrelle relaxing in my home while I play for him. What a dream it is, to hear his soft sighs over my songs.

An hour passes quickly, and I only realize it's passed at all because Elira gives me the signal that she's finished up, tapping her fingertips on the side of the piano in the corner of my vision. I trail my playing to a stop and rise from the bench, looking over at Cain as he sits up, looking far sleepier than I've ever seen. His face is a rosy pink, his lids low over his eyes, every edge to him rounded and soft. I adore it, and him. *Gods.*

I glance away at the realization of the blanket covering his waist, swallowing a bit forcefully. "You can put the robe back on, if you don't feel like getting totally dressed. I have more to treat you to."

Cain yawns, rubbing his eyes with one hand before he grabs the robe, slipping it on. "Where to next?"

With a smile, I reach over to take his hand and lead him to the small library down the hall—which is made up of four bookshelves, a velvet couch and loveseat across from them, and matte black walls, making it feel considerably cozy with the low-lighting of the chandelier hanging above the center of the room. A new wooden coffee table sits in front of the couch, covered by a draping white tablecloth as well as a chocolate fountain, fruits, cookies, and cake squares all spread on golden dishes. To the left of the fountain, a wide charcuterie board with various meats, cheeses, crackers, and vegetables is spread out neatly, in case we grow tired of the chocolate.

Cain's eyes widen at the sight, immediately taking one of the thin, wooden sticks beside the dishes to spear a strawberry and hold it under the waves of chocolate.

"You're so sweet," he murmurs, leaning over to press a kiss to the corner of my lips as I dip a strawberry too. Before he can move, I quickly turn my head to capture his mouth in mine, imagining the taste of the sweets on him mingling with his warmth.

When I lean back, I place the strawberry on my tongue and relish the cool sweetness of the fruit as it meets the warmth of the liquid chocolate. "I hope you know I'm doing this to show you *this* is how you deserve to be treated. Not the way Irsa or anyone else thinks. You don't need to be kept like a bird in a cage—you deserve to be treated like the royalty you are." I shrug, shaking my head. "I may be mad for thinking that way, but it's how I feel."

"I'm glad *someone* sees what I'm worth." Cain mutters, placing another strawberry in his mouth. "Is there more after this?"

"After this, you and I will be relaxing in the hot spring in the backyard,. I discovered it a few weeks into my stay here, and it seems comfortable," I say as I lean across Cain's lap, taking a few pieces of cheese and shifting back over to eat them. His eyes sparkle in a specifically dangerous way that I feel in my core, and I glance down to his hand as it finds its way onto my thigh.

We eat in quiet for a little while, until Cain leans back and shakes his head. "I don't think I can eat anymore, good Gods."

I laugh, standing up and slipping away from the grip of his hand on my thigh. "Come with me, then."

He follows a step behind as I walk out of the room, heading to the kitchen to grab the bottle of wine we drank from over dinner. I hum as I lead Cain outside, down a smooth stone path that meets a circle of stone bricks around a cracked and mossy fountain in the center of the rose garden. The velvet petals seem to bloom wider as we pass, extending their leaves and thorns in our direction, and I grace them by brushing my fingertips over their surfaces.

Cain smiles as he does the same, eyeing the fountain. "You know, it almost seems like you copied our garden with all these roses."

I shake my head, laughing. "They were already here when I arrived, Cain. And besides, I wouldn't do it to *copy* you, I would do it because they make me think of you.

He rolls his eyes playfully as he loops his arm through mine, leaning into my shoulder as we walk, chuckling to himself. "Suuure, you would."

My fingertips tap a thread of a song as it works its way through my mind, coupled with the guttural calls from the ravens lining my rooftop. I glance back at them, eyeing the shadows of their bodies, the slight tinge of purple I can barely see in the darkness of their feathers. One chatters at me, and I restrain the urge to chatter back.

A few fly to the trees around the hot spring, watching over us.

The spring is a few feet outside of the last section of rose bushes and isn't very large—probably only big enough to fit the both of us—with clear blue, almost teal-colored water, dotted by small groupings of lotus-covered lily pads. It is surprisingly close to the gnarled garden I have yet to neaten up, which I swear I can smell from this distance. Or, well, at least the orange trees.

Cain looks over the soft red blanket I spread out alongside the water's edge, his gaze crossing the small picnic basket holding more chocolate-dipped strawberries and a pair of wine glasses. "You put a lot of thought into this," he remarks, his voice touched with awe.

Nodding, I lean down to pour us both a glass of wine, then cork the bottle and look back at him. "When it comes to you, I put a lot of thought into everything."

He slips the silk robe from his shoulders as I pause to watch as he steps down into the steaming water. His body is still so slender and so *pretty,* sprinkled with freckles on his shoulders and slightly reddened by the massage. Impossibly breathtaking as ever, making it hard for me to consider undressing, to even be *seen* naked beside him.

Cain looks up at me, eyeing where my hands rest on my slacks. "Are you coming?"

I force a deep breath, closing my eyes. "Yes, sorry. I... had to gather the courage, truthfully."

"Don't be nervous, Dae. You're pretty," Cain says as he sits down, leaning an arm on a stone lining the edge of the spring and picking up his glass of wine. He takes a singular sip before setting it down again, smiling fondly at me.

"Hush," I murmur, swiftly slipping off my clothes and neatly folding each piece in a pile. The water is perfectly hot when I step in beside him, flooding my body with a comforting heat that I don't mind one bit.

"What if I don't?" A smirk crosses his face as he moves in front of me, bracketing my thighs and caging me in. A moment later, his hand rises from the blue and brushes carefully across the scar on my throat, leaving behind a cooling trail of droplets over my skin.

Cain looks like he wants to say more, his mouth opening before he shakes his head, tracing his fingertips along the length of his throat. "I'm sorry," he murmurs as an obvious shudder runs through me, withdrawing his hand to brush it across the other scars crossing my body. Some from my trainings, some self-inflicted, some from the attack on the carriage the night before I found him. It is such a careful thing, so oddly intimate, making my hands shake.

He's being *so* gentle too, and no one but him has ever touched me like that.

I swallow hard, leaning back to pick up our glasses, offering one to Cain before sipping from my own. If he's going to keep touching me like this, I *definitely* need a drink—especially when the feeling alone nearly brought tears to my eyes. I've never had anyone do it like that. Not even my brief ex-boyfriend overseas. He was gentle, sure, but it was so *different.*

Cain touches me in an exploratory way, as if he's appreciating every piece, taking the time to learn my body and care for the way I react.

My ex touched me in a way that was never as thorough as him, and always meant he wanted something out of it.

I sigh, closing my eyes, and Cain gingerly shifts forward to catch the sound as it escapes from my lips. In this moment, things are beautiful, and the outside world is quickly forgotten as he kisses me. It's gentle, it's sweet, it's quiet as a butterfly's wings and haunting at the same time. His lips are on mine, his mouth against me, his hands on my skin. He tastes like the dryness of the red wine and the chocolate from moments before, and I chase it like an animal.

All things are as they should be, even for a moment.

29

— • —

SITTING SIDE by side on the blanket, sipping wine and eating strawberries and letting the breeze dry us off, feels *comfortable*.

I never thought I would ever feel this way, especially nude—I hate being looked at, which is one thing I've never been able to escape, because I can't even stand for my own eyes to see my body. But, being looked at by someone like Cain is different. It's special, and I'm only now coming to understand it.

Having Cain look at me with patience and understanding isn't something he does, I know this now. From his past with the club and from what I've heard in trailing rumors, he's considered to be a sexual being by nature, but I know now that was because it was *easy* for him to be that way. He used that because it was expected, and because it helped him deal with other things.

I know now that this is as different for him, as it is for me.

The sunset passes into the deep blue shades of night, causing goosebumps to creep up my arms with the cooling air. I glance over to Cain, studying him closely, finding it a little surprising how quickly he turns to face me once he notices I'm looking. He reaches over to the basket and plucks a singular strawberry from it, raising it to my lips. "Here."

I take it between my teeth and smile, finding warmth in my cheeks yet again.

Something is odd about that feeling as well. I had learned for so long it was seemingly bad to feel anything beyond emptiness, to be a shell who followed Morgana's every footstep. Now, I think I'm carefully breaking free, even as a changed man—and something about it feels so nice.

I'm *loved*. I'm *cared for*.

And so many other things.

I lean back on my hands and sigh in a dreamy way, finishing the last bite of strawberry before reaching over to offer Cain one as well. His soft lips brush against my fingers, sending a wave of hungry sparks through my stomach.

"What else do you have planned?" Cain murmurs once he finishes it, tracing a circle over my chest.

"A nice bath for you, dinner, and then we can go to bed."

He nods, settling himself to straddle my lap. "You know, you've been treating me so nice all day, I should do something for you too, shouldn't I? I was thinking maybe you could bite me, since you haven't yet."

His fair skin looks pretty against the gold, red, and green of the necklace I gave him earlier. It makes my mouth water, seeing the jewels there, imagining what they might look like with blood dripping over them. "That isn't expected of you, but you do know how much I would appreciate it."

Cain smiles, playful and sultry, like he knows *exactly* how much I want it. "So?"

I watch as he tilts his head, sweeping his hair over his right shoulder and out of the way of his throat. My stomach growls instantly, growing with a need I haven't felt in forever. "It's going to hurt, you know," I murmur, and it comes out hoarse.

He shifts forward, moving his hips against mine ever so slightly. "I figured."

My breath leaves my lips shakily as I lean forward, pressing my mouth to the space of his collarbone where the cold chain rests over it. He tenses a little, running a hand up my spine—clawing into my skin with his sharpened fingernails when I finally sink my teeth into him. A gasp, his body tensing as I hold him close to me, drinking in the rush of his blood.

"It hurts," he whispers, though he does not pull away.

"*I know,*" I murmur back in his mind, lightly petting his back as I reach my magic out to his. "*Just relax.*"

Cain's breath hitches, his hips twitching. "Yes, sir."

With the taste of him on my tongue, it's terribly easy for my magic to latch onto him, plunging me through the heat of his flames and pushing further. Another gasp leaves his lips, followed by a breathy whimper when my jaws clench down a little harder.

My darkness soars through him, dragging along new waves of pleasure and pain that I cast along, shivering with my own want.

He plunges me into the grim embrace of desire, pulling me viciously into depths I will never climb out from. Need wells up in my hips with every lap of his blood, causing an erection I know damn well he can feel.

His body relaxes against mine, and I smile against his skin. "*Oh,*" is all he manages to say, attempting to press his hips into mine a bit more. He's unsurprisingly hard against me, searching for relief, and I know just what will give it to him. I reach a hand down to line my length with his entrance, sliding into him a little unevenly due to the lack of lubrication.

My hands find their way to him, thumbs digging into his hips, but they don't stay there long. They run up his back, tangle in his curls and pull, allowing me to relish in the arch of his spine and the moan he lets out.

The feeling of him coupled with his taste makes me groan, finally releasing his skin from my teeth so I can fuck him better. I lean back for a split second to eye him before taking him by the hips and flipping us over in one swift motion, eagerly setting a hungering pace. The blanket tangles under us as I reposition myself, pushing away what is left of the strawberries, kissing Cain as deep as I can.

I'm far more drunk off of Cain than I was from any of the wine we've had so far.

His is a taste I am all too eager to get addicted to.

I'm not sure how long we spend out there, but the mix of Cain's blood and the wine has left a pleasant little buzz in my veins when we return to the manor. By the time I started to pay attention, the stars were glittering in full, the moon was bathing us in her pale light, and fireflies had begun to appear from the whispering trees.

I watch them until we walk inside, leading Cain directly to the first bathroom on the main floor—smiling at the sight of the candles lining the countertop around the sink, the rose petals scattered across the pink and gold steaming water, the two robes folded neatly for us on a shelf hanging off the wall. Lavender coats the air, mingling with rose to make a perfectly sweet bath.

I nod to myself in approval as Cain slips off his robe once more, hesitantly doing the same and folding my clothes up again.

Years-long habits never fade.

Cain sits on the edge of the tub, skimming his fingertips through the petals as I kneel down in front of him. He looks at me with softness in his eyes, extending a hand to gingerly cup my chin and tilt it up in his direction, churning my insides with butterflies. Staring up at him, my heart misses thousands of beats before it jolts once in my chest. My mind screams with all the wonders of him, screams with the realization that I truly came back for him and him only. Not my family, just Cain Sidrelle.

He hums, tilting his head. "What are you doing, Dae?"

I shrug, allowing my jaw to be held as he drags the pad of his thumb across my lower lip. Sitting at his feet like this feels like worship, like I am nothing more than an acolyte knelt before a god of fiery beauty. "I think I'm obsessed with you."

"Well, you're in luck—I feel the same way," Cain replies, a fond little smile twitching at his lips as his eyes drop down to my mouth.

A light laugh leaves me, followed by a surprised exhale when he presses his thumb against one of my fangs. One hot drop of blood wells up from it and falls onto the pad of my tongue, one I eagerly swallow down, a singular cannibalism.

He drags me up into a kiss and carefully slips into the water, leaving enough room for me to sit across from him.

I welcome the heat of the water as I sink into it, sighing at the same time and leaning back against the sides of the white claw-foot tub.

Cain's hand brushes over my knee, following a thin scar across it. "This has been really, really nice. Thank you."

I sheepishly nod in return, watching his hand move back and forth over my skin, tracing the skeletal kneecap with his sharp fingernail. "I felt you needed to be shown what you truly deserved from another person, and to learn what you like most. I don't know... people seem to just use you for things. I don't want to do that. I'm glad you enjoyed your day."

He nods, sighing dreamily. "I appreciate it more than you know."

My hands fall still on Cain's knees, following the angles of how they're bent, admiring him for a moment before my smile fades from my face. I don't mean for it to, but my mind keeps prodding me. "I kept thinking I'm too cruel for you, especially now. My hands are bloodstained, and yet somehow, you still let me touch you."

"I don't care how stained your hands are, Dae. You came back for me, and that tells me everything," Cain answers reassuringly, placing his hand over where mine shakes against his knee. "And I'm not worried about you being cruel, because you never have been to me. In fact, I've never quite met someone like you before."

I pause, laughing breezily. "Is it funny if I say the same thing?"

His smile grows brighter, softer, affectionate. "Maybe it can be true for both of us." He pauses for a moment, eyes meeting my own. "Should you go see your family?"

I hadn't even thought of it.

"Soon, yes. But right now, all I need is to be by your side." I shake my head, smiling warmly at him. "I'll go soon enough."

Cain nods, kissing my cheek. "I like the sound of that."

As we sit together, my mind calms for only a moment. Everything I can possibly want is here, and everything is taken care of. My family still loves me. Cain and I are... something, but I have him and that's all that matters. I don't need to know what we are, as long as he's by my side.

I am impossibly alive, alive, alive.

I let Cain drag me into another kiss, and in it I explain all that words can't, as if I could tell him all I'm thinking through that alone. The way it is instantly reciprocated draws a warm smile on my face, my slow-beating heart pounding an uncertain rhythm in my chest. Knocking away, reminding me it's still there.

I have Cain—and in truth, he is all I need. I would kill for him, fall for him, I would throw myself from the highest building for him. Whatever Cain asked, I would do it gladly.

After a combination of the comfortable bath and more kisses than I could ever imagine having, we sprawl out in the well-trimmed grass in the fenced-in yard outside and stare up at the sky together as the evening colors slowly shift into night. Neither of us say a word, neither of us so much as *breathe* as we turn to face each other. Minutes pass as our gazes meet, and for once, I can't make myself look away.

He must notice, because his eyes light up. "You're looking at me." Whispered, almost awed.

I laugh, softly, smiling at his expression. "How could I do anything else?"

The world feels enormous in this moment, but so is whatever we are—a tenderness so wide and so deep it had created a fissure in our hearts and souls, one that revived me from my own grave.

I didn't mean for all of this to happen. It just so happened Cain wanted me too, and I had to break a few rules to give him that. To give him everything. To give him, maybe oddly, *me.*

And so, under the glittering stars, constellations, and an abundance of glowing colors stretching and sprawling across the sky, I show him my feelings as I lean in closer to him.

First, by tracing it over a palm.

Second, the back of the hand.

Third, arm, collarbone, sternum, back up to throat.

Over, and over, and over.

ACKNOWLEDGEMENTS

The Skeletons In Our Closet has been a many-years-long project that I couldn't be more glad I didn't give up on, ever since that very first draft in 2022. This book and its sequel are absolutely stories from and for my heart, as are these characters. I couldn't be happier to have shared it with all of you, finally!

Now, onto the sappy bit:

First, to my beloved. Without you, these characters wouldn't exist, this book wouldn't exist. I wrote this story for you, and I hope it's lived up to every little thing you've thought it would. You believing in my every step of writing this book has been everything I needed, and now that it's finally here, I'm glad you did. I love you, every little bit of you—to us, and to these beautiful boys we've created.

To my parents. You two have pushed me along every time I've thought about writing, and supported me every which way when it came to my books. To Mom: thank you for being just as excited as me when it came to my books (even if you might not read them because of the subject matter, haha). To Dad: don't worry, I'm not only writing "thanks for your support!" this time! Thank you for always getting a copy of my books and demanding I sign them, it never fails to make me smile. I love you both!

To the Boys. You two have also pushed me along with your support, whether or not you know I wrote this little bit for you. Your endless confidence and excitement about my writing has meant a lot, and I love you both for it.

To Mawce. You have absolutely become a much-needed friend in the writing world for me, and I will never be able to tell you how much I appreciate your friendship. From answering my dumbest questions to wild fanart to BEING MY EDITOR, you're the best and I care about you so much! Your endless supply of knowledge and love for my writing has been so so helpful to the development of this book.

To my writing friends. I don't know where I would've been without you. I spent a lot of my time in the writing world floating by myself for the first year or so, until I met all of you! To Shane, for always being my most rabid hypeman & for always showering me in the biggest support and love. To Charlie, for being there when I needed a shoulder & for hyping up all my crazy ideas.To Gabby & Lilliana, you both & Charlie were absolutely what I needed in writer friends after a while, and I needed to make sure you knew I appreciate you! I love your energy and constant love!

To Alx, for always being just as insane as me and being there to hype everything. To Harper, for delivering me to the of of the best discord servers I could've ever been in. To Morgan and Ronan, for always being excited to talk about whatever and dealing with me popping up at random times with something out of pocket. To Nico, for absolutely hyping the HELL out of my cover with me with every update, and sharing in my excitement over both of our works.

To Kate, Kristin, Alexis, and Nicole. Yes, you get one too! Thank you for being you, for supporting and loving me, and for pushing me with your excitement for this book to keep going with publishing it. All of your hype about the little sneak peeks I'd show or teasers I'd give about this has really helped push me along, so I love you guys and appreciate you more than you know. I'm not sure how I would've managed to get it out without all of you too.

To Therese. Thank you beyond words for making me such a beautiful cover, and for dealing with my unhinged responses to it. I appreciate you more than I've told you, and I'm so grateful I get to work/be friends with you!

To Quinton. I honestly couldn't have gotten this book out there without all of your tremendous help. You don't know how much I appreciate you handling all of my wild questions and just your absolute kindness with helping me out! You're truly an out of this world person and I am so eternally grateful to have you as a friend (and a mentor)!!

And thank *you*, for taking the time to read my beloved book! I wouldn't be able to do this without you too!